Extended Play

Extended Play

The Elastic Book of Music

Edited by Gary Couzens

Extended Play

ISBN-10: 0-9548812-9-X

ISBN-13: 978-0-9548812-9-0

Printed in Bristol by MRT Services

Typeset by Andrew Hook

Published by:

Elastic Press
85 Gertrude Road
Norwich
UK

elasticpress@elasticpress.com
www.elasticpress.com

Table of contents

Intro

Jean-Jacques Burnel

People often ask me where the songs come from. I would like to answer, from the imagination; from a deep well of experience and fantasy. The truth, however, may also be more mundane and be dictated by the physical limitations of the composer. In other words the imagination may well be boundless but the skills at the writer's disposal may be limited. But if they did come from experience and fantasy would the same ideas be interpreted in a completely different way by others? I would like to think so, because experience is not just the mental filing of events and facts, it is the interpretation and catalyst for an unlimited number of thoughts that can only be defined by its creator, yet completely transformed by those who hear it. Within the arts, those of us who are inspired by another art form are almost creating progeny from already incestuous relationships although, paradoxically, the product goes toward increasing the gene pool rather than narrowing it.

Songs and music have often been inspired by literature and here, within these pages, the literature is conversely inspired by songs and music. It only remains to be seen how the writers' imaginations trigger the imagination of each reader. In theory there are no limits.

JJ Burnel, 2006

The Little Drummer Boy

Marion Arnott

'But hark! My pulse like a soft drum
Beats my approach, tells thee I come.'
Henry King

Francis Xavier Sweeney learned to jump sideways when he was too big to hide in the meter cupboard in the hall. When he was small and heard the key in the lock and smelled the pub smell coming in, he used to dive in there and pull the little door behind him. In the close warm dark, holding the door and his breath at the same time, he could hear the click of the electricity meter – *click click click* – steady like a tiny heartbeat, and somehow the sound of heavy feet and swearing, and of things being knocked over, swung into the same thin rhythm. His Mum's crying didn't. Slap slap and noisy sobbing. Slap. Slap. Her shrillness rose above the tick of his heart and the meter and made his insides twist with a hot sharp pain. Darkness filled him up inside, even his head, so that he couldn't see or hear. He tried to breathe out the thick black air but it stuck in his chest and began to sparkle with little glittery bits. This was nearly jumping sideways, although he didn't know that yet.

The first time sideways happened was when Daddy hanged the puppy. Mrs. Brunton's dog Sheba had puppies and Frankie went every day after school to see them. The old woman lived just up the road, and gave him cake and sandwiches. She always said the same thing as the school dinner lady did when she piled extra on his plate: 'You need feeding up, Frankie.'

1

Mrs. Brunton was really clean, from her white curly hair all the way down to her to her snow white trainers. The house smelled of lemon polish and cakes baking. She made him wash his hands and face before she let him eat, and he had to sit on a newspaper placed on the white painted chair at her kitchen table. But that was OK. There were spam sandwiches, or maybe tuna mayonnaise, and then fruit cake. He could eat and watch the puppies in Sheba's basket. Sheba was black and tan with ears that bent over halfway and fur like feathers. Her eyes were whisky coloured and all soft when she looked at her babies. At first they were half naked wee wriggly things that whimpered and scrambled over each other to get at Sheba for milk, but soon their fur thickened and their ears cocked up and their eyes were bright and looking at everything. Frankie and Mrs. Brunton sat together, she laughing and he rocking with longing as they tumbled out of the basket one after the other. Poor Sheba kept going after them, nudging and nipping them back in.

"She's not hurting them, Frankie. She's a good wee mother. She'd never hurt them."

Frankie hadn't asked, but Mrs. Brunton was good at reading his silences.

"What about their Dad?"

"Pups are nothing to do with him. Don't even know who he is."

Frankie decided that dogs were clever creatures. Except that Sheba didn't know she was going to lose her pups. She lay with them, licking and giving little nips to cheeky ones while Mrs. Brunton talked about finding homes for them. Frankie held his breath and was filled with a longing so fierce it hurt. If he asked her...she liked him...she made him cakes...maybe she'd...

But when he looked up she was gazing at him sadly.

"Frankie, they take a lot of looking after. And I don't think your Dad..."

Inside, Frankie closed up tight as a clam and he didn't ask her for a puppy. There was never any point in wanting anything.

He didn't visit for a few days, but he missed his sandwiches and milk: Mum didn't get home till late and it was a long time from school dinner. Besides, he was desperate to see the pups. When he slouched to her door, Mrs. Brunton let him in and asked him where he'd been. He only shrugged and she said no more. She was used to his silences.

Cheese sandwiches today and a chocolate biscuit. No cake. She must have thought he wasn't coming. She talked non stop, rattling on about the tricks the pups had got up to. Frankie stared big eyed at the little animals. All seven of them were scrambling about the floor, yipping and sliding on the lino. It seemed as though there were dozens of them, they were so all over the place. Two of them were having a tug of war with an old knotted tea towel. They were funny – growling seriously, trying to frighten each other off. Sheba lay and watched with a steady gaze. Then the doorbell rang. Mrs. Brunton looked out the window.

"Window cleaner," she announced and went out to fetch her purse.

Frankie was ready to go home when she returned. He swung his school bag over his shoulder.

"Away already, Frankie?"

He nodded and headed for the door. Sheba padded after him but Mrs. Brunton shut the door. Frankie heard Sheba give a long low whine, and then he was running, his heart pounding. He shot out of the close like a bullet, ran all the way up the street, into his own close, and up the three flights of stairs. His heart was drumming by the time he'd let himself into the flat and slammed the door behind him.

The pup was scared. Frankie held it in his hands and gave its floppy ears a gentle tug and scratch. Sheba loved it when Mrs. Brunton did that, but the pup only whimpered more. The sound was appallingly loud in his little room. He folded up his school sweatshirt and put it and the puppy in the drawer under his bed. That was a good hiding place. When the drawer was closed, the whining was muffled. He stood in the hall outside his door, listening, but he couldn't hear the little dog at all. Everything would be fine.

There wasn't much in the kitchen to eat, but he knew puppies needed feeding often. He upended the biscuit tin onto a plate and mixed the stale crumbs with a little water. That would keep the pup happy until tea time when he could smuggle something off his own plate. He was coaxing his little doggie friend to eat the crumbs when the doorbell rang. In the empty flat, it was strident as a fire alarm. Frankie clutched the pup to him and held his breath. Someone rattled the letter box.

"Frankie! Are you there?"

Mrs. Brunton.

"Frankie Sweeney! I know you're in there! Answer the door."

The banging and rattling and shouting went on for an age, but Frankie sat motionless with the pup pressed to his cheek. When it stopped, he crept to the window, stood up on tiptoe, and looked down into the street. Mrs. Brunton's white head was bobbing away down towards her own close. She looked funny – her white trainers flashed back and forward, back and forward. Her lacy wool scarf fluttered behind her.

Dad found the pup of course. It was the pup's fault, not Frankie's. Its whining was frantically loud, almost a howl. Frankie hid it in the drawer and piled his puffa jacket on top when he heard Dad come in, but when he looked round, Dad was in the doorway.

"What's that noise? What have you got in there?"

He was speaking too quietly. Mum always said that was a sign of him building up, ready to blow.

Frankie couldn't speak. The darkness was filling his mouth, choking him. His tongue felt like a big lump of sponge. He couldn't move it. His heart drummed and made his shirt flutter on his chest.

"Answer me when I speak to you!"

Quiet. Hissing.

Two long strides into the room. Frankie on the floor. Puffa jacket thrown at him. Loud miserable howls from puppy. Dad shaking puppy in his face. Dad slapping him with puppy.

"Where did you get it?"

Close to Frankie's ear. Answer me, Answer me. Answer me. Spittle on Frankie's face. Blood coming from the puppy's eye. Frankie choking and trying to swallow. Frankie wetting himself. Punch in the thigh from Dad.

"You should still be in nappies, filthy wee bastard."

Punch.

"Answer me when I speak to you!"

Mum came to the door. She drew deeply on her cigarette and went away again. Dad snatched up Frankie's school tie. He stood up and hefted the pup from hand to hand.

"Answer me."

Frankie wept soundlessly as Dad knotted the tie round the pup's neck. Gently he lowered the struggling animal to Frankie's eye level.

4

He jerked it up and down like a yo-yo, then side to side like the pendulum on a clock. Tick. Tock. Tick. Tock. Frankie's heart caught the rhythm. The dog was jerked faster and faster. Tick. Tick. Tick. Like a watch, like his heart racing to keep up. The little animal's cries stabbed his ears. It spun helplessly round and round, its paws grappling wildly with empty air. The blood from its eye splashed on Frankie's face. One of its claws caught his cheek. Frankie couldn't breathe.

Then suddenly he wasn't there any more.

One minute he was swelling and swelling inside, all thin and stretched and going to split open, then suddenly he was out through his mouth. Pop. Out of his skin. Jumping sideways meant floating like a bubble. He was lighter and cooler than air, floating high above, looking down on himself on the floor in the wet patch, looking down on Dad and the puppy. He could see and hear, but he wasn't afraid.

He heard the doorbell ring, fire alarm loud. He saw through the wall which was clear like polythene – Mum at the door – policeman and Mrs. Brunton – Mr. Welsh from next door with his big Alsatian dog, just passing by and stopping to look. The puppy's cries were weaker now, little wavelets of snuffling whines, but Mrs. Brunton heard and pushed past Mum.

"My God! My God!"

Mrs. Brunton burst into tears. Frankie had taken his eyes off Dad and hadn't seen him hang the pup from the hook on the back of the door. The animal was still now, small paws curled in towards its chest, eyes slit shut. The only movement was the blood trickling from its eye. Dad was bending over Frankie, rubbing at his wrist. He looked up bewildered at the policeman.

"He fainted. Frankie fainted when I came in and caught him tormenting the puppy. I can't wake him up."

Mrs. Brunton lifted the pup down and drew it close to her chest.

"Is it your dog, Mrs. Brunton? I don't know what gets into the boy sometimes, I really don't."

Dad sounded really upset.

Mr. Welsh and his Alsatian came in. The dog whined and growled when it smelled death. Mr. Welsh swore at Frankie lying on the floor. Mum lit a cigarette and told him to mind his language.

Jumping back in was painful. He didn't really want to go back inside himself, but once the policeman and Mrs. Brunton had gone away, and Dad had settled in front of the TV, it just happened. He felt pain throbbing in his leg. His face burned where the pup had clawed. Suddenly, he felt himself cramming back in. When he opened his eyes, he was lying on his bed in the dark, the pup's bleeding face hanging in the air above him. The sight of it made Frankie want to go sideways again, but he didn't know how to make it happen yet. Instead he lay and thought about being light and cool as air and high above everything. It was a good way to be.

Spelling was never Frankie's strong point, in spite of Dad helping. Dad was a good speller and wanted Frankie to be the same.

'Spell ferociously,' he would say, or whatever '-ious' word came into his head as he paced in front of Frankie.

"F-E-R-O-S-H-U-SH."

Sometimes he laughed at Frankie because Frankie couldn't help being stupid. Sometimes he got angry because he wanted a son he could be proud of. Then Frankie wouldn't even be able to spell it wrong because his tongue swelled up in his mouth and made it too dry to speak. There might be a cuff on the back of the head then; or maybe something hot on his skin like when Dad asked him to spell Francis Xavier Sweeney while he stirred sugar into his coffee.

"What comes after 'X', Frankie?"

Silence.

"After 'X'?"

He stirred and stirred, – *clink-clink-clink* – and Frankie's heart began to drum its crazy swinging rhythm. Dad pressed the back of the hot spoon on Frankie's hand.

"….Dad, Dad …"

"Dad! Dad!" echoed back at him in a falsetto whine. "What comes after 'X', Frankie?"

"X…Y…Z."

"So you've got a voice after all," Dad said in wonderment. Luckily he laughed.

Frankie was afraid of spelling, even when Dad wasn't there. The teacher at school gave them words to learn and then came round the class. The worst time was the week after the puppy died.

"Kitten, Shaun."

"Miss, K-I-T-T-E-N."

"Good. Mitten, Tracy."

"M-I-T-T-E-N."

Sweets handed to the children who got their word right.

"Sitting, David."

"Miss, S-I-T-T-I-N-G."

"Oh, very good. We're doing well with our double Ts today. Frankie, try bitten."

Frankie sat silent. His heart drummed in his chest. The wild beat rose higher, into his throat – he could feel it pulsing there, and at his temples, and in the veins in his wrists. Everyone waited. All eyes were on him.

"Come on, Frankie, give it a try."

Frankie opened his mouth but no letters came out. Inside his head felt like birds' wings flapping. Paul Devaney put his hand up.

"Miss, Miss, I know a word Frankie can spell. Puppy."

A snigger shot round the class like lightning. Miss Thomas waved Paul to silence and shifted her gaze to Siobhan.

"You try 'bitten', Siobhan."

"But, Miss – Frankie knows all about puppies. He killed one. He really did…"

Somebody jeered. Paul nodded his head vehemently. A murmur of agreement lapped at Frankie's ears. It sounded like a sea of hisses and a feeble whine, both at the same time. In his mind, he saw two little slit eyes, one bleeding, and two small paws curled into a furry chest. The drumming in his chest got louder and louder until it drowned out the excitement of the class and beat back the thin autumn sunlight coming in the window, leaving him alone in a pounding darkness. He could feel himself stretching inside, stretching and thinning and ready to snap, and then POP! He was out, away from the drumming and the flapping in his head, high above Miss Thomas, looking down at her butterfly hair clasp. She put down the jar of sweets and hurried towards Frankie at his desk. His eyes were wide and staring, but he wasn't seeing anything. How could he when there was nobody in there? Miss Thomas waved her hand in front of Frankie's eyes, then she touched his shoulder and gave him a gentle shake. She stepped back.

"Siobhan, go and ask Mrs. Grey to come in here, please."

Frankie hovered, enjoying the commotion. The class was silent, frightened, he thought. Miss Thomas was frowning but pretending there was nothing wrong. Mrs. Grey, stout and comfy, arrived and tried waving her hand before Frankie's eyes.

"It's nearly playtime. Let the class go out now," she muttered.

Frankie watched the class file out, Siobhan full of her own importance because she had to go and fetch the school first aider. Miss Thomas was upset, wondering what was wrong with him.

"I heard he killed the pup with a knife – slit its throat," she said, fluttering a sheet of paper in his face.

"No, the jannie says he hung it with his school tie."

The teachers exchanged glances and then let their gaze fall on the tie neatly knotted round Frankie's neck. Mrs. Grey shuddered. "They've requested an appointment from psychological services."

Miss Thomas snorted. "Oh, good. Six months from now we'll get another report saying he suffers from communication difficulties…"

Frankie was bored. He drifted towards the window, wondering if he would feel warm if he went into the sunbeam. He didn't. He couldn't feel anything, except that now he was light and cool and golden. A buzzing noise attracted his attention – a bee. It was crawling along the window ledge, tired out by the sun. He drifted closer.

"You're the spelling bee," he chortled to himself. The bee was angry at dying. It was losing strength, because of last night's cold, Miss Thomas had said. "They die off in the autumn," she said, "and they are dangerous then and likely to sting. Don't go near."

But it couldn't sting Frankie. He wafted across the room like a puff of golden smoke, and peered into its eyes. There were dozens of them, banks and banks of eyes full of hard black light. He wanted to know what it was looking at, if it could see him, but it was struggling to crawl away. He followed, and it grew increasingly desperate, its fat heavy body rolling and trying fruitlessly to take off. Frankie drew back and the bee lay still; when he came forward, it tried to fly again. Its buzzing was frantic and he felt its anger and fear enter him. His heart boomed with its rage. Sting. He wished he could sting. He would sting everyone. Everyone. He pursed his lips and buzzed a bit. The spelling bee did the same. Frankie floated a little closer still and suddenly he felt heavy. He was fat and heavy and soaked in yellow sunlight and trying to fly. His body vibrated with buzzing as he rolled and fanned wings. The buzzing was horrible in his ears. He thought hard and made his heart drum loud and clear. Boom. Boom. Boom. The buzzing died to a noise like summer and as far away. Frankie was strong and angry. Up. He was up in the air, rolling from side to side, unable to fly straight, but he was up and flying.

The teachers and the first aider had gathered round Frankie's desk. The first aider was filling in a form.

"This beats me," she said. "Query petit mal. Query fugue state. Query catalepsy, catatonia, narcolepsy and God knows what all."

The three of them looked funny to Frankie – long and thin and curved out of shape. Like people in the House of Funny Mirrors. The bee's eye view of the world. He smiled to himself. Miss Thomas's neck was like a swan's, bendy like a snake. Even Mrs. Grey was skinny. Frankie flew closer and closer. The first aider swatted at him with the form and he felt a rush of buzzing fury. Sting. Her cheek was soft and powdered, easy to pierce. A flash of sheer joy exhilarated him as she yelped and staggered backwards. He buzzed loudly and swooped around her head in triumph. Then he felt his strength ebb and only just managed to steer himself back to the window ledge. His anger was dying with the bee. No point in hanging round in there. He kicked himself free and drifted up to the ceiling again. Mrs. Grey was trying to get the first aider's sting out with a needle. Miss Thomas was still flapping paper at Frankie. He saw Frankie's eyelids flutter and felt himself being drawn back inside. He tried to drift back, tried to jump sideways, but Frankie was swallowing him up alive. The drumming of his heart slowed and quietened to the tiny tick of a watch. Feeble Frankie. Tick. Tick. Tick. Feeble.

Miss Thomas pressed wet tissues to his forehead. Water dripped into his eye. For a second, she looked as she had done through the bee's eyes, but then Frankie blinked and she was herself again.

"All right, Frankie? Don't worry. Your Dad is on his way."

From somewhere in the back of his mind, out of a pit of darkness, swelled a loud shrieking 'No-o-o-o-o'.

After school, Paul Devaney and friends were waiting for him round the corner from the school. When he got home, he had to clean up the blood and hide his torn shirt or Dad would have been angry that yet again he hadn't stood up for himself. But he'd tried. He'd tried to jump sideways and escape. But his heart had nearly stopped with fright at the sound of the jeering music of their taunts, and without that heart beat banging wildly in his chest, he was trapped inside himself. No golden puff of smoke for Frankie...no floating upwards cool as air...

The drum changed all that. The drum happened because Dad phoned the school to complain when Frankie didn't get a part in the class Nativity play. No use for Miss Thomas to say that Frankie was barred for filling the Baby Jesus doll with water so that it peed itself and made the Virgin Mary cry; useless to say that he could not read the script or remember any lines and would spoil the whole play; useless to say that the other children treated him like a pariah and he might be better off in the audience. Mr Sweeney would have none of it.

And so in the weeks before Christmas, Miss Thomas gave Frankie a little tin drum. He had to stand amongst the angels, shepherds, and the Three Kings from the Orient gathered round the edges of the stage and be a musical prop. Paul Devaney wasn't happy. He was Joseph and was supposed to knock at the Inn door asking for lodgings. Except he couldn't really knock at the door because it was cardboard and would fall down. So he had to shout,

"KNOCK! KNOCK! Is there anybody in the Inn?"

"KNOCK! KNOCK! Is there any room in the Inn?"

"KNOCK! KNOCK! Will someone let us in the Inn?"

He had been chosen because he could shout *Knock! Knock!* louder than anyone else in the class. But when Frankie got the drum, Paul wasn't allowed to shout *Knock! Knock!* any more. Frankie had to tap it on the drum with a wooden drum stick.

He memorised his part:

Joseph: three steps up to the door. Halt. Then Tap! Tap! on the drum.

Count to twelve, then Tap! Tap! again.

Then the same again.

Miss Thomas crouched at the side of the stage, counting the beat for him, so he couldn't go wrong. At first Frankie hung back among the shepherds, his head bowed, trying to avoid Paul Devaney's glare. Paul was furious because he loved to shout Knock! Knock! His tormenting made Frankie fumble with the drum and come in with the beat at the wrong time.

"You'd better get it right, Sweeney," Paul said every time he passed Frankie. And if the teacher wasn't looking, he knuckled Frankie's back as well.

But he needn't have worried – Frankie got it right in the end because a strange thing happened when he held the drum. It was royal blue with white painted Xs all round it and hung round his neck by a scarlet silk cord, smooth and shiny and sleek. The drum felt warm in his hands when he held it. The sticks fitted on to his hands like extra fingers. When he tapped, he felt a thrill go right up his arm. The tingle spread throughout his body until his feet tapped and his head went from side to side. He practised tapping in patterns – two loud, one quiet. Two quiet one loud. Two sticks tapping together, sometimes loud and sometimes quiet. Even when Miss Thomas put the drum away in the cupboard, he sat tapping with his pencil. And when she told him to stop it, he tapped with his fingers. And when she told him to stop that, he heard it in his head anyway. He could tap in time to his heart, which made him happy and relaxed; he could batter out fear until he was empty of it; he could let hot hate travel down his arm and into the sticks until they had a life of their own and drummed at a furious rate. Miss Thomas fetched the music teacher to hear him. He thought Frankie had talent. Maybe they would do something about teaching him after the Christmas holidays.

Mrs. Grey was so impressed that she presented him with a short blue jacket with silver buttons, and a pair of white trousers. Her nephew had been a page boy at a big wedding, she said, but the outfit was just right for a little drummer boy. Frankie thought his uniform looked a lot better than the striped and chequered towels the shepherds and Joseph had to wear round their heads. Paul said he looked like a gay boy, but Frankie didn't care. It all felt right to him.

Miss Thomas wouldn't let him take the drum home, which was a shame because he needed it. He was still having nightmares about the puppy. When he closed his eyes at night, the little dog's face appeared, all scrunched up and dead. Paul Devaney was there too – 'Puppy Killer! Puppy Killer!' knuckling Frankie till his back ached. He could hear his Dad hissing at him, and see his face twisted with anger while he swung the pup from side to side at the end of the tie. Sometimes, the dead pup's eyes sprang open and looked at him sadly, crying tears of blood. Other times he felt the tie tightening round his own neck like thin sharp wire, and dreamed that Dad was hanging *him* by it. He couldn't breathe then and his head filled up with black sparkle. One night he even got up and loosened the nails that held the hook to his door so that it wouldn't take his weight. Just in case Dad came in. Then he sat and cried.

But those terrible nights came to an end when he managed to smuggle the drum sticks home. When everyone else was asleep, he sat up in bed in the dark and drummed and drummed on the cover of an old magazine, faster and faster till the pup and his Dad were driven from sight, till the fear and shakiness drained down through the sticks and into the darkness of his bedroom. He filled the room with the black glitter that seeped out of his head and when he was empty of it, opened the window and let the breeze blow it away. The room felt cool and airy then, and he could sleep with his heart beating in a slow comfortable rhythm. Or he could go out.

Going out was a great adventure. There was a park on the other side of town. He'd seen it from a bus once, but he'd never been there. Now he could go whenever he liked. It was a big park with crags and a waterfall, and a fast flowing river which gurgled under trees. He found a children's farm there. That was a good place. He could get into the sheds and cages and look at the sleepy animals. Once he jumped inside a goose which was used as a watchdog. He liked waddling about and hissing at anything which came near. Old alkies came and sat drinking in the park at night. He liked to chase them, hissing and running at them. Sometimes they fell over and couldn't get back up again and he would stand over them, hissing and flapping until the park keeper came. There was a fox too in one of the enclosures. She had cubs, russet coloured with bright curious eyes. He liked to go inside one and spend the night nestled up to the mummy fox. He felt dozy and warm in the silvery winter moonlight, being watched over by his furry Mum.

Sometimes he followed the river to the bridge and hovered under there. He could watch rabbits coming to the bank in the dawn to drink, although he didn't like their faces close up. Their teeth were yellow and ugly. There were loads of creatures under the bridge. He visited a rat's nest once. He never jumped inside a rat though – he didn't like them. The bridge had lamps which stayed lit all night. He discovered that he could slide down the beams of light then skip across the stones in the water.

More and more, he hated it when Frankie woke up and called him back. He hated going back inside.

The gym was full of Mums and Dads on the night of the play. The wall bars were bright with tinsel and paper chains. And there was a Christmas tree at the back of the gym. Frankie liked its warm red and green and gold lights twinkling in the dimly lit hall. He and the other children stood behind the curtains which hid their platform and peeped out at the audience murmuring on the other side. Frankie saw Dad talking to the head teacher. She was laughing. They all liked Dad – he didn't know why. Mum was still outside in the playground, smoking a last few cigarettes before the show began. Siobhan and the others waved at their parents in the audience. Everyone cooed and smiled at their own child and everyone else's child, although Frankie thought that the Mummy fox, although she didn't smile, felt safer to be with. Frankie decided he'd better wave at Dad to be the same as the others. He was rewarded with a bright smile and a friendly wave. Then he saw Mr. Welsh and his big Alsatian dog, Roxy, and ducked back behind the curtain. Since the night of the puppy, Mr. Welsh scowled whenever he saw Frankie, and if he had a drink in him, called him bad names. Roxy, responding to a muttered command, always snarled at him, showing big white fangs.

Frankie's legs trembled. He was afraid of Mr. Welsh and Roxy. He ran his fingers round the rim of his drum then lifted the sticks, stroked the warm smooth wood, and calmed himself. The Virgin Mary pointedly inspected the Jesus doll and shook it to make sure there was no water inside before she wrapped it in a blue baby blanket. Frankie saw Paul watching. Unusually brave, Frankie wanted to tell her that it was Paul who had mishandled Baby Jesus and blamed him, but Paul held up his sharp white knuckles and Frankie was silent.

Cameras flashed when the curtains slid back with a loud creak and people clapped and cheered until the piano thumped into the first song; "Tired and weary, Mary hugged her little baby…"

The Virgin stood, head drooping under its blue headdress, and cuddled the Jesus doll. Joseph stepped – ONE TWO THREE – up to the

Inn door. Frankie beat the drum twice and Joseph yelled: "Is there anyone in the Inn?"

Frankie counted to twelve. Twelve heartbeats exactly. He beat the drum twice, louder this time. Miss Thomas smiled approval.

"Is there any room in the Inn?"

Twelve heartbeats. Two beats on the drum. Then a flourish and a roll and long tinny tattoo. Frankie's hands had a life of their own, or the sticks did. Joseph's demand to be let into the Inn was overwhelmed by the noise. The audience applauded until they saw that Joseph had burst into tears and run off the stage. I-made-him-run-I-made-him-run – Frankie beat out a triumph song. The Virgin stood bewildered and dangled Jesus by the arm. The blue blanket fell to the floor. Frankie kept drumming. Miss Thomas was calling him from the side of the platform – Frankie! Frankie! Stop! – but she'd stopped him once too often and he kept on going. Finally the head teacher closed the curtains. Frankie, his head light and his sticks flying, marched round and round in his blue jacket, feeling the power of the drums surge through him, enjoying the way the other children scattered before him. Finally, Miss Thomas and the head teacher lifted him between them and carted him off to the changing room. They made him sit there while they went and started the play all over again. This time Paul was to shout Knock! Knock!

"I'll get you later, Sweeney," Paul muttered through clenched teeth when he passed the changing room door. "You're for the kicking of your life!"

Frankie hardly heard him. His head was full of warm Christmas light and wild free drumming. His feet and hands twitched, tapping to the beat of an invisible drum. Still he felt shut in and so he jumped sideways, right out of himself and up in the air. It was easy, so easy, after the drum had loosed his spirit. He looked down at his other self, slumped limply on a bench, his silver buttons gleaming softly. Frankie was filled with irritation. He hated that Frankie, everybody's punchbag; he hated living in that scrawny body, hated being afraid all the time. So much better to be OUT! He drifted towards the gym. He knew, he just knew, that Paul would give him that kicking later and Frankie would stand there and take it and cry and cry and cry like a baby. Disgusted, he wafted though the wall and took up a position at the back of the hall. Joseph and Mary had found the stable and the choir of angels was singing *Away In A Manger*. The audience, sorry for the little boy who had been so upset, clapped encouragingly every time Joseph opened his mouth. Joseph thrust out his chest and strutted, the star of the show. Frankie's anger rose up in him like bubbles, making him light headed. Like a plume of red smoke, he billowed down to the front of the gym. Mr. Welsh was sitting there with Roxy lying quietly at his feet. The dog looked up as he approached and gave a subdued whine. Frankie looked into big brown intelligent eyes. The dog knew he was there. She whined again. Mr. Welsh scratched at her ears and shushed her. Frankie grinned. She didn't look very happy, not in the mood to snarl or show teeth. On impulse, he jumped sideways into Roxy, just to find out how afraid she was. The colours of the world dimmed and faded. Frankie looked about the gym and saw shades of grey. Strange. The gym smelled different too – a thick choking pall of perfume and sweat and old socks and damp wool nipped at his nose. People stank.

On stage, Joseph was accepting the jewelled boxes from the three wise men who were singing *We Three Kings of Orient Are*.

"Spell Orient," Dad had said when Frankie told him about the play. He was flicking his lighter – off, on, off, on – and staring into the flame. Frankie had stammered and stuttered and only got as far as 'O' when Dad lost patience with him and pressed the hot top of the lighter into the small of his back. Frankie had screamed once and been slapped for it. His mother had turned back to the cooker and lit another cigarette. She hadn't spoken to him until Dad went out. "Try not to annoy him, Frankie," was all she said.

A low growl rose in Frankie's throat. He felt his hackles rise and a powerful tension in his muscular shoulders. He wanted to spring, to tear, to bite. His back stiffened and his great heavy tail thumped on the floor. Joseph stepped to the front of the platform to command the heavenly choir to sing for Baby Jesus. They had only just begun *The First Noel* when Frankie sprang. Snarling and snapping, he leapt through the air and flung his full weight at Joseph. Terrified screams provoked him. Joseph's flailing arms enraged him. He seized the hem of Joseph's gown and tore it in two, then leapt again for the tea towel on his head. It was pinned there with kirby grips. He tugged and hauled, snarling and growling, until the grips and towel came away, bringing hair with it. The towel was red checked, like the ones the puppies fought over.

15

Frankie almost burst with rage. He snapped at Joseph's swinging fists, tore at his exposed calf. Mr. Welsh was shouting, 'Roxy! Roxy! Down!' But Frankie had tasted blood and wanted to howl and rip and shred. Mr. Welsh got him by the collar and tried to pull him off the screaming child. Frankie bit him too, sank his teeth right into his hand and worried ferociously. His own vicious growling was music in his ears. It took three men to haul him away from Joseph, who promptly fainted. The fun was over. Frankie jumped sideways and watched from above as the fight suddenly drained from Roxy. She lay down, whining, and seemed bewildered. There was blood on her muzzle and a splash on her chest. She looked up in his direction and flattened her ears. No one else noticed that.

Parents stormed the platform and snatched up their sobbing children. Miss Thomas was crying and fussing over Joseph. 'Go on, then,' Frankie thought. 'Go on then – start your play again.'

But the hall was clear in minutes. Frankie was left alone, standing among the angels' tinsel haloes which had all fallen to the floor in the panic. He wondered where his own parents were. Then he realised they would be with the other Frankie. He floated back to the changing room. Sure enough, there they were.

"He's fainted again," his Dad was saying. "What's he fainting for? Nobody bit him! He never even saw anything!"

Mum reached for her cigarettes and lit one.

"No smoking on the premises," Mrs. Grey said, looking up from Joseph who was weeping noisily on a bench, almost as loudly as his mother. Frankie's Mum scuttled silently out of the gym and headed for the playground.

"You can't smoke anywhere on Council property," Mrs. Grey called after her, but she turned back to Joseph. "Your Dad's coming with the car," she said. "Won't be long till the doctor sees you."

Dad was shaking Frankie's shoulder. "Come on, son. Time to go home."

Sullenly, Frankie hovered in the doorway. He didn't feel like going back in. He wouldn't go back in till he felt like it. Dad lifted him in his arms and turned to Mrs. Grey. "Best get this wee soldier home, eh?"

Mrs. Grey smiled thinly. "And what is the doctor saying about Frankie's funny turns?"

"They're investigating," Dad said. "But you know how it is. These things take forever."

Liar. Bloody liar. Frankie had never been near a doctor. He watched his father cross the playground. His body was limp as usual, the legs hanging down over Dad's arm. His blue trainers bumped against father's hip with every step he took. The coloured lights in the heels flashed on and off every time the trainers bounced against bone. Frankie-glow-in-the-dark. He decided to go for a prowl before he went home.

Frankie ended up down by the river again. He hung in the air under the bridge, listening to the rush of the water and the slap of waves against the piers. He could see the frost hardening along the walkway, but under the bridge the weeds and damp kept the ground soft and sour smelling. He saw rats, scavenging and scurrying and disliked their malicious beady eyes and pink whippy tails. One of them scampered out from under the bridge and ran along the walkway. Frankie heard a whirr of wings, so quiet as to be almost silent, and saw a flash of deadly speed. An owl. A big owl with a heart shaped face! It plunged from the sky, straight down, claws extended, and snatched up the rat. In an instant, Frankie was inside it, gliding silently through the air high above the glistening frost. Three broad silent flaps of his wings and he was perched on a beam under the bridge, hearing the tiny crunch of small bones. The owl tore and ate and Frankie felt its heart, smaller and quieter than his own, but stronger somehow. It wasn't afraid – that was it. The owl wasn't afraid. Everything was as it should be – he hunted, killed, ate, and was calm. The owl preened and then launched itself into space again. The power of wings startled Frankie – he glided, swooped, and the only sound was the whistle of wind ruffling his feathers. He flitted from one side of the bridge to the other, scanning the ground below for prey. Rats. Mice. Once the owl had heard the rustle of small paws, the clatter of a claw on paving, the small animals had no chance…
He was enjoying himself, wondering if it was possible to fly right up to the moon, when he sensed a weakening of his will. Frankie was waking up! He struggled to ignore the flickering return to consciousness, but could not. Frankie was waking up and getting stronger. He was sucked out of the owl and drawn back along the river bank, back into the town,

past the place behind the park where the alkies hung out, past the high tenements with their neat squares of light warming the gloom. He travelled like a dark strong wind, back home, to his street, to his tenement, to his flat, to his room. Frankie was lying on the floor, moaning quietly. His eyes flickered and he sat up. Frankie and Frankie were reunited.

He could hear raised voices from the kitchen.

"That kid's a fuckin' freak and he never got that from my side of the family. I only need to look at you to see where the weakness came from."

He couldn't hear his mother's reply – she gabbled when she was frightened, a rapid meaningless gush of words.

"Have you got any ciggies? I'm out. What do you mean, no? Did you smoke them all?"

Dad's voice was incredulous. Outraged. Offended. Frankie's heart began to race. They were at it again. He climbed into his bed and pulled the covers over his head, and the pillow over the covers. But the voice went on, ranting and working itself up, ready to blow. He wished he had his drum sticks, he wished he could drum himself out of here. But he was stuck where he was, hearing it all.

Slap. Slap. Squeal. Don't, Frank, don't.

Frankie pressed his face into his mattress, clamped the ends of his pillow over his ears. But he could hear her crying.

"Come in and look at your freaky son. Come and look at what you landed me with."

His father's feet stamped along the hall, accompanied by a dragging noise and his mother's whimpering. His room door burst open and the light went on. Frankie flattened himself, trying to be invisible, but a rough hand pulled the blankets off the bed.

"Look at him!"

Slap.

"Frank! Don't! You'll wake him up!"

"I should be so lucky! He's a fucking ZOMBIE! The living dead! Like you!"

Slap.

Frankie's heart nearly stopped with fright. He wet himself, and groaned when he heard his father's shout of disgust.

"You haven't even got him house trained yet!"

A hand tore the pillow away and flung it aside. Then it grabbed a handful of Frankie's hair and shook his head from side to side. He felt roots tear. He heard his mother panting and then slinking out of the room. She'd left him! She always left him! Dad hauled him upright by the hair and shook him some more so that his head battered off the headboard. He couldn't breathe for fright and pain. The room turned black, his body numbed, and then he was out. He didn't know how it happened but it did. He stood back, watching his father punch him. Punch after punch after punch.

He slipped away, unable to bear the sight. He went to the kitchen. His Mum was there as usual. She was raking through the ashtray, looking for a big ciggie end. She found one, lit it with a shaky hand, and stood with her back to the sink, drawing deeply, trying to get the smoke into her lungs. Frankie was angry. He didn't have his cool light feeling. He was earthbound somehow, not able to get out. The banging from next door went on and on. Finally his mother went to the door.

"Frank! Frank! The neighbours will be up in a minute."

His father came storming through.

"You trying to tell me what I can and can't do in my own house?"

"No, no…"

His father stopped mid rant.

"I thought you had no cigarettes left?"

Mum stood staring stupidly at the lighted tip of her cigarette.

"I don't, Frank. I don't. It's a fag end. From the ashtray."

Dad snatched the cigarette from her hand and stubbed it out on her neck. Rage convulsed Frankie, and quick as lightning he jumped inside Dad. His trick had to be good for something besides hunting rats. He would stop Dad doing this. He would. But it didn't turn out like that.

Inside Dad, he found himself gripping his Mum's arm. Her soft squishy flesh annoyed him. The smell of fear on her stinking sweat annoyed him. Her wide fearful eyes annoyed him. Christ, the only time she had any expression was when she was afraid. He dug fingers into her arm and was filled with a fierce glee. Dad hissed abuse, quietly, into her ear. She was crying. Dad's irritation with her ran through Frankie like electricity. Why didn't she….? Why couldn't she… be like a Mum! Be like a real woman? Be anything other than this whey faced trembling good-for-nothing…The sound of slaps invigorated him, let his contempt out. It was a lot like drumming. His Dad's heart was big and strong and swept Frankie into its venomous rhythm. Mum slumped to the floor, trying to pull herself up by holding on to the table leg.

Dad stepped back, tired by his own onslaught, but Frankie wasn't through yet. He made Dad swing his feet, swing his arms, made him swear all the worst words Frankie had ever heard. Blows and cries energised him. Dad was his puppet now, punching where Frankie led, kicking where he lunged.

You and your cigarettes, Frankie thought, you stood and watched and smoked and watched and smoked…You never cared what he did so long as it wasn't to you.

She was crumpled on the floor now, weeping, clutching herself. The sight infuriated him. His father's heavy breathing was loud in his ears. Frankie understood the meaning of triumph then – to beat and kick and let your anger out and face no consequences. This is what it would be like to be grown up. This is what he would be like. Dad sank on to a chair and started searching through the ashtray for another fag end. Frankie's exultation faded suddenly. Dad was sullen and shamed – Frankie could feel it in the dullness which descended on him.

"Get to your bed, Mary," he said wearily.

Mum sort of slid upright and sidled out of the room. Dad sagged in the chair and his mind emptied of his racing fury. Frankie didn't like the feeling of vacancy. It was as if without his anger Dad was no one. He jumped out and hovered, looking down at the top of his father's head as he lit a half inch of cigarette and inhaled deeply. He was feeling sorry for himself – Frankie could see it in the slump of his shoulders. He moved through the hall and peeped through into his mother's bedroom. She was feeling sorry for herself too, lying on the bed and staring at the ceiling. He was sick of the pair of them. They were more than he could stand. He went out of the window and into the frosty night. It was black out there, black and dark but clean with frost and cold. The slates on the roofs glittered, the windows all around him glowed with warm light from Christmas trees. He drifted up and down the street, not sure what he wanted to do. He wished he'd stayed with the owl. There was something pure about an owl's kill, done without rancour or venom, done without confusion and red rage, done because that was the way things were. It was a better way to be than anything Frankie had seen. He stayed out for hours, visiting his old haunts, expecting to be called back at any moment when Frankie woke up. He even went into Mrs. Brunton's house. She was asleep in her old fashioned bed with the satin coverlet. Sheba lay on an old mat across the bottom of the bed, snoring gently.

She whimpered in her sleep when Frankie drifted by and half opened an eye. But she only sighed and fell asleep again. Frankie settled in the corner watching the old woman sleep. She had been his friend, she had been kind. He knew she'd never known what it was to be full of a killing rage because she was soft and gentle inside. He jumped into her to feel what that was like. Her heart was calm and steady, soothing, a quiet beat on a kindly drum. He stayed in her, feeling himself grow light and airy and golden again. He wished he could stay with Mrs. Brunton. He'd be a better boy then, he knew he would.

An icy pink dawn was tinting the window when he was startled by the sound of sirens. Mrs. Brunton was too. She sat up and called Sheba. An ambulance siren. It filled the empty street with its racket. Mrs. Brunton went to her window. The ambulance had stopped outside his close. Mum! She'd been bleeding a lot! She'd been pale as milk. He watched as ambulance men opened up the back of their vehicle. Mr. Welsh was standing nearby, pointing behind him. The medics disappeared into the close. Then a police car came roaring up with its blue light on. The police went into the close too. Frankie, frozen to the spot, watched the drama unfold.

Mrs. Brunton drew her dressing gown round her against the cold and then a shrill cry broke from her.

"My God! My God! It's wee Frankie!"

He saw a stretcher with a small figure laid out on it. He saw the police dragging his father, handcuffed, out to the car. Mum came out next. They didn't seem sure whether to put her in the ambulance or the Panda. In the end, she went into the ambulance. Frankie jumped through the window and into the street. He was inside the ambulance in a flash. His body lay on a bed, and the ambulance man was trying to breathe into his mouth. His mate was saying that it was pointless, too late. Frankie looked down at himself. His face was battered out of shape. Thick black clots of blood matted his hair. There would be no getting back inside Frankie. He knew that right away. But where would he go now?

"Either of you got a cigarette?"

Mum. She hardly looked at him, seemed to be trying to pretend he wasn't there.

"You can't smoke in here, Missus."

She began to snivel.

"All I want is a smoke. Is it too much to ask?"

The ambulance man ignored her and drew the blanket up over Frankie's face.

"Is he dead?" The ambulance man ignored her some more. She lowered her voice confidentially. "I always knew he'd go too far one of these days. This was always going to happen. It could just as easily have been me, you know. Just as likely to be me as him."

Frankie jumped out of the ambulance. He had no connection here. He chased after the Panda car all the way to the police station. His Dad was explaining to the big silver haired sergeant that they had the wrong guilty party – his wife wasn't quite right in the head. He'd come home and found her covered in blood and his little son dead in his bed. He should never have left them alone. He was going to have to carry the guilt of that till the day he died. Frankie could tell that the police sergeant wasn't very impressed. His hard gaze was knowing and weary. Frankie followed them down to the cells. There were a lot of stairs. He could feel a dull anger warming the sergeant's body. He could feel the heat of it. On impulse, he jumped into him. Sure enough, the big man was angry. He had it well under control, so it wasn't like Dad's anger. But his blood was thick and heavy with it. Frankie thought of drum rolls. Loud long drum rolls. The sergeant's heart began to beat in time. Thump. Thump. Thump. Frankie drummed pain and fear into the rhythm of hate. The veins at the sergeant's temple pulsed visibly. Frankie felt him get light headed with it. Suddenly, the sergeant's foot lashed out, kicked Dad's legs from under him and sent him crashing headlong to the bottom of the stairs.

Frankie grinned at his father's protests. He protested all the way along the corridor, and kept it up while he was locked in a cell. It was a sour place, dirty and stained, and it delighted Frankie because Dad was always so fussy about being clean. His cell mate was asleep. Frankie peered down at him. Big and ugly with a battle scarred face. His knuckles were raw from a fight. Frankie jumped in and drummed him awake. The man glared balefully at Dad.

"Who the fuck are you? And what do you think you're playing at, waking me up?"

Dad was afraid. Frankie grinned happily. This was going to be fun. And it was, all night long.

In the afternoon, Frankie cruised down to the river again and hung about the bridge. He realised that he didn't belong nowhere – he belonged everywhere. He knew where Paul lived, and Mr. Welsh, and Mum. He could find his father whenever he wanted – prison walls were no barrier to him. And then there was Mummy fox, and the owl, and the goose. He hovered golden in the weak winter sunlight. The gurgle of fast flowing water pleased him, and the slap of the waves on stone. The hard blue sky above was like glass and the frost on the grass diamond bright. Sky and water and frost were free things that came and went as they pleased, unstoppable, unforgiving, and so was Frankie. He was full to the brim with the joy of being dead forever.

Sexual Heaney

Gary Lightbody

I don't think I connected the two, music and literature I mean, until I read *Digging* by Seamus Heaney. It was the first time I heard music in words without the music being there already. I was sixteen years old and had been idly strumming the guitar with varying results for two years. The instrument at that point seemed alien in my hands but that was the year I discovered two things that changed my life forever: Seamus Heaney and Nirvana. Forget Walter Matthau and Jack Lemmon.

Cobain's music was visceral and furious at times but it belied his egg-shell heart and I found some of the same contradictions in Heaney. However in Heaney there seemed an emotional honesty I always presumed Cobain was hiding, or at least distorting, from the world. It was that honesty I followed in my writing from that minute to this.

Of course I was sixteen then, as green as spring and my ears wet with all the things I didn't yet know but something made me grab hold of those two disparate wires and force them together sparking. My parents will attest, hearing those early songs I was writing thunder and dirge up from the basement, that it took a long time for me to find any semblance of voice of my own but the wheels were turning at least. I still listen to Nirvana from time to time and I'm still as avid a fan of Heaney as ever. So these, my early catalysts, still connect me to something special. Or maybe I'm hopelessly/hopefully connected to them.

From that point for me music was as much about the words as it was about the melody. It's hard for a song to be truly great without honesty and that is something I learned from reading Heaney. A poet.

Last Song

Andrew Humphrey

"You just fancy her," Cal says. "You'd have stopped listening ten minutes ago if she was a moose."

"A moose," I say. "You have such a way with words."

"It's a gift," he says.

I'm whispering but Cal is too pissed to worry about such niceties and heads are beginning to turn. I lead him back towards the bar.

"Whassup?" he says.

"People are trying to listen. You've got a voice like a jackhammer."

We're in *Spencer's Bar*, a club set in a twelfth century crypt on King Street. On Friday nights one half of the L-shaped bar is used for live music. Anyone can put their name down and play a fifteen-minute set. Understandably the quality can be patchy. You get established acts trying new material and complete beginners fulfilling their guitar-hero fantasies. And all kinds of stuff in between; eclectic, experimental, exceptional, sometimes awful. But almost always interesting. Whatever the quality Friday nights at *Spencer's* are cool. It's often packed. The setting – vaulted stone ceilings, dimly lit corners, a slightly pissed sense of history – lends itself to the music and generates an atmosphere of benign expectation. You often get the sensation that something special is about to happen. It never does, of course, but the feeling is nice while it lasts.

A table comes free by the bar and I guide Cal into the nearest chair then buy him another pint. Cal's my older brother. He's got the looks, the money, the luck. I've got…I'm not sure what I've got.

By the time I hand him his drink he's chatting up a couple of students who've made the mistake of wandering past his eye line. You get a lot of students at *Spencer's*. Loads of women, mostly young. That's the main reason we come here, I suppose, whatever I say about the atmosphere. Cal, with his looks and his tan and his floppy blond hair, and me trailing behind, trying to feed off the scraps. Mother must be so proud.

Cal's t-shirt is pulled up as he shows the nearest girl – blond, casually beautiful, ridiculously low-slung jeans and a top short enough to reveal a flat stomach and a navel adorned with a golden stud – an eight inch scar that stops just below his breastbone.

"Great White. Just off the Barrier Reef." He looks at me as I sit opposite him. "Isn't that right, Josh? I'm lucky to be alive."

The blond girl runs a finger along Cal's scar.

"Ringland Hills," I say. "Just off the A47. You fell out of a tree and cried like a girl. Mind you, you were only eleven."

The blond laughs. Her friend – brunette, pretty enough – smiles slowly and tries to hold my gaze. Instead I glance at Cal again. He nods, his grin off centre. "Nice one, Josh."

"I'll leave you to it," I stand again. "Nature calls."

On the way to the toilets there's a side door that leads to the music area. I ease through it quietly, careful not to disturb the view of the bearded man who sits on a stool just inside the entrance.

The girl we were watching earlier is still playing. A single spotlight picks her out. She stands on the tiny stage, just her and an acoustic guitar that seems too big for her and a voice that quivers constantly but never quite breaks. The song itself is Aimee Mann-lite; spiky, ironic, a sense of loss, yearning, disappointment. The usual. But still…

It ends suddenly. Her use of the guitar has been understated throughout and the lyrics seem to stop halfway through a verse. There is a small silence then a smear of polite applause. Usually the acts at *Spencer's* bring an army of friends along with them, ensuring a raucous response when their set finishes. She obviously hasn't bothered. But the lukewarm reception she receives doesn't appear to worry her. She stands for a moment – small, sharp-featured. Short, spiky hair hennaed to within an inch of its life – then mumbles a quiet, *that's it* and disappears behind the stage.

I stare at the space she's vacated. I haven't even clapped. Her music is…almost instantly forgotten, actually. Cal is right, I fancy her. So I'm shallow. Sue me.

"Twat," Cal says.

The pretty students are nowhere to be seen.

I sit next to him. "I'm fine. Thanks."

"You're a fucking liability." He looks vaguely sullen, but then he always does when he's drunk.

"Do you remember her name?"

"What?"

"The girl we were watching. The one you reckon I fancied. Did you catch her name?"

He squints at me. He's trying to think of something witty to say. Eventually he blinks slowly and grunts and says, "Lesbian."

"I take it that's a no."

"Don't worry, little brother. She'll be back."

"Why do you say that?"

"She was shit, wasn't she? Where else is she going to play?"

I find her in the car park, loading her guitar into the rear of a battered Fiesta. Cal's moved on to the *Waterfront* and I decided to leave him to it. He didn't put up much of a fight. Probably thought he'd have better luck without his liability of a brother for company.

It's cold – well, it's February, it's entitled to be – and the car park and pavements sparkle with frost. The river Wensum runs through King Street and the smell of it hangs in the freezing air.

I have to pass her Fiesta to get to my car. I hesitate and she turns towards me with understandable wariness. She is even prettier close up with features sharp enough to cut. Her eyes are bigger than I remember, but hooded, watchful.

"Great set," I say.

She slams the hatch shut and locks it. "It was crap." I start to protest but she interrupts me. "Anyway, you only saw half of it."

"A bit more than…"

"You and your boyfriend sneaked out."

"Actually, he's my brother."

Her head tilts. "Really? The pretty boy?"

"Well…"

"But you crept back in, didn't you? Caught the last two minutes. That was nice of you."

Jesus. Cal is obviously an amateur as far as sarcasm is concerned. But at least she's noticed me. Not that there is anything else in her voice or in any of her words to offer me the slightest morsel of encouragement. But still. Oaks grow from tiny acorns, don't they? I mean, *really* tiny acorns…

She steps towards me, holds out a hand. "Sorry. My name's Lucy."

It's a small hand, surprisingly warm. "Josh."

"Josh," she says slowly. She stares at her car as though it is suddenly fascinating. "You are hitting on me, aren't you, Josh?"

I'm stunned but I try to hide it. "I thought I was being polite."

"Polite." Her eyes are on me again. They are disconcerting. "I don't really do polite. Anyway, I've got a boyfriend."

"Of course you have."

"Of course," she says.

Bollocks, I think. But it's liberating, not giving a shit. "I'd have thought he'd be here. Lending moral support. Giving you a hand."

"I said I had a boyfriend. I didn't say he wasn't a useless wanker."

"He must be," I say.

"He's at the hospital. His dad's dying."

"What? Shit, I'm sorry…"

She leans forward, touches my arm. "I'm lying. I do that. I'm not a very nice person."

"No," I say.

She walks to the driver's door and unlocks it. She wears a sweater over a cotton dress. She doesn't seem cold. My breath turns to smoke as I speak, her's doesn't. "I'll be here again. In a month or so. New songs. Better songs." Her expression becomes vague. "Better everything."

"Cal said that you would be."

"Cal's your…brother."

"Yep. My brother."

She makes a face. "But he *is* gay, right?"

God, I can't wait to tell him. "He's fighting it."

She gives a short laugh. It's harsh, ostensibly unattractive, but it makes the hair on my balls tingle.

I'm still smiling as I watch her car turn onto King Street.

*

Cal played in a band for a while, when he was in his early twenties. This was in the mid-nineties when Oasis and Blur were cool and most new bands tried to mimic one or the other of them. Nero – I know, crap name; Cal's idea, obviously – were a curious mix of both and were good enough to earn a contract with a minor label and release a couple of albums, both of which drew respectful reviews before bombing predictably.

Cal played lead guitar and sang. He's a good guitarist, could be much better than good if he ever put his heart into it. He practiced his guitar solos, though. He insisted that every Nero song had at least one solo and he milked them for all they were worth; the poses, the faces. Textbook stuff. Watchable enough, I suppose. Up to a point. As usual, it was all about Cal.

He has a good voice, too. A lovely voice, actually. But he overdoes it. Not in a good, Jeff Buckley-type way, but in a way that makes people look at him and think…what a twat.

For a year Nero toured pretty much non-stop, throughout Britain and Europe. I travelled with them across Germany for a couple of weeks. It was numbing. The gigs were a relief from the hours spent on motorways and in motel rooms. The highlight was a gig on the outskirts of Stuttgart, in some chilly box of a municipal building. For some reason songs that I grown to know so well they barely registered seemed suddenly imbued with fresh meaning. Every note was perfect, singular, part of a wonderful whole. For two hours the band, the increasingly hysterical crowd and myself, were on exactly the same frequency. For once, Nero rocked.

I wondered if it was simply my own perception but afterwards the band were on the same high – natural, for once – and even Cal was beaming, generous, normal and I almost loved him.

The next evening Nero were once more functional, efficient, just getting the job done and two days later I went home. After another fortnight Cal was home too and Nero were no more.

He was tired, he said. Bored. Rock and roll wasn't all it was cracked up to be. Even sex and drugs get tedious after a while, apparently. And Cal doesn't do addiction, just as he doesn't do commitment or giving a shit.

*

Three weeks later Cal and I crunch our way to *Spencer's* across pavements clogged with inches of fresh snow. Norwich city centre is hyper-quiet, abandoned.

"It'll be cancelled," Cal says. "This is a waste of time."

"The show must go on. They'll find a way."

I wish that Cal would stop moaning, wish that he hadn't accompanied me at all. I've had a feeling all day that Lucy will be at *Spencer's* tonight and if she is I'd rather Cal wasn't there to spoil things for me. I'm quite capable of doing that myself.

It's not particularly cold now the wind has dropped and the last of the snow clouds have scudded eastwards. If it weren't for Cal this would be fun, walking through this hushed, suspended world.

He's in a foul mood. A girl he met a fortnight earlier dumped him via a text message just after lunch. It took her two weeks to discover that beneath the movie star looks lies…nothing much. No hidden depths. He really is every bit as shallow as he seems. Actually, I have no idea what her reasons were, I don't even remember her name. But I expect it's a pretty good guess.

He looks so pathetic that even *I* feel a stab of pity for him. "You can always borrow a guitar, play a couple of Nero's greatest hits, if the worst comes to the worst."

Cal is quiet for a moment as we slow approaching the downhill gradient of Music House Lane. As our path flattens again he says, "I've been thinking about that, actually. Putting my name down for a set. Just to keep my hand in."

"That'll be a fifteen minute guitar solo, then."

"You make it sound like a bad thing."

"Might as well just get up on stage and have a wank."

"I'm pretty sure that's against house rules."

Spencer's car park isn't entirely empty, which is encouraging. We enter the bar, which is dotted with regulars. The sound of a guitar being tuned drifts across from the music area.

"See," I say. "Packed."

"Right," Cal says. We fetch our drinks and chose a seat. "No sign of *her*, though, is there?"

"I've got no idea who you're talking about."

Cal snorts into his Guinness.

I flick a beer mat at him. "Anyway, you sold your guitars."

"Change the subject, why don't you."

"And amps. No point putting your name down without an axe. Man."

Cal shrugs. "I'll have a word with dad. He'll come up with the cash."

"I thought you were minted."

"Yeah, but it's all tied up. You know how it is."

"You know that I don't. Mum and dad aren't made of money."

This is so manifestly untrue that Cal doesn't even bother replying. Dad is a heart specialist who spends most of the week at his London practice. Mum is something high up in the County Council. I'm not sure of her title. I don't think she is. It seems to change most weeks, anyway. They live in a suitably luxurious house on Judges Walk that Cal is very much looking forward to inheriting one day. They belong to the golf club and the tennis club and all sorts of other shit that I suppose they are entitled to and that seem to make them happy. Cal still lives with them and sponges off them remorselessly. He has acquired squatter's right to mum's BMW. She's been forced to splash out on a new 4x4. Poor mum. I long ago decided that I would make my own way. I work in admin for a software developer, live in a council flat off Grove Road, drive a beat up Datsun. What a hero.

We wander over to the music room and watch a guy with waist-length blond hair play guitar left-handed and sing plangently about something or other. He goes on a bit so we fetch another drink and chat to Scot, the Australian behind the bar, and to Lenny, a dapper man with a neat goatee, who was playing steel guitar before either of us were born.

We sit down again and Cal says, "I had a look at the list. Her name's not down."

"You don't even know her name."

"Lucy. You've mentioned her a couple of times."

"Right. You needn't look so pleased. Just because she thinks you're gay."

"Fuck off, Josh."

I lean towards him, say earnestly, "And there's nothing wrong…"

"I know, I know," he snaps. "But the point is, I'm not gay. Not remotely. I've got my reputation to think of."

"I think he doth protest too much," I say softly and he looks at me and says, 'What?' and I shrug and then Lucy walks in.

"Speak of the Devil," Cal says. I stand and hit my knee against the table. "For Christ's sake. Don't seem so bloody keen."

"I'm fine," I say. I nod at Lucy and she nods back. She seems to be alone, apart from her guitar, which she places awkwardly next to the coat-rack. There is something different about her, but it's not her clothes, which are still take-it-or-leave-it-hippy-grunge, or her predictably spiky hair. It's in her face and eyes, I think. She looks…honed, ready for anything. She glows.

"Josh," she says, as she passes our table. "And this must be Cal. The…"

"My brother," I say, taking her arm and steering her towards the bar. I feel Cal's eyes on my back.

Scot looks at me expectantly. "Drink?" I say to Lucy and her eyes meet mine and I'm lost. "Shit," I say.

"What?"

"You were right, I was hitting on you. And you've been pretty much all I can think about. I know I'm being extremely uncool, but…oh, fuck it."

Scot laughs. Lucy doesn't, which is something. She says, "Wow. I'm impressed." She doesn't sound it and I don't blame her. "I'll have a JD and coke."

Scot's still chuckling as he fetches it. "Your name's not on the list. Didn't think we'd see you tonight."

"You've checked already? Be still my beating heart."

"Actually, Cal…"

"I phoned earlier. They've had some cancellations, unsurprisingly, given the weather. I was happy to step into the breach."

"You said something about new songs?"

"Four new songs. I wrote them today."

"Today?"

"Yup." Her eyes are brimming with…something. Confidence? Glee? It's hard to tell but I can't look away from them. Her face is angled towards mine. Her mouth is small, even when she's smiling.

"But you lie, don't you? That's what you said."

"And you remembered? How sweet." She takes a tiny sip of her drink then licks her lips. "But I'm not lying now."

"And I should believe that, because…?"

"I see your point. It's a bugger, isn't it?"

"I wouldn't know," I say. "I've always been pathologically honest."

"Not that it's anything to be proud of. It's very over-rated, the truth."

"I'll take your word for it. No boyfriend again?"

She turns so that her back is against the bar. "My, you are observant. He's gone to a better place."

"A better place?"

"Mundesley."

"Mundesley?"

"He runs a drop in centre for drug addicts. Quite a lot of them in Mundesley, apparently."

"Not much else to do, I expect. But it's hardly the end of the world. No reason…"

"He's a twat. I dumped him."

"Right."

She turns her face towards mine. Her eyes are dark and wicked, her voice bone-dry. "And I'm obsessed with you, Josh. That posh voice and those puppy-eyes. I keep getting wet thinking about you…"

"Don't take the piss."

"Why not? It's a free country."

I can hear Scot laughing again. Cal is nowhere to be seen, which is something of a bonus.

Lucy tugs my sleeve. "So what public school did you go to?"

Still avoiding her gaze I say, "And I thought I hid it so well."

"Better than your brother."

Now I do look at her, sharply. "You've never even spoken to him."

"I've seen him about. Listened to him. I've *noticed* him, Josh. Anyone would."

"What do you mean?"

Her voice changes. She speaks slowly. "He's beautiful, isn't he?"

"Beautiful."

"To look at. He's bloody gorgeous."

I nip my eyes shut, open them again. "Yeah, I think I get the point."

"Bitter as a lemon."

"But it's all show, isn't it? On the inside…"

"Inside?" Disdain is back, her default setting. "Who gives a fuck about what's inside?"

I look at her hard, trying to work out if she's taking the piss or not.

Then she glances over my shoulder. "Trevor's calling me. I'm on. You going to watch the whole set this time?"

She's already pushing past me. "Wouldn't miss it for the world," I say.

Cal's standing by the rear wall and I join him. The music room is about two-thirds full, which isn't bad for this early in the evening.

"Didn't think you'd bother," I say. "You weren't very impressed last time."

"I've got bugger all else to do." He waits a beat. "And yes, I did hear you make a prat of yourself at the bar. I was ashamed to be your brother."

"Hardly for the first time, Cal."

"It's as though you set out to achieve the polar opposite of cool. Which you did. Well done."

I say nothing.

Lucy is introduced and the lights dim. I brace myself, expect to be mildly embarrassed. But…

The change is obvious from the first chord she plays which shimmers like something tangible and blurs into a gorgeous intro to a song of such iridescent sweetness…

And her voice. It's real now, a physical presence stalking the room, raising the hairs on every neck, stopping conversations, commanding attention. It is cool and pure and note perfect.

And the songs are about…well, loss, yearning, disappointment. But it's different now. They matter. There's an elegiac urgency to them, a sense that every word was written specifically for you. Even Cal feels it. He watches, rapt.

Four songs. All sublime and as close to perfect as you'd want to get. Then she stops. The silence seems obscene. The room erupts. People stand. A woman close to me is crying. I haven't seen anything like it at

Spencer's before. Cal is clapping like an idiot, but then so am I. His expression, for once unguarded, without irony, is of pure joy. He looks child-like, actually, and it seems odd seeing him like that. I can't remember it happening before, even when he *was* a child.

I turn back to the stage and Lucy is smiling. She's looking straight at Cal. At first I think she's looking at me, but of course she bloody isn't.

*

Six months after Nero split up I discovered that their demise was due to more than simply Cal's boredom.

I bumped into Mick, their bass player, in a pub in Cawston, a tiny village next to Reepham. I'd just finished playing cricket and most of the team stopped off for a quick drink before we returned to Norwich.

I didn't recognise him at first. He was working the fruit machine, so his back was to me. His hair was longer than I remembered and he'd gained a little weight. It was his voice that gave him away.

I was moaning to one of our opening batsman about the shocking bias of the local umpire when Mick said, 'You useless, fucking bastard,' to the fruit machine. The voice was flat, laconic, vaguely Northern and I recognised it immediately. I made my excuses and joined him by the machine.

"You always were crap at gambling, Mick."

He did a double take that made me grin then shook his head and said, "I thought you were dead."

That did for the grin. "Nice to see you, too."

He shrugged, turned on his stool so that he faced me full on. He looked older. His features were weathered. He wore a badly trimmed beard and it didn't suit him. "That's what Cal said, last time I saw him. Mind you, I was about to beat the shit out of the useless fucker."

"He said I was dead?"

"Dying. Meningitis. So I only hit him once."

"And you believed him?"

"He was pretty convincing."

"He would be if his arse was at stake."

"I could have checked, I suppose. Wouldn't have been difficult. But I found I didn't really give a shit. No offence."

"None taken."

I bought us both a drink and we sat at a corner table. I watched as Mick fixed himself a roll-up. His fingers, although thick and blunt, were nimble enough. Just as well, I suppose, considering that he was a bass player. But they were rough, like his face, beaten. He saw me looking.

"I'm a brickie now, Josh. With my dad. He always wanted me to join the family firm. I've had my fifteen minutes, haven't I?"

"More than most get, Mick."

He nodded at me. I was still wearing my whites. "Call me Sherlock, but I reckon you've been playing cricket."

"Nothing gets past you."

"Give the village a hiding, did you?"

"Yeah, it was pretty easy."

"They're crap. I turn out for them sometimes, when they're desperate. How did you do?"

"Quick thirty-odd," I said. "A couple of sixes."

"Short boundaries, aren't they?"

"Dodgy pitch, though. And umpires."

"Shite bowling, though."

"Pity you didn't play. Might have got my fifty."

"I'd have knocked your head off, mate."

"That's a bit harsh, Mick."

He took a long drag of his cigarette and blew the smoke past my shoulder. "Sins of the brother and all that."

"I don't think that's quite right."

"Whatever."

We drank in silence for a while then I asked him exactly what his problem was.

He stubbed out his cigarette and started to roll another. "I bear a grudge. Always have."

"Against Cal?"

"Now who's Sherlock?"

"He said he left you in the shit. But you could have carried on, the three of you." Mick's eyes are on the roll-up. "Might have been better, actually. Less self-indulgent. Chris has got as good a voice as Cal…"

I stopped when I realised that Mick had stopped rolling his cigarette and was staring straight at me.

"You're full of shit." His voice was pinched, even drier than usual.

"What?"

He took a deep breath and placed both hands face down on the table. For the first time I noticed the tension in his shoulders and arms. "I'm not a fucking idiot." He said it slowly, with equal emphasis on each word.

"I never thought…"

A large hand shot forward and grabbed my wrist. His grip was predictably strong. He gave my forearm a squeeze then eased off a little to show he was holding something back. "Are you telling me you don't know?"

I tried to reclaim my arm but failed embarrassingly. "Know what?"

He looked hard into my face then released his grip. "Your brother is something else, isn't he?"

"What the fuck are you talking about, Mick?"

I felt a hand on my shoulder. I jerked backwards. It was Andy, the captain of our cricket team. "Are you ok, Josh?"

"I'm fine," I lied.

He looked at Mick for a moment but didn't hold his gaze. "We're off in minute."

I remembered that my car was back in Norwich and that I needed a lift.

"I'll be there in a sec."

Andy nodded and left me to it.

Mick was working on his cigarette again.

"Answer the question," I said. "What are you talking about?"

His face had closed down. His voice was Fen-flat and final. "Ask Cal," he said.

But I never did.

*

The buzz that Lucy's extraordinary set generated follows her into the bar. She's at the centre of a knot of people. She seems normal as she smiles and answers questions. I suppose that the sarcasm has been tucked away for a while. Perhaps she reserves it just for me. It's an arrogant thought and I bat it away.

"You've got competition," Cal says.

"Just the usual," I say, and something in my voice makes him look at me.

"What are you talking about?"

"You must have noticed the way she looks at you."

"What? The chick who thinks I'm gay?"

I tell him what she said to me.

"And who can blame her?" He shrugs as he speaks but I can see that he's pleased. "Anyway, she's not my type, Josh. You've got nothing to worry about."

I'm just behind him as we fight our way to the bar. I can see the streaks of sweat in his blond hair. "And if she was your type? And I liked her?"

He glances back at me, shoots me a feral grin. "I'd fuck her in a heartbeat. You know that."

Indeed I do.

We find a seat and after a while Lucy joins us.

"Little Miss Popular," I say.

"What did you think?" She still glows but it's muted now.

"You were awesome, frankly," I say.

"Told you I would be."

She scrapes a chair back and sits between us.

"So what was it?" Cal says. "Coke? Speed? What?"

"Cal," I say.

"I mean, no offence, but you were shit last time you were here. How else do you explain the improvement? If you were a racehorse they'd be running all sorts of tests."

Lucy rests her chin on her palm and aims Cal a smile of deceptive sweetness. "Jealous?"

Cal leans forward. "Look at her eyes. The pupils are well dilated."

"Leave it Cal," I say.

"I've never taken a drug in my life."

"Very rock and roll," Cal says.

They are still looking at each other.

"It reminded me of Stuttgart," I say, and Cal's gaze snaps onto me as I knew it would.

"What happened in Stuttgart?" Lucy says.

"Cal's band played their best gig there. Tonight felt similar."

"Cal was in a band?"

"You didn't know?" Cal says, disgusted.

"You were hardly a household name. Anyway, it was probably before Lucy's time."

Before Lucy can speak Cal launches into a ten minute monologue about Nero. Or more specifically about how Nero revolved around him and his general all round brilliance. I tune out for fear of vomiting. In the distance a folk band are murdering *Fairytale of New York* to a muted reception. Not that I'd envy anyone following Lucy tonight.

When I tune back in again Lucy is saying, "That's a great idea."

"What's a great idea?" I say.

"We're getting together," Cal says. "Going to write some songs. We thought a little electric guitar might beef her sound up a little. Something understated."

"Understated? You don't know the fucking meaning of the word." I realise that my voice is embarrassingly high and that people are looking at me. "Lucy, this is some kind of joke, right? You don't need this…" I wave a hand at Cal and search for the word. "…Oaf."

"Easy," Lucy says. "You'll have a stroke." She laughs as she stands. "I'm going to the loo."

After a moment I stand as well. I say 'Cunt' into Cal's face as I pass him.

"It's all about the music, man," he says mildly.

I take a pint of Guinness and go and sit by the river so that I can feel sorry for myself properly. I look across the cold, dark water to the Riverside Development, the multi-coloured and over-priced houses and flats that back on to a multitude of depressingly trendy nightclubs and bars. It's busier now, despite the weather, and clusters of woefully under-dressed young people gather and shout and laugh and drink and ready themselves for action. A shaven-headed teenager in a *Fred Perry* shirt spots me. He points at me and I hear a cackle of laughter. I raise my pint in his direction and say, 'Fuck off', under my breath.

After ten minutes my glass is almost empty and I realise that, unsurprisingly, I am quite cold. I watch a pair of swans sail past. A pillock from the other side of the river throws something at them. He misses by a long way and the swans ignore him. I stand and wave at him and call him a wanker, which is pretty brave considering that there's a river between us. I suddenly hope that he can't swim. But he simply makes a number of suggestive hand signals and disappears from sight. "My hero," Lucy says and I nearly jump out of my skin. She brushes snow off the wooden bench and sits next to me. "Sulking," she says. "Such an attractive trait."

"I'm just astonished that you've fallen for my brother's bullshit."

"Why? It's not as though you know anything about me, Josh. Is it?" She speaks evenly and her words make perfect sense. But that's not the point. "Anyway, we're not talking about marriage. I only want to fuck him."

"And that makes me feel so much better."

"And why should I care how you feel?"

I toss my empty glass into the river. "Just fuck off, then."

Lucy laughs. "That's better."

It starts to snow again, lightly at first then thick chunks of the stuff that I brush away from my eyes and mouth. I look at Lucy. The snow doesn't appear to be settling on her at all.

"Still here?" I say.

"I don't feel the cold." She nods at the river. "My mother drowned herself in the Wensum."

"Great."

"You don't believe me?"

"I don't give a shit either way."

"I think she thought she was Virginia Woolf. She used to write as well. Poetry. Awful stuff. She used to make me read it. Embarrassing. She couldn't understand why it wasn't published. I told her, it's because it's shit." She leans forward. I'm trying to ignore her, but I can't. "Dad had long gone so it was her brother that broke the news. I saw him waiting for me at the school gate and I knew what had happened. It took her four goes to get it right. She always was bloody useless."

"How old were you?"

"I didn't think you cared?" I stare at the cold water and say nothing.

"Fourteen. I never went to school again. I stayed with Uncle David for a while, but…it didn't work out. So I squatted for a bit, then got myself a council house. Been there ever since. Eight years."

"You're twenty-two?"

"Twenty-three."

"You look older."

"Charmer."

The snow has eased again and the air is still and vinegar-sharp. Lucy puts a hand on my thigh and squeezes. "I *am* a bitch."

"I think I'd worked that out."

"I'd only ever hurt you. You know that too, don't you?" I nod. "But you'd have me in an instant, if I gave you the chance."

"Perhaps you flatter yourself."

She removes her hand from my lap and I breathe again. "I don't think so. Maybe I'm saving you from yourself."

"What a princess."

She stands suddenly. "You're freezing to death. Let's get inside."

"Whatever," I say.

Back inside *Spencer's* Lucy buys me a drink and we sit in a quiet corner. Cal is nowhere to be seen.

Lucy looks at me with what appears to be pity. "So what's up with you? Don't you like nice girls?"

"What sort of question is that?"

"Are they too easy for you? Do you need to suffer a bit? Have you got *issues*, Josh?" Her big eyes sparkle as she taunts me.

"Something like that," I say softly and Lucy eases off a little.

"They bore you? Or you enjoy getting hurt. Maybe you're just fucked up, like the rest of us."

"Yeah. A bit of each. It seems you have all the answers."

She sits back suddenly. "I don't even know the questions." Her voice is smaller, normal and for the briefest moment she appears almost vulnerable. Then the mask slides back into place and her eyes meet mine again. "What?"

"Nothing."

"Think you can find the real me?" She leans against me. "Do you think you can save me, Josh?"

There's only so much sneering even I can take. I stand. "I'm off."

"I'll walk with you."

"Best wait for Cal."

She stands as well so that I can squeeze past her. She smells of freshly turned earth, which is odd. Odder still, it is pleasant and it arouses me.

Before I leave she says, "Will you watch me play again?"

"With Cal?"

"Perhaps."

I nod.

"Do you want to know why I was so good tonight?"

"Surprise me."

"Sacrifice."

I suddenly feel tired. "You mean, practice, giving things up…"

"I mean sacrifice. Blood. Killing things." Her eyes are bright but she isn't smiling.

"You're too much," I say, and leave her to it.

*

When Cal was twelve he killed a stray cat. I was eight and he made me watch. It was an old tabby that haunted the park that backed on to our old semi-detached. He latched onto us for a week or so during the summer holidays. We fed him scraps, mucked about with him. He was a scruffy, skinny wreck of a cat but I grew to like him. I noticed that Cal was rougher with him than I was, but…that was just Cal. He was like that with other kids, too, particularly the younger, smaller ones. He was like it with me.

It was almost dusk and we sat in a small glade in the centre of the park's tiny wooded area. The cat was fussing at the crust of a cheese sandwich I'd given him. I was telling Cal, yet again, that we should name him.

"No point," Cal said. He pushed his trainer against the cat's flank. "He's old, Josh. He'll be dead soon."

"He's not that old. We could look after him. Mum wouldn't mind." Even at the age of eight I recognised that Cal could be cruel. I learned to be wary of him sometimes, but that evening he was in a good mood and there was no hint of what he was about to do.

He leant across and stroked the cat's head. Then he stood and picked him up by the scruff of his neck. The cat squirmed and mewled as Cal adjusted his grip until his hand was around the cat's throat.

I stood, too. "What are you doing, Cal?"

The cat spat and thrashed, but Cal held him firmly, at arms length. I thought of fireworks, suddenly, randomly, then I saw the muscles on Cal's forearm tighten and I ran for him. I shouted his name and he grabbed the collar of my t-shirt so that it bunched around my throat and I couldn't move.

The cat was jerking more and more quickly now, but the movements seemed unreal, cartoon-like. His screams were high pitched and continuous. I couldn't make any noise, Cal's grip on my throat was too tight, but I was crying hard and snot and tears streamed onto my brother's hand.

When the cat was still and quiet Cal dropped him onto the ground. His face turned towards mine and for the first time I felt scared for myself.

"I can do the same to you," he said, softly. "I can stop your crying, too."

His grip tightened briefly then he let me go. I scrambled over to the cat, but found that I couldn't touch it.

Cal was walking away from me. "It's just a cat, Josh. You should grow up."

It was getting dark and I was frightened. I followed my brother home.

Later, when Cal was out of the way, I told dad what had happened.

He looked serious, but not particularly interested. "You expect me to believe that?"

"I saw it." I tugged at his hand. "The cat must still…"

He pulled away from me. "You must stop being so jealous of your brother."

I started to say something else, then stopped. Even at eight I knew when I was beaten.

"Go and have your bath," he said. As I reached the door he called, "And not a word to your mother."

Later they both saw the scratches on Cal's arm, but neither mentioned them.

I met Matt in the city centre on a chilly October Tuesday. Matt was Nero's drummer.

"The only drummer I've known who wasn't a fucking nutter," Cal once said.

We shook hands outside *Starbucks*. Matt is slightly built with fair, thinning hair and wide-set eyes that are blue and innocent.

"It's good to see you," I said, and meant it. I'd always liked Matt. Everybody did. He was warm, friendly, kind. 'He's got a good heart,' Mick once said. It was intended as an insult, but you take the point.

We sat outside, although it was cold and rain threatened. Matt asked me about myself and listened to the answers carefully, as though he gave a shit.

It was pleasant for a while. He told me that he was training to be a social worker. That he didn't miss Nero, was glad when it ended. He preferred real life, he said. Helping people.

Then he fiddled with his collar, sat forward in his white plastic seat, his face changing. "I suppose this is about Chris?"

"Chris?"

Chris was Nero's rhythm guitarist. He sang a bit and co-wrote the songs with Cal. He doubled up as the band's manager as well. Not the wisest decision they ever made. He was a volatile manic-depressive with an ego that dwarfed even Cal's. He was addicted to an impressively wide range of chemical substances and he had problems with gambling, relationships, life. In retrospect, perhaps not management material.

"Not a total shock, I know, but still…" He shook his head sadly. The breeze stiffened, ruffling the sleeves of his sweater. "But when you actually hear it, man…"

"News? What are you talking about, Matt?"

He saw the expression on my face. I had 'bewilderment' down pat by now. "You really don't know?"

"It seems it's my year for not knowing."

"Chris is dead. Hanged himself in his bedsit, more than a week ago."

"Bedsit?" For some reason that word made more impact than the obvious ones.

"The horses, Josh. He lost everything. Even mummy and daddy couldn't bale him out any more."

"Jesus." I studied the remains of my latte. "A week ago."

"There was an obit in the Guardian, Josh. A tiny one, but…unbelievable, really. Would I warrant an obit? Would Mick? Chris would have loved that."

"Funeral?"

"Last Monday. Family only."

I nodded. "Poor Chris. Not that I ever liked him, but…" I let the words tail off.

"He was a hard man to like."

"But at least you tried, Matt." He shrugged diffidently. "But for all his problems I would never have thought…"

Matt said nothing.

"I mean, he was always in debt," I said. Matt's face changed and his eyes slid away from mine. Something in my head clicked and I took a punt. "Maybe Stuttgart was the last straw."

After a moment he said, "I suppose it was obvious that Cal would tell you. You always were inseparable."

I bristled. "Hardly."

His gaze was equable, amused. "You're joking. I could never understand it. It's not as though you even like each other." He must have caught something in my expression because his voice softened. "Cal's trouble, Josh. I'm sorry, but it's true. You need some distance from him. You're a nice guy. Make some friends…"

"Things are different now," I lied. "I hardly see him. We've got our own lives." My voice was stiff and awkward. Matt nodded and said nothing. "Anyway," I said. "Stuttgart."

"Oh. Yeah." He rubbed the downy stubble on his chin. "Couldn't have helped. Presumably even Chris had a conscience tucked away somewhere."

"Presumably."

His eyes fixed onto mine and his expression became earnest. "It's been hard, actually. For me, I mean. The guilt. You know I'm a Christian?"

"You mentioned it."

"It doesn't sit well. I'm not…I mean, I try and lead a good life, but it's a hard thing to get past."

"It must be."

He was quiet for a moment. "You're a good man, Josh."

"I am?"

"You haven't judged me. I appreciate that." I mumbled something. "But it was wrong of Cal to burden you."

"I'm his brother."

"And you'll keep his secret?"

"What else can I do? Anyway, he was a bit hazy as far as the details were concerned."

His expression sharpened. "How hazy?"

I shrugged. "It's hard, I suppose. Re-living it."

"I suppose." His face became thoughtful.

I was caught so deeply in my lie I didn't know what to say.

Matt left shortly afterwards. We shook hands, said we'd keep in touch. I haven't seen him since.

*

It's a Sunday afternoon, four weeks after Lucy played her amazing set at *Spencer's*. We're in Waterloo Park, Lucy, Cal and I. Lucy is standing by the river's edge, annoying the ducks. Cal and I sit on a wooden bench a little way back. The weather is quiet, anonymous, mild. The mist that has gathered above the surface of the water spills towards us.

"Thanks for coming, man," Cal says.

I'm quiet for a moment as I try to remember the last time he thanked me. "No problem." I haven't seen much of him recently as he's been busy with Lucy. I've missed him, which surprises and worries me.

Cal puffs out his cheeks. We both watch Lucy as she starts a conversation with a shabbily dressed elderly man who is feeding the ducks bread out of a brown paper bag.

"She's freaking me out," he says. He shoots me a half grin that doesn't convince at all.

"You've been seeing a lot of her. Mum was wondering if she needed to get a new hat."

He doesn't smile, doesn't rise to the bait. "I've never met anyone like her."

I start to sing *It Must Be Love* by Madness but he doesn't hit me or anything.

He checks that she's out of earshot and says, "Do you know what she does?"

"Look, if this is about sex, I don't…"

He shakes his head impatiently. "No." His expression clears. "Although it *is* fucking mind blowing."

"Enough already."

"I'm sorry. No…" He hesitates, looks at his hands. "She writes down every conversation she has in an exercise book."

I look at his face but he's watching Lucy. She appears to be singing. The old man is laughing nervously. "You're taking the piss."

"Every conversation." He points towards her. "Whatever she's wittering on about with the old boy, she'll write that up. Everything she's said to you, to me. I've seen her do it. She has a room full of books crammed with the stuff."

"She can't remember everything she…"

He shrugs, offers me another wan smile. "I suppose not. But she has a bloody good try. You spoke to her in the car park at *Spencer's* the first time you met her?" I nod hesitantly. "Some bollocks about her boyfriend's father being on his death bed? A little dig about me being gay?"

"Something like that."

"She showed me it. Timed and dated."

"It's just like keeping a diary," I say. I hunch deeper into my jacket.

"It's not like a diary, Josh. It's like the script of her fucking life." He leans forward, props his elbows on his knees. "She started after her mum died."

"So she says."

"What does that mean?"

"She lies, Cal. You must have noticed."

"Sure. But not this time."

I say nothing.

After a moment Cal says, "She says it's all recorded anyway."

"What?"

"Everything we say."

"You mean, Big Brother…"

"No, not like that." He pats the seat. "By the wood of this bench. By the earth and the water. By the walls of the houses we live in. Every word we speak, every thought. Absorbed, recorded."

"That's what she believes?"

"Yes. Fervently. And one day we will work out how play it all back. How to translate. She believes we will be able to play back everything that was ever said."

"Fuck," I say.

"And that's not all…"

Lucy is walking towards us.

"You two talking about me?" she says.

We both shake our heads and say no at the same time.

*

After I saw Matt I decided to forget about Stuttgart. It was obvious something bad had happened and that Cal was at the centre of it, but…what difference did it make? I kept thinking back to the day of the gig and the mood of the band when I caught up with them just before they went on stage. They were nervous, but that wasn't unusual. Cal and Chris were a bit hyper, but then, when weren't they?

I thought about asking Cal. Of course I did. But what was the point?

I suppose he was always a bully. The incident with the cat has stayed with me, naturally enough. But other memories have dipped below the surface and refused to budge. Small cruelties, I think. A casual, off-hand spitefulness. All so utterly denied by my parents that at times I questioned my own eyesight. I wasn't jealous, exactly. It seemed entirely normal that they should dote on Cal and dismiss me. It was all I ever knew.

And yet I craved his company. And his approval. I didn't get it very often but when I did I would glow with pride for days.

When I was about twelve three older boys chased me through the park, caught me just before I got to the main road and gave me good kicking. Later the same evening Cal confronted them outside the local Off-Licence. I watched from a distance as he hurled himself at them. He got a couple of good shots in and drew blood before the biggest of the boys – and they were the same age as Cal – dragged him to the ground and pummelled him with feet and fists. When they relented enough so that he could stagger upright, he punched the big lad in the face, breaking his nose. They gave him another beating and he took it without making a sound. If some adults hadn't broken it up minutes later I think they might have killed him.

He stumbled over to me, asked me why I was crying. He looked broken. An arm hung at an odd angle. One eye was closed and grotesquely swollen. When he grinned his teeth were filmed with blood. "That'll teach the fuckers to mess with my brother," he said.

I loved him then. He spent a week in hospital, which was something else my parents could never forgive me for.

*

It's the first week of spring and I'm at *Spencer's* again waiting for Cal and Lucy to play a set together.

I'm at the bar, chatting to Scot, waiting for them to come on.

"It must be hard," he says, "seeing them together all the time." He passes me my pint, tosses another regular a bag of honey-roasted peanuts.

It takes me a moment to work out what he's talking about. "Not really. Not now." And it's the truth. I like my brother better now that he's with Lucy. He's quieter, more thoughtful. Actually, sometimes he appears haunted. I see him less, but he seeks my company now, seems to value it. Need it, even. It feels almost as though I am the older brother.

As for Lucy, she's…well, she's as mad as a spanner.

"Cute, though," Scot says. I wonder if he's reading my thoughts.

"Cute's not everything," I say.

"You reckon?" He angles me a wry Aussie grin. I return it then turn my back on him as he serves a cluster of students.

Lucy sings beautifully. Cal plays with astonishing subtlety and understatement. Together they are superlatively good. The best thing I've heard for years. The crowd, awestruck, obviously agree.

I watch with hurt pride. Lucy *is* cute. Her eyes linger on mine a couple of times as she sings and my heart twists in my chest. I am drizzled in glorious self-pity. It is warm and seductive and I let it have its way with me for a minute or two then I shrug it aside.

I think of the look in Cal's eyes the last time I spoke to him. Of the pinched expression on his face, the edge to his voice. The way he winced when Lucy called him on his mobile. Wanted to know where he was, who he was with. Then he left without a word. It was only a lunchtime drink, that was all. I had the feeling there was something he wanted to tell me but he never got around to it.

When they finish Lucy turns to Cal and kisses him on the mouth. He takes a step back, almost trips over his amp in his attempt to avoid her.

*

Mum and dad hated Cal and Lucy's relationship. They blamed me for it, which wasn't much of a surprise.

They turned up at my door unannounced on a Saturday afternoon in early March.

"What a pleasant surprise," I said, as they squeezed past me in the narrow hallway of my flat. Even though it was the weekend they were both immaculately dressed; father in a linen suit and silk tie, mother in a honey-coloured woollen dress. He smelled of expensive cologne. She was checking her lipstick as she eased into the living room. They both exuded distaste, disappointment.

"You haven't decorated," dad said.

"Tea? Coffee?" I said. "Stale biscuits?"

I was watching Sky Sports News, but dad switched it off. I waited for mum to do the usual mum thing and check for dust on all visible surfaces, but she didn't bother. She turned on her heel in the middle of the room and looked into my face.

"How about drugs?" I said. "Soft, hard. All tastes catered for."

"That's not funny," my mother said.

"The ceiling is yellow," father said. "And the paper is peeling."

"You can sit down," I said. "The sofa is clean enough. I doubt you'll catch anything."

They remained standing and so did I.

"I take it this is about Cal?"

Mum picked up a novel, *From Blue to Black* by Joel Lane, then dropped it again as though it was contaminated. "It's about that girl."

"I take it you mean Lucy."

"The one you introduced him to."

"That's not quite…"

"She won't do at all," father said.

"Have you met her?" I said.

They exchanged a glance.

"She came to lunch last Sunday," dad said.

"Thanks for the invite."

"Believe me, you didn't miss anything."

"I think there's something wrong with her," mum said.

I tried to imagine Lucy sitting at a dinner table with my parents. I felt a surge of pity for my brother.

"You're speaking to the wrong son," I said.

"She doesn't work."

"Neither does Cal."

"But, her family…"

Dad said, "You know about her mother?" I nodded. "These things can run in families."

"You're the doctor."

"I'm worried about the effect she's having on Cal."

"He is a sensitive soul," I said. They ignored the sarcasm. Actually, they ignored me, but then that was par for the course.

"She kept talking about marriage. Children." I wondered if mum knew how much older she looked when she frowned. "Lots of children."

"She's winding you up," I said.

"What?"

"It's what she does. She makes things up." They both looked at me blankly. "She lies."

"Lies? And you knew this? And still you encouraged…"

"Don't put this on me."

"Don't raise your voice to your mother." His voice was sharp, familiar, and I felt the years peel away.

"You can both go now."

They exchanged another glance, a longer one.

"We need you to talk to Cal," mum said.

"Why?"

"Because he's not talking to us."

"What have you done?"

She hesitated. "We made a…misjudgement."

I waited.

"I offered her money," dad said.

"What?"

"It's what she's after, surely even you can see that. So I cut to the chase." He glared at me. "I offered her £2000 to leave Cal alone."

"And what did she say?"

They both stared at the floor.

*

"I told him to fuck off," Lucy said.

We were in my local. Cal was at the bar.

"Subtle," I said. "Not that I blame you."

"They're quite a pair, your parents." I wouldn't meet her eyes. "I really loathed them."

"I think it's fair to say the feeling's mutual."

"They hated me before they met me."

I nodded, conceding the point. Cal brought our drinks.

"No more Sunday dinner invites, then?" I said.

He shuddered. "It was a nightmare."

"I thought it was fun," Lucy said.

"I thought dad was going to have a stroke."

"Pity he didn't," Lucy said. "They can shout quite loudly, can't they, your mum and dad?"

Cal looked at me. "It didn't help that she kept laughing at them."

"I wish I'd been there."

"So do I," Cal said.

"It's a lovely house, isn't it?" Lucy said. "It will be yours one day, won't it, sweetheart?"

"Ours," I said.

Cal looked at the floor. Lucy smiled into her drink.

"Anyway," I said, "if you don't call mum and dad soon, you'll have no inheritance at all."

"Yeah, I'll call them. Better let them know I've moved in with Lucy."

I stared at him. "Really?"

"Where do you think I've been staying?"

Lucy was gazing dreamily at the wall. "He's a good looking man, though, isn't he? Your dad. For his age."

"Where the hell did that come from?" Cal said.

"I offered to blow him. Before lunch, when you were in the garden with your mum."

Cal's face turned the colour of brick. "What?"

"I thought it might make him like me."

I felt as though I was watching a play. "Strangely, he never mentioned that."

"I'm not sure he knew what I was talking about. He didn't say anything. Just smiled. Didn't rule it out, though."

Cal kicked his chair away and stormed to the toilet.

Lucy leant forward and touched my knee. "He'll be fine. He knows what I'm like."

I looked at her and didn't speak.

*

After their set Lucy, Cal and I sit by the river. It's the warmest day of the year so far and the air is like seasoned velvet. Cal sits quietly. He looks exhausted. Lucy bounces with energy. Her eyes shine darkly. She stands, takes my hand, pulls so that I stand too.

"Say it again."

"You were awesome, Lucy."

She hugs me. She takes her time over it and I feel the flatness of her stomach and the pressure of her breasts against my chest. Cal takes a long drink from his pint and stares out at the motionless water.

I ease her away a fraction. "It's about time you recorded something."

"Next week," Lucy says. She releases me, turns towards Cal. "Isn't that right?" He nods. She looks back at me. "He's going to call some old contacts. See if he can get a tour together. Just local stuff at first."

"Sounds good."

There's a sound behind us and Trevor appears. "I need you two back inside," he says. "To play the final set. By popular demand. I might just get lynched if you don't."

"Great." Lucy skips towards him. "Come on, Cal."

Cal doesn't move. "I can't, Luce. I feel like shit. You do it. Use my electric if you want. You'll be great."

Her face changes slightly, but she only hesitates for a moment. Halfway down the path she calls back. "Come and watch, then."

"Be there in a minute," Cal says.

After she's gone the tension in his shoulders eases visibly. I sit next to him.

"I should leave her," he says.

"So why don't you?"

"It's not that easy."

"I don't see why not. You can stay with me for a while, if you can't face mum and dad."

His head tilts towards mine. "Thanks, bro. But that's not it." He holds his hands out, palms upward. In the artificial light I see the trace of rust-coloured stains embedded in the joints of his fingers. "Blood. I had to clean up after her."

"What are you talking about?"

"She kills things, Josh."

Something clicks. "Sacrifice."

"You knew?"

"She said something once. I didn't take much notice."

"Neither did I. When she told me to buy her a rabbit, I thought she wanted a pet. Instead she killed it with a hammer."

"Tonight?"

"No. A few weeks back, when we first wrote together. She needed inspiration, she said. And that was how she got it."

"Jesus."

He sits back, exhales slowly. "Tonight I found a dog for her. A stray, off the estate. We fed the poor old bastard then she cut its throat with an electric carving knife. That's why we were so good. Or that's what she thinks. She's done it since she was a kid. If she felt bad, if she needed luck, anything, she'd kill something. An insect, a bird, an animal."

"Get out. Now."

"I can't."

"What's she got on you, Cal?"

He stares at me bleakly. "What do you think?"

As we walk back to *Spencer's* a memory stirs. "It was only a dog, Cal."

"What?"

"You've got a bit of previous as far as animals are concerned."

"I'm not in the mood for this. You'll have to translate."

"Eaton Park. Twenty years ago."

His stride shortens. The front door to *Spencer's* is only yards away.

"You mean, the cat?"

"Yeah. The cat."

Now he stops, faces me. His expression softens. "But you killed the cat, Josh."

56

Our eyes lock. I start to speak but the bar door bursts open and Lucy is there, eyes blazing.

She points at Cal. "Where the fuck have you been?"

*

Lucy lived in a large semi-detached council house on the Lakenham estate. I turned up at her door a week before she and Cal played at *Spencer's*.

She ushered me inside. "Cal's not here. He's patching things up with your parents." She angled her head as she looked at me. "But you know that, don't you?"

"Yes."

"You want to get me on my own?" She was as cute as ever in a cut-off t-shirt and a short skirt.

"Right again." I looked around. The hallway was dark and smelled of damp. Two large rooms led off it. There was a kitchen ahead of me, to the right, and a wide set of stairs straight ahead. I thought of my tiny flat. "This place is massive. How did you swing it with the council?"

"I was living with this guy. A divorcee. Two kids. This was his place."

"What happened to them?"

"Dunno. They left. It's in my name now."

"Just like that?"

She wrinkled her nose. "This is boring. Do you want some tea or something?"

The living room was neater and cleaner than I expected. The scent of something earthy lingered beneath the smell of pine and lemon.

She handed me a mug of tea and sat next to me on the sofa.

"Are you worried about your big brother?"

"A bit."

"And with good cause." She tucked a leg beneath her buttocks, sat so that her left knee touched mine.

"Why did you let him move in with you?"

"Why not? Don't worry, it won't be forever. Your time will come."

"That's not what this is about."

"Don't you want Cal's sloppy seconds?"

"Lucy."

"Wouldn't be the first time. Would it?"

"It's easy to mock."

"Fun, too."

She was half-turned towards me. I took her left breast in my hand and squeezed it hard. Then I stood, linked my hands behind the back of my head.

"I'm sorry. I don't know what came over me."

"It was nice. You didn't have to stop."

"Please…"

"I find you so much more attractive now."

Her expression was guileless. "What?"

"Since Cal filled me in on your hidden depths."

"I have no idea what you are talking about."

"Modest, too." She reached a hand towards me but I ignored it. "And you seem such a nice boy."

"You're freaking me out."

She stood. "Come upstairs with me."

"I already told you…"

"Not for that." She shot me a hammy wink. "Unless you change your mind. No. I want to show you something."

I followed her up the stairs. She opened the first door on the left and we stepped into the room. It was of medium size, presumably intended as a spare bedroom. It was two-thirds full of archive boxes. They were stacked almost to the ceiling and arranged in small clusters so that every box was accessible with a little effort. Each box was lidded and had two dates – from and to – written on the side in black magic marker. I lifted the lid of the nearest box. It was full to the brim with exercise books of various sizes and colours.

"Cal told me about this."

"I know. He couldn't get his head around it."

"Really."

"It's no big deal."

"It's weird, Lucy."

"It's the past made real."

"Hardly."

"Words define us."

"Do they? I thought that talk was cheap. It's what we do that matters."

"Words are concrete. Stone." For the first time since I met her it didn't seem as though she was taking the piss. "Everything we see or seem is but a dream within a dream." I stared at her blankly. "Edgar Allan Poe."

"Good for him."

She gestured at the boxes. "They keep my past alive."

"And that's a good thing?"

"It's my reality."

"But you lie, Lucy."

"Not here."

I held my hands up. "Whatever. Fascinating as this…"

She took a step towards me. "Don't you want to look, Josh?" I hesitated and she touched my arm. "It's all here. Just the words, though. No context, no explanations. You have to use your imagination, if you've got one."

"I don't…"

"The stuff with my uncle, for example. You have to read between the lines. It's mostly him talking. I was a good little girl. I didn't speak with my mouth full."

I didn't say anything, didn't rise to the bait.

She opened one of the boxes closest to her. "This is almost all Cal. Loads of stuff about you. Your dark side. Your little secrets. Your childhood. Tell me you're not interested, Josh?"

"This is a game."

"For once, it isn't," she said.

"I've got to go."

"You disappoint me."

"You'll get used to it," I said.

*

I put an arm across Lucy's chest. She presses against it, but with little weight. I look more closely at her face. There is no real heat in her eyes. Her fury appears manufactured.

I turn towards Cal. He's backing away.

"I'm gone," he says.

I nod. He walks towards his car.

Lucy says, "He should have been watching me."

Trevor lurks behind her. His expression is harassed, confused. I shake my head and he shrugs and goes back into the bar.

"You don't own him," I say to Lucy.

She gazes over my shoulder. Her eyes are bigger than ever. I think of something Cal said once about drugs, and wonder. We hear a car engine turn, catch, accelerate.

She relaxes against my arm and her face changes. "I don't even want to own him."

"Then let him go."

"What do you think I've been trying to do?"

"That's not the way he tells it."

"The way I've been treating him, I can't believe he's still around."

I take a step away from her.

"None of this is my problem."

"You've only just realised that?"

I rub my mouth. The air seems hushed, waiting for something. I can smell Lucy, and the river. "Apparently."

"I know about Stuttgart," she says. She speaks casually, her eyes averted.

I watch her face. "That's not my problem either."

She cocks her head. Her smile is slow and careful. "Really?"

I start to walk away from her.

"I have my car," she says. "I'll run you home."

"I'll walk."

"Your choice," she says.

*

Two days later I saw my brother for the last time. He came to my door in the middle of a dull, damp afternoon. He was wearing the same clothes he had worn Friday night and he was unshaven.

"Where the hell have you been?"

"I don't honestly know." I stood aside so that he could enter the flat, but he shook his head. "I'm not staying, man."

"Why not? Let me get you something to eat, a change of clothes."

"I'm fine."

"You look like shit."

"I could do with some cash."

"Have you seen Lucy?"

"No."

"Mum and dad?"

"No. Have you got any money, Josh?"

I dug a couple of twenties out of a pocket and gave them to him.

"I'm sorry. That won't get you far."

"It doesn't matter."

He looked old, defeated. "You're running away?"

"Nothing gets past my little brother."

"Why?"

"I told Lucy about Stuttgart."

"I know."

"She told you?"

"I still don't know…"

"Josh." His eyes were on mine. "Enough."

The pitch of his voice was higher now and mine rose to meet it. "What?"

"She's a loose cannon. At some point there will be repercussions."

"You don't have to run. Mum and dad will…"

"For fuck's sake!" He put his hands on his head.

"Easy."

"I'm running from you, man."

"I don't understand."

He took a step towards me and I moved backwards, catching my arm on the doorframe. I thought he was going to hit me but his arms slid around my neck and he held me tightly. I felt his stubble against my cheek. "I still love you, you crazy bastard." My shoulder muffled his voice. When he pulled away from me his eyes were wet.

He didn't look back as he walked to the gate then down the path. I wanted to say something but I didn't. I watched him until he disappeared from sight. Then I followed.

*

Lucy is in the kitchen, stirring a spoonful of marmite into a saucepan full of fresh pasta.

"Thanks for knocking," she says.

"The door was unlocked."

"That's hardly the point."

She tips the pasta into a large bowl and sits at the kitchen table. The room stinks of marmite.

"What the hell is that?"

"Comfort food," Lucy says.

"That's your idea of comfort?"

"Amongst other things. What are you doing here, Josh?"

She seems washed out, muted. As though her volume has been turned down.

"Cal turned up at my door a little while ago. I think he's been sleeping in his car."

"Well, it's a big car, isn't it? Comfy."

"You don't give a shit?"

She swallows a mouthful of food, wipes a trace of marmite from her top lip. "I was looking forward to recording something. And he's a good fuck. Still. Easy come, easy go."

I sit at the table. I've not been sleeping well and it's starting to catch up with me. My head feels close to bursting. It's crammed full of…stuff. Years of it. I can hold it back, just about, but I'm not sure for how much longer.

"Get me the book."

"What book?"

"You know what book."

She chews slowly. "Let me finish my dinner."

"GET THE FUCKING BOOK!"

She stands, smiling. "Are you sure you need it?"

I study the grain of the pine table until she leaves the room. I reach across and take the half-empty bowl of pasta and hurl it against the far wall.

Lucy comes back into the kitchen.

"Temper, temper," she says, and slides a pale blue exercise book in front of me and I start to read it.

*

The thing is, reality is subjective. History is simply opinion, perspective. The same applies to our personal history. The past is just as susceptible to flux, to dislocation as the present or future. Unless Lucy was right, of course, and everything is stored, recorded for future generations. But she wasn't right. Not about that, not about anything.

Throughout my life – and with increasing regularity as the years have passed – I have felt that I am being filmed. That I am the subject of some cosmic documentary. That a director lurks, to the side of me, just out of sight. This feeling became overwhelming when I discovered that my brother was dead. It was something that I had fantasised about constantly when I was younger, when my parents' lives so obviously revolved around their oldest son. Fantasies of such intensity that I would come to from a daydream and greet my brother's living, breathing presence with open astonishment.

I can still feel his stubble against my cheek, his breath on my face. But faced with the reality – although you know how I feel about reality – I felt the glare of that camera again. It was as though a script was being nudged in front of me. I read it reluctantly.

But scripts can be edited. Everything is subject to revision.

*

I throw the book at Lucy. She's leant against the doorframe, hands tucked into the waistband of her jeans. It hits her knee and falls to the floor. She ignores it.

"Bullshit."

"This from the man who never lies?"

"Cal's delusional. You both are. I was out all day."

"But you snuck back. With a friend. Cal and Chris interrupted you." She has come alive again, it seems. The sun is low now and the light that slants in through the kitchen window hits Lucy full on and her outline shimmers. "Mike and Matt didn't even see you. They just helped Cal clean up. But then he was always cleaning up after you, wasn't he?"

"Made up stories."

"What's the big deal? She was a prostitute, right? And it's not as though anybody has even missed her."

"I don't have to listen to this." But I don't move, so perhaps I do.

"Denial ain't just a river in Egypt, baby."

"But I spent a year trying to…" My hands curl into fists. "Why would I do that?"

She's by the table now, out of the light. I can smell her. I see the obsidian glitter in her eyes, the set of her small, soft mouth.

"Because you're as fucked up as I am, sweetie."

I stand because I know she wants me to. She comes against me and my arms circle her waist unbidden.

"Jesus, the heat coming off you. What have you done?" She arches backwards a fraction so that she can meet my eyes. "I know that look." Then, slowly, her lip curling, "I know what you've done."

When she kisses me she tastes of rotting fruit. Of sweetness and corruption.

"You can't get around me like that," I say.

But, of course, she can. Does.

When I wake it is dark and I ache all over. Lucy lays motionless beside me. I dress quickly and step onto the landing. I open the door to the spare bedroom, the room full of exercise books. I stack two archive boxes one atop the other and carry them downstairs and out through the back door so that I can stack them on the lawn. I do this again and again until the room is empty and I no longer ache. Until the lawn is full and the eastern sky is streaked with layers of crimson and cream.

Etcetera, Etcetera...

Sean "Grasshopper" Mackowiak

We met Bob Creeley in the late 1980's when we were kicking around Buffalo (where he taught at SUNY Buffalo for 37 years), and were immediately drawn in by his rhythm of thought, the musical necessity of his poetry. His innocent, ideal words proposed that he and his readers (or listeners) play out a rapprochement together, just as Ornette Coleman's Congeniality does with sound. The moment of self discovery often leads to a collective discovery; the impermanence of permanence.

His innocence often left him open to ridicule (we know the feeling), especially by the tough Bukowski, but actually Creeley and Bukowski's intensions in writing were actually not so different, i.e., expressing thoughts in an anti-academic form of writing (in the voice of the street), a 'naked poetry.'

The Beats and the Black Mountain Poets (both of which Creeley was associated with) called for a stripping away of conventional rhyme, meter, and shape in order to achieve a pure form of expression. Bob Creeley's "FORM IS NEVER MORE THAN AN EXTENSION OF CONTENT," (1950) became a most influential formulation of this idea of 'naked poetry' and has been mirrored in the works of Jackson Pollack, Jack Kerouac, Allen Ginsberg, Robert Frank, Ornette Coleman, Don Cherry, Marlon Brando, James Dean, etc. etc. (Bob loved to say 'etcetera, etcetera, etcetera.')

This idea, "FORM IS NEVER MORE THAN AN EXTENSION OF CONTENT", was central to the formation of Mercury Rev, and is present in our musical communications to this day. In other words, we would like to celebrate that there is a congeniality of feelings that are present in the audience as well as the performer; an invisible connection. We would like to thank Bob for this realization and for all of his encouraging and enlightening words through the years. Bob died on March 30, 2005 in Odessa, Texas. We'll miss him dearly.

Tremolando

Becky Done

Prelude

It was the sensation of horse hair grating against gut that Joseph loved the most. He lifted his bow, balanced it neatly between fat forefinger and thumb, and dug it in at the heel. Shutting his eyes, he smelt the sharp puff of rosin as he filled the gloomy flat with the rawness of his first note.

He liked to slot the violin underneath his chin, scratchy with the untidiness of week-old stubble, and let his bow decide for him. Yesterday it had been Bruch, today, Elgar. *Salut d'amour*. He smiled, closed his eyes, and thought of Tamsin.

He remembered the first time he had seen her play. She had been much younger, almost too young. He had watched over her shoulder, half-distracted by those long, tumbling curls, gypsy-dark, which threatened to snag on the fine tuners. But then the notes had catapulted, unrestrained, from her slim fingers, and he had felt a high rush of exhilaration. Had he found a female Perlman? The new Vanessa Mae?

Years later, they had attended Perlman's birthday concert together at the Festival Hall. They drank too much gin in the bar, sat tightly side by side, knees almost touching, but not quite. She had plaited her hair that evening, wound it tightly down against her head, exposing spots of flesh he had never seen before. He wanted to reach out and touch them, feel their newness, but instead he simply glanced at her from time to time, watching her face tighten and relax with the flow of Perlman's bow, and it saddened him slightly that her excitement was not for him. Perlman had been magnificent.

The memory jolted Joseph from his daydream, and he released the violin from his shoulder, hooked the bow over the ledge on his music stand. He turned stiffly in his chair to check the clock, before setting the instrument down on his father's oversized silk handkerchief and struggling to his feet. Doing so, he dislodged a pile of yellowing newspapers with his left slipper, and they slid over his manuscript, obscuring it entirely.

He had been writing it for years, intricate pencil markings on an assortment of ancient paper. It was almost a concerto now, and he hoped that one day it would be premièred by one of the big ensembles. He had played with most of them – Covent Garden, the BBC concert orchestra, the RPO – before he turned to teaching, and now his greatest wish was to hear his own concerto swell to fill a concert hall. He imagined Tamsin sitting beside him, spellbound and proud.

Shaking his head, Joseph reached for a tumbler, and quite steadily, for it was still only ten past five, poured himself a good measure of single malt.

Staccato

She would not tell him. There was no point even considering the possibility, Tamsin decided, letting her violin case thud gently against the inside of one thigh. The Tube ground gently to a halt at Leytonstone and she lowered her gaze to avoid meeting the eye of two young mothers, who climbed on with pushchairs and stood very close to her. One stunk of booze, Tamsin recognised. What sort of a mother..? But the Tube was moving again and the women started talking about their children, one of whom was evidently having toilet problems. 'Left a great stinking turd...'

Tamsin shut her eyes quickly, her mind unleashing the opening bassoon solo from *The Rite of Spring* over their conversation. She relaxed, temporarily jaundiced from the flickering lights overhead. Tamsin found Stravinsky to be useful in most situations.

It was not the only secret she kept from Joseph. She still hadn't told him her father was dead. This was mainly because Joseph had, over time, become a sort of natural replacement for him, and in view of this, she felt that mourning him would seem insensitive – cruel, even. She hadn't seen her father for almost thirty years; she had been a toddler when he left. So on the night she received the telephone call, she had simply gone to rehearsal at Joseph's flat, the same as any other night, and drunk a little more of his whisky than normal. She had wanted to tell him – she still did – but the months had slipped by.

She couldn't quite bring herself to tell him about Neil, either. She could imagine the look of horror on his face, which he would temper quickly, of course, with a quiet nod and a shuffle in the direction of his drinks cabinet. Later, he would probably ask her to explain what it was she saw in someone so unreliable, so unpredictable. *Maybe because my love life needs a jump start,* she thought, dreaming of Neil's hungry smile, his double-take good looks. It made a welcome change to dreaming about crotchets and semitones.

But, this news – this other news – was bigger. She knew this would be more important to Joseph than anything she could say about Neil, or her father. This, she had to tell him.

It was not that she thought he would be angry. Joseph rarely got angry with her. No, he would feel...

A billboard caught her eye as the Tube pulled into the station. *Don't neglect your underarms,* an underweight model in her underwear was telling her.

That was it – neglect. Joseph would feel neglected. Worse, if possible. He would feel utterly surpassed.

Rhapsody

Neil hurried out of the Underground and into the cool dark of South Woodford in September. *Fuck me, Tamsin's got beautiful tits. Why did I never realise before?* He peered again, a little closer. *Oh fuck. Don't tell me that's a mole. A cute little Madonna-like mole on her left tit? What could be more perfect than that?*

He folded the photo gently in two, and smiled at the man standing outside Raj's Wine Store. *Alright, you've got your own fucking wine shop,* Neil thought, *but tonight, Matthew, I'm going to fuck Tamsin Price.*

He gave Raj a little fuck-you wave and tried not to ruin his temporary fantasy by thinking about Joseph. Tamsin had almost spoilt everything by making Neil swear he wouldn't tell him. She treated Joseph like a frail father; he was like a battery-farmed egg in the palm of an animal rights activist. *Just fucking tell him*, he had fumed internally. *Crack him, and watch him spit yolk and albumen all over that crappy symphony he's writing.*

Neil knew the challenge was part of the attraction, the challenge to distract Tamsin away from her compulsive consideration of Joseph's feelings. All he had to do was offer her something irresistible. It was a bit like fishing, Neil pondered, as he walked.

He wished he wasn't on his way to the old man's flat, worrying about being late for rehearsal. He wished he was on his way to Tamsin's Hackney townhouse, ready to knock on her front door and seduce his way to her bedroom. Failing that, he would be happy just to stare at her left breast all night. So long as that was really a mole, and not a speck of dirt. Neil rubbed the photo, just to be sure.

Divisi

There was something different about Tamsin tonight, Joseph observed. She arrived eating pitta bread and talking quickly. (Tamsin normally hated eating in public, and was not one for chattering nonsense). She was wearing green too, a colour she claimed she hated, because it reminded her of hospitals.

"Joseph?"

"Sorry..." Joseph shook his head and leaned back against the kitchen work surface, gripping its rounded edge for support. He felt a little strange.

"Are you out of wine? A whisky would be fine..."

Joseph almost laughed. *Out of wine.* She spoke as if he was a university student, or worse, someone who worked in television!

Last year, Joseph had employed a wine consultant, who had filled his spare bedroom with enough of the stuff to see the century out. He had not, of course, revealed this to Tamsin. That would be like explaining to an audience exactly how he, the composer, had arrived at the diminuendo in bar 36, movement four. Joseph detested such

Brechtian bulldozing of artistic magic.

"Neil's late," Tamsin commented as Joseph retrieved a half-drunk bottle of Australian Shiraz from behind several tins of food. Tinned macaroni cheese mostly, artificial food, enough to supply his mind with temporary energy, and, he hoped, a little creativity. Extracting the Shiraz was like finding gold in mud. He smiled briefly as he remembered the story of the elderly Hungarian who discovered a genuine Stradivarius hidden in his late father's chicken coop.

"Lovely," Tamsin nodded in approval without looking, as he waved the bottle at her.

She didn't see him as he filled the glass and offered it to her. She had moved towards the large living room window, and had gently raised the corner of his net curtain between finger and thumb. She was examining the road.

"He'll be here," Joseph mumbled, letting his palm warm the wine. What was wrong with her?

Stringendo

Roseanna bumped into Neil on the stairs and was instantly amused by his interesting pastel jumper and foreign aftershave. He had called her the night before, announced his intentions towards Tamsin. Roseanna had simply laughed and hung up. She realised later she was slightly insulted that Neil had forewarned her, as if he thought he still mattered to her in that way. *Enjoy it*, she told herself, hoping he would mess it up somehow, and provide her with a particularly satisfying, passive revenge. *I mean, Tamsin for God's sake!* It would never last.

Personally, Roseanna thought this latest obsession of Neil's was less to do with Tamsin herself, and more about liking to fuck women who could read music. He had dated tone-deaf women before, and it had always ended in disaster.

Joseph's front door stuck slightly. Roseanna couldn't remember it raining recently. Neil leaned across her, pushing, pushing, and suddenly the door obeyed.

Tamsin appeared immediately. "Oh hi!" she said casually – smiling, smiling – "everything alright?"

Roseanna toyed briefly with the idea of taunting her – *Neil picked me up, we stopped for a drink on the way* – but he was too quick for her. "Central line," he said, with a grin and a quick roll of his eyes. Tamsin smiled back at him, as if they shared some sort of secret.

Joseph was standing in the kitchen doorway, his mouth slightly ajar, breathlessness ageing him beyond his sixty years.

"Hi," Roseanna murmured, passing him to set up, but he was looking beyond her, towards Tamsin, regarding her as if she were a particularly puzzling crossword clue.

Roseanna felt a slight twinge of – was it sympathy? – and moved back towards the old man. "Joseph." She touched him lightly on the arm, and he flinched as if she had stung him. "Are you ready?" He nodded briefly in the direction of his own Stradivarius. She nodded back, and for a second she felt as if they understood each other.

Roseanna reached for her usual chair, sitting neatly against the wall where she had left it two days previously. She bent down to remove whatever was lying on top of it – a white napkin, decorated boldly with splashes of red. She picked it up, but froze as she realised it wasn't patterned. It was stained – covered – with blood.

She looked up sharply as Joseph shuffled towards his chair. It was the slippers, not his age, which made him shuffle like that; they were too big for him. For a moment she teetered on the edge of questioning him, but now Neil was laughing at something Tamsin was saying, everyone was sitting down ready to play, and the moment passed. Roseanna placed the napkin on the edge of the bookcase.

Had the old man been trying to kill himself?

Vivace

Roseanna was out of time, and Tamsin was sure it was deliberate. They played this piece so often – it was hardly challenging. It was Haydn.

She looked across at Joseph. He was absorbed, but the crinkle across his forehead wasn't concentration, it was irritation. His dignified demeanour reminded her of a motionless horse trying to flick flies away with its forelock.

She kept playing. Neil was sure to point Roseanna's error out before long. Tamsin wondered if he had talked to Roseanna yet, told her it was all over for good? She hoped so; but part of her suspected that Neil still saw the whole thing as a bit of a game. Not that Tamsin minded, at this stage, if it was. She was pretty sure their affair was purely lust-driven. Neil was a dick-led sort of a man.

Neil stopped playing abruptly, lowering his bow so it rested on the floor. He shifted the cello between his legs. Tamsin pressed her lips together, watching.

"Roseanna, fuck it..."

Roseanna frowned slightly. "Fuck what? Fuck you?"

Tamsin felt an unexpected sting of resentment as she watched Roseanna brush the pure blonde crop away from her eyes, pronounce her words very exactly, with freshly moistened lips. She wasn't afraid of admitting Roseanna was beautiful – there was no reason to pretend that Neil had been attracted to her for her brains. She worked in a cocktail bar near Liverpool Street station; Neil had met her by clamping a sweaty hand on her rear. She had slapped him, hard enough to leave a mark (they used to relate the story with such pride) and somehow it had led to a discussion of Roseanna's musical talents. Joseph, Tamsin and Neil had been hunting for a viola player for months, but Tamsin remembered feeling faintly shocked when Neil bought Roseanna along to a rehearsal one evening. She had worn perfume that smelt strongly of windowsill herbs, and had stunned Joseph by attempting to play with gum in her mouth.

But Roseanna had proved more than capable, and at last they were able to form a quartet. They had named themselves *Viol,* and began to have moderate success, acquiring a steady stream of bookings for functions, and considering at one point the possibility of making a CD, but Tamsin had continued to worry that Roseanna lacked the passion to really *read* the music. It wasn't, after all, just a case of translating from score to bow, and Roseanna seemed unwilling to try and evaluate her performance. She utterly lacked, Tamsin felt, the enthusiasm, the curiosity, to peel the layers from the stave.

Neil rapped violently on Roseanna's score with his bow, started pointing out her mistakes with a raised voice. Straightaway, Joseph caught Tamsin's eye, as he usually did when Neil and Roseanna started to argue. But tonight it was slightly different. He hadn't just happened to catch her eye, she thought; he had been waiting, probably for minutes, until she looked at him. She knew he was trying to communicate with her – *Is there something wrong? Is there something you're hiding from me?* There was always something, Tamsin thought, as she bent forward and scribbled nonsense on her score to avoid his eye. Whoever really ever knows the whole truth?

Agitato

I'll take her to Austria, Neil thought. *That's what I'll do. I'll take her to Salzburg and drown her in cum and Mozart.* He had planned to take Roseanna there once, until he realised she didn't care enough about Mozart or music to warrant the air fare. Roseanna was the child of a pushy mother – the sort who forced her daughter to play in recitals just so she could sit in the front row, the sort who made her practice viola instead of homework, the sort who, eventually, drove her to fuck men like Neil. Tamsin's mother hadn't been pushy enough. It was Joseph who had done the pushing – Joseph, Tamsin's music teacher at secondary school, who had identified her talent and encouraged her. Joseph, who since meeting Tamsin had given up teaching at schools because he had recognised in time, thank God, what he was capable of. Neil didn't want to think about that. He didn't want to remember that Joseph had given up his job – the job he had adored most of his adult life, the job he had excelled at – in order to hold onto Tamsin.

Con fuoco

Joseph watched Tamsin's expression as her face began to crumple with irritation. *Neil should know better*, he thought, listening to Roseanna play worse than before. *We should be playing something more challenging. Roseanna's clearly bored.*

Joseph frequently experienced feelings of frustration, fury even, with Neil. It had come to blows on several occasions, mostly when Neil was joking around, distracting everyone, not taking *Viol* seriously. During one performance at a wedding some years ago, Neil had started laughing during *The Four Seasons*. Joseph had jumped, furiously, to his feet, and the pair had grappled viciously. Tamsin, the darling, had carried on playing as if nothing was wrong, and fortunately most of the wedding guests were so drunk by this point they were convinced it was all part of the show. While Joseph attempted to pummel the left edge of Neil's jaw, a small crowd of revellers gathered around them, clapping and whooping. Roseanna had completely disappeared, Tamsin carried on sawing away at Vivaldi, and the fight had only ended when Joseph fell onto a glass and it splintered into his thigh. He needed fourteen stitches. *Viol* disbanded for a month.

Joseph began to feel that familiar sensation of rage building now, in his chest. He felt a compulsion to fight again with Neil – but this time he wanted to win. The boy was too cocky, too fond of bullying Roseanna.

Joseph had always suspected Tamsin had a soft spot for Roseanna. Tamsin had been nine when her younger sister Jade died on holiday in Crete after hitting her head on a diving board. Tamsin had tried to stem the flow of blood with a Winnie the Pooh beach towel; Piglet had been stained red.

An hour later, the *rondo* drew to a close. It was 8pm, and everybody seemed in a rush to leave. Neil, especially, seemed on edge. Joseph hoped Tamsin would stay for a while. She did sometimes – they would share whisky and water, eat cheddar cheese on crackers and watch poorly written ITV dramas about the police. The flat was always filled with sound, ready to be absorbed – the television, the taxis impatiently halted at the traffic lights beneath the living room window, Joseph's laboured breathing. A CD would whirr in the background, despite the television – Kabalevsky, perhaps, or something grander, something like *Finlandia*. No sound in the world could tear Joseph's ear away from music.

He stood now, watching Tamsin put her coat on, wanting to say something, but feeling too unsettled. Neil was standing behind her; he was probably going to walk with her to the Tube.

"Well, see you tomorrow." Tamsin was gripping her music case – pale blue leather, the same one she had been holding on her very first day as Joseph's pupil. It made him ache to see it. He remembered the clumsy way she used to stuff her music into it with slim, hurrying hands – the scores covered with his pencil scribble, typed letters notifying her mother of this audition, that recital. And now it hung at her side, brushing against one denim-covered leg, and Joseph felt inexplicably desperate.

Neil stepped forward and put an arm around Tamsin's shoulders. "Come on." Joseph saw him squeeze her, as if checking her for ripeness. And suddenly, what he felt was fear. He saw what was about to happen, and it terrified him.

"I meant to give you something," he lied, suddenly.

Tamsin looked quizzical. "Oh?" She smiled, already grateful, perhaps expecting him to produce a CD, a piece of her favourite music, some fresh strings, perhaps, that she would pay him for later, but suddenly her smile froze. "Oh my God. What the hell is that?" She moved quickly, picked up the stained napkin. Inside, Joseph panicked, but his face revealed nothing. "Shiraz," he replied, stiffly.

"Wine?"

"Yes." A quick glance in Neil's direction warned him the lie was unconvincing.

"You never drink wine by yourself. You drink whisky. Did you cut yourself?"

"Cut myself? No. I knocked a bottle over, that's all."

"Joseph..." She looked over her shoulder, and for a moment Joseph thought she was asking Neil for help, but instead Neil took some sort of invisible cue and left the flat, beckoning Roseanna with him. Joseph thought he heard Roseanna complaining, childlike, as Neil shut the door behind them – "But I found it..."

Tamsin moved closer. Joseph wanted to shut his eyes. *Not too close.*

"Joseph, what is this?" She put her nose to the napkin. "This is dried blood."

"A nosebleed."

"You said it was wine. Why would you be ashamed of a nosebleed?" She took another step, and suddenly her face looked like a little round apple, illuminated by the dim bulb in its ancient green shade. Her nose cast an awkward shadow across her mouth. She gripped the napkin with pale fingers. "Tell me now, or..."

"Tamsin, it's getting late. Unless... would you like a snack?"

She looked almost insulted. "Just tell me what's going on."

It had happened three nights ago. He had been drunk, very drunk, and thinking of Tamsin. But not Tamsin the adult. Sixteen-year-old Tamsin kept floating into his mind, positioned nervously in school uniform, bow poised to play the first note of Massenet's *Meditation*. He had tried to drown the image in whisky, ease his mental nausea, but he could not. He began to remember how something had changed in him that day; he recalled the shame, disgust and fear that compelled him to resign the following week.

He had tripped up trying to reach the bathroom. Vomiting over the welcome mat, he hadn't noticed the wound to his stomach until the next morning, when he dislodged a thick crust from the skin, and it started to ooze. He had grabbed the napkin, soaking it with blood before flinging it angrily to the corner of the room. The rest of the day had been spent in a haze of Dvořák and single malt.

"I fell." *Please God, if you exist, forgive me.*

"You fell?" Tamsin questioned. Her tone was disbelieving, like a social worker's.

"I fell," he repeated, nodding. It was the truth, after all.

"Well...how?"

"I was drunk, I fell down. How else would it happen?"

"I don't know. I don't know. I have to go." She looked briefly towards the door and he knew she meant Neil.

"Do you?"

She ignored him. "I have to go." She didn't say where.

"Okay." He watched her slip the napkin into her pocket. What was she doing?

She shrugged. "You'll need to clean it properly or it'll ruin."

"Don't be ridiculous, Tamsin. I was going to throw it out."

"No need. I'll clean it for you." She reached out, a cool hand on his rapidly heating arm. "It's no problem."

Rubato

This is it, Neil thought. *It really is. I've never seen Tamsin's place before. Well, okay, I'm more interested in seeing her naked. Can she tell? Can she tell I've no interest in Picasso posters and A.S. Byatt novels?*

"Well, this is me," she announced, pushing the door open. Neil didn't care. He didn't care if it was her house, her neighbour's house, her best friend's house – fuck me, he would have been happy to do it at Joseph's flat, right there on the fucking sofa. Let the old man see it all hang out. Let him see what he was missing and what he didn't stand a chance of getting.

Tamsin was talking about door widths. "...going to replace them at some point. I'm no fan of DIY, though."

DIY. Doors. Okay. Neil smiled. "Well, if you need some muscle..."

It was meant to be sexually loaded but she took it literally, smiling.

"Thanks." Neil followed her into the living room. *Red sofa, lots of books, fuck me, hundreds of fucking books. This girl obviously hasn't had enough sex.*

"Bit of a library, I know," she was saying, "but I can assure you, I haven't read them all."

"Thank God for that." Neil scanned her collection without interest. De Beauvoir, Morante, Dante, Michelangelo. He could spot no English authors. He thought about asking her why, feigning interest, but she was already talking.

"Are you hungry?"

Neil contemplated wiggling his eyebrows suggestively, but he knew he couldn't really get away with it – Tamsin was classier than that, classier than Roseanna. "Not really. But if you are, feel free."

"Oh, no. I'm not. I'll just put this in the fridge."

By now, Neil's mouth was awash with saliva. *Oh fuck. She's talking about saving her bloody pitta bread. Please, forget the fridge. Forget your fucking pitta bread. Please, let's just...*

She shut the fridge and turned to face him. "Now."

"Now." Neil moved towards her. He could feel his cock stirring. He had been trying to keep his eyes from her breasts ever since she removed her coat by the door; she was wearing that fantastic green top which showed her off to perfection...

"I'm really worried about Joseph."

Joseph?

A tempo

Christ, Neil was volatile, Tamsin thought, removing her earrings and gently bathing her wrist in icy water. She knew he had a temper, having witnessed him engage in many, many arguments with Roseanna, but she hadn't expected anger to overpower *their* evening together.

It had started with the napkin. Tamsin had withdrawn it nervously from her pocket, showed it to Neil, wanting to talk about it, but Neil had snapped tersely, "I've seen it already and I'm not remotely concerned."

Tamsin had asked him how, how he couldn't worry after all these years, after the increasing signs of alcoholism...and then things got out of hand.

After he had slammed the door, and things had gone very quiet, Tamsin's neighbour Claire knocked gently. "Tamsin," she called through the letterbox, "are you okay?"

Tamsin glowed red with shame. Claire had three children under five – she and Neil had probably woken them, caused no end of problems. "Yes. Of course. I'm sorry. My friend was drunk."

"He sounded angry." Claire looked worried, and seemed to scan Tamsin's body for bruises, injuries. Neil had twisted her wrist, slapped her. But she had iced everything and consequently, she had nothing to show for it.

"Yes, he was. But he'll be okay."

"I hope so," Claire said doubtfully. "Are you sure you're alright?"

Tamsin tried a reassuring smile. "Yes, I promise. Neil's a musician, he's very passionate."

"Passion is no excuse for violence."

Surely it's the only excuse? wondered Tamsin. "I know, Claire."

"Goodnight then." Claire gave her a *don't let that bastard back round here* look.

Tamsin nodded obediently and shut the door, before heading straight for the kitchen. She poured herself a small glass of Shiraz and thought of Joseph and then her sister, turning the stained napkin over and over in her hands.

Adagio

Tamsin forgave Neil the second she woke up. She even suspected she may have forgiven him before she went to bed. She couldn't think why she had provoked him with a discussion of Joseph. After all, Neil seemed to have something against him at the moment, something she didn't understand, but saw in his eyes every time the old man offered him whisky and Neil declined in favour of his own cigarettes. Why on earth had she thought that Neil would be sympathetic? There always seemed to be something between them in rehearsals these days. They had frequent disagreements over dynamics and tempo, choice of rosin, Bach versus Handel. Some arguments had threatened to get out of hand. There was no denying Neil to be a very talented cellist, but he was lacking in discipline, sensitivity, depth of interpretation. Musically, he was perfectly matched to Roseanna, Tamsin thought, as she checked the time and got up to put the coffee on. To Neil, a piece was either his showcase or it wasn't.

Perhaps it was for this reason that Neil had never shown much interest in playing professionally or auditioning for larger ensembles, in earning money or making music his career. He liked the occasional booking, and he seemed to need the discipline of regular rehearsal – unconsciously sensing its value, perhaps – but he never auditioned, or aspired to anything beyond Joseph's quartet.

Maybe she could help him – inspire him, jolt him out of stalemate. The prospect of a full-blown relationship with Neil fascinated her. She could picture them messing about together, Sunday mornings, in her flat. She would play violin, Neil would recite Kerouac and stew magic mushrooms in her art deco kitchen. She would listen to him play long mournful passages of Elgar on the cello; they'd smoke cigarettes together in the bath.

Tamsin smiled to herself as she dialled Neil's number. She just hoped he had calmed down.

Dolce

They met for an early lunch in the park. It was a windy day, not really suitable for alfresco dining. Neil was distracted by the prospect of having to apologise, despite the fact that Tamsin had not sounded particularly pissed off on the phone. He hoped that the vile weather might provide them with an alternative topic of conversation.

She was waiting for him on the agreed bench, curls blown in all four directions, her cheeks pink, dressed in an orange coat and matching earrings. Neil observed with some amusement that she looked a bit like a fortune-teller.

He opened his mouth to say something, but realised that the truthful reason for his outburst would hardly please her. The basic truth was that he had wanted to fuck her, badly. It had been like smelling coffee first thing in the morning – the very sight of her, the very feeling of her near to him, had resulted in an overpowering craving for a shot of Tamsin to his bloodstream. Well, to his loins, actually.

But instead, she had pottered around, fretting about Joseph, and Neil had experienced the caffeine-addict's jitters, making him edgy, ready to let fly.

He opened his mouth now to say – what? – but Tamsin laid a hand on his arm and spoke instead. "I've got something to tell you."

She didn't seem to want an explanation. Neil felt slightly perturbed. He wasn't used to having zero effect. "Go on." He suspected, darkly, that this was going to involve Joseph.

"I auditioned for the RPO – The Royal Philharmonic," she clarified, not needing to, "and I got through." The words tumbled from her mouth like an aria. "Nobody else knows."

Neil was confused. Why was she telling him? Why hadn't she told the old man? "Well done."

"I'm going to have to withdraw from the quartet."

That was why. Neil wanted to laugh. This would finish Joseph, absolutely finish him. "He'll find out, you know," he warned, without needing to mention Joseph's name. "He's like a bloody Red Indian, spends his whole time listening for horses."

"What?" Tamsin looked puzzled.

"Ear to the ground." It was true. Joseph lived alone, seeing no-one but his quartet from week to week, yet he had still managed to retain a bewildering number of contacts from his days as a concert violinist.

Neil opened his arms to hug her. It didn't come easily to him but he knew it was what she wanted. And he was right. She fell into his arms with relief, folding into him, smelling of shampoo and Pear's soap. "Thank you," she said.

"No problem," he replied, although he had no idea why she was thanking him. The physical contact made him stir once again. The frustration burnt him.

Rondo

The sky was grey and thunderous. Joseph had no appointments, and the hours until rehearsal stretched out ahead of him, long and laborious,

Handel's *Messiah* translated into time.

He moved over to the bookcase and extracted *Bennett's History of the Violin*, drawing it out by its thin white spine. It had been a birthday present from Tamsin, when at last she had reached the age where marking a teacher's birthday could be considered appropriate. He didn't think much of the book, or its author, but he liked to open it occasionally and run his eye over Tamsin's scribble on the inside cover. *Many Happy Returns – for a favourite teacher. T x*

Joseph slid the book back between its neighbours – *The Oxford Companion to Classical Music*, and *Kennedy: Maestro or Maverick?* – raising a smile at the latter. He knew Kennedy well – they used to mix in the same circles – and he could answer that question without having to read a book.

Beneath the shelving was a mahogany cupboard. Joseph knelt on the edge of the rug, turned the cupboard's little key, sitting stiff in its lock, and opened one of the doors. He reached inside and slowly withdrew the violin case, feeling its delicious weight. His breathing became more rapid suddenly – perhaps it was the strong smell of the cupboard's interior, locked in on itself for months, sometimes years at a time, the combined odour of stale polish and ripe mahogany. Joseph glanced briefly inside, at the many piles of his own discarded manuscripts – mostly music, but occasionally, poetry. His hands wobbled slightly as he rested the violin case on the patch of faded rug at his knees.

Flicking both clasps upwards, he raised the lid, moved the silk scarf aside, rediscovering the elegance of polished spruce and maple. He drew the instrument out steadily, rubbed a forefinger along its strings, imagined the dents they would make in fresh fingers. He pictured Tamsin lifting it to her shoulder for the first time, the look on her face as she clasped its neck, pushing the chin rest under her jaw. He imagined himself placing a score in front of her, watching her play. She might play for hours, he thought, and he would watch the sweat gather on her smooth, pale forehead, making little patches in the armpits of her cotton top, forming small moons under her breasts. In his mind she set her jaw, climbing the octaves on her new fingerboard; he could almost smell the rosin forming crusts along the clean strings. The folds of her long skirt would sway; he would set a metronome and watch her strain against it. He wanted to conduct her, to command her.

Outside, a taxi sounded its horn and Joseph heard shouting. Wrenched from his reverie, he set down the violin and got slowly to his feet, feeling his knees creak. He had not yet found a time to present her with the gift, wanting the magnitude of the occasion to match the gesture. He had commissioned his late friend James Perch to craft the violin for Tamsin, and since James' death on a lethal stretch of A–road in Devon, instruments with his signature were now of considerable value. Perhaps, Joseph pondered, as he poured himself a whisky, he held back because in his mind there was only one occasion which would ever be truly fitting.

Appassionato

Roseanna had spent lunchtime serving cocktails to Neil. He was drunk already, talking about Tamsin, disappointed by the fact that she wasn't going to be an easy lay. Neil wasn't a man who put in effort very willingly.

Roseanna leant over the bar, listening to him slur, and she thought how lucky it was that Neil had been born with such a natural talent for music. Had he been required to work hard at it, to make actual sacrifices for his art, he would undoubtedly be occupying a squat in Mile End, snorting cocaine for breakfast and stuffing notes into women's knickers every night. Ironically enough, it was the routine and monotony of Joseph's quartet that kept Neil sane, enabling him to hold down a job and appear normal to the outside world. As he continued to talk, Roseanna noticed him sniffing slightly, and she peered more closely at his face. There was a light dusting of white powder on his upper lip.

They left soon afterwards, Roseanna telling her boss she had a headache, and they made it (just) to her bedsit off the Dalston Road. Neil clawed her as they climbed the stairs, scratching out his hunger over her body with his fingers. His touch was pleading for something only she knew how to give. She knew what it meant. Neil had no interest in conversation or self-improvement, in success or personal growth. Neil's touch said 'Fuck me'; Tamsin thought it said 'I want to get to know you.' Roseanna smiled. Misreading men like Neil was fatal.

They didn't mention Tamsin again. Neil didn't know guilt, he didn't know responsibility. He only knew his body, his needs, his drug dealer.

But he knew her too. As they stumbled into the kitchen, his hands grappling at her bra strap, she caught sight of the untouched cheesecake she had left out on the side to defrost. Oh yes, she thought, as their mouths met, you'll block my arteries and kill me eventually, but by God, you taste good.

They made it to bed, and afterwards, limbs still entangled, Neil reached into her bedside cabinet for her cigarettes. "I think you're jealous," he said, lighting up.

He always started off like that, trying to provoke a reaction from her, as if she were a cat. She ignored him for a while, staring steadily up at the creeping blot of damp across the high ceiling. "I don't pity you Neil," she said, eventually, truthfully. "Do you want me to pity you?"

"You do," he corrected her, dragging hard on his cigarette.

"You want pity; you don't deserve it. You want Tamsin? You'll never get her."

The crispness in her voice must have irritated him; he rolled over and pushed the lit cigarette into her arm. She cried out, tears falling instantly, forcing him off her, rushing to the window. She lifted the sash, gasped air.

Neil watched her from the bed, shook his head, re-lit the same cigarette. "Maybe I don't want her."

Yes, he did, but if he had her, just once, his interest would evaporate like fog. Tamsin was a passing phase, yet he came back to Roseanna time and time again.

All he needed to do was sleep with Tamsin once, and conversely, he would belong to her again. The burn started to blister, forming a thick yellow crust, round and small like a little golden sun on her skin. He had marked his passion out on her, his territory.

Subito

The doorbell rang at four. Joseph had just settled down to a plate of salad and eggs in front of a mindless antiquing programme. He swore as he got to his feet, suspecting his downstairs neighbour, Ben, of losing his keys yet again. Ben had supplied Joseph with three copies of his keys when he moved in, and had already lost two.

It was Tamsin.

"Hello," Joseph said simply, ignoring the jerk he felt in his stomach.

"Joseph, could I come in please? I need to talk to you."

"Of course." He held the door wide, let her pass. She looked shaken, as if she had been blown to his front door by the wind. He hoped this wasn't about the napkin.

"Joseph." Tamsin set down her old familiar bag with the bright stitching, resting it in the dent on the sofa where he had been sitting. She spotted the plate of salad and eggs. "Oh – you were just about to eat."

"It's salad," Joseph replied. "There's no danger of it getting cold."

"Well, look, Joseph. I've got something to tell you."

"Tell me then." He felt as if something was washing about in the pit of his stomach, and was half-expecting Tamsin to announce a boyfriend, a move to Wales, or something equally disturbing.

"I had an audition," she announced shakily, seemingly unable to look at him. She began to rub at a sticky patch on his table, probably spilt whisky, wetting her finger against her tongue and then rubbing hard. "I had an audition for the RPO. I got in."

"Tamsin. That's wonderful news. Isn't that what you've been working towards – " he smiled what he hoped was a reassuring smile, "– since you were eleven years old?"

"Everything's going to change," Tamsin said, quietly, apologetically, "I'm sorry."

He wished she would look at him. "Yes, it is. It is." Joseph nodded and rubbed his chin, which bristled with the sharpness of a thousand tiny hairs. He nodded again. "Everything is going to change. But you shouldn't be apologising – we should be celebrating. It's wonderful news."

"Joseph," Tamsin said, and she still wouldn't look at him, "the reason I didn't tell you about the audition..."

Joseph laughed softly, and regarded his salad, sitting limply on the plate, on top of this morning's *Telegraph*. "I knew, Tamsin. I knew about your audition."

Finally she looked up. "Oh."

"I didn't know whether or not you were successful, of course. I didn't want to." It was not entirely true – his fingers had wavered over the phone for weeks – but he had a firm grasp of audition ethics. He wouldn't have risked her respect. In a way, Joseph thought, as he felt her already slipping away from him, her respect was all he had.

"Anyway," Tamsin carried on, and he sensed this was not all she had come to say, "I didn't tell you because I didn't want to raise your hopes. It was enough raising my own, let alone..."

"Is there something else?" Joseph interrupted suddenly, a little more abruptly than he meant to.

Tamsin looked almost frightened, as if he had delved into her head and plucked her thoughts like fruit. She hesitated, but only for a second.

"Yes," she whirled, suddenly breathless, "Neil and I are seeing each other."

Cadenza

Joseph regarded her for a few seconds. "I have something for you," he said, moving towards his bookcase. "I'd been saving it for a special occasion..."

He knelt down in front of the cupboard beneath the shelves, turned the key and drew out a violin case. It looked new; Tamsin didn't recognise it at all. He moved over to the table under the window and set it down. "This is for you."

Tamsin hesitated for just a second, but curiosity drew her to his side, and she gently opened the case. The smell of varnished spruce was immediate; it was the colour of burnt sugar – the surface of a crème brûlée. With a gasp she touched the taut new strings, the clean pegs, the perfectly carved f-holes. She wanted to pick it up and stroke it.

"I had James Perch make it for you. It should fit you perfectly."

"James? James has been dead for years," Tamsin faltered, confused.

"I've had it a long time," he said, "I've been waiting for the right occasion."

She felt deeply and instantly unworthy. She had kept things from him, distracted herself with Neil, lost focus, lost professionalism. And now he was rewarding her with this thing, this priceless thing, whose weight of meaning she could almost feel in her arms. She lifted the violin to her chin and imagined raising a bow with it. The effect was overwhelming, and she knew she would cry.

"Joseph..."

"I'd really like it," he said, "if you would use it and make it yours.

To mark this new era...in your career."

He meant to say, *in our lives*, Tamsin thought, shaking her head. The movement released a few dark hairs which floated under the strings, through the f-holes and into the hollow belly of the instrument. "I just don't know what to say."

Joseph shrugged woolly shoulders. "That doesn't matter."

"May I?" Tamsin gestured towards his bow, hanging lifelessly on the music stand between them.

Joseph nodded, saying nothing, and Tamsin lifted the violin to her shoulder. It needed her own shoulder-rest to be perfect, but it was so nearly there, it didn't matter. She dug the bow in, played a solitary note.

Tranquillo

She looked Romany, Joseph observed, with her dark curls and silver jewellery, skin still freckled from the summer. Her eyes were shut but her body moved fluidly to her own sound. Joseph hoped she would never stop.

He tried not to think about Neil. He suspected the boy's motivations, but he didn't worry too much. For one, he didn't credit Neil with enough intelligence to know what he had in Tamsin and secondly, he trusted Tamsin's good sense. Joseph suspected Neil was still seeing Roseanna, but he would not be baited; he would say nothing. Things would take their own, natural course. The right and proper course.

He was suddenly overwhelmed by the impulse to kiss her.

Accelerando

Neil's phone rang as Roseanna made them both coffee. Caffeine was the only drug she had available. She heard the phone ring, heard Neil say one or two words at the most, and then she heard the creak of the bed as he raised himself from it.

"I have to go."

He wanted her to ask where, but she didn't. She just shrugged and carried on making the coffee.

"Did you hear me? I have to go. I have to..." He trailed off. She listened to the familiar sound of him hunting about for his clothes. She heard him swear a couple of times, open her drawer, pocket her cigarettes. She padded back through to the bedroom and watched him pull his boots on.

"See you tonight." He looked blank for a moment. "At Joseph's?"

He laughed then, gently, as if she was missing something. "Yeah, see you tonight." He got up, kissed her hard. "Later." He looked at her for a couple of seconds, but as if he was thinking about something else. Then he turned and left the flat, banging the door behind him.

She listened to the sound of his boots as he thudded down all three floors. She watched him scuff his way across the browned grass beneath her window.

Fortissimo

He's almost thirty years older than her. The thought of it was vile. Foul. He had always suspected the old man of harbouring thoughts like these, but to act on them? Tamsin had confirmed what made him feel sick to his stomach.

Straightaway he had identified the regret in her voice, which turned into panic as she realised what she had done in telling him. She had pleaded with him, trying to make him promise to do nothing. But by then it was too late – it was no longer to do with her, it was between him and Joseph.

It was time to make it all happen.

He climbed the cold concrete steps to the old man's front door, the welcome mat sitting smugly on the step, angering him. He rang the bell three times in quick succession. Joseph wasn't long – probably thought it was Tamsin come back for him, the dickhead.

He said nothing, simply held the door open. Neil returned his silence, pushing past him into the flat. It smelt of eggs. The curtain was flapping at the window, blowing a stiff breeze between them both.

"This is not your business," Joseph announced eventually, coldly. Neil could read his disappointment – Tamsin had betrayed him. One nil Neil.

"It is. It's between you and me, you bloody idiot."

"No," Joseph said firmly, and said nothing more, but he moved away slightly, edging towards the window. For safety, maybe, witnesses?

There was nothing that angered Neil more in the world than cowardice.

Presto

Joseph was left gripping the scroll of the violin in his hand. It had splintered away from the rest of the instrument as Neil had torn it from him, and he had watched helplessly as he smashed it against the door. Joseph knew that this had little to do with Tamsin. They hadn't even mentioned her name. This was about years of silent anger between father and son, unspoken rifts, drug abuse, violence. Neil wanted to harm him, and he didn't mind much how he did it.

It was Joseph's own fault that the violin lay smashed. He had destroyed it himself, when he kissed her. Now he felt nothing but shame – shame that after all these years he had demonstrated such a lack of self-restraint. Every aspect of his life had been down to discipline, and he had crumbled at the most crucial point; the *crescendo* had flattened him.

He wished he had had the quick thinking to force the case handle into her hand at the last minute. If she had felt it there in her palm, he was sure she would not have tried to return it – she would have fled, clutching it. The violin would have been safe, at least, and perhaps some day years from now, she might have opened the case and remembered him. But now it was no more than a handful of splinters scattered across his table, the manuscript, the rug. One piece had landed neatly in a sticky whisky glass. Joseph eyed it from where he lay on the floor. He couldn't tell which part it came from. The wood bowed slightly – a rib, perhaps?

They had been working up to this their whole lives, he realised, as a trickle of blood settled in the fold at the corner of his mouth. The inevitability of the whole thing was constant, like the tick of the metronome.

He couldn't move – the pain in his side was too great – but he needed to, desperately. "Neil," he gasped, as he attempted to inch his frame along the floor. He felt like an elderly seal trying to flee dogs. "Please, son. Don't."

Neil's face was contorted now. Anger had been replaced by something else, something far worse. "You have no right whatsoever to call me son, you bastard."

Joseph gasped. The pain in his ribs was growing. It felt as if acid was gnawing the bone. *I can't talk to you like this,* he wanted to plead. *Help me up, give me a couple of hours, we'll talk. We'll talk, son.*

"You watched my mother die and you did nothing."

Joseph swallowed a sudden wash of bile that had surged into his mouth. "No, Neil. No. It was what she wanted."

"Don't fucking lie to me."

"Neil, it's the truth. Your mother..." But the pain was too great and his body folded. As his face met the carpet, something in Neil's expression caught his attention. Had the boy taken something?

"Neil," he began, steadily, "are you on something? What have you taken? Come on, you can tell me. What is it?" He tried desperately to remember what Neil had taken in the past. "Is it...acid? Es? Cocaine?"

Neil laughed a shrill, manic laugh. "Yeah, good one. Keep them coming."

Please don't, Joseph pleaded silently with his son. *Please don't do it.*

But he knew it was too late. There had been no talk, only music, for years. They had sat in opposite seats for a lifetime, playing from the same score but forgetting what had gone before, regarding each other with unspoken hatred, burying their thoughts in sheet music.

"You watched her die. Now watch me."

Joseph disobeyed, panicked, shut his eyes. When he opened them – hoping, hoping – Neil was gone. From the street below, Joseph heard car horns and swearing, horrified exclamations, a woman's scream. Ten minutes later, an ambulance siren.

And then a knock at the door.

Intermezzo

"I'm sorry," was all he said.

They were sitting in Joseph's living room, the night before Neil's funeral, and for the first time that Tamsin could remember, no music was playing. Silence was almost a relief; she needed to map out her thoughts.

She had come here to comfort him, but how could she? His life had disintegrated, leaving only crumbs, traces of a former existence, soaking up the blood. What else could he feel but sorrow and despair?

She was glad she had not seen Neil's body. The thought of it brought back images of her sister Jade, floating bloated and lifeless in a Greek swimming pool, leaking blood. She did not want to remember Neil as crumpled and deformed, flesh seeping from skin, face blackened from the fall. When she shut her eyes, she still saw his confidence, talent, undeniable charm. He was fucked up, she knew that, but wasn't everybody?

The police had questioned all three of them. Nobody had seen it coming. Tamsin had blamed herself, then Roseanna briefly, then Joseph, then herself again.

She needed to ask him. She wasn't even sure why, but the question had burnt her every day from inside, like a lit match. "Joseph, did Neil jump?"

She was almost too afraid to hear the answer, not because she expected an admission of guilt, but because she understood how terrible the question was.

Joseph paused for a couple of seconds, but he didn't seem surprised. "You mean, did I push him?"

She nodded silently, ashamed.

"Well then, here it is: Neil jumped. I trust you Tamsin; I trust your reasons for asking."

"Joseph, I'm sorry."

"My wife..." But he couldn't finish.

Tamsin knew that Joseph had helped his wife Lucy to die. She had been a fine cello player, just like her son, and they had listened to du Pré play Elgar's cello concerto in E minor as she lost her life. Tamsin pictured Joseph gripping Lucy's hand as he gripped hers now, tears falling onto a limp white arm.

"Will Roseanna come to the funeral?" he asked, hopeful but doubtful.

"I don't know."

"I started everything, didn't I?" he said despairingly. "With that kiss."

Tamsin reddened slightly. "Don't." They had talked about this too many times; it had yet to make either of them feel better.

"But it angered him. I don't know what I was thinking..."

"Joseph, it was all down to me! I should never have told Neil about the kiss. I was out of my mind – I just panicked, thought he might be able to read you better than I could. If there's anybody to blame for Neil's death, it's me."

He didn't seem to hear her, or, if he did, he didn't agree. "Please, Tamsin. Forgive me. Please."

"I do," she said, softly, squeezing his hand again, seeing nothing to forgive. "Oh," she added, remembering, slipping a hand into her pocket, "I brought this back for you. It's clean." She placed Joseph's once-stained napkin on his knee. It was white again, folded and ironed, and it smelt of soap.

"Thank you. You really didn't need..." He paused. "Will you play at the funeral tomorrow?"

Tamsin hesitated. "I don't know if I can. I'm terrible at funerals." She had left her father's funeral after only five minutes, overcome with shaking and sweat. The vicar had called her a disgrace.

"Joseph," she began, and she was telling him before she realised it, "my father died. It was six months ago. I didn't know how to tell you."

Joseph nodded. "Oh, Tamsin. I'm sorry."

"Don't be. I'm sorry I didn't tell you earlier. I couldn't..."

Joseph shook his head. "It's okay. I understand. I couldn't think how I was going to tell you Neil had died..." A few solitary tears fell as he blinked.

How could she show Joseph she did not blame him? How could she say sorry to Neil one last time?

"Okay," she assented, with a nod, "I'll play."

Diminuendo

The street lamps were beginning to fire up, dotted like beacons around the estate, matching perfectly the orange of the sunset which squatted over the horizon. Tamsin spotted Roseanna sitting on the wide windowsill in her kitchen, blowing little puffs of smoke into the air, watching them form neat little clouds in front of her before they dispersed into the dusk. In the gloom, Tamsin could see that Roseanna had not spotted her; she climbed the stairs to her flat and knocked on the door.

Roseanna took a long while to answer, but eventually, she was there, wearing nothing but an oversized t-shirt in sky blue.

"I wanted to see you," Tamsin explained, almost shy. It had been weeks. "How are you?"

Roseanna said nothing, shrugged slightly. She was regarding Tamsin as though she had forgotten who she was. Tamsin wondered if she should remind her.

"Can I come in?"

Roseanna nodded, and held the door wide. Tamsin slipped through it into the hallway and made her way towards the kitchen. The flat was very hot, and smelt almost sterile, as if it were barely being used – to sleep in perhaps, but little more. There was no evidence of food or activity of any sort. Roseanna looked ill and very thin.

"Are you okay?"

Roseanna shook her head, said nothing, but waved a bottle of something in Tamsin's direction. Tamsin couldn't quite see the label – was it vodka? – but declined anyway. They stood facing each other in the middle of the kitchen.

"Roseanna...Joseph would love to see you. He wants to make sure you're alright."

"I'm alright." Her voice sounded muffled, as if she was speaking through fog.

"I'm so sorry. I don't know what to say."

Roseanna nodded, lit another cigarette. She resumed her seat on the windowsill again and nodded towards the door. "Neil left through that door. That was the last time I ever saw him."

Tamsin felt accused, and bowed her head. "I know."

"Neil told me he was going to do this years ago."

Her words hung on the air, before slowly turning into silence. Tamsin wanted to stop them, grab them back, shake them. "What?"

Roseanna seemed to examine her fingers. "He planned it years ago. Revenge on Joseph. For Neil's mum."

Tamsin's hands flew to her mouth. "Oh my God," she breathed.

"And before you ask, there was no point in telling anybody. Once Neil made up his mind about something...God, the bloke was a ticking fucking time bomb."

Tamsin exhaled, trying to understand. "So you just waited..."

"I tried to make him get help, see somebody. He had some crappy mental health specialist on his case for a while."

"What happened?"

Roseanna shook her head and tapped the end of her cigarette. "The specialist? Committed suicide."

Tamsin shook her head. "No..."

Roseanna shrugged. "I'm telling you. If Joseph had known, nothing would have changed."

Tamsin started to babble. "But they could have made amends, they could have...sorted things out. If he'd known, Joseph would have tried harder, I know he would." But she saw from Roseanna's face that she was missing the point.

"It was too late for that, Tam. You'll think about it, and you'll realise I'm right. That was how he had always planned to go, like that. One day. I just didn't think he'd do it so soon."

"He probably didn't either, Roseanna," said Tamsin softly and sadly, feeling guilt-ridden.

The two girls were silent in the kitchen for a few moments, listening to the hum-click of the boiler.

Tamsin needed to leave. Her head was beginning to pound from the enormity of what she'd heard. She took a breath, tried to think practically. "Is there anything I can do? Is there anything you need?" Roseanna shook her head.

Another uncertain pause. "Do you want me to stay?"

"No." Roseanna continued to stare out of the window. "You could take that rubbish bag downstairs on your way out if you like. There's bins outside, blue ones."

"Okay." Tamsin made her way towards the door, and then hesitated. Should she hug her, say sorry again, tell her everything would be alright?

"Can I tell Joseph...?"

She nodded. "Yes, if you like. If you think it will make a difference."

Would it make a difference, a positive one? Tamsin wondered. She hoped so. She had to tell him. She no longer wanted to keep anything from him.

"Bye Roseanna." Tamsin lifted the bag from the hallway and left the flat. As she made her way down the stairs and reached the patch of worn grass where the bins stood, she happened to glance inside the bag at its contents: a navy blue knitted sweater. *The Grapes of Wrath*. Two Kafka paperbacks, a CD of Debussy chamber music. Tamsin reeled. This was all Neil's.

She hesitated. She couldn't throw this away. She had to show Joseph, at least, to see if there was anything he wanted to salvage.

Something made her glance upwards. Roseanna was still seated at the window, but this time she wasn't staring blankly at the horizon. She was looking down at Tamsin, and her eyes said, *please*.

Tamsin heaved the bag into the bin, smiled softly at Roseanna, and left, swallowed gradually by the gloom as she walked.

Finale

Joseph sat on the Schwedenplatz, raised a hot cup to his lips and scorched his tongue with coffee. He had come here against the advice of four consultants, but as the only person whose wishes mattered to him was now absorbed elsewhere, he had seen no good reason to stay in London. He wanted to die in the company of those he knew best. Familiar, old, faithful friends.

He had spent the last few months walking in the steps of Haydn, attending recitals at the Musikverein, taking walks along the canal and drinking coffee, as he did now, on the Schwedenplatz. He had spent long days admiring the Baroque architecture, imagining his namesake, the great Joseph Haydn, doing the same before failing health prevented him. Failing health was almost preventing Joseph. He had been here for almost one year now. The doctors had given him eight months. He felt almost proud.

Neil's boot in his stomach had been the catalyst for the ugly cancerous growth; he was sure of it. He had told nobody except Tamsin, in a letter, although he had revealed nothing of his whereabouts. She would probably guess, but his secrecy allowed her the excuse of ignorance, enabled her to get on with her life and career without guilt. He had asked her to forget him, to forget *Viol*, to forget Neil; he hoped she had taken his advice, though deep down, he doubted it.

Joseph had bought an English music magazine from a bookshop on his way to the square that morning. He opened it now, letting the pages flap in the breeze that came in off the canal. He turned several pages, gratefully savouring the news from a past life. He read about a Britten memorial concert, the programme for the Proms, some gossip about Charlotte Church.

Suddenly his heart began to pump more forcefully. He squinted to check the words, reading them through more slowly, and then again. The ache in his stomach relented for a few seconds, and then resurfaced as he shifted in his seat. Joseph smiled, ignoring the pain.

The Royal Philharmonic are to première this month Concerto No. 1 in D Minor, by little-known composer but one time pupil of the Royal College, Joseph Fenner, the article read. *Fenner is believed to be based in Austria at present, but rights to the piece are granted to viola player Tamsin Price, currently performing with the orchestra. Music Director Daniele Gatti commented...*

Joseph leaned back in his chair and shut his eyes, hearing the chatter of German around him, feeling the sun across his cheekbones. For a split second, he recognised true joy. It was a strange, unique feeling, but, briefly, it filled him utterly. He met death's steely glare, and suddenly, he was no longer afraid.

Watch What You Say

Rebekah Delgado

I had to think hard about this one, but on reflection I realised that some of my lyrics had been affected by the books and poems I have read. I first remember something clicking – in terms of lyric-writing – when I learnt about iambic pentameter in *Mr Bleaney* (Larkin). I realised that when used the right way, words can create their own rhythm.

Then there were the French writers that struck a chord with me (no pun intended). *Les Justes* by Camus was fascinating in the fact that it tried to balance philosophy and its practical application when wanting to instigate change. *Therese* by Mauriac spoke to me of tragedy without the melodrama; quiet tragedy that knows its name but doesn't speak out. As did *The Grapes of Wrath* by Steinbeck. I also liked Ibsen and Chekhov for similarly non-indulgent reasons: being driven along by something bigger than yourself that you have no control over, but not wallowing unnecessarily in your pain.

Voltaire (particularly *Candide*) helped me see society and its strange evolution of thought through a historical perspective (as did the first two Anne Rice vampire chronicles). Our song *FUUK* tries to follow along from that: 'Leave a path behind for those who follow, 'cos we're the predecessors of tomorrow'. Another good writer is Jon Savage, although he has a tendency to get lost in his own rhetoric. His *England's Dreaming* also influenced that song: 'History's made by the ones who say no'.

Quentin Crisp's diaries are illuminating not only in the acute observations of American culture, but also in cross-generational comparisons. Using the term 'post-modern' tentatively, so much of our current artistic output seems to be a cross-cultural reinvention of something that went before (more so than ever before), and that inspired the *FUUK* line: 'Our soundtrack is a bootleg life, so turn the volume up high'.

I know many other people in bands who don't hold much importance to lyrics and care mostly for the music. Without pontificating, to me, they are just as important as each other. Whether abstract or concrete, I try to write lyrics that can stand fast against the foe (with a wry smile).

Some Obscure Lesion of the Heart

Nels Stanley

The music business is a cruel and shallow money trench, a long plastic hallway where thieves and pimps run free, and good men die like dogs. There is also a negative side.

-- Hunter S. Thompson.

"Pulsing skronk, mate."

"Say what?"

"That's what the kids are into. Not this folksy shit. Pulsing skronk." He sipped lager from a plastic cup, wiped a moustache of foam from his upper lip onto his Aphex Twin T-shirt and stared past my ear at the ranks of Marshalls lined up by the stage. "Glitchcore. Multi-wavelength subsonics. High-end divebomber BPMs." He grinned, exposing yellow teeth caried from long-time speed use. He smelled like death. "Not jangly fucking love songs sung by a bunch of Art School wankers. I mean, who do they think they are? The Boo Fucking Radleys?"

"Thanks. I'll bear that in mind," I said, looking around desperately for someone to save me. Not twenty feet away, a group of identical looking young men in flared trousers and boring shirts stood on stage while the guitarist threw a tantrum about monitor levels. The sound engineer lit his third joint of the afternoon and settled into his Anais Nin book. Their manager was nowhere to be seen, thank God; a few roadies – all of them earnest, aloof young men in Beta Band T-shirts and brick-thick bifocals – sneered their displeasure at me. Cunts, I thought uncharitably, then felt a pang of remorse; mustn't speak ill of virgins, my mother said. Words to that effect, anyway.

My new friend ripped the cellophane off a pack of *Embassy No. 1*'s with his teeth then proffered the spittle-drenched packet. I politely declined. He shrugged, and turned to watch the band, who were now arguing about the time signature *I Hung My Head* was written in.

"It's five/nine, Charles. Any prick could tell that." The lead guitarist, resplendent in a frightful green velvet shirt, shook wispy blond fringe from his eyes and stroked his acne-spattered chin. "Or maybe nine/five. Not seven/ten, at any rate. It's a fucking Sting song, not Miles Davis."

My new friend nudged me in the shoulder.

"What are you here for, then? With the band, are you?"

The question. It haunts my days and pursues me down the Stygian corridors of night. I scraped my foot on the floor, bummed a ciggie and lit it off his. Then I looked around, to make sure there was no-one within earshot. The band jangled out the intro to *An Englishman In New York*, stumbled over a chord change. The singer swore into the mike, spun about on his heel and stomped off-stage. Everybody was safely ignoring me.

"I'm a hack," I whispered. The temperature of the room dropped seventy degrees. My new friend stiffened, a look on his face like he was about to whip the cigarette from my mouth and stamp on it. The roadies swivelled like they were all on castors, sneering at me in unison. The smell of the place suddenly filled my nostrils, ghosts of Old Holborn from a million roll-ups and sweat from a hundred thousand armpits. It seemed to solidify in my throat. My stomach churned. I grinned and hurried away, heading for the street, for light, for life.

*

Safe in the car. Mix tape slotted in. Head back against headrest; Nick Cave screaming; rain falling Biblically, making a nice streaky effect on the windscreen. Finish the ciggie. Wind window down an inch, flick butt out. Watch shoppers straggle about between the puddles. Nothing to do for three hours but sit and think and worry vaguely about not having a real job.

A knock on the window. My new friend leered into my car.

"Cor Jesus," he said. "Let us in for fuck's sake."

I thought briefly about date rape and Rohypnol and whether or not you could soak an Embassy No. 1 in it, then opened the passenger door. He flopped into the seat, then broke wind loud enough to drown out the Bad Seeds.

"Into that, are you?" he said, as I turned the stereo down enough to make conversation possible.

"Into what?" I asked, on the defensive.

"Fucking Goth," he said, lighting another cigarette. He pronounced it 'Goff'. Of course.

"Actually, I don't mind some of it. It's..." I looked out into the street. A small child stood outside an ironmonger's, pressing their head against the window, unmindful of the rain, trying to bore through the plate glass by force of will to get at all the lovely shiny things in the window display. "Look. I like lots of stuff. Taste in music is subjective, all right? There's no right or wrong. There's stuff people like that they simply cannot defend on a rational basis. I just get paid to sneer in print, that's all."

He drew reflectively on his smoke, flicked ash onto the floor.

"Nice speech. Prepare that, did you?"

"Actually, no. No I fucking didn't."

The rain pattered madly on the roof. The reek of cheap cigarettes, lager and a T-shirt probably not washed since Kurt Cobain was alive filled the car.

"S'no biggie. I prefer something with a bit more oomph meself." He stuck a chubby finger in his ear, twiddled it about then withdrew it. A glistening lump of something thick and yellow adhered to the tip. He wiped it on his sagging trackie bottoms. I tried not to gag. "Y'know..."

"High-end divebomber BPMs?"

He grinned, nodded once like a dog-owner whose Pomeranian has just performed a long-practised trick.

"Yeah. Like I said, pulsing skronk."

*

It turned out his name was Adam, and he had a band. This was not surprising; everyone I've ever met at a gig has a band. Sometimes two or three. You can tell from the expression, eventually – two parts glazed to one part drug-damaged. He pressed his mobile number into my hand later that evening, while the band I was there to see self-destructed on-stage and a riot ensued around us.

It started when they ripped into the opening chords of *I Hung My Head*, the set-closer. The singer missed his cue and failed to come in on time, and instead of just carrying the thing on and bringing the riff back to the beginning again the lead guitarist screamed into his microphone and smashed his semi-acoustic Rickenbacker into match wood like an anaemic teenage Pete Townshend. The singer immediately leapt upon him and pushed him to the floor; the bassist went to separate them, got tangled in the MIDI output trailing out of the keyboard and fell screaming on top, dragging about two grand's worth of vintage Moog down with him. By this point everyone in the room was cheering, which made a nice change from their essentially passive attitude during the rest of the gig. Security made a few inconclusive moves toward the stage, warily keeping an eye on the now animated crowd; the keyboard player shrieked a primal scream and, wielding the fallen bassist's axe like, well, an axe, attempted to get one back for the rhythm section. He missed his target as the singer rolled across the stage, and the bass slipped from his hands, sailing out over the front row with an almost balletic grace. We watched it describe a graceful arc, shining and twinkling as it passed through the spotlights, then it thudded into a fourteen year old girl's forehead. She went down screaming. Seventeen of her mates stormed the stage, incensed to a righteous wrath. Security tried to hold them back but the wave of students washed over them like time. The mob dragged the guitarist off the recumbent vocalist and beat the snot out of him. A vast howl rose and reverberated around the club, a dropped-D power chord you could feel in your bowels, then everyone went mad, tearing at each other, the furnishings, the band and staff with commendable impartiality. The keyboard player crept away, safe in his anonymity.

Adam and I sheltered beneath a long low table at the side of the room while a seething mass of bodies whirled around the dance floor. The splintering of wood and shrieks of feedback bled into screams and the sound of shattering bone. A heavy glass ashtray skidded across the floor like an ice hockey puck, coming to rest about two inches from my nose. Adam slipped his fag packet into my grasp then grabbed the ashtray and waded into the fray.

I kept my head down and cursed that I had forgotten to bring my camera. On the inside flap of the packet was scribbled a mobile phone number; there were still two ciggies inside. I shrugged and put it in my pocket.

*

Days I hardly saw, recollected at this remove, gain a sheen of nostalgia, a fond patina that at the time they sorely lacked. The days I spent either unconscious, recovering from the previous night's excesses, or – usually fruitlessly – chasing after cheques. The nights I spent listening to a variety of bands in a variety of venues, all of which put the appellation 'toilet' to shame. There was some decent stuff out there – there always is, there always will be – but none of the guys and girls making the stuff ever seemed to be the ones with fiscal remuneration, the big shiny tour buses, the legions of hangers-on bearing solid silver trays piled high with cocaine, the good-looking groupies. As ever, those who enjoyed some measure of record company largesse all seemed to sound like an act who'd sold a few records eighteen months' previously; every other sod gets to headline the Joiners' Arms, Southampton, just under the railway bridge, and are conveyed about the country by Transit van.

*

It's a question I get asked often, so I'll answer it now, before you start to wonder; I grew up listening to Nina Simone and Peggy Lee, subtly affected by the sound of my mother singing over the lazy beats and smoky vocals in her cracked wailing voice. My old man listened to David Whitfield and Marty Robbins, real warbling shitkicker stuff, so hearing my mother's music came as a kind of epiphany.

One of my few recurring dreams involves my mother pushing the vacuum around the floor, wailing along to *Fever*, missing every note and fucking loving it, every single cracked tuneless syllable she sang sending a little thrill coursing along my nerve endings. In the dream I can see myself; I'm maybe four or five, looking up from a book and swaying in time to the music, a look on my face that couldn't possibly have been there, a look that I've only seen on the faces of those who were far gone in the revels of Ecstasy or undergoing an orgasm. I see myself get up to dance with her, and we pirouette and gavotte around the living room of our old bungalow, passing the hose of the vacuum cleaner back and forth: a woman in her late forties who should've been too old to bear a child and her only son. We laugh as I try and fail to sing the backing vocal on time. Then the music segues into *Black Is The Colour (Of My True Love's Hair)*, and perfectly in synch we slow to a mock-movie star end-of-the-night shimmy, breaking away laughing as the last sombre piano chords roll out of the speakers, and then she picks me up and hugs me, and I bury my face in her hair, breathing in her faint smells of dust and feminine sweat and beeswax furniture polish.

The scene normally shifts at this point, and I see myself at age fourteen, sitting by her hospital bed, and I'm singing *Save Me* to her, completely out of time, the off-time whoops of the song rendered awkward and joyless without that pulsing bass line, those biscuit-tin drums, behind it. Her eyes are closed, and I guess the morphine spares her both from the feel of the cancer eating out her insides and the less serious but rather more pressing issue of my voice, which is quavering and breaking and as tuneless as her own, the sheer enthusiasm with which I'm singing making it all the more awful, like an extraordinarily ugly man in an exquisitely tailored suit.

Thankfully the dream ends there, dissolving in a haze of medical tubing and my pimply adolescent self warbling out of tune. The scene fades to a haze the exact colour that my mother's skin had gone by this point, a kind of washed-out grey like mist on a winter's morning. I wake up clutching at the bedclothes, foul with my own sweat, sobbing desperately into the duvet. The LCD of the alarm clock wavers from my tears, milk bottles clink on doorsteps. Someone wheelspins an overpowered car in the distance.

My old man ensured that he got his way with the music for her funeral; if I'm quite sure of anything it's that *Nearer My God To Thee* would not have been the top choice for her send-off.

*

"Right, shut the fuck up." The lead singer fiddles with his guitar. Short and chunky, a crew-cut like a Mexican featherweight and heavy-duty tatts crawling over thick forearms. "No, shut the fuck up, because if you don't this one'll be out of time, and I don't mean out of time in a good, Fugazi-out-of-time kind of way, I mean out of time as in..."

He pauses, scratches at his buzz-cut. A shard of feedback pulses through the club. The mosh pit has thrown us, battered and euphoric, up on the shores of the encore, and here we wait as Mclusky – who are on their 'Mclusky Do Dallas' tour, with Steve Albini looming godlike and shadowy on rhythm guitar – try and keep their machinelike precision for just a few moments more.

"I mean out of time as in... Well. Shit."

The crowd explodes. The bass line chugs in like the tide, surging then receding. A few people surf over the sea of outstretched hands then are hauled out by security, striking Jesus Christ poses as they are borne away to have the shit kicked out of them in the corridor by the toilets.

A few hundred people buzzing on various chemical highs cut with enough adrenalin to wake up Jimi Hendrix, smashing themselves to pieces out of the sheer fucking joy of being alive, trapped in a sweat box while a riff like a pneumatic drill hollows out their brains.

All this, and I didn't even have to pay to get in. I shall construct the review a few hours later, hunched over my keyboard, my ears ringing with the ghosts of tinnitus, reeking of cheap cigarettes and cheaper lager, my pulse still throbbing to the beat, the words falling from my fingers onto the keyboard, a spliff I rolled to send me to sleep sitting almost untouched in the ashtray at my elbow.

Sometimes, not often, but sometimes, it almost seemed like all the rest of the shit was worth it.

*

One morning, still hollowed out by lack of sleep and a hangover that felt like I had a member of Slipknot living in my head, I tottered across my flat, from pile of promo CDs to heap of discarded T-shirts. I didn't know what I was searching for – I barely knew where I was – so I dipped my hand into a haphazard stack of recently delivered singles and without looking slid it into the CD player.

A synthesised backing track, handclaps, 'tastefully' restrained guitar. Robbie Williams' anaemic voice following it, half-singing, half-talking. Something about not wanting to rock, DJ.

A howl of pain and rage, a vicious kick that sent the CD player toppling off the amp, pulling cables free. Robbie died with a pop. Clutching my foot and stumbling now, I hauled my jacket out from the debris, rifling through it for something to smoke, anything, half a joint secreted in an inside pocket, anything...

My hand clutched on a flattened cardboard cuboid. Hauling my treasure free with a little cry of triumph, enthusiasm only slightly dampened when I saw the white and red packaging isn't actually a deck of Marlboro's; still can't be helped, gotta be something to smoke in there, please God let there be something to smoke in...

A few dried-up shreds of tobacco fluttered to my unspeakably fouled carpet. I was about to screw the packet up and launch it across the room when I noticed the number scrawled in biro on the inner flap.

There's no name.

Mental processes fogged by lack of caffeine and nicotine, eyesight queered by the proximity of the hour to midday, a thought struck: could be a girl.

Jesus, it could be a girl. I consider how unlikely this is for a second, then decide it's gotta be worth a shot. I find my mobile phone and punch the number into it, saving to the address book under the name *Mystery Suitor*.

If it's not, I thought, I can always hang up on them.

*

"Yeah. I signed Laibach. Really. They insisted on holding the signing of the contract at midnight in a Belsize Park squat, surrounded by dying winos and people shooting up. First they subjected me to a reading of an eleven page, single-spaced document outlining their political agenda and beliefs, then they lit candles and we signed. No, not in their own blood. Bit of a letdown, all in all..."

*

"Right. We need something for the cover."

"Have you heard Seagull Screaming Kiss Her Kiss Her's new album?"

"Hmm. Girly surf-rock's a bit passé, isn't it? I mean, Kim Deal was doing it all better years ago."

"True, but they're both worth a fuck."

"Really?"

"Un-huh."

"Let's stick them on the cover, then."

Pause. Sound of cocaine being vacuumed up a rolled-up banknote.

"D'you think, if we offer them a couple of hundred quid, they'll get their tits out?"

"I'll get on the phone to their management."

*

"Hullo. I'm on the guest list."

Two steroid addled gorillas with arms as big as my thighs and bigger tits than my last two girlfriends glowered from beneath their Cro-Magnon mono-brows.

"Not on the list."

"Ah-hahaha." Pause, while I try to ascertain a better strategy. "Look, would you mind actually checking? I'm not trying to put you out, but I spoke to Andy – "

"Who the fuck's Andy?"

Rolling my eyes I took in the shuffling queue of kids in hoodies and baggy jeans shivering in the drizzle, the row of shitty cars parked on the double-yellows outside, the fizzing neon of the club's sign, the way the soft rain caught in the sodium glow. It all looked a bit like a Tom Waits album cover.

"Andy is the tour manager. Of the headline act. Look, if you can wait a sec, I'll give him a ring, I've got his number in my mobile – "

A threatening step down the concrete stairs. "If you pull out a shooter I'll stick it so far up your arse you'll blow your nose with it." The little piggy eyes were squinting, probably because they had to maintain a conversation for longer than fifteen seconds and his cerebral cortex was overheating. I backed away, holding my hands out in what I hoped was a conciliatory gesture.

"Look mate, I know you're only doing your job, really I do, but if you'd just check the guest list, I'm meant to be reviewing the show tonight, so – "

Another step. I could smell cheap after-shave and the nandrolene coming off them in waves, and it loosened something in my stomach.

Sneering young faces leered from the queue, enjoying the pre-show festivities. A sweepstake was probably being held at this moment, to see if the bouncers were just going to break my arms and legs or do that and rape me too.

"Please check the guest list, I know everyone tries it on mate, but really my name's on there, I spoke – "

"Now you're speaking to me." I craned my neck and studied the stubbled underside of his chin.

"Yes, yes I am."

"And I'm saying: Fuck off." A hand the size of God pushed me in the chest, sending me staggering half-a-dozen paces down the pavement.

"Would it really be that much trouble to check – "

"You." Another push. "Are." Another push. "Not." Another push. "Getting." Another, and now we're a good thirty feet from the club. "In." I'm already moving: duck and slide, slip to the left then dodge right, under the outstretched hand and around, curse these fucking cigarettes as breath shortens and the chest tightens, fuck I've made it, I've made it, I'm in, I'm –

Straight into the second bouncer, who just had to stick out his foot and I sailed through the air until I came to rest against the door of a battered Ford Escort with an impact that knocked the wind from me.

A ragged cheer from the line of paying punters. A swift kick in the ribs from one of my tormentors, to make sure I've got the point.

"Thanks very much," I said weakly, but no-one seemed to hear or at least, to care.

*

Five minutes to four on a dreary late-winter afternoon. It had been raining for what felt like twelve years. Fishing the remote for the stereo out from under my head, I thumbed the control until The Ramones hammered from the speakers. Singing *I Don't Want To Live This Life Anymore*. Tommy's (or was it Marky's?) back-beat vibrates the eyeballs in my skull. Sinuses hollowed out from the caustic bleaching effect of too much cocaine, liver swollen and kidneys aching from too much alcohol, vision fuzzy from lack of sleep. Numbness creeping into extremities.

Another perfect day.

Roll off sofa. Find cigarettes. Find lighter. Curse, because there are no lighters in the flat. Throw piles of CDs and identical black T-shirts around room in effort to find one; stand back a moment, lathered in sweat, chest heaving with exertion, head spinning. Realise that room seems unchanged, despite orgy of destruction. Light cigarette from gas ring on cooker. Set fire to hair. Kick cooker.

I took another look at the room. What I need, I decided, somewhat blearily but with admirable joi de vivre, is a woman. I racked my brains. After ten minutes of this I had a headache and the eyes of my big Johnny Cash poster seemed to be following me around the room, The Man In Black's craggy, speed-scarred skin attaining an awful luminosity, every hair of his impossibly perfect quiff mocking my singed barnet.

The Bruvvers segued into the cod reggae of *Not My Place In The Nine-To-Five World*.

I found my phone underneath a big wad of PR printouts. Called up the phone book.

Jane. Hasn't spoken to me since I got drunk and threw up at her record label's Christmas party. On her cleavage.

Joanne. Hasn't slept with me since I slept with Katie.

Katie. Hasn't slept with me since she found out I was already sleeping with Joanne. Did not, however, find out I was sleeping with Siobhan.

Siobhan! No, no; not at all. She's on tour with Napalm Death.

Mystery Suitor.

My eyes crossed with effort of recollection; synapses fused. Who the Hell, I thought, is Mystery Suitor?

Oh well. Here goes nothing. Push the button. Wait, as connection is dialled.

No such number, no such phone. An eerie electronic whistling, like something that you might expect the old Warp Records label to put out. Throw phone at pile of CDs. Watch as phone lands in takeaway cartons.

And begins to ring.

*

What does the digital music revolution mean to you?

"You what?"

Er. What does the digital music revolution mean to you?

"What do you mean?"

109

Well. People can now, er, buy your albums without, you know, going down the shops, and –

"But nobody buys my records anyway."

No, true, but if they did, then how d'you think it would affect you?

"Uh. Well. The punters'd be a bit lonelier, wouldn't they? And... And fatter and that."

Right. How about your song writing process?

"What?"

How has the digital music revolution affected your song writing?

"Are you taking the piss?"

No, no, really, I mean, you might, I don't know, write songs... Er, purely for the... You know, downloading market...

"What, like *56K Modem Blues*? *You Wiped Me From The Hard Disk Of Your Life*? Don't be a twat."

But you might not write long songs any more, in case –

"Don't be stupid. I've never written anything longer than two minutes, anyway. I'm lazy."

Okay. Have you got any cocaine?

"No. Fuck off."

*

I gingerly picked over the detritus coating my floor, and pulled the phone from its resting place. ID withheld. Charming.

"Hi."

"Yo. Who's this?" A man's voice, early twenties. I could hear something playing softly in the background, a strange fluting synth-laden noise.

I was thrown: "Hang on, I'm meant to say 'Who's this?' I mean, you phoned me."

"But you phoned me first."

"Did I?" A pause, while I try to gather my thoughts. "No I didn't."

"You fucking did. I got your number off the scanner."

"Look, mate, I don't know what your game is – "

"Oh right, I'm really going to be randomly dialling numbers aren't I? I mean, that's the first thing I thought when I got up this morning, 'Right Adam, better make sure you get some credit on your phone 'cos this afternoon there's some complete strangers you gotta bug – '"

"Excuse me?"

"Really, I mean, all the fun of the fucking fair. Jesus. How sad d'you think I am?"

"Er, I don't know. Look, did you say your name's Adam?"

"There's nothing better than being fucking sworn at by an unidentified voice calling out from the ether. I mean, it's how I spend my spare time anyway, so why wouldn't I?"

"Hello? I'm really very sorry, but could you please be quiet, please?"

"Right, don't worry about it. Courtesy's just out the fucking window, isn't it? When my old man told me that I never believed him, but now I – "

I thumbed the disconnect button and threw the phone at the wall.

It bounced behind the sofa, where after a second it began to ring. I took a deep steadying breath, stalked over to it and answered.

"Pulsing skronk?"

"High-end divebomber BPMs."

"Indeed."

"We're playing a gig down at *Thekla*. Next Tuesday. If you wanna come. Know where that is?"

"Ha, do I know where *Thekla* is? Are The Ramones all dead?"

"Er, three of them, I think. But they had more than one rhythm section. So I'm not sure. It's hard to tell. Why do you ask?"

"Don't worry. I know where it is."

"Fuck yeah."

*

Ring-ring-ring.

"Hello, it's _____ from _____ PR."

"PR? Aaaarrrrrrrgggggggggghhhhhhh!"

"No, wait, you interviewed Mikey last night, right? How'd you think the interview'll come out, then? I mean, did they come across well?"

"PR? Aaaarrrrrrrgggggggggghhhhhhh!"

"Right, right. Well. I'll let you get back to work, then. Let me know if you, uh, need anything. Anything at all..."

"Ahem. Sorry, did you say 'anything at all'?"

"Er. Yeah."

"*Anything* at all? I mean, 'scuse me for being Mr Pedantic here, but would you be offering me...favourable treatment, for a kindly stance on your charges in the interview due to appear in Fashionable If Clueless Rock Magazine? Perks, even?"

"Well, I wouldn't go so far as to say that, but..."

"Hmmm?"

"Well. Yes. That's about the size of it. How about it, then?"

"One moment. Could you outline a few of these, uh, 'favours'? You know, you don't have to come out and like say exactly what you mean, but you could hint."

"Right. Okay. How about... Free tickets to see Limp Bizkit play Wembley. A limited competition-winner only signed CD flexipak edition of The Strokes' latest single. His'n'hers Hives' sweatshirts. Er. Jack White's plectrum?"

"Okay, thanks, don't worry – "

"No, wait! Don't hang up! Look, how about guest list to every single London launch party and piss-up we've got scheduled for the next six months?"

"Plus one?"

"Certainly, certainly."

"Hmmm. Will there be booze?"

"Streams of it. Fucking rivers. Veritable oceans."

"*Free* booze?"

"Does Fred Durst look like a cunt wearing that cap?"

"Right on. I'll, hahaha, *see what I can do* about that interview, yes?"

"Oh yes, very much appreciated. I'll stick the swag in the post. Don't worry about the guest list, just turn up. You'll be on. All right?"

"Fuckin' A."

"Fuckin' A indeed."

Put phone down. Realise that you didn't actually interview any band last night, nor indeed for the last week, since you described the Sub-Editor's best mate's band as 'a bloody awful Jam covers act'.

Sigh, and start checking E-mail to see when the next piss-up is.

*

Thekla is not only the best-named club in Britain, it's also the coolest. I mean, really: it's a hundred foot long boat, parked up at Bristol's East

Dock, peeling blue paint off to scatter across the frontage of the restaurants and wine bars of the Ballardian multi-million pound development that has spread like a neon cancer across the waterfront. Just as an aside, there are more people sleeping rough under the neon and the fifty foot high modern art sculptures than I have ever seen, anywhere, including Thailand. If I stopped to give money to every one, I'd be broke in about five minutes, and only ten per cent of the poor fucks would receive any spare change. What can you do? Stop and talk to the guys with the crazy stares and the dogs on strings, the girls with missing teeth, matted dreads and filthy blankets; roll a smoke, share a toke. Pass the time for a minute, shake some hands before turning away and trudging into the light, guilt stopping up your throat.

Walk up to *Thekla* along the sea-front and you can hear the bands tuning up, fragments of guitar and bass rolling out across the night, undercut by the soft lapping of the water against the hull. On a quiet Tuesday night at the dead dog-end of November, it's quite something.

Inside, they've hollowed out the thing so that the bands actually play below the waterline, with the crowd pushing up in front or arrayed around one of the gantries that run along at the level of an upper deck above the dance-floor. The toilets appear not to have been touched since the place was ocean-going and freezing-cold blasts of air that reek of shit occasionally swirl about near the stage, providing a welcome relief from the thick heavy smell of the Calor-gas heaters they use to keep the temperature above zero.

I passed a flyer pasted to a rivet-strewn bulkhead.

TONIGHT:
SLAVES TO LOVE/THEE OBSCURANTISTS/SOLOTH
DOORS 9PM
FIVE SQUID.

The bar staff all wear identical stripy jerseys for that 'nautical' look; I smiled at a girl with filthy dreads and enough metal in her face to qualify as bionic as she poured me a Guinness.

"Three quid," she snarled.

Adam's band, SOLOTH, were up first. I hung around at the bar as they ambled on, four young guys in shorts that came down past their knees and enough obscure band T-shirts to get them jobs at a second-hand record shop. Adam waddled up to a mike that was set up Lemmy style, requiring him to stand on tiptoe like a man looking over a high wall. He appeared to be wearing the same clothes as he wore the last time I had seen him. It was dark, but I don't think he'd washed them. He shouted out 'One-two-three-four...'

SOLOTH sounded like...

I mean, really, there were obvious traces of...

There was *melody* in there, really, I'm sure of it...

They sounded...

Like...

Like...

A typical song: imagine a Harrier jump jet firing up its engines. Now imagine you've stuck your head inside the air intake. The whistling noise that strobes up past the point of endurance and rattles your fillings suddenly stretches and distorts, pulling the air apart with a noise like a sheet of steel being torn in half by God.

Then the guitars kick in, cheap Yamahas set to 'razor-blade'. Over it and under it, pursuing a threnody of their own, synths and DAT tapes emit a sound like the world coming apart, an organic howl of pain and rage distilled into feedback and various unidentifiable whooshing noises. At this juncture the drummer starts on a spazzing attack like someone has spiked his medication   and an old 808 drum-machine provides blasts of spin-cycle fills, juddering and twitching in an apparently random fashion. The bass shakes something loose inside your bowels.

Then Adam started to sing, in a voice that sounded so utterly alien, so impossibly other that I spilled my drink. Ignoring concepts as pedestrian as 'choruses' or 'verses', his voice transformed by some electronic trickery into an amalgamation of Kevin Shields' morphine-duvet croon and Tim Buckley's siren whine, he didn't so much slur his vocal as fold the words around each other, creating a net of sound that pulled at something you thought you'd forgotten inside your chest. Music full of pain and rage, tinged with regret and swathed in reverb.

There were only fifteen other people in the place; thirty seconds into the first number a girl standing with her boyfriend near the back started snapping her fingers along to an imaginary beat with infinite contempt, then shook her head and stomped off toward the exit. The volume was such that in the darkness at the sides of the stage it almost seemed that something coiled, thrashing half-formed appendages at the edges of the spotlights, shimmering then disappearing into the banks of dry ice, an entity formed of distortion pulling itself free from the hole made in the world by the music, clawing its way into the light from something sucking and primal beneath. Then it was gone, and I promised myself I'd do less drugs in future. A few people tried to mosh, got confused by the time-changes and stood there, slack-jawed, staring off into space. In the hushed, echoing moments between the slabs of shrieking noise that passed for songs a skinny intense-looking guy with a shaved head turned to his mate and mouthed the words 'Fucking torture music.'

I had to agree. As well as with the woman with the mohican who said, apropos of not much at all, that 'this is what they do to you in Guantanamo Bay, isn't it?'

Personally, I loved it.

They saved all their energy up for the last number, an angular thing that hammered along in a spectacular thrash-out, the band beating the jagged ends of the song against the hull of the ship until it broke, then dropping their instruments and shuffling off-stage without a word.

By that time there was only me and another slight figure standing on the dance floor. I turned to them as the band left, the last lingering note still vibrating in my skull:

"They rule!"

She looked up, pale and haunted beneath a shoulder-length shock of mousy blonde hair, her big dark eyes set in a face seemingly too narrow to contain them. She looked a bit like one of the aliens that were supposed to have landed at Roswell, only wearing baseball boots and *Levis*. She looked me up and down, slowly. I wondered if the tingling sensation nagging at my extremities was the result of listening to SOLOTH or because her gaze was unreadable. Then she huddled down inside her thick fleecy skater top, shivered hugely from battered *Converses* to black plastic Alice band.

"They're... They're... It's like... Springsteen at the *Woodhaven Swim Club*. This is like watching The Clash at the *100 Club*!" I waved my hands in nonsensical patterns in the air. "I mean…Fuck. The Manic Street Preachers busking outside Cardiff Uni. Joy Division at *Pips* in Manchester. You know?"

"They weren't bad. I could do with a drink, though."

While I was thinking if I could get an unsolicited review of an unknown band with no A&R and no commercially viable singles into one of my usual haunts, parts of my brain unused for far too long began to fizz and jump up and down behind my eyes, trying to attract my attention.

"Who couldn't?" I flashed her a grin, then hoped I didn't sound too stupid. "May I?"

"Red Stripe, thanks. They sell it in cans."

"Rock'n'roll." I cringed as I walked back toward the bar, shoulder-blades twitching under my jacket like I'd just turned my back on a sniper.

"Guinness and a Red Stripe, please."

I paid and turned around, and she was standing by my elbow, still staring inquisitively up into my face. I tried smiling again, but then thought better of it and aimed for carefully neutral.

"What did you think of the band, then?" I said, as I lit a cigarette.

She shrugged, took a sip of her beer then said: "They didn't do too bad. Adam's vocals were a little off."

"Really?" I boggled.

"Yeah. Missed a few notes." She sipped at her beer again, then gave a disarmingly girlish giggle. "I'm so sorry. My name's Virginia, but everyone calls me Vinnie." She stuck out a slim hand, which I shook, marvelling at the delicacy of the bone structure of her wrist. I'm a sucker for women's wrists. Don't ask. "Thank you for the drink."

"My pleasure." I risked a smile, and she did not scream and run from the club. I took this as a good sign. She kept looking directly into my face, which I was unused to. In the music industry someone staring at you normally means that the person you are speaking to is about to sack you or – in the case of bouncers and roadies – beat the crap out of you.

"I'm not really interested in the other bands on the bill," she said, "but if you want we can go and fuck somewhere."

I opened my mouth to say something clever and tipped my Guinness down my sleeve.

*

Dictaphone tape found stuffed down the side of the sofa, October 2002:

So. Why all the ancient Christian and Judean symbols on the artwork for the new record, then?

"It's... A symbolism thing."

Ah. Turning into Tool, are we? Or have you found God?

"Hah. No. It's just that we wanted to iterate that all these words, all these chords, every beat, everything, they've all been used before, right? Y'know, if not in the order in which we used them, then certainly... They've all been used. I wanted to connect that idea to the power of those symbols, to the archetypal underlying power of them."

What?

"Well, people might not know what they mean, but they'll know that they mean something, right?"

Er, right. But...

"Yes, if people don't know exactly what they mean, they'll still be reassured that they stand for something. That they're *meant* to stand for something else."

Okay. Enough of that. Can you set me up with a date?

"What?"

Well, your bass player's fit as fuck. No, don't do that. Mark, listen mate...

<sound of movement, muffled swearing>

Fuck. He's fucked off. Jesus. That went well, I thought.

*

She climbed all over me in a deserted alleyway behind the Beefeater opposite the dock, jumping up into my arms and affixing her face to mine while taxis inched along the road outside and my hands turned to stone in the cold. I fumbled at her small breasts through her thick top, and she began to move against me with increasing abandon, her hands knitted together behind my head. I staggered back until I was resting against cold brick, filthy water streaming down a quarter inch from my face.

"You know," I managed to mumble, when she came up for air, "this is the most fun I've ever had with my clothes on."

She pushed her tongue down my throat, the lager on her breath raising the hairs along the back of my neck. I moved my groin against hers, and she moaned somewhere back in her throat and squeezed me tighter between her thighs. She let go of my neck with one hand and started working at my fly.

I wasn't really in a position to complain.

*

She left me fumbling with my zipper. I shuddered in the cold, fighting against a feeling of unreality. The grim concrete of the buildings around me seemed to lour against the invisible sky; mist clung to the tops of buildings, rolling in off the sea. I staggered from the alleyway and trundled back to the club.

The second band were on; as I crossed the road I could hear them cranking out some kind of by-the-numbers Emo, post-hardcore radio-friendly 'punk' for people who didn't like loud noises, the sort of stuff peddled by college-boy virgins with too many Weezer records. Thee Obscurantists: waste of a perfectly good name.

Inside and the dance-floor was filling: fat boys with crew-cuts, hardcore T-shirts and neck tattoos; fourteen year old girls with half their heads shaved, chain-smoking roll-ups as the speed peaked too early; the occasional pretty, skinny boy carrying a canvas record bag over his shoulder, pushing his NHS spectacles up the bridge of his nose with a self-conscious gesture and trying to look serious yet available. A couple of kids in filthy, oversized hoodies and baseball caps sat behind the merchandise table, passed a joint back and forth and eyed the crowd evilly over their overpriced T-shirts and albums burnt on rewritable CDs. I let myself be pushed around, milling underneath the beat, staring a second too long at the young girls who returned my gaze with deadened hard-eyed looks that made me flinch. Suddenly I was standing at the front of the stage, the over-cranked amps giving off a smell of melted plastic and burning dust, the bass reverberating around my head. I needed another drink.

"Don't you find it's funny that some boys are only comfortable rubbing up against one another in the context of a mosh-pit?"

The voice cut through the noise, inveigling its way to my ears via some strange trick of acoustics. I looked around and saw Adam, short hair plastered to his head, a slight grin playing over his features, pulling on a bottle of lager. Clasped underneath his sweat-stained armpit and cuddling up to his bulk, Vinnie looked even smaller, as if she shrunk in his presence.

"Rock'n'roll is inherently gay. Or at least masturbatory," Vinnie mused, a sly, satisfied look on her face. "It's obvious: you get all these young boys charged up with adrenaline and hormones, and they all rub each other all over and then, because everyone's so fucking macho... Well. All that *energy* has to go somewhere, doesn't it?"

"Good gig," I managed weakly.

Adam shrugged.

"We've played better."

I nodded slowly, letting myself get shoved around by uncaring elbows, unable to take my eyes off the young girl by his side. She matched my stare, and looking into her eyes was like being presented with some fabulous empty pit that stretches down forever. Then, in the shadows, in the darkness, you think you see something stir.

"I'm Vinnie," she said, extending a pale hand.

"Hello," I managed, my mouth a desert, my heart stuttering in my chest.

"What did you really think of the show?" she asked. "I heard you're a writer."

I blinked.

"It was... Okay."

"Really?" Adam, for all his earlier bravado, seemed genuinely pleased. He beamed out at me from within that gross prison of flesh. I tried not to look at Vinnie.

"Yeah. Your vocals were a little off, maybe?"

"See," said Vinnie, elbowing Adam in the folds of flesh hanging off his ribs. "Told you."

"Fuck this shit," said Adam, and necked the rest of his lager. "Let's go hit a club."

*

Criticism, as someone who was ineffably dull once said, is a passive activity. It's only a bit more active than listening to music, and rather down the scale from dancing to a band in a club or surfing over the top of a crowd. Nowhere near the creative act of writing, recording, making an album. We hacks know this. It burns beneath our skin like a maddening itch that won't go away. Some of us are driven to claw at the sore point where our own basically futile existence intersects the body with bad behaviour, a ludicrously inflated sense of our own worth or chips on both shoulders. We have to develop personality problems to paper over the enormous gaping holes thwarted desire has made in our actual personalities.

Because... Well. The sort of person driven to do this thing, to spend five, ten, however many years sending off unsolicited reviews to sub-editors – who have better things to do than reading illegible semiliterate screeds from geeks, like doling out the blow-jobs and finding a new drug dealer – in the pathetic hope that someone somewhere will print their drivel, the sort of person who will willingly stand at the front in a space you couldn't rear a hamster in, going deaf, getting bruised by drunken slam-dancing and spat on by drummers night after night with no guarantee or hope of reward, that sort of person is basically a little fucked-up. It's visible in the way they carry themselves. We all wear a furtive rodent air that comes from preying on something we used to get off on in the hope that one day we can exploit it. We all dream of selling the ruin of our lives to buy ourselves a leg-up the ladder to more exclusive pastures, where the cocaine has less bicarb in it and the dressing rooms stink a little less of failure, fear and cheap cigarettes.

We all worship at the altar of Lester Bangs, aping and emulating with crazed enthusiasm a man who was dead at the age of thirty-three, a bloated sack of chemical dependencies who reeled from breakdown to breakdown like a unicycle wobbling around the lip of an enormous abyss. We welcome it; we want it. We need it. We can taste it.

Eventually, if you're crazed and stupid enough, if you keep beating your head against closed doors, someone will take pity on you and start publishing some of your drivel. They do this, I suspect, in the hope that having seen some of your bullshit in print, you'll smile happily and go away. This rarely works.

The first time you see something that you wrote used anonymously on an advertisement by a faceless multinational corporation to flog shiny slivers of plastic to children and adults who should know better then it's time to give up. There are no more mountains left to climb; those peaks you can see looming up in the ionosphere, stark against a blood-red sky, that's only the reflection of your own ego shining back at you, amplified and swollen with your own hubris.

If rock'n'roll has a creed, it's this: live fast, die young. Leave a good-looking corpse, the old lie tells us. But few are that lucky. And if rock music is the world's biggest Death Cult, the ultimate narcissistic shrine to beautiful loserdom ever dreamt up by a marketing machine powered by broken dreams and steered by idiots, then rock criticism is only the pale shadow, the queered reflection of same. It's a pointless endeavour. It's not dancing about architecture, it's mime in a pitch-black room. The only people who read rock criticism and take it in are fledgling rock critics, the desperate wannabes who will one day replace you, already picking over your corpse and stealing your worst excesses to use in their own tortuous bullshit.

And anyway, the pay's crap. Anyone who gets into it for the money is probably better off opening up a dry-cleaners or something. It'd be a more fulfilling job, I'm sure.

*

We ended up in a scuzzy dive nestling beneath a motorway flyover, where they served warm *Stella* in plastic pint glasses and played hideously arcane techno that sounded like a 4 a.m. car alarm. I made my excuses and left after a few drinks, unable to stand any longer the shy, matey proximity of Adam and Vinnie's awful knowing silence, the reek of cheap aftershave wafting off the soft *Ben Sherman* shirts and the sight of so much cleavage glistening with sweat and fake tan. The Godawful music. I caught the last train home and climbed into bed at dawn, bad dreams chasing me down corridors of sleep, a slick queasy feeling in my gut and the marine, animal smell of her clinging to my skin.

I busied myself, over the next few days, with ephemera: a phoner that had to take place at midnight with the California-based bassist of a once-notorious industrial metal act; a stack of single reviews for a website that didn't pay, because I owed the owner a favour. Trying to keep my mind off those eyes, the deliciously fragile body that I had only felt through layers of clothes... I slept even less than was normal for me, and laboured through my waking hours under a curious sense of foreboding, dreading the call from Adam yet willing his girlfriend to bug him about phoning up that interesting young writer they saw at the gig the other night.

He eventually called on a Saturday afternoon while I was in the shower, and left a message on my answering machine telling me to meet him that evening, that we had to 'catch up'. He mentioned the time and venue, and I replayed the message a dozen times, listening to his voice for any hint that he knew of my inadvertent betrayal, hearing only the same weirdly synthetic fluting music beneath his terse greeting and mumbled instructions. I wrote the details down on the back of a white label promo CD, then sat in my darkened flat listening to old Nick Cave piano ballads, songs of fire and death, remorse and romance.

*

It turned out to be a cold but clear day, a slight drizzle borne along by the wind and splattering against my skin. Every single person I met on the street seemed to have the same vacant, mongoloid stare; I began to wonder if I'd grown an extra head, or if something had been introduced to the water supply.

We were due to meet in a nasty theme pub, part of a chain that had been buying up local boozers and refitting them. In this particular case it involved the addition of lots of stripped varnished pine, about half a ton of fake horse brasses and various framed sepia photographs, taken sometime in the early days of the previous century and purportedly showing local views of the day. I sat down at a small round table and stared at the photographs while I drank my coffee, but for the life of me I couldn't think of the places where they had been taken. The geography was all wrong; if they had climbed up on *this* hill and taken that shot, why could you see the back of buildings that faced the hill? Such considerations began to make me nervous; I hoped it was just because I had to speak to Adam again. The pub was nearly full, the hubbub of people's voices and the damp they carried in from the street making the too-warm air thick and uncomfortable. I thought about lighting a cigarette, decided against it. A table of loud boys in lurid sportswear exploded in raucous laughter, the harsh lights shining off shaved heads and heavy, fake-looking gold jewellery. Even their football shirts seemed aggressive, the slogans and logos of sponsors like a threat or a challenge. Many pints were drunk, one of them stole another's baseball cap and it was passed around the table, leaving its owner scrabbling in its wake, crashing into nearby tables, always a step behind it.

"There's little in this life more stupid than the sight of a man chasing after his hat."

I started, knocking my empty coffee cup over. It rolled around the table on its edge, describing a teetering parabola along the rim.

She caught it before it hit the floor, of course. She snatched it out of the air with a practised ease, a slow easy grin on her thin lips. I couldn't help but try and match her stare, to meet her eyes; if they were as dark as the night I met her, now they also seemed strangely green, a dull shade of jade that I found mesmerising. She reached across me to replace the coffee cup on the table, pushing so close that I gasped and winced at the same time, then she walked slowly around the table and sat down opposite, a death-camp slim teenage girl in regulation over-sized skater wear, her hair scraped back into a ponytail secured with a black scrunchy. I sat looking at her, wondering what to say.

"Aren't you going to say hello?"

I bit my lip.

"Yes. Hello." I reached forward, stretched out my hand to her. She looked at it with a vague air of disappointment.

"Mmm. Warm. You were a lot warmer the other night."

I shrugged.

"I don't really know the convention."

"What convention?"

"When two people...." I stopped. When two people what? When two people who have fucked meet again in an over-lit barn without a jukebox, and one of them wasn't expecting it? I tried again.

"I'm sorry, I didn't expect you to be... I didn't know."

"Ha. None of us ever do."

"True. But about you, I mean. About you and..."

"Ah. Guilt." She sat back and crossed her legs, her hands clasped in her lap. She seemed obscurely happy, like she was getting to do something she'd looked forward to for a long time. I realised all at once how vulnerable I felt sitting here in the middle of a big crowd of people, and I wondered why.

"I wouldn't worry about it," she was saying. "People fuck up all the time. There's not a lot you can do about it. I mean, it'd wear you out, wouldn't it? It'd just wear the heart right out of you."

I shook my head. I couldn't precisely grasp what she was talking about.

"It's okay," she went on, as if she could read my internal dialogue straight through my skin, "I can see your dilemma." She patted my hand gently. I snatched it away.

"Oh really?" I was suddenly angry; I felt she was presuming a little too much. I began to feel slightly paranoid, as if she had engineered the entire situation for reasons too impenetrable for me to fathom. I felt stupid, used in a nebulous, undefined manner. "Just what is my dilemma, pray?"

"You like Adam's band, and feel guilty because you've fucked me. What you want to know is whether or not we're going to fuck again, and how that's going to affect your standing with Adam. You're possibly thinking about riding him all the way to... I don't know." She shook her head. "Fame and fortune? Is that it?"

I sat up in my chair and craned my neck about the pub. "Where's Adam? Is this all a put-up? What's going on?"

She laughed. "He couldn't make it. Genuinely. He's busy. His boss had a big contract come in, and he's had to stay behind to look after it."

That snagged my attention. "Where does he work?"

"Dry cleaners. Down the High Street." She grinned, then stopped and hugged herself as if cold, thin arms nearly lost in her voluminous sweatshirt. "S'not very glamorous is it? Not very... Rock'n'roll."

I said nothing, just sat there and played with my cigarettes. There it was again; why do all the ones with talent have to work shit jobs? Why is it only the narcissistic poseurs who have any success? I sighed.

"Nothing is, really."

"Oh yeah? Been to many parties lately, have we?"

I ignored that one.

"No, come on. You can whine about it. Just don't expect any sympathy. How many gigs you get to go to, a year?"

"A few."

"Yeah? How many?"

I thought for a moment.

"I don't know. More than a hundred. Less than three hundred."

"And you don't have to pay?"

I shook my head.

"Enjoy it, do you?"

I couldn't think about an answer. The situation seemed to want to pull itself out of shape. I toyed with the idea of seeing if Vinnie wanted to continue our 'relationship'. I thought briefly of illicit meetings behind speaker stacks, in the back of Transit vans. A few seconds of carnality snatched in the moments when I wouldn't be fawning over her boyfriend.

"What are you getting out of this, Vinnie?"

"Me?" A trick of the light as she smiled, a simple obfuscation of vision that made it seem, for a moment, that something rippled through the depthless green of her eyes. "Why, I'm The Girl. I hang on his arm, generate friction –" under the table, she slid her hand up my thigh. I coughed, and tried to concentrate "– between him and his band-mates. Between him and..." Her fingers crept higher. "Other interested parties. Besides, I quite like playing The Muse. It's a giggle. All you gotta do is wipe their foreheads, maybe mop up their sick. Make sure they've got enough ciggies to keep them up all night. Pine after them when they go off in a funk. Then luxuriate in the glory of the creation."

"You make it sound... I don't know. Romantic. With a capital R."

"Isn't that the point?" She lowered her chin. Her cheekbones were so sharp I could've cut my hand on them.

"I think I'd better go see Adam," I said.

"Really?" She suddenly seemed distracted, staring past me at something in the corner. Her hand slipped from my groin. I turned in my chair, followed her gaze; an old couple hunched forward over a small table had taken one of the photographs off the walls and were examining it. The man scratched at his flat cap while his wife spoke earnestly at him. He didn't look up, or even seem to acknowledge her existence. A pint of bitter sat untouched in front of him; it seemed nearly all head.

I turned back to Vinnie. But she had gone. The chair opposite had been pushed back close to the table, and the boys in tracksuits were singing a song that I didn't recognise, pints in the air, a scene from fifty years ago spilling Kronenbourg on plastic beer-mats.

*

Ian Curtis' muse, and the person most often mentioned when people talk about his suicide, was a girl named Annick Honoré. She was Belgian, and he met her on tour, on one of the trackless lonely nights in a faraway town where he knew no-one but the three other members of his band, had nothing to do but sit around and get fucked up for the nth time. Ms. Honoré – of whom I believe no photograph has ever been published – is not painted in a particularly favourable light in *Touching From A Distance*, the biography written by Ian's wife, Deborah. Even Mrs Curtis seems to know little about her; she's one of those figures transmogrified by prurient rock iconography from an ordinary life with its shabby infidelities and tiny betrayals into part of a streaking myth with all the resonance and tragedy of an Ancient Greek play. I wonder sometimes about her, where she is now, what she has to say to the death cult which has created from the tiniest details a whole persona in her missing image to mock, to vilify, even to aspire to.

Rock's canon is littered with them, of course: Nancy Spungen, smacked-up and cracked-up, giggling while Sid pissed himself away, just a smear of bad makeup and the reputation of a villainess left to cover the reality of just another fuck-up only as special as you or I, playing out her life under a spotlight that rendered the skin translucent and bared every part of her to the slavering world.

I don't want to talk about Kurt and Courtney, inextricably linked forever, like Sam'n'Dave or cookies'n'cream, inseparable in their infamy; one's face immortalised on T-shirts worn by kids who weren't even born when he redecorated his bathroom with his brain, staring out through the heroin haze forever, the other relegated to the gossip magazines and tabloid showbiz pages.

Though it merits inclusion, I'm not sure I want to talk about the way rock'n'roll itself decimates women, reduces them to bit parts, walking cleavage or walk-ons in the endless, reverberating fucking *stories* that we create of simple lives twisted and distorted by the weight of too much bullshit and not enough common sense. I mean, let's face it: Polly Harvey or Tori Amos are the exceptions, rather than the rules, right? Name another woman who actually sells records but keeps her tits covered up?

And don't say Lulu.

I think at times of Richey Edwards, just another Valley Boy with a big heart and an eating disorder, who thought he could change the world with Sylvia Plath poems and old Clash records. I think of the pictures of his slate-blue Vauxhall Cavalier, a rep's car, a bog-standard family man 1600 cc saloon, parked empty by the Severn Bridge, the plastic wheel-trims already stolen off the wheels. I think of the revulsion that he inspires even now in some quarters; in my darker moments I think it's probably because he had such a boring demise: no guns, no murders, no drugs, no suicide notes with dodgy quotations from Neil Young (Neil Young, Neil fucking Young), not even any evidence that it was actually a demise. Or because he owned a boring car. Just a boring Welsh lad with a philosophy degree and some cool tattoos. Couldn't even play guitar. I was listening to Radio One the night Steve Lamacq challenged him live on air, heard Steve's intake of breath as Richie carved '4 REAL' in his arm. I've often thought since whether I'd have tried to stop him, if I had been interviewing him. Whether or not I'd have the guts to slap him, shake him and scream in his face. I like to think I'd not have grabbed a camera and immortalised the fucking moment for the NME. I pray that I would not have.

I still listen to *The Holy Bible* or *Closer* or *In Utero*. You'd think that my misgivings about this, my angst, my aidos in the face of my own moral culpability – I bought the magazines, listened to the music, wore the T-shirts, I grew up and ended up hounding other poor sods – would induce a reluctance to listen to the albums in which you can hear the awful certainty of their progenitor's doom bearing down in the silences between the tracks, in the scream of every guitar solo, in every tortured shriek torn from a larynx marked to die too soon.

But of course, those are the records I love best.

See? World's biggest Death Cult.

*

Past fried chicken outlets with names that are 'amusing' riffs on a certain famous fast-food outlet, past failing pound shops selling a variety of knocked-off plastic tat, past gaggles of teenaged girls all talking at once in identical voices into tiny plastic phones. Step in a puddle, feel the water soak into your sock. Light another cigarette as the wind changes direction and brings the whiff of exhaust smoke to your nose. An old lady, bent in half by the weight of the years, turns and looks at me, fixing me to the pavement with a gaze undimmed despite the cataracts crawling over the surface of her eyes. I wonder if she's ever been to a gig, felt the bass thrum in her blood and the over-amped excess drive her mad, ever fucked to music while so high the chords seem to choreograph your movements. Probably not, I decide; Daniel O'Donnell, maybe, but no rock'n'roll for her. Probably one didn't do stuff like that when she was young, it was something that, hidebound by propriety and delusions of self-sacrifice, she left to her children.

She is whistling. I realise that I recognise the tune. The song is *Time*, by Tom Waits. I throw my head back and laugh. When I stop, there's a small space cleared around me. I look at the faces, all of them careful to avoid my eyes, then I push my way through the crowds. I am going to see Adam, not on-stage, not in the environment where something that lurks within pushes its way through his skin, desperate to be seen, feeding on the spotlights and the cheers. Let him have it, if he wants it. At that precise moment, I'm done with it.

I stand on the pavement, staring into the mist obscuring the window. I push open the door, sniff back the harsh smells of steam and cleaning solvent. He looks up from behind the till. He doesn't seem surprised. I walk over, and extend my hand.

"Hullo mate. Playing any gigs soon?"

"Course we are. We're a fucking band."

"Mind if I turn up?"

He looks at me for a moment.

Then he smiles.

"Pulsing skronk, mate."

"There's just one thing."

"Yeah?"

I don't ever say it, of course. A customer jangled the bell as they entered. I stepped aside, looked over my shoulder. Vinnie didn't even look at me as she passed, just walked straight over and clasped both hands behind Adam's head and dragged him forward into a long, lingering kiss. I stared at the racks of suits dangling from plastic hangers, at advertisements for key-cutting and shoe-repairs.

Then I slipped back out onto the street, humming a Pogues' song about a broken heart.

Living In A Bear Suit

Iain Ross

I stuck a piece of paper on my bedroom wall the other day; it said, in bold portentous script: 'THE GREAT ENGLISH NOVEL', just like that. I'd decided I was going to write the lyrics for our next album, and they were to be both a blazing critique and heart-warming celebration of everything great and piss-poor in our squalid and plucky little island. Set against squalling indie punk and heart-rending melodies, of course. Martin Amis: move aside, Will Self: shut it, Dickens: do one. I would be the new Morrissey, the next Jarvis Cocker, a modern-age sage, beloved by both MTV2 and Radio 4...

But then I realised that, despite even having once written a song (*drinkink*) extolling the virtues of devouring literature till it leaks from your very pores, I've barely read a whole book, I'm a fraud. Jane Austen makes me puke, I mean *physically gag*. He's a fantastic little wizard but I can't get through a whole Salman Rushdie. *Ulysses* made my guts twitch after about twenty pages, I haven't got the stamina. If I've absorbed anything in my sorry little life from both high art and lowlife cultural rummaging, it's been filtered through the lens of that most maligned and sweaty-palmed of genres. Science-scumming-Fiction.

Most SF, like most of everything, is turgid and pointless, but Philip K Dick's novels have crystallised all I've ever thought about the world, all I've ever wanted to express musically: cacophonous joy and anger and fear.

I can't think of anyone whose work more encapsulates the same kind of 'broken future' I try to set my songs in. These are parallel universes, or worlds set just slightly in the future, where the same walking follies of our own time (us) come up against, not the sci-fi staples of spaceships or aliens or Cold War histrionics, but drug paranoia, malfunctioning technology, failing to get the girl *again*. His short stories are hilarious, full of bleak humour and the desire to reach out for some comfort before the government have you brainwashed, or nanobots eat your innards. He was nuts and a genius and I can't get enough of him.

What a noble and beautiful idea: the desperation to cling on to the tiniest sliver of whatever it is that makes us decent and human, whilst the world around us implodes in clamour and brutality. How do you put *that* in a pop song?

fight Music

Tim Nickels

I

After the air raid, I go to a grey and green room that smells of pencil shavings. An anglepoise throws a yellow miniature moon onto the linoleum. Long shelves of manuscript; a little platform on wheels. Wall clocks created from viola carcasses. Photographs, signed scores; the frames and glass repaired with buttery adhesive tape.

Far away a piano stops and starts; stops. A second piano answers. Forlorn, too late.

Professor Gnessin pares an acorn husk into a small glass of sugary hot water. Her starched shirt cuff wipes the excess from my résumé as she surveys me, lips thin and disappearing into their arrow-shaped chin. Is Professor Gnessin willowy? Or as thin and shrill as a clarinet reed? The lips sip with distaste before they open into a lopsided smile. She leans her bony elbows on the desk and nods me to a broken chair. A finger hovers over the Dictaphone and she motions me to begin.

»

Yes? Am I speaking loud enough? Well, my father didn't die in the war like the other dads. He drove trucks out of Agapova where the salt Green Sea gives way to fresh water and the crawfish have their home. A troop carrier drove out of the darkness as Dad thundered down a steep incline through fir trees. He was carrying ten tonnes of water and crawfish and couldn't stop. Didn't stand a chance. The water became a living thing, rocketing onwards as the truck tried to brake. The soldiers were hooking crawfish fragments out of the telephone wires with bayonets. My mother told friends that her husband had soared a little higher.

And so my life in music began.

||

A train rattles into a tunnel within the foundations of the building. It sounds even closer than the remaining piano in its determined *decrescendo*.

Until today, I have never seen a train.

"*Your life in music*, Victorvna Yudelvna? You mean you had a life before?" The professor is good natured, her small eyes merry. Her questioning of my vocation is light but I sense there are more than two of us participating in this interview. I glance at the green walls, as thin as the professor's chuckle.

I lean forward – and very much aware of her thumb on the || button – I hiss: "My secret history, professor. You will be aware of how I have arrived at this juncture."

She is even more amused. "Good lord. And how fifteen year-old girls speak these days. This *juncture*? At your age it's all arrival and departure, isn't it. And most of them desperately dramatic. Every week's a new doorway. Each year an eternity."

"Why? How old are you, Professor Gnessin?"

"Precisely three times your age. Forty-five last birthday."

"Old."

"Older than the national average, granted. And you're well nosy for a co-op girl."

"Farm girl. We had our own farm ten kilometres from the village."

"Living in your own shit and not the state's?"

"No shit at all. Me, my mother and my sisters saw to that. We worked sixteen hours a day to keep the chicken sheds clean."

"Mutation rate?" She has her pencil out.

"Between fifteen and twenty per cent. Far better than those city farms."

"And your sisters. Not musical in any way?"

"You know they weren't."

"Nor mathematical."

"No. And nor was I until Dad died."

The piano painfully works through some scales. A touch of melody. Something in C Minor.

"So your secret history. I'm waiting." The professor's finger settles on the Dictaphone. "I'll re-wind. Let's start at the beginning."

«« »

I was delivered to my family on my third day on earth, muslined and shivering. The midwife was silent, the ambulance driver a bundle of talkative nerves. The money would arrive soon, she said. Go out and plan what you're going to do with it. A new shed for the chickens with a sprinkler system for antibiotics. Or perhaps a down payment on a mini-tractor from the new factory. And it went without saying that the family's land would go unseeded by land mines. Families like ours, she said, needn't be put on the ten year list. We were eligible already. Cinema news reels mentioned our names in hushed tones. Newspapers manipulated our images amongst those of the Governing Committee. Family members were already heroes of the state.

My mother was pale after they drove away; her irises the colour of lemons as she looked down at me.

She tried to smile but the war had been going on too long.

‖

"Tell me about your non-musical, non-mathematical sisters. They're both dead now, aren't they."

"Rimma's dead. She died in the Hasmal anthrax attack. Elice is still alive. She works in a barracks canteen somewhere in the south. I haven't seen her for years."

"You write to Elice?"

"No, she can't read."

"Nor count either, I'd be bound."

"Hardly unusual these days."

"Continue."

»

My two elder sisters were four and six then. They smiled gleefully into the little tin crib that Mum had set up in the kitchen. The eldest – Elice – had dark hair and walked like one of the chickens with stiff movements and nodding head. She was Daddy's favourite, sitting up in the cab and humming as he played the bazouki –

||

"You said they weren't musical."

"They weren't. Do you teach bazouki at the Conservatoire?"

"Point taken."

»

Her sister Rimma never stopped talking. Or writing. She was bright. That's why the Committee sent her to the Codes Department.

||

"You said they weren't mathematical."

"They weren't. However, Rimma's position in the Department was reactive: a foil to the code breaker alphas using inverted logic. Essentially non-logic. That's why she was transferred to the Hasmal listening post. Have you ever played chess against someone who merely knows the moves as opposed to the classic strategies?"

"Yes. It's hellish."

"Exactly. Rimma's non-logic has probably shortened this war by as much as thirty years."

"I'm suitably sobered." A swift bleak smile. "Schooling?"

»

Rimma and me used to walk out to Madame Stok's house near the village twice a week. She liked Rimma but I know I was her favourite. She would set Rimma exercises with the other girls – spelling and graphs – while she let me sit on the back step and drink pop –

||

"You're a quaint one. You mean lemonade?"

»

Yes. My mother had eyes the colour of lemons and I drank lemonade with Madame Stok during lessons and my favourite sister died horrifically. Are you joining some dots with that pencil and paper? Anyway. Madame was more of a conversationalist than a teacher. She would lay out concepts. We'd be staring out across the great plain almost as far as the Green Sea and she would ask me if I thought there was such a thing as solid light. And did I know that the ancient Greeks believed our ability to see was because our eyeballs emitted light beams? And she talked to me about – about –

||

The old coldness pours back into my head. My tongue shrivels and numbs. Professor Gnessin looks at me with an expression of utter non-surprise before deftly flourishing the steel wastebasket for me to vomit in.

"I know, Victorvna. The suppressants are still kicking in. Don't worry. You'll soon learn to think freely here. Madame Stok talked to you about music."

A heavy curtain seems to have been pulled back. I almost laugh, take the tissue she hands me. "Yes. She talked to me. About music."

»

She talked to me about music. About the place where mind and soul collide. Where numbers take on the soft cloaks of angels. Sequence, rhythm. Charles Ives, Benny Goodman, Alice Faye, Mama Cass. Madame had no instruments though. Her little schoolhouse held a blackboard and five chairs. She had a funny hairless cat and her voice was odd. Very deep. But somehow she managed to conjure melodies in my head. Was she a witch? I used to stand in the farmyard at night looking for her broomstick as I watched the satellites strafe each other with laser fire. I counted the stars and started to consider each one a musical note. Is this madness?

||

"Yes. But I understand. Madame Stok was one of my finest Academicians. I'd like to tell you that she's here. But I won't lie." The professor refills the little glass from her kettle. "A little more of your family?"

»

Dad was away a lot, of course. Sometimes he would bring us a crawfish, one of the damaged or handicapped ones. He used to make a fire in the farmyard and we'd pretend we were pioneers. Elice would rake the charcoal until it was white hot. Dad played that bloody bazouki while my mother shuffled and danced, one arm above her head, the other gathering up her skirts, bare feet sliding back and forth in the mud. Dad would carry her off into the engine shed and we'd rush to listen and peer through chinks in the door. They knew we were listening. Dad's penis was huge and when they'd finished Mum used to piss on him.

||

The piano has fallen silent.
    "Good lord. And *how* fifteen year-old girls speak these days. And did anyone come to see you?"
    "See *me*?"
    "See *you*. Not them. *You*."

»

A couple of times before I was ten perhaps. They came in a minibus, an Opel maybe. I had a feeling they were touring around and just happened upon me. Usually two – a woman and a girl not much older than me. They took skin and nail scrapings and poked about under my tongue and seemed to already know that I could identify my mother's eye colour aged three days. Infantile prescience, you know.

||

"I know."

The first piano begins again.

»

They gave me pills for the constipation but seemed disappointed that I wasn't ambidextrous –

||

"You are now."

»

– I wasn't then – and made known their satisfaction that I'd passed through puberty at the age of eight. Some of us never get pubescent out on the farms. And then they'd drive off. Mum was just in the room next door but they never even attempted to speak to her.

||

"Did the Committee send any money in the end?"

»

No. Dad said he'd got a bit of a promotion at the haulage co-op. But I reckon he was making it up. But Mum loved me. I know that. She never differentiated between the other two girls and her little Victorvy. She loved me –

||

"I'm stopping the tape but the interview isn't over."

I won't cry. "Where is she, professor?" She thinks I'll cry but I won't.

"In the city. She's safe. You'll be seeing her soon."

"I don't believe you."

The professor begins to chuckle, her coathanger shoulders heaving, tiny acorn fragments in her bent teeth.

"Actually – you're right not to believe me. I'm telling you a lie. Your mother has been informed that her daughter Victorvna Yudelvna has been returned to the Fostering Institute on account of her blabbing about you and your talents to the neighbours. She's allowed to write you letters. But I don't suppose you'll be reading them."

"You look stupid with a grin." I can feel the hot tears now.

"I look stupider without one. My chin is weak. Bad teeth distract the viewer."

"*More stupid*, professor. Your grammar is appalling."

"I am a musician. Proceed, little Victorvy. How did you learn of your father's death?"

»

It was funny. I walked alone to school as usual on the Thursday. Rimma was already dead by now. Madame Stok sat by herself in the schoolroom with a pot of tea and the cat. It was called Munsk, I remember. The cat. She took me out to the back step but didn't offer me lemonade. My tummy really ached for it but she wouldn't pour any. Instead, she hauled me into an outhouse and locked the door. I thought about Mum and Dad in the engine shed. Madame had occasionally commented in her curiously deep voice on my changing body in terms of gestation dynamics. However, I was no less disturbed when she pulled a tarpaulin off something I'd never seen before. But I can hear one now.

||

"A piano?"

»

An upright piano. She led me gently, making a thing of dusting the stool and opening the lid. The keyboard was covered in crawling June bugs – there must have been a way in through the back. I remember looking at the keys and wondering if they were black and white pupae. The bugs were in my hair but I ignored them. "Play, Victorvna," she said. Well, I tried. I'd never seen or heard anything like it. She took my hands and showed me how to make sounds. I enjoyed the way my fingers were able to splay across the keys, from sharp to sharp. I suppose I did some rudimentary scales. Madame then instructed me to stop and look out of the window. She told me that my father had been killed very suddenly and very painfully and that I would never see him again.

||

"Proceed."

»

The notes fell into place. I was crying, of course – but more through this mad rush of – of creation. This something out of nothing. I didn't know it was music. Madame Stok left the recorder running and walked out across the grasslands and left me. I never saw her again either. Munsk sat in the sun and watched me through the doorway. She rolled and chased her stringy tail in the dust and provided me with my rhythm.

||

Professor Gnessin holds up the disk. "It has a lot of coiled drama. Rah rah rah raah. You crash right in, don't you."

"My impetus was sudden. I'd had a shock. But the motif just uncoiled from my body. As if, as if – "

"As if it had always been there?"

"As if it had always been there."

»

||

"Could you say that again? I need it on tape." The professor offers a cough of embarrassment. "It's, er, relevant to a minor funding issue."

»

As if it had always been there. Well, I walked home carrying that disk – even though I had no means of playing it when I got there. And it's sat on the mantelpiece next to Dad's picture ever since. Three and a bit years? And last Saturday, true to form, the minibus pulls up when there's no one in the house but me. I'm dumped at a railway station and spend half a week in a wagon full of beets and bison manure. And now I find myself sitting at your desk next to a bin of sick watching you make that mad little glass of acorn tea while I haven't eaten since God knows when.

• «««

"And how fifteen year-old girls speak these days. Arrivals and departures, departures and arrivals. Bisons and beets? Life's so unfair. Dear me. My tea's gone quite cold listening to you." The professor has stopped the machine, rewinds and raises her voice ever so slightly. "Clarabella Veronni?"

A tall girl – at least a metre and a half – opens the door and steps into the room.

"Clarabella. Please take our new Academician to the dormitories. She's had a long journey – beets and bison, don't y'know – and the day tomorrow may seem longer."

They can probably hear my stomach in that basement tunnel. "Food?"

"Take heart, Victorvna Yudelvna. We breakfast early."

Clarabella Veronni might be smiling as she goes ahead with my knapsack.

I wearily rise and pause in the doorway. "Professor Gnessin. My father's death was an accident. Tell me it wasn't meant to happen."

The anglepoise is switched off and the room plunges into darkness behind me.

II

Dawn stares in, the colour of my mother's lemon eyes.

There are no curtains. The glazing is uni-polarised so that light can enter but not depart: a directive from the Aerial Bombardment Sub-Committee. How do I know this? I don't. I'm making it up. Madame

Stok and her cat sucked something out of my head and three years of rubbish has piled in to fill the gap. And not just my own. I've pushed the sensors off my brow while I slept. A gentle putter inside my head tells me the earbuds are still secure: Professor Gnessin and her thin walls would have made sure of it.

I slide up the mattress and rest my head against the wall; feel the frozen limb of the metal bedstead against my neck. Flecks of pinkish-beige paint lie on the pillow. I find my spectacles in their case beneath it and put them on. The fuzz shapes resolve into sleepers: thirty? Forty? The big light from the single window halos their breath; starkly highlights freckles and the occasional melanoma.

"Quick! Put them back on!"

It's the tall girl Clarabella hissing in the bed next to me, whacking her own sensored brow like a mad baby bird. "Shitsop will make you sleep on a plank, Victorvna Yudelvna."

I fumble and find the little suckers. They adhere eagerly, undeterred by my swiftly raised eyebrows.

"Shitsop?"

"Mrs Shiltsoff. Eugenia Larissa's sister says she actually has balls. Shitsop hauled Eugenia Larissa off to Sick Bay and showed her once."

Eugenia's sister – a girl of ten with a naked scalp – nods her head vigorously several beds away.

"Eugenia is obviously highly observant." The paint flecks begin to annoy me.

"Too observant. They transferred her to the Surveillance Section but the Yankees caught her en route and now she has no eyes."

"You're joking."

"Or legs. Ssh!"

The other girls have begun to stir at our exchange but Clarabella's warning is enough to shut them up.

In the silence, I listen to the city's morning: the train in its tunnel, the croak of a helicopter. Water pipes, quiet weeping from the beds. A sort of purring cry from the corridor: not urgent, repetitious; a set of wheels. The door opens and – through half-closed lids – I see a small figure in a wheelchair float in. The chair deftly weaves its way among the untidy array of bedsteads and comes to rest beside me. My eyes are tight closed now.

"So, Victorvna Yudelvna." The voice is thin, immature; the mind behind seeming to hold an infinite age. "What do farm girls dream of? Something pretty good if they have to wear their glasses in bed."

A dry chaffing hand is on my cheek and my spectacles are gone. My eyes are so tightly shut I'll have crow's feet for a week.

"Wire rims. A little bit in the old style, eh girls?" Silence. "*Eh, girls?*"

"Yes, Mrs Shiltsoff." A single voice. Poor girl. I bet it's Eugenia's bald sister.

"Well, a voice. And not such a good one. I hear your sister's had a bad time with the Yankees, Georgievna Larissa." God, it *is* Eugenia's sister. "Lost some limbs and her eyeballs. Dear oh dear, how careless. Come, come."

My lids crack open to let in a little lemon light. I see Shitsop in profile, her face almost level with mine as I sit upon my high hospital bed. It is a child's face, finely featured; the hair full, coarse, complexly dressed perhaps in the style of the 1900s; earlobes holding pearl drop earrings. Yet she has the voice of a woman. The eyes of a woman as she swivels them suddenly on me, shows her teeth in the briefest of smiles and turns back to Georgievna.

"When I say come come I really do mean... come." She holds up a hand to Georgievna and the girl mutely slips down onto the freezing floor and works her way towards Mrs Shiltsoff.

Startling child-in-woman Mrs Shiltsoff.

Georgievna is before the wheelchair now and – bully for her – she looks Mrs Shiltsoff straight in the face. Mrs Shiltsoff turns my spectacles in her hands. I only have the one pair. They used to belong to Rimma.

"Give me your voice, Georgievna Larissa."

Georgievna is silent and now begins to bow her head.

"Your voice, girl. You know I can take it if I want to. Here, farmer. Give her your chamber pot."

Chamber pot? I didn't know I had one. I wish someone had bloody told me. I look under the bed. There it is. I haul it out and hand it to the girl. Her hand is steadier than mine. Her eyes are smiling. Her eyes tell me not to worry as she puts the pot on Shitsop's lap and kneels.

Georgievna has a couple of goes, coughs and nearly kills herself. In the end she gets it with two fingers stuffed down her throat. She wretches, wretches again and suddenly it's there. I smell the acridness of bile for the second time in twelve hours.

Shitsop shows me the chamber pot with that quick grin before she wheels away to oversee breakfast. She takes my spectacles with her.

I'll never forget peering in: there it was in its little soup of sick.

The voice of Georgievna Larissa.

*

There is practice before breakfast.

I expect to be lead into the bowels of the building where I heard last night's pianos. But a blue-overalled woman with a scarf around her neck conducts me up the bare stairs. She carries a music case. The walls are covered with further photographs of the musically gifted and probably dead. She pauses on a landing with a window that looks out over a bombed shoe factory; leans on the sill and points back to a curled monochrome picture pinned to the plaster. The photo's emulsion is cracked. It features a boy and girl; he with guitar, she with dulcimer. They sit in an orchard surrounded by fallen apples.

"Couldn't you just eat them?" My guide is enthusiastic. Her voice is slow and precise.

"Apples or children?" I wonder if she can hear my stomach rumbling.

I look out and down on the scattered shoes: hundreds or thousands of mismatched pairs clouding the wasteland as far as the shrunken river. All of them waiting for feet that will never be born.

The practice room is windowless, the ceiling covered in egg boxes. The room contains an upright *Klemt & Sons* piano, a stool, metronome and a family of spiders low down in one corner. I find this out when I examine the floor. The floor and wall are painted the same colour but even close inspection fails to tell me what that colour is.

I wonder if I'll get my glasses back.

The woman – I suppose she's middle-aged – hands me a single sheet from the music case and departs.

I study the music. I peer closer, have to screw my eyes up. It looks normal enough. Simple even. Just a few notes. Something in C Minor. It's quite similar to my audition piece. But as I begin to play, I become confused. The notes could almost be the spider's relatives: they vibrate when I look too hard at them; fade into the white paper as I try to casually interpret with a sly sideways glance.

The metronome is broken. I play nothing.

The woman returns. She tightens her scarf in an unconscious gesture; takes the manuscript back and locks the door behind us. "How did you get on, miss? I could hear some very pretty music in the corridor."

We climb a further flight towards breakfast. I might just live another day.

"Fine. Very good. I can't believe how easily I took to it."

*

Georgievna Larissa sits in the corner of the canteen at a small table by herself. The voice – still in its chamber pot womb – sits between her spoon and fork. The tabletop is scattered with her fingernails: now that's what you call rotten luck. She sucks lemonade through a straw that connects to a hole in her throat. Following voice loss, Georgievna's mouth swallowed its own tongue and the nurses had to carry out a tracheotomy. Georgievna Larissa sucks steadily in spite of hiccoughs.

"Poor Georgievna. Quietest girl in the Conservatoire," says Clarabella as she tries to make a meal of her oats and water. Her observation is without slant or judgment.

The girls around me keep their heads down, intent on the round ceramic universes before them. The oatmeal is surprisingly good, in spite of a metallic undertaste. We are almost queens at breakfast: women in blue overalls run around with trays and tea towels. My guide fills the urn in the corner. I catch her eye and realise she's a good deal older than I thought.

The same age as my father might have been.

While much of my mind wanders, a smaller part understands that Clarabella is a focus of attention. She sits beside me, a light bulb in the dim morning, not always speaking but the first to be turned to if there's any listening to be done. She listens now as a dark girl called Dulcie reads an official trawler report from the Finnish Ocean. The girl's family live on a ship that circles the eternal day of higher latitudes. They are pirates plundering the lochs of fish farmers; releasing and stealing the domesticated cod; allowing them to spread their viral contagions amidst the deep seas.

"I'd like to be a fisherman," says Clarabella suddenly. "Not just fish. Anything from the water. Oysters, crawfish. How about you, Victorvna Yudelvna?" Her turn to me is even more sudden.

"I don't know." The cereal fibres catch in my throat. "We're so far from the sea here. Seafood has to be fresh."

"But you can use transports. Even now." This from Yergeniya, a girl with permanent earbuds.

"But the trains are so slow." Lizan, a long-limbed redhead from the south somewhere.

"You mean the roads *aren't*?" Aja: black staring eyes.

"Well, the rivers aren't much good anymore. My mother fought river fever all her life. Her guts glow like a lantern." Kara: skinny limbs, large hands. I notice her fingernails hinge away from their cuticles.

"People will find a way if they want to dine on crawfish. Am I right, little Victorvy?" Clarabella dwells at the centre of her halo in the canteen, the others just watchers looking in.

"You're right." I don't mean to cry. "You're really really right."

There's a light pressure on the bridge of my nose, the hooks of my ears.

I open my eyes to find I can see.

Clarabella leans closer to ensure the new glasses fit snugly. I am fascinated by her face: the tight skin stretched on finely-furred cheeks. Freckles, nostrils wide like a pony. Legs longer than she knows what to do with. Is she pretty?

Clarabella smiles at me. Blue-grey eyes.

Yes, she's pretty.

"What's the time, Victorvna Yudelvna?"

I glance at the canteen clock through my spectacles.

"07.25, Clarabella Veronni."

"Five minutes to go, girls. Might as well make a start for the shelter."

*

The air raid is early.

We barely reach the bomb shelter before it's over.

On the way down Georgievna Larissa trips over a body. She can't scream. I gather her voice into my hanky and we carry on just as the big landing window implodes. It's one of the old-fashioned sonic weapons and its hum carries through the steel superstructure of the building long after the munition has discharged. I have Georgievna in my arms and we fall down the stairwell. Her body is full of glass. I am aware that Clarabella observes this even as we all run and trip and scream. Little Aja actually stops for a proper wee in the janitor's doorway. Heroic or foolish, Clarabella holds the iron door open for us wearing the world's biggest grin.

There could be a hundred in here: pupils, staff, the blue overalls. A piano sits in one corner below a row of steel helmets. Yergeniya has her earbuds plugged into the News Service and screams a running commentary.

"Our forces are triumphant! The slack-jawed Yankees are running across the sky faster than they have come, driven by our heroic pilots as a shepherdess drives her sheep. But not to any green field go the Yankees, but into a burning place of kerosene and cordite and irradiated munitions. Damn their tiny cocks! We are victorious! Victory! Victory!"

A beaming Professor Gnessin squats on a rations box at the piano. "Well done, Yergeniya. An excellent précis of the broadcast. And I hear the All Clear sounding so it's time to start our lessons. But not without a stirring rendition of the Imperial Anthem. Come on girls. Let's show Victorvna Yudelvna how we conduct ourselves in the war zone!"

As the professor strikes up, all the faces turn towards me and the body of Georgievna Larissa still cradled in my arms.

"Look," calls Clarabella above the singing. She toes a loose flex on the floor. "Bloody radio's not even plugged in."

*

The lemon dawn has given way to grey mid-morning. Smoke hangs over the city.

I lay Georgievna's cold body out in the deserted Sick Bay. The room's as empty as its large dispensing cabinet. Where can everyone be? I look through an archway into what seems to be the nurses' station. That chamber there might be an operating theatre. From behind a large set of double doors I hear echoing shouts and splashes. A sharp smell of disinfectant.

I leave Georgievna's voice on the night stand: pinkishly organic, moistly mechanical.

*

As we sit and wait for class in the boarded-up lecture theatre, I ask Clarabella about the double doors.

She brushes her forearms, arranges her notation manuals. "Water polo." She almost looks at me. "The nurses can't get enough of it."

Water polo? What the hell's that?

Doctor Kaulay arrives in a cloud of spilt manuscripts and we have an hour of ensemble theory before break time. The girls have explained that ensemble means playing with others: I consider the lonely practice room with its egg box ceiling – presumably a deterrent to prevent those mysterious *others* from hearing your music.

Doctor Kaulay is a brightly plaintive graduate of the Conservatoire. The Conservatoire is her existence. That year twixt graduation and a return to doctoral residency was the worst of her life. A wasteland. In fact the theory lesson is pretty much taken up entirely by that nest of horrors that was Life Beyond The Conservatoire.

Doctor Kaulay continues to chunter on as she oversees our break. A side door is unlocked and we find ourselves on a shattered netball court beneath exhausted lime trees. Needless to say, the doctor is able to recall a time when the lime trees were over-burdened with sap and the court possessed more lines than a geometry lesson.

We are placed on salvage duty. It is explained that the metal rain that drops from the sky during aerial bombardment is valuable and can be turned against the enemy.

The girls have a system. Aja and red-headed Lizan work the Geiger counters while Kara scrabbles on her knees, those great hands spread out on the tarmac like the rippling whiskers of catfish. By break's end, they have quite a haul of ball bearings. Yergeniya and a small girl called Calli follow Clarabella as she douses the ejected aviation fuel with sand before sweeping the result into great leather satchels for recycling. I laugh as I discover the satchels have been home to clutches of yellow frogs. They jerk away across the broken ground, doubtless smelling the river. Most seem to be copulating on the run – but Yergeniya removes her earbuds to explain that they are actually Siamese twins, cursed to

147

drag a comatose sibling through their stunted tiny lives.

The bell sounds and Doctor Kaulay goes inside. I am about to turn in too when a movement catches my eye beyond the high fence. Mrs Shiltsoff weaves between piles of steaming debris on a course roughly parallel with that of the amphibians. She makes good progress: some of the concrete must be red hot.

Professor Gnessin lingers at the side door: her face colour matches that of her starched cuffs. The professor calls us inside, her manner vague: she watches Mrs Shiltsoff go, and presently slinks down to the fence and scratches around until she finds a badger hole. She crouches in and catches a thread of her dark gown on the razor wire; disentangles, straightens and jogs after the wheelchair.

Clarabella and I are the only ones left in the playground. She holds a frog in her left palm and gently strokes it and its twin in the half-light of morning. In the dull brightness, her irises are almost transparent. More blue than grey in the out-of-doors. "Just another unexploded bomb, I expect. They can't get the fuses right lately."

I can't stop looking at Clarabella. She smiles slowly and says: "Can you run, farm girl?"

"Chicken girl. We kept chickens."

Before we slip under the wire, she lets her frog go. It darts across the netball court; pauses to drink from a puddle of aviation fuel.

*

Shitsop and the professor have made good progress. Their silhouettes are barely discernible through the oily smoke. The sun is a disc that slips in and out of visibility.

Clarabella yells back that the area we're running across is the collapsed metro entrance – part of the tunnel system that I heard below the professor's study last night. The dust is heavy yet still hangs; phosphorus sticks smoulder and steal oxygen from the air. Tram ponies limp and whimper on the superheated black-top.

Clarabella stops, rests hands on knees, tries not to breathe too deeply. "It must have been a ground detonation. Air rounds are much cleaner."

A pair of naked legs hangs from a lamp post; only one limb has a stocking. A moving staircases – I learnt the term on my train journey into the city – is miraculously still moving. It snakes up from below and unravels into a clattering coil. Rationing leaflets and those for special travel privileges are beginning to helix up into the air, buffeted by the heat underground.

"It *is* a bomb! I can hear it. Come on, Victorvy..."

She uses a pile of travelling trunks to scramble up a wall that used to be a roof, the tiles lacerating her long legs. I make to go around – realise the grizzly reason for her clambering – and hoist myself up after her. I can hear screams, but not from this ruined ticket office; there's no one left here.

They come from the river.

"Wait, Clarabella. You're bigger than me. Just wait..."

She stretches an arm down, dust catching the fine blond hairs. "Mind your hands. The piano needs them for later, cowlick."

"Chickenlick."

She just catches my fingers and hauls me up in such a painful grip that I almost cry again: I'm obviously being punished for my insolence.

From here we can see clearly down to the nearly-dry river. Clarabella quickly points and I listen: the Food Committee factories; a couple of Dulcie's beached pirate trawlers with their riverine camouflage. The abandoned zoo and an old bridge that they've never bothered to bomb, the piles allegedly filled with our own high explosive ready for the Yankee's final push. To the east, we can see the remains of two other music academies that were built too close together. They know better now. The blackened masonry looks like my near-broken fingers feel. Clarabella used to attend the nearest one: she says she can see her dormitory window with its new transparent walls.

Shitsop circles something half-sunk in the river mud about fifty metres off. At every circumlocution, she gives the object a hefty whack with a piece of driftwood she's found. Shitsop's been pretty fearless, obviously gambling that the mud will remain stony enough to prevent her chair from sinking.

Professor Gnessin advises from firmer ground. Her voice whips up to us on a thermal. "Do you think we can save it?"

"I'm not sure. It's still responding." Shitsop circles and gives the bomb an almighty wallop.

The bomb screams again.

*

We sprint back to the netball court where the blue overalls are assembling equipment: a gurney and tarpaulins. My practise room guide is with them. She carries sandwiches in greaseproof paper and a bottle of lemonade.

The woman's all concern. "Shouldn't you be at lessons, Victorvna Yudelvna? It's time for accompanist vocations. And I'm surprised at *you*, Clarabella Veronni."

But she passes on through the fence, her concern eclipsed by the riverside discovery.

Clarabella kicks at the molten asphalt. "You've got to keep an eye on Erica."

"Erica?"

"Yeah. She used to be a Yankee. Didn't you clock the paunch?"

"She's stick thin."

"In her brain, silly. Too much flab and wastage."

"How did she end up here?"

"The usual. Wandered over the border. Had the operation. Debriefed and put to work in the service sector. Anything to be a tiny fragment of our glorious revolution." She looks right at me. "It's funny though..."

We tread on frogs, gelatinous and snappy. I'm not exactly laughing.

Clarabella continues: "She hasn't got the glow. The super fanaticism that makes them defect. She's got a sort of lazy look."

As we reach the side door, I turn back one last time. Erica has paused on the ruins of the ticket office to slug back lemonade.

*

The Vocational Accompanist Module is taken by Professor Gnessin herself. She's a little late to class and her fingernails are filthy. She sends Dulcie off for a bowl of water.

The professor's delivery is flat, the small eyes distracted. "The accompanist often goes ahead of the principle. The accompanist is the scene-setter but not the scene itself. There is a withdrawal, a return, a replication of the principle's motif."

She sits and steeples her fingers over the desk, skin moist as a yellow frog's above her thin top lip. She ponders the blotter. Dulcie returns, but the bowl and towels are ignored.

"A suitable metaphor would be that of a thermobaric air-fuel weapon. Consider the accompanist as the initial discharge of fuel, that mist of ethylene oxide that must be laid down so the principle – acting as the primary charge – can ignite and deflagrate. As we know, a thermobaric impulse can initiate pressure spikes within internal organs of over three-hundred pounds per square inch. The accompanist/principle relationship should have no less an impact. Erica?"

Erica peers through the celluloid window in the classroom door.

Professor Gnessin rises. "Unfortunately I'm needed on other business, girls. Aja, please take over the class."

Aja's black eyes are ready to pop from her head as the professor scurries away.

*

The talk over luncheon is especially small as we stir our blue soup and fight over paprika. The blueness of the soup has long ceased to be a viable topic for the others. I am curtly told by know-it-all Yergeniya that the Food Committee steals it from the sky and boils it in their factories by the river. I look at Clarabella but she doesn't look at me. She's taken up with Lizan at the far end of the table.

Gnessin and Shitsop hurry through. I hear a snatched dialogue but am unsure which is which, so hissed is the exchange:

...Does this mean our own programmes can be accelerated?... ...Doubtful. The technologies are so different... ...Surely there must be some concordance... ...Well, you try talking to it. I can't understand a word it's trying to say...

They are gone, a gaggle of blue overalls travelling in their wake.

Blue soup, blue overalls.

I rub my bruised hand and notice that a fine blue sweat has pooled on my fingertips. I try to draw on the plastic table top.

I might write my name but I can't quite remember it.

*

I'm on the floor in the corridor, my dress covered in sick. My eyes feel like great throbbing nuts. I've been dreaming of Georgievna Larissa, laid out on her bed back in the dormitory. Except her legs are missing and I just know that I'll find them on top of the lamp post in Professor Gnessin's office. The same lamp post where she hangs all the melted mis-matched shoes. I can smell the professor's wastebasket and it smells of me.

Clarabella kneels close by. Lizan is there: she has an elastic bandage around her neck; it leaks a little.

I vomit, blue and acrid. This is more than last night. I'm soaked. The girls pull me up and drag me to the washrooms. Lizan scrubs my dress in a basin while Clarabella looks after my spectacles and keeps my head down the toilet. The sick keeps on coming. I half expect frogs. I stagger out and lean against the cubicle to a round of applause.

Lizan turns back, laughingly works bauxite into my dress. "You'd better stay in the bog. It'll be coming out the other end soon."

She's probably right. I can feel my intestines distending, a worm uncoiling downwards across my stomach. I catch Clarabella looking at me as I stand in front of the mirror. I'll need my spare vest.

"Big old agricultural thing isn't she, Liz? Elevate your mighty arms, Victorvna Yudelvna."

They seem thick and yellow as I raise them under the strip light; old chicken beak scars, a flash of hair in the armpits.

Lizan has stopped scrubbing. They both stare at me as I look at myself in the glass. Suddenly, I can smell the oil from dad's engine shed. The smell of the animals; my mother squatting over his face...

The tall girl gently touches my elbow, slides her finger down the arm.

"I'm not feeling too well, Clarabella... What are you..."

"Nothing, Victorvy." She delicately holds the sweaty, calcified strands between thumb and forefinger. "Just bloody jealous, that's all."

I absorb the other girls' bodies as if for the first time: flat and unrounded, lithe and destined for some other purpose.

I stumble back into the cubicle and only later realise that Lizan's voice once belonged to Georgievna Larissa.

III

The practise will be even easier this morning.

In my weeks at the Conservatoire, I have discovered a rhythm both to my life and to my music. The air raids and the oatmeal and the theory and the reality.

Erica again leads me to the room of egg boxes. She seems anxious that I might forget the way. The music seems the same – and yet I now notice pencilled annotations that must have been there all the time. Erica sits on a second stool in the corner and watches me as I make the spider notes come together. I activate the metronome but she swiftly leans over to lever it off.

"You won't need that, miss. You'll find the rhythm in your mind."

She seems very sure about that. I run through a couple of cascades then turn to her.

"Erica?"

"Yes, Victorvna Yudelvna."

"Where do you come from?"

I don't need the metronome to count the beats between question and reply.

"One of the outer dependencies. Near the Green Sea. An Asiatic you've never heard of."

Liar.

"You speak our language very well."

"Thank you. I had a very good teacher. Mrs Shiltsoff. She has great patience." The scarf is loose this morning and I watch the Adam's apple as it bobs. "Small c and small m, miss."

"Sorry?"

"You've written C Minor in the margin with a big C and a big M. A small c and a small m are fine for your purpose."

My purpose? I had no recollection of writing C Minor. I had no pencil. "So why's it fine for my purpose, Erica."

"It's quicker." Bob, bob went the neck. "It's quicker, Miss Victorvna."

*

I crouch beside the dispensing cabinet and hear Shitsop's voice behind the double doors. It's like a buzzy squib amongst the water and echoes. She's been questioning the bomb for weeks in its own language. The bomb chatters and screams. It must be in unimaginable pain now. Professor Gnessin's voice requests thermobaric data. Demands knowledge of their fight music. Will the bomb submit or will they have to kill it? The bomb wails as the professor opens the doors and steps into Sick Bay. Behind her I see the rippled reflections of water against an aquamarine ceiling.

The professor has a high colour. There is a muskiness about her. She falls onto one of the beds; knots her hands into her skirt and pulls it up over the bird-thin thighs.

When she sleeps, I slip away.

*

"So tell me about your father."

"You know about him. You knew about him that first morning at breakfast."

"I just listen. They tell me to listen." Clarabella and I sit top to toe on my high bed in the early evening. We darn asbestos hoof socks for the tram ponies. Kara's been losing her hair for the past week and is confined to the dormitory. We keep her company as she lies in the bed next to ours, looking at the ceiling. Her big hands are folded across our ball of coarse wool. Her fingernails have all gone and Mrs Shiltsoff has told us her voice is taking well.

Otter meat for supper and no one's feeling good.

"And what about *your* father, Clarabella?"

"No, that's too easy. You need to try harder. You should say: And I suppose you don't want to talk about your father, Clarabella Veronni."

"I bet he's some neutered arse wipe in a minority groups sub-committee."

"Brilliant! You're *good*."

"She's good." Kara's new voice has a smile in it.

Clarabella jumps off the bed. "For that, you deserve a special treat. I'll take you to him. He lives in the city – "

"He *lives* in the *city*?"

"Yep. Even works at the Conservatoire – but he comes and goes so early you'll never notice him. Officially, he's not on the books. Music's not his real job but it keeps the crusts from crawling off his table. Come on, Kara Reginid. All of us."

She slips some packages from under her mattress into the tubes of Kara's bedstead, kicks away the locking pin and has left the dormitory before I've even had time to put my sandals on.

*

The goods elevator complains on its cables as we descend through the layers of the building. The stamp issued by the Committee of Public Safety is taped to the control panel and was signed seventeen years ago.

"Faster, Kara? Faster?!" Clarabella's a demon, her teeth bared, her blond hair sticking up like a scarecrow.

We hit the ground floor and the gates groan open. A sudden silence.

"Check for blueys, Vic."

"Where do Gnessin and Shitsop sleep?"

"With each other probably. And they summon Kaulay to tickle their toes on alternate Wednesdays. Now poke your nose out and see if the coast is clear."

I peer into the dank corridor and realise my glasses could do with a good clean. But apart from a fire bucket the corridor's empty and we propel Kara down a ramp and into the rear courtyard. It's full of rubbish. Broken upright pianos are stacked on the cobbles, several piled upon one another. Picture frames and glass tanks and oxygen bottles. Mummified birds in a cardboard box. And something white on a wheeled stretcher. I move closer. The object glows in the dimness. Clarabella has matches and we both jump in the sudden light.

"Gosh, what is it? Some sort of giant salamander? It must be a metre long."

I strike another match as she strokes the flowery external gills, the stubby paws that could almost be hands. The body is quite desiccated and the head has been severely beaten. But I can still smell the river mud. And disinfectant.

Abruptly, Clarabella loses interest and climbs up onto the pianos. She cries with laughter as she thrashes at the strings through their naked broken backs. She plays until the blood must shine on her knuckles. I join her to take the rhythm and follow her lead as she continues to work the melody. Accompanist and principle. Kara goes at the bedstead with a big spoon. We fashion a bleak boogie-woogie out there in the twilight courtyard.

We'd howl at the moon if there was one.

*

The hole through the fence has been shored up – but we manage to find another. I strain my ears but the whole city is wrapped in nothing. The daytime raids accentuate the nocturnal silence. Something catches in my hair: a moth or June bug drawn by our residual radiation. Perhaps they were living in the pianos.

We're on the other side of the underground station and there's less debris. A few trams venture down the street, headlights slitted for the black-out, their ponies' hooves muffled. The drivers are as nervous as we to be out after dark. The Committee's curfew regulations have been left deliberately vague.

The sidewalks are wide in this part of the city – Clarabella tells me there used to be a street market here – and we've room enough to push Kara along. One of the bedstead's wheels has seized and our navigation is erratic: several times we career into piles of rubbish or carcasses.

And the bloody frogs are everywhere.

"Here."

I realise I've been mesmerised by the semi-gloom – the blind lamp posts, the fleets of confused insects – and Clarabella's cry makes me start. We stop by a wide shop front: boarded-up plate glass either side of a short passageway that ends in a door. The boards display repeated fly posters advertising Pioneers' Day Special Offers on Bicycles. Clarabella skips up the passage and knocks: a rhythmic tattoo that carries meaning. I look at Kara but she sleeps. I stroke her eyebrows but she doesn't stir.

The door opens a fraction and I realise it's a curious one, the shape of a bullet in profile, pointed at the top. A tatter of paper is pinned to the wood: *962110 Kovarskaya 48*. An orange splinter of light streaks out across the sidewalk. Someone holds the ring handle: I can only see an outline against the warm luminescence. The door is wider than it looks and we push the bed in.

Immediately, my senses are engulfed: an overwhelming stink of beeswax and damp tapestries. The light – a single source that depends from a chain in the high roof – is sheathed in a copper and jade cocoon above a table of once-milky linen. Our feet make gentle crunching sounds as we enter and I glance down to see that the stone floor is covered in large skeletal dry leaves. Chickens live in a corner and I find myself kneeling amongst them, stroking their broken beaks as easily as I stroked the sick girl's eyebrows.

Clarabella is unscrewing parts of Kara's bedstead. "Don't worry. Victorvna Yudelvna's a whizz with chickens."

I notice our door-opener is nervously considering me from a distance. He is a man, tall like his daughter; a nail-biter with a long black beard and large forehead; dark robes over a bony body. Down at chicken level as I am, I notice he is shoeless.

"I can see she has a way." The voice is quite high: it has music in it. "That one – the one with the thick neck – what is wrong? She no longer lays. Don't cut your knees on the palm leaves."

Clarabella pulls out compressed bread and dried oatmeal from the metal tubing and goes into a room beyond the lantern.

I carefully crouch and cradle the bird. It has dull eyes and its crop is inflamed. A beak blackened by faeces.

"Do the others hurt it, Master Veronni?"

My knowledge of his identity catches him out. "Yes. Why yes, Victorvna Yudelvna. She never gets any grain, that one."

"The others know. She has distemper. Have you noticed the white eyes. She can see very little and can smell nothing."

I hand him the bird and he takes it as if it were a child. "Thank you. Thank you. I'll just put it with – with the others." He quietly slips into the room beyond the beautiful light and presently returns with tea. He is followed by Clarabella and two other girls – one a miniature version of Clarabella, the other even smaller, staggering under a mess of dark hair above over-sized gumboots. They carry cups and saucers and small plates of bread and cake.

"Allow me to introduce my other children. Dulciana..." – the mini-Clarabella puts down her tray and curtsies – "...and Bourdon." The littlest grins widely and with great kindness and I know her father will be safe in old age. "Pour the tea, Clarabella. See I've put an extra cup for your little friend in the bed. Be careful, her ears seem very dry. Victorvna Yudelvna, you will sit up with me."

I take his proffered hand and he leads me into a dim corner away from the chickens. Apart from my father, I've never been so close to a man. We sit on a long bench together and he lifts the stained lid of a double keyboard. The ivory keys are worn and have tiny chips like old teeth. A candle is lit and dusted with powder: the fragrance is overwhelming. "They don't have myrrh at the Conservatoire, do they. Do you like it?"

Clarabella calls over with a mouth full of cake: "Dad's a piano tuner. He comes in at 4 o'clock every morning. Takes the same route we took to get here."

"Don't eat and talk, Clara. Bourdon, come and pump."

The tiny girl jumps to her work eagerly, almost trips in her big boots. She leans on a sprung stool, see-sawing once she gains her rhythm with the bellows.

"Used to just plug it into the mains once. Right! How many fingers?" Master Veronni has his fisted hand in the air.

The delighted children all answer 'Three!' in a rush, with Clarabella perhaps taking the advantage.

He winks at me as his left hand – which indeed is missing a finger – slides across to a peg beside the upper keyboard. The peg is marked *Clarabella*.

"We call them 'stops', Victorvna Yudelvna. Even though, in a manner of speaking, they actually make the organ go..." And as the girl pumps the organ and the thin man begins to play, I notice the other stops: *Dulciana, Bourdon*. And yet more: *Lieblich Gedackt, Open Diapason...*

He watches me. "Don't worry. I'm not planning on having any more kids. I have some compassion. Do you like Vidor's toccatas? He's a bit mathematical..." His right hand is at the upper keyboard, ascending and descending in eighths; the bare feet move more slowly over the long pedals. Square wooden pipes the breadth of a torso transmit resonances through the organ stool.

It's marvellous. I've never heard anything like it.

Abruptly, the music stops mid-beat. He raises his feet; puts his hands behind his head. "Or maybe you prefer Miles Davis? I have some records."

"Madame Stok – my teacher back in the country – liked Alice Faye."

"Ah, yes." He strikes up Vidor again, this time more quietly. "*Speaking Confidentially... I've Got My Love To Keep Me Warm...* She was a very natural contralto. Do you play those songs at the Conservatoire? Dulciana! Bring our guest some tea."

"No. Just our scales. And there's a short practice piece we have to do before breakfast. In C Minor."

"Beethoven's magic key? He was addicted to it. Why don't you play it for me? I'll stop in for you."

He pushes the stops home and slides across the bench.

"It's *molto mosso* with a *sostenuto* at the end."

"Good lord. And *how* fifteen year-old girls speak these days." Master Veronni regards me unblinkingly.

"Um. It has to be very exact. I'm not sure – "

"Try. I'm sure you're better than that crotchet-tangled Clarabella."

A hunk of tea-moistened cake hits Master Veronni on the ear.

So I do try, my hands relaxing in the presence of this comfortable man who seems to want nothing more than to make me feel better about myself. I start to take the notes in on an unconscious level. They no longer register as notes in my brain. No longer are they spiders of physicality. They are deeper, so much deeper than that.

I stretch my hands and play.

Master Veronni's gnawed fingernails slide across his lips as he rocks to and fro, hums and anticipates the melody that he obviously knows so well.

*

They're all waiting when the elevator reaches dormitory level.

The girls and the blue overalls; Professor Gnessin, Doctor Kaulay and tutors hitherto unseen. Mrs Shiltsoff promenades up and down and says nothing as Erica heaves the lift doors open. We nudge the bedstead into the corridor and Lizan slips forward and seems on the brink of speaking; Yergeniya hovers too, almost there yet still deep within the world of her earbuds.

Shitsop pauses, leans up to rest her hand on Kara's barely moving chest; brushes the skin scales from her forehead.

And the next person she looks at is me.

"You. Farm girl. You will hold vigil over Kara Reginid tonight." Her eyes turn elsewhere. "Clarabella Veronni, you will know how disappointed I am. You are responsible. You are the senior girl here. There will be punishment."

Clarabella grips the bedstead tightly. I thought she would answer. Where is the girl of glory who thrashed those twilight pianos, that food fighter? She seems slighter; seems younger even than her little sisters.

The eyes swivel back. Shitsop's like a demon, her speech bursts like hot poison. "She *is* responsible isn't she, Victorvna Yudelvna? *Isn't* she. You're not answering so I know it's her fault. Don't speak. Don't defend her."

My mouth won't open. I know Clarabella's blue-grey eyes are clinging to me but I can only look at the floor. God! I'm still thinking about the colour of her eyes! A nausea plays with my stomach. I fold my arms across my chest, sure that everyone can see.

My throat feels like there's glue in it.

"There *will* be punishment, Clarabella Veronni. We shall talk tomorrow." Shitsop beckons me closer; her low voice is husky, the ear pearls try to hypnotise. Deep inside, the last and strongest part of me thinks: *You won't have me, you ancient bitch baby. I am for another.* But Mrs Shiltsoff merely purrs, as if in the presence of proud parents: "You are one of the best here, child. I cannot punish you as I do the others. Watch this poorly girl and do not be afraid. Erica will bring you a stool and some warm milk."

And then she is gone. And soon I am alone in the corridor with Kara and her travelling sick bed.

I wonder what Clarabella's face looked like as her friends dragged her back to the dormitory. I peer into the nighttime window pane and behold the ghostly face of the chicken girl, etched as it is with misery and a sudden knowledge of loneliness.

*

"Kara play now. Kara ready to deploy."

I have been dozing; the milk has sewn my dreams with a thread of sourness.

"Kara play now. Kara play fight music."

I'm thrown by the spluttering on/off kerosene light at the end of the corridor.

"Kara Reginid?" I am fully awake now and stand over her. Her eyes are wide open. The irises have lost all their pigment. They are not even the colour of lemons. I look directly into them; they've mislaid their sheen, almost as if the fabric of the eyeball has thickened. She spits teeth and I hold her head to prevent choking. She's really agitated now. The nailless fingers are working at her ears. Compared to those of Master Veronni, the fingers are smooth and slightly translucent; nearly fused, almost joined...

I hold her arms down but she's taken on an impossible strength and thrashes like the eel her mother might have landed on the riverbank. She scratches an ear away. She shrieks. She sneezes snot onto my dress; a moment passes and implodes before I realise she's blown her nose off.

I don't cry out. I am not afraid. Shitsop was right.

The other ear sloughs away and I flail like a fool beneath the bed trying to retrieve it.

Somewhere, at a great distance – or so it seems – the passage doors open and Mrs Shiltsoff is here, murmuring to Kara, stroking my hair as I scrabble on the floor.

Erica is behind her and Kara is wheeled away, a white shining vision gasping for breath; something caught between earth and ocean; a pale barking sea lion.

"Kara play now. Kara request ordnance status. Kara play fight music."

*

Erica makes no mention of the previous night as she hands me the music. I give a reasonable performance. It's in me now. The time at the organ seems to dwell in a long ago somewhere else. I try to hold the memory.

Erica slips me a ticket as we leave the practice room.

"Report to Professor Gnessin's study. She will want to speak to you before you leave. Then walk to the bus depot. It's not far – just beyond the underground station in the same street as Master Veronni's church. The bus driver will understand and will know what to do. Go. Breakfast and go. Remember your purpose."

The girls are bitches in the showers; they taunt me with boot polish painted on their stupid little hairless quims. They use towels like bullwhips. Clarabella's bed has not been slept in and nobody will tell me anything.

And so I sit at a table by myself in the canteen and ponder the ticket. But I feel a curious new strength. The night has been a long one. I'm aware of the watchers but I'm in a different place now. I hoped to journey with another but I think I'll be travelling alone.

I turn the ticket over. My name is there in pencil:

vic

Small letters.

*

Master Veronni pokes his beard out of the passageway as I hurry past and grabs the strap of my haversack.

"Steady there, Victorvna Yudelvna!"

I wave my ticket. His approach is so playful that I'm mute in his presence.

"I know where you're going. I've been to the Conservatoire. Just pop inside, won't you?"

The interior seems bigger in the dim morning. High windows shaft in the rancid light, turning the palm leaves into shadow ripples across the floor.

He invites me to sit at the organ but makes no move to lift the cover.

"I want you to be kind to Clarabella. She knows so little."

I'm thrown. "But Clarabella's so clever. She's been at the Conservatoire so much longer than I. She's knows everything."

"She's learnt many things during her time there. But how much did you know even before you'd heard of this city?"

I thought about Madame Stok's house and her hairless cat: she talked to me about music. *About the place where mind and soul collide...*

Master Veronni rises and goes to stand by a hole in the wall above his chickens.

"Clarabella would do anything in the world for you. And one day she'll probably have to." He gestures me to join him. "Look through this and tell me what you see."

I stare into the hole: it's set at shoulder height and is perhaps a half metre tall, a little narrower in width. It has been cut clean through a major structural wall of the building. Through it I can see the soiled linen table; that amber lamp of much magnificence.

"This is silly, Master Veronni. All you need do is step around this buttress. Why burrow a hole?"

"Because it concentrates the mind, my girl. They call it a hagioscope. Literally, a viewer of saints. It forms a frame for God's glory. It's also a blast blind for the building: let off an explosive in the hagioscope and nothing would happen." Now that's a funny fact to tell a fifteen-year old – but he continues urgently: "Again, what do you see?"

I see the lamp, of course. And part of a window that seems to be held together by bits of string. And something that looks like a black carpenter's nail hanging from a hook midway up the wall. It is bent into a right angle; something is wrapped around one half.

Something that gleams.

"I see you've noticed it. That's my priest's ring. They came and broke the door down and hacked my finger off and threw it in the toilet. Ransacked the church's gold to manufacture Committee members' pacemakers and then tried to blow up the building by stuffing nitro-glycerine... *guess where*?"

I notice the scorch marks inside the hagioscope for the first time and Mr Veronni continues:

"Even then I was better than them. I traced the pipes and the forgotten underground streams of this city. I crawled like an ant over the shit stink of their sewerage farms. And I found it. I bloody found it. I staggered back here more dead than alive and hung it up on the wall. And..." He smiles into the middle distance: Dulciana and Bourdon hover, shy in the daylight. "...And my children were waiting for me. My precious children."

He speaks quietly now and I realise that he must have a knowledge of what has passed between Clarabella and myself. "In future times, you will need to concentrate your mind. This moment is one you must remember, Victorvna Yudelvna."

*

There's no one on the bus but me and the driver.

At first I think she's too busy snapping cashews and flooring the clutch to save fuel to say much.

I'm drowsily grateful after the long night. The industrial chimneys seem to form prison bars across the eastern sky, their belchings too heavy to drift. Smoke slides down the chimneys like black treacle. Fumes swirl and choke the older buildings into invisibility.

Our route takes us through a triumphant arch to some long-ago battle: words and symbols circle briefly above our heads and are gone. The arch is mid-way through its demolition: massive blocks are being craned down onto pony-drawn palettes.

"And when they run out of ponies they'll just use people. Same as it ever was." The driver has me in her mirror. "The greatest battle this city has ever seen. Makes the Yankees look like insects."

We are in an area of tent towns and low buildings covered in pipes. Memory snapshots: mounds of artificial limbs and battle tanks, split muzzles pointing to the sky; overturned helicopters on off-ramps. An old couple in thick anoraks waltzing in a car park. The sudden beauty of an oak tree in full and green leaf in the middle of a traffic island. Endless allotments sprouting dwarfish ingredients.

A bulldozer filling in an excavation in a field of excavations.

"They're not what you think, Victorvna Yudelvna. Most of the bodies have already been atomised. But people have got to have somewhere to go and mourn. Look. That's my house. The red one." The driver nods to a shack amongst others within the confines of a missile silo. The silo's twin doors have been welded half-open by rust. Lines of washing dangle between them. She snorts: "Laundry's buggered if someone remembers the codes."

*

And so the country:

My land. My place.

A plain runs for a hundred kilometres before softly colliding with a low range of mountains. The bus follows a river, loses it then finds it again. The bulrushes grow strongly. Plum orchards and plantations of trees for the winter festival. Co-operatives with their heavy horses; tables by the roadside with honey for sale. I want to buy one and the driver stops.

"But I have no money."

"Just show the old girl your ticket."

I do so and the wizened face gazes up with a mixture of terror and joy. I think she blesses me in the old language.

I sit on the big back seat and dip my finger in the jar as we cross an old causeway into an avenue of cypress trees; tall, undiminished. Parkland beckons: a lake, figures picnicking or doing eurythmics. A little beyond, a large villa; nearer, a running track and facilities for field sports. An open-air cinema and swimming pool.

The bus comes to a halt. I can hear girls laughing and splashing. I step down onto the unmade road and call up through sweet sticky lips. "Do I wait here for you to take me back?"

But the driver turns around and is gone, our brief connection severed.

Clever how she knew my name.

The sun plays tricks in the settling dust and I almost giggle to be out of doors. Perhaps they have some chickens here. I must have consumed half a jar of honey: the world glistens and vibrates before me.

A gasping wheeze makes me turn and Mrs Shiltsoff stands before me, her crooked shoulders level with my waist.

"Hello, Victorvna Yudelvna. Take some tea with me, will you?"

*

The leg-irons are quite modern but she's obviously in pain. The smile she favours me with is a fixed one.

We pass the crowded swimming pool: the girls are muscled and well-tanned and seem so at home in the water. There must be thousands of gallons of it. And it's so clear.

"Do you play water polo, little Victorvy?"

Ah, water polo.

"No, Mrs Shiltsoff. I'm afraid I don't even swim."

"Really? You might surprise yourself."

She moves as if to push me in. The girls wait, upward-turned faces stretched in anticipation. She reaches up and brushes something off my shoulder. "Maybe later, dear."

We manage to avoid a hail of javelins as we cross the cinder track. "Bloody little Junos. They think they're pretty tough." Her complaint is good-natured. "I bet Clarabella Veronni would love it. All the girls are so athletic."

I am unswayed. She'll have to try harder. "Is everyone a musician here?"

"Of course. They come from academies from all over the country. And a couple of the dependencies too. Recreation is important."

We reach the villa's verandah and she offers me a seat while carefully crouching herself into the waiting wheelchair. I put my honey on the table between us. I'm in a sort of gentle joyous stupor, made lazy by the sunshine and cut grass and distant friendly voices.

"Clarabella? Come here will you."

A figure undips out of the shadows, walks in short studied steps.

She stands in her black vest and running shorts; eyes turned towards the swimming pool, lank hair tied back with an elastic band.

Her neck is bandaged.

I surprise myself; my jumbled mouth actually speaks: "Long? Have you been here..?"

"No. Not long at all." Shitsop's tone is light. "Nip and get some tea and pastries, there's a good girl."

Clarabella trots into the house.

Mrs Shiltsoff smiles. "I used to be a clever girl too."

"Is Clarabella clever?" What is this mad game she's playing?

"I'm talking about you. I'm reading your thoughts. You were thinking how clever you are."

And I suppose I was, sitting there and looking out at the beautiful grounds in the less-lemon sunshine.

"But things change, Victorvy. Do you see the lake where they're doing their exercises? A meteorite crashed there a thousand years ago and wiped out all life within five hundred kilometres. The world went through a mini ice age. Growth rings from trees are very close and dense from that period – and consequently the wood from them makes the finest violins. Thank you, Clarabella Veronni."

The tall girl places a tray on our table. I search the beautiful eyes in vain. She comes around behind me and I'm aware of her hand on the back of my seat. It smells of disinfectant.

Mrs Shiltsoff pours tea and chatters while I cut the baklava.

"When I first entered the Conservatoire the tutors tried to change

me. They thought they were clever, they thought I would just give in."
She smiles with her woman-child lips. The sugar tongs drop from her
tiny fingers onto the tablecloth and she leaves them there. "I resisted and
look what happened. A seventy year heart in a toddler body. I'm getting
polio now because I didn't get it when I was younger. They tell me I
could die from meningitis at any moment. You have to do what we say.
Don't fight it, girl."

I realise my hand has unconsciously gone to my throat.

"Hah! Your own voice is perfect for your purpose, Victorvna
Yudelvna. You've got a real talent! It's only the drones and blind grubs
who need help along the way."

The wicker chair groans under Clarabella's grip.

Shitsop peers intently above my head. "Yes. Once upon a time, a
girl called Clarabella was my chief principle. A beautiful girl with a
precious musical ability. So precious. But now she's just an
accompanist. *Your* accompanist, Victorvy. Sink into change. Change
can be beautiful." Shitsop is almost radiant as she gently helps me lay
the daft little cake knife back on the table.

Presently, I take a sip from the steaming cup but I already know.

Shitsop smiles. "Oh? Does your tea taste a little odd?"

*

After the interview, I look for a piano.

I leave them together on the verandah; Clarabella has been
permitted to sit and finish off my baklava. I hope my honey helps her
throat.

I seem to have regained a little of my mood from the bus journey.
There is a wonderful warmth in the air. A golden anticipation. Soon, I
discover an empty lodge among several behind the main building.
Pyjamas in my size have been laid out on the bed. I can't wait to play.

Maybe tomorrow.

*

in the centre of the night i unsleep. no. No. in the middle of the night i
wake up. come on, vic –

Come on, Victorvy.

The dream was one of tininess, of shrinkage, of tight tree rings. Of efficiency through density. And in the dense darkness, my hair's an oily mess, my pyjamas soaked. I'd made up a bed of blankets on the lodge balcony; had fallen asleep while the summer evening was still light. I slept with swimming pool laughter.

I sleep again. I wake.

i wake. I wake and go inside to the bathroom, run water over my head and unravel my hairs from the plug hole. i sit. I sit on the loo but nothing comes. my My my image seems unclear in the mirror. i stand in a haze. i remove my spectacles and can see better without them. they are left by the basin as i ignite a hurricane lamp and carry it onto the balcony. i extinguish it. the darkness takes on a green brightness far stronger than a flame.

without thinking, i focus on the leaf of a plum tree 8.3 kilometres away. the leaf is one of eighteen million two hundred thousand and seventy-one in the whole orchard. this particular tree is besieged by a cloud of june bugs with an average wing frequency of 23.9 mhz. only one of them is a male, leaping out of my spectrum as a fiery crimson. i can smell clara Clara clarabella's disinfectant as she plays water polo in the steaming pool.

i want to play my music. in c minor.

refocusing, i see i have a new bedmate. a siamese frog is ailing on my balcony pillow. i slip under the blanket and help it onto my palm. the four eyes are wide but i realise it's too late. my senses already trace its failing cardiology and renal systems; can map the flood of carbon dioxide through the tiny bodies. but there's something else. the corpses continue to shiver: and a third frog struggles out from the ruins of its parents.

change. change can be beautiful.

with a mighty hop it is gone.

i gather my fingernails into a little pyramid and try to sleep.

*

professor gnessin picks me up three days later. I've learnt to swim and can throw a javelin like a young juno. i haven't talked with mrs shiltsoff since our tea. i may have seen clarabella holding her breath in the shallow end.

the professor puts my haversack in the boot and opens the minibus door for me. "cat got your tongue, victorvy?"

"it *is* a bit swollen, professor."

"does it still hurt?

"no. hurt went on the first day. everything feels condensed."

"good. you must start upon your exercises. erica's got the practice room ready. we've installed a heater. you'll start to feel the cold more now. nothing will get in the way of your Music."

we drive between poplars and plum orchards. i can see sun spots; the solar flares buzz. i soak up my last day in the country.

i won't be coming again.

IV

life is simple now. barely have to think. drink tea and lemonade with erica and practice. bunk has been placed in recital room. never have to leave. notes are in my body now. notes of Music. they are like blinking. sequence is natural to me. "hey, vic, you'll do," erica says. she smiles and is kind. "one more time, vic, one more time." and vic plays the sequence ten more times. c minor. g, g, g – e. f, f, f – d. easy.

*

feel good. feel better. like tea. warm enough for Music. blue woman-man smiles, says play again. i play twenty times twenty. g g g – e. f f f – d. sleep now. no. sleep now.

*

100 x 100 i play good i play same for days ggge fffd ggge fffd ggge fffd i play fight Music rah rah rah raah

V

i am in a swimming place.
  i float without pain.
  there are shadows. others.

my tongue has become detached; a thick slug suddenly huge inside my mouth. i spit it out and watch it spiral to the bottom of the big tank. a movement dashes out and grabs it; consumes my tongue, that most intimate piece of me, in great heaving swallows.

grubtown. ignore them, vic. kara hangs beside me and is beautiful. her head is grey and streamlined; microscopic air bubbles catch in her tiny auricular openings.

grubtown?

the failures. failed their studies and are now no longer fed. they scrap for what they can. you're looking good. do you mind?

kara elongates her fin and scratches at my eye. scales flicker away in the dimness like pinkish-beige paint. i remember that. why do i remember that? i blink and my eyelids slide like curtains.

battle-proof. like armour. you'll need them. come and meet the others.

we cruise over grubtown in a cloud of skin fragments.

do we play Music here?

no. kara smiles. she has no teeth. *we've been waiting for you to show us.*

*

they circle just below the surface, glorious in their diversity.

they glitter.

aja has a wonderful set of long semaphore-ready fins while dulcie and calli sport light-sensitive antennae on their mouths: they swim upside down and taste the air with their arrays.

and dear georgievna larissa, round and fat like a brown expressionless balloon; her progress dependent on the eddies of others.

but aren't you dead, georgievna?

dulcie answers, her eye telescoping down to me. *don't bother with her. she can't understand you. watch.*

she rockets down from the surface to fasten on georgievna like a lamprey. muscles ripple their way along dulcie's body as she sucks in the protein.

she feeds us. that is her purpose. aja furls her fins around georgievna and takes a large bite from the hind-quarters. *her nervous system has been dismantled. she feels nothing.*

i look into the eyes of georgievna larissa and remember her voice and how light she felt in my arms. *and the rest of the class? where are they?*

yergeniya's still outside. slow learner. the others are in grubtown. dulcie regurgitates. *never made it up here. lizan and whatshername. nor that other girl. you remember. the tall one.*

*

a plastic keyboard suckers to the side of the tank. i don't need to use it. i know the Music. i swim around it for days. i know they're watching me. kara and the others. and above the surface are the hazy walkways; an ever-moving wheelchair, keening and restless. groans from the double doors carry sharply through the water.

i try not to think of clarabella. i hover over grubtown and blank her out. but i know she must be able to see me. i take bites from georgievna and casually let them fall.

georgievna tastes like honey, her scales sweet and sugary.

*

unknown days. weeks.

dulcie and calli have left the tank for further training. aja too. kara is still here but keeps to herself; lays dummy mines on the further side of the swimming pool.

my ears drop off – it's taken longer than usual – and i am distraught. kara swims closer. her presence has a harder edge.

but without ears how can i sing my song, kara? how will i know if i sing too loud?

you've still got little holes, vic. they're cute. let me poke you.

we tread water while kara works a flipper into what's left of my ear. *you're tickling.*

some sensation then. look. you're growing wings. that's more than i've got.

she clicks her voice box.

i can still hear you, kara.

you only need ears in the air. vibrations carry much further in the water. have you done your practice today?

the waiting keyboard shimmers through refracted light.

*

unknown weeks. months?

they drop yergeniya in. she resists, tries to clamber out only to sink away to the bottom, unable to inflate her float sac. a steel hoop plunges down and stops her progress just short of grubtown.

...i resisted and look what happened...

yergeniya is dumped on a slipway, half in and out of the water. i peck at her malformed feet but soon lose interest.

*

clarabella? clarabella?

surely years have passed now.

i am squeezing georgievna's tail till it comes off, leaking viscous bones. i chew and regurgitate georgievna into grubtown.

clarabella. i love you.

decades later, there is nothing left but georgievna's eyes, unblinking pale marbles suspended midway between bottom and surface, slaves to neutral buoyancy.

clarabella.

yes.

georgievna's eyes hang between us. clarabella gently slides them aside. she is still slender, a freckly white salamander all multi-lidded blue-grey eyes and gliding vanes. i let her lick my lips like i wanted her to lick the honey from them. she sucks every milligram of nutrient.

we settle at the keyboard together, select c minor, play the eight letter sequence and are immediately summoned to the surface.

principle and accompanist.

VI

i'm ready for the drop. the blower's belly hatch is open. battlefield fog scuds below us. clarabella is in a cradle beside me, breathes hard through external gills. our co-ordinates are presently unknown, will be fed through sensors when we enter fight Music. the territory below remains classified. clarabella prepares to freeze herself for the drop. from 7000 metres, we will plummet through the crust above the long-drained artesian wells of a secret city, our vanes spinning us into the crystallised soil ten metres below the surface. as night seeps over the war zone, our bodies will reactivate their bloodstreams to dowse us in the chemicals that will warm our brains into wakefulness. we will unscrew ourselves from the soil and continue in hibernation for a further fortnight as our wings – which would not have survived the freezing process – mature inside their chalky membranes. and inside me the bomb will grow.

*

i wake and clarabella has gone. she has struggled up through the topsoil and i follow her tunnel to the surface. lemon sky, smoke grey. i crouch in a crater, allow my wings to dry too quickly. i snatch a frog and eat it. its still wriggling body nudges the thermobaric weapon inside me. i am ready and beacon gnessin to boot fight Music. she is angry. i have failed to discipline my accompanist. gnessin's system start-up is jagged. my vision whites-out and the Music has me

*

fight Music | thermal glide + vic glides too | rise 3 km in 2 min | enemy airshot + girders from satellite platforms | swerve beneath barrage line | breathe hard | try to keep larynxes at 97.2 like gnes has told vic | smoke spiral change to fog as firestorm vacuum drags flames 1/2 way round planet | hope clar has bead on enemy fireships | diversion far below | liz + yerg | zip over tank traps | contrails like icicles | yerg resists fight Music | vic concern | vic dip | dip again | wings well-angled | leading edge air flow sparks w/electricity | create radar-absorbing plasma pulse | sing w/joy + run through scales | rah rah rah raah | hot air rises up to meet vic | vic invisible | sensors from below | yerg loses head to pylons | liz flies on | knows voice not hers + probably won't sync | tracer lacerates stabiliser + vic drops 500 m | re-triangulate | comsat off-line | request clar support | static only | smell river | turn w | wsw | w into sunset | lemon sun | vic reaches line | drop to 30 | 20 | 10 m | wings retract | sacrifice front legs to razor wire | shit say vic don't resist | engorge float sacs w/battle gas + slide across mud | flooded slit trench |

vic cough cough | sonar bursts into life | fills vic's mind w/1000 echoes | trench bottom | bones + shrapnel | loam + leeches | beyond walls vic senses dugouts | see/sense soldiers as they rush w/stethoscopes to track vic's progress | brightness | clar must have hit main magazine | cordite stings eyes | 2 frogmen wait | wear plastic egg box-suits to confuse vic's sonar | they are stealthy defenders | arm w/yank's last + finest weapon | gnes warn vic | they have devil in a bottle | wave it in front of vic | taunt vic | laugh at vic's nakedness | vic laugh back + sing | laugh + sing fight Music as vic's tail thrashes + turns their bones to rubber | sewer pipe | vic slip through | coil bone structure | stretch spleen | float sacs | fart battle gas | clar is behind | clar has found vic | vic feel clar's bead on vic's back | feel good so good | co-ordinates come through for final assault | feel bead on back red hot | clar sings private transmission uses abort codes | battle won vic | battle over | vic sings back | battle on clar | objective not satisfied | bead is hotter hot hot |

*

force-quit fight Music. clarabella's weapons have fragmented my left shoulder; i sense a re-phasing of microwaves for a headshot. reaching a sewerage sub-station, i haul myself up; unzip and activate my morphine gland. a glow beneath the water; i duck and fold as a force beam slices out and liquefies the metal cylinders behind me. morphine tickles my throat. i slide back in but clarabella has already gone up the pipe. she leads. the principle. i scrape my shiny hide through the last 200 metres as professor gnessin re-connects, force boots fight Music

*

confirm vic | confirm | 200 | 150 | 100 | 50 m | switch throat to manual | cough | cough | 15 secs | confirm vic | civil grid ref 962110 k/kaya 48 | through toilet cistern | diphtheria + dead chickens | slip around door + clar is there with rotor weapons | pieces missing from my side | my beautiful tail | clar has man | protects man | kill him clar | kill men | activate fuel atomiser prior to detonation | G | G | G | fail |

*

clarabella has me on the floor, pins me, pummels my broken body. the little children scream, their father tries to wrench away the blast pack. but i have the fight Music. my purpose. my focus. i stand and flex and they drop from me like the leaves of a plum tree

*

vic will win | Music's in my head | my throat sings the fight Music pitch perfect | beethoven 5th | rah rah rah raah | G | G | G | E | fuel atomiser activated | ethylene oxide fills church | prepare 2ndry charge in head | ready for deflagration | 300 psi | 300°c | 3 km/s blast | beethoven 5th | morse v for victory | i am victory | i am victorvna yudelvna + i sing fight Music | Music is part of me | F | F | F | D | rah rah rah raah | my focus | chicken girl crawl up into hole | vic die now

Half Magic

Lene Lovich

Dust. In the silence, the particles rotate, floating on a phantom breeze. A wide channel of sunlight cuts through a guarded window. The dust falls. It falls on the madman and me. Suddenly, there is an itch beneath my faded red coat. My skin burns and the unseen rope around my neck pulls me forward. I am tied to the madman, I go where he goes.

Baptised in the dust, we enter the holy place. It is unnaturally quiet and cold. As we move across the floor I trace the delicate marble veins with my hard shoes. We walk on, towards a mighty altar in the centre of the room where a grey woman stands. Our echoing steps disturb the others who sit in the stillness. They look pale and weak against the towering shelves filled with books. I blink twice. They won't help me.

The grey woman knows we are here, but continues her search through a long wooden box. The madman fixes his eyes on her. His thin lips distort and I feel a terrible power rising. The demon inside him inflates his chest, his powerful arms thicken. "Where are the Christian myths," he bellows.

The grey woman raises an eyebrow, but otherwise remains unmoved. She points to a separate section on the other side of the room. "Myths, legends, devotional texts and comparative religious studies – on the left," she replies.

He growls. His eyes dart to the left and back again. Soon the room will fill with raging curses and things will get broken, or worse. Nothing happens.

The grey woman looks down at me. "The children's section is over there," she says kindly.

My father is now on the other side of the room. At once, I feel the rope loosen. The woman smiles. She extends her hand, encouraging me to accept her direction. For a moment I remain still, then I rush to the low shelves. My fingers touch the books. They feel good. I scan page after page, hunting for images, my reading skills being rather poor. There are strange and beautiful worlds here: *Alice in Wonderland*, *Grimm's Fairy Tales*, *The Water Babies* and more...

For years, my imperfect mind struggled with the words. Nobody understood my uncontrollable urge to do everything backwards. In time, with a lot of effort, I learned how to concentrate, though it was a while before I was able to finish a whole book: *Half Magic*, by Edward Eager. Now, I write songs. I sing about the things I see in my head and my problems with communicating and other things too. Reading about strange happenings and unusual characters has always made me feel better. I am not alone.

Everybody needs a refuge from the ordinary
Everybody needs to breathe
It's a necessary dip into the unknown ocean
It's essential fantasy

Excerpt from *Gothica*, by Lene Lovich, from the album *Shadows and Dust* (Stereosociety.com)

First and Last and Always

Emma Lee

I have a map inside my head. A map of either brilliant or first-and-only versions of various songs. It starts: Hamburg *Sister Ray*, Newcastle *Nine While Nine*, Blackburn *Stairway to Heaven*, Wembley *Temple of Love*, Brixton Academy *Ribbons*... OK, I'll be the first to admit I'm a fanatic. How many other people would seriously get up at ridiculous hours on weekends to wear out shoe leather around record fairs in search of that unique piece of memorabilia, that limited edition format? I had a knack: visiting a different town I invariably found a new fair to visit. Perhaps obsessive is nearer the word.

Ironically I'm not even old enough to have heard the earlier songs live. Let's face it, I was eight years old when Andrew Eldritch formed the original Sisters of Mercy line-up and recorded the first single *Damage Done*.

It's Dad's fault really. I'd bounced out of bed on my tenth birthday and scurried downstairs, probably making enough noise to wake the neighbours as I never was light-footed. There was nothing downstairs to even suggest it was my birthday: no cards left at my place at the table, no presents piled in the lounge. I poured cereal into a bowl, added milk and ate, thinking that maybe the postman would have come by the time I'd finished.

He hadn't. So I slunk back upstairs and into the record room. Strictly it was the spare bedroom but Dad had put up customised shelving and stored his jazz records there. I was only allowed to touch records in certain sections: bog standard releases of Ella Fitzgerald's songs. The others only Dad handled, holding them with reverence as if offering a prayer before placing them on the turntable as if they were as fragile as one of Mum's glass ornaments. I didn't feel like playing anything.

"Well, there's the birthday girl, then!"

Dad's voice had startled me.

"Come on!"

That's how I always remember him: his tall, thin frame half-turned in the doorway, ready to race me back to my room. Sun from the landing window picking out the flecks of grey in his dark hair, but the grin on his face made him look like a boy eager to share in opening my presents.

He was irresistible. I got up and raced to my room, narrowly beating him and skidding to a stop just in front of a huge box of wrapping paper. I ripped it off. Dad sat on his hands to stop himself helping me. I knew it was a cabinet for a stereo as soon as I got a glimpse of the mahogany veneer covered chipboard underneath the paper. I also knew the cabinet wouldn't be empty. A proper grown-up's stereo instead of the ghetto blasters I'd had so far.

I flung my arms around Dad, "Thank you!"

He couldn't stop grinning.

He never saw my twelfth birthday.

Small wonder then I was subsequently attracted to the black cover with a red mock-snakeskin streak with the band's name and album title, *First and Last and Always*. I bought it then played it to death. Then discovered there was a limited edition gatefold version, plus a Japanese import...

I get mocked. I go out and someone, usually male, will eventually comment, "You don't like *them* do you?", leaving me wondering why I'd bother wasting money on a tee shirt of a band I didn't like. I guess at gigs I'm too busy checking out the merchandise or pushing my way down to the front of the stage to take much notice of anyone in the audience. And at record fairs, well, if it's not vinyl...

As Brixton Academy had been fogged in dry ice, I felt disorientated coming out into the normal people and traffic fumes of London. Even so I noticed him immediately: slender frame, naturally dark hair, pale complexion and clear blue eyes looking perplexed at a flat tyre. I offered to help. He surprised I'd want to risk breaking a nail. But I'd learnt to drive as soon as I could and it was no use ringing Mum if I'd got a flat – she would not have risked a broken nail – so I'd soon learnt basic car maintenance. He offered me a lift home and wrote his name, Oliver, and phone number on a piece of paper and joked about not letting me out of the car until I gave him mine. I doubted I'd hear from him again. Although he was the first fan who didn't compare me with Morticia Addams. I guess my long, dark hair and dark eyes invite the comparison, but it gets tedious. I also shared her alleged vital statistics, 36-26-36, something else most men eyed up. It wasn't until I'd closed my door behind me that I heard him drive off.

Oliver invited me for a drink. We went clubbing afterwards and he insisted on driving me home. He hadn't drunk alcohol and I'd only had a couple so it felt safe. We chatted about music, discovering we shared tastes. He was a student too, final year of business studies. He'd frowned a bit when I said mechanical engineering, muttering something about not being very practical. I reassured him it didn't matter. He slipped his arm around my shoulders and I leaned into him, grateful that here was someone I could talk to, who seemed to see beyond the vital statistics.

We saw each other a few more times before I invited Oliver in for coffee. He admired my record collection. So I started talking about them, where I'd picked up various rarities, what I thought of the live recordings. Oliver stopped me for a kiss. Light years away from his spacious flat, he expressed surprise that a thin mattress spread across two wooden pallets in my tiny bedsit could actually be comfortable.

We kissed again. I tasted breath freshening mint, smelt a subtle lingering of aftershave, hair gel and newly-laundered clothes with a faint overlayer of dry ice, cigarette smoke and damp air. He complimented my outfit: a long, black jersey dress, the leather jacket having been left on the threadbare but clean floor. He'd declined coffee, an unsurprising decision in hindsight, so I wasn't sure what to do.

He put *First and Last and Always* on my record player and laid me down on my bed. I undid his shirt, kissing exposed flesh and sliding his belt undone. He responded in kind, undressing me slowly. Our love-making gentle, satisfying. He lay still for ages with me curled up, legs entwined, arms around each other, with his eyes closed afterwards.

When he opened them, I moved away, assuming he'd get up and go.

"Could I stay?" he asked.

"'Course," I said softly.

"You sound surprised."

"I thought you'd go." I moved back.

"Where? Back to an empty apartment when I could stay here with you?"

"Well, if you put it like that..."

He grinned and kissed me. "You're so uncomplicated. And that's a compliment."

Waking up inspired a reprise of last night's performance. Sunlight filtered in through the thin curtains, making the room less dingy.

"Breakfast?" I asked hesitantly.

He smiled. "Back to mine. We'll shower and I'll get you breakfast."

He slid his clothes back on while I got a pair of black jeans and a black shirt off the rail and dug out fresh underwear from a small chest.

Oliver was still smiling when we got back to his car. Naively I was wondering what kind of student lived in an apartment block with underground car-parking when the carpeted elevator – it was too smart to be called a lift – stopped at one of the upper floors. The plants in the pots that were spaced at intervals along the corridor were real. I was thinking back to my bedsit: wide enough for a single bed, desk and clothing rail with just enough space for my stereo cabinet and stacks of record boxes.

Oliver opened the door. I pinched myself. I was looking into a loft-style apartment with exposed brick, decorative timber beams and a wall of windows hidden by thick, pale green drapes. I liked the drapes: it would have felt horribly exposed without them drawn.

Oliver grabbed my hand and pulled me in. I couldn't help staring at his top of the range stereo and the shelves of records next to it. His record collection may not have been as impressive, but I looked at him again, sure my eyes had been as wide as seven inch singles.

His lips covered mine and I responded to his kiss, letting it blot out the generously proportioned lounge, the thick oatmeal-coloured carpet, the chocolate brown sofa and armchairs that weren't faux leather, the large antique desk in front of the windows and the TV set that looked more like a cinema screen.

"You're hesitating."

I wanted to run away. If Oliver wasn't holding my hand, I would have done.

"Don't. I could buy you a diamond-encrusted dress and it would be loose change. Don't let it intimidate you. You're here because I want you to be. Not because I'm showing off or want to slum it for a while with a poor little girl. It's really not like that. I can't help who am I."

I let go of his hand and walked over to the desk, then around the sofa and up to the TV. I couldn't bring myself to touch any of it. I returned to Oliver.

He held me in his arms. "Please don't go."

"It's not what I thought. But if you had all this, why did you stay at mine last night?"

"Because I wanted to see who you were. I wanted you to see me before you saw all this. I wanted... I want us to connect as two individuals. I want us not to be about money. Sure, it buys you things, it makes life more luxurious, but it complicates things. You can't be sure people hang around because of you or because of what you can shower them with." He kissed my forehead. "Shower. We were going to shower and have breakfast."

The bathroom was three times the size of my bedsit. Showering took at least twice as long, involving lots of kissing and caressing. He preferred holding me close, his arms behind me, stroking my back. It wasn't until he picked up a towel that I noticed. Along the inside of his left arm was a long scar that ran from his wrist to his elbow. I reached out and traced it with my finger.

He looked alarmed then quickly looked down, letting his fringe fall over his face. 'An old scar,' was said in such a way it was clear he didn't want me to ask anymore about it.

"Must have been a deep cut," having opened my mouth to ask how he'd done it, I had to say something to cover myself.

"It was."

I quickly dressed and dragged a brush through my hair as Oliver went to his bedroom to get dressed. I took the opportunity to study his record collection. He had the standard releases, the imports and the official limited editions, but not the bootlegs and live recordings.

"Records again," he grinned, returning in a clean pair of jeans, ironed shirt and with his hair gelled into place.

I felt scruffy. "You don't mind?"

"Be my guest. Let's get breakfast." He put his jacket on. I must have looked baffled because he chided, "If you can tear yourself away..."

I slipped my jacket back on. Breakfast, it turned out, was bought at a nearby coffee shop: skinny lattes and Danish pastries.

"I have to be at the record shop in half an hour," I said.

He frowned.

"I work there."

"Sorry. I'm being dim, aren't I? I should've known."

I shrugged. "No. Just a different planet, that's all."

"I do want to see you again."

"If you don't mind me asking, where does the money come from? You're a student, with no job, after all."

Oliver sighed. "My father's a financier. Worth... well... He bought the apartment to put me in while I studied. He tops up my bank account regularly. I'm under pressure to follow suit. I don't think it's me."

"What would you prefer to do?"

Oliver shrugged. "That's the complicated part. I don't really know." He fiddled with a spoon, turning it over and over in his hand.

I let it go. "I'd like to get re-acquainted with your records."

"OK." He grinned. "Pick you up tonight. I'll take you to dinner."

Of course, after that, we always went back to his flat. I ended up moving in: meant the money from my part-time job in a record store didn't have to go on rent. Kept my records separate from Oliver's, to start with. I think I did intend to merge them eventually, but Oliver's had no logical order. He just pulled out the records he wanted to play and left them propped by the side of the stereo until he got fed up and simply stacked the records with the others at random. If he wanted to play a certain song, he'd spend ages looking for it.

One morning he proudly presented me with a round of unburnt toast. "I think I'm learning." He was wearing the chef's apron I'd bought him and still had his sleeves rolled up.

"You're doing well," I said, joining him at the breakfast bar.

"I love learning all this stuff you just do. You're very patient with me."

I shrugged. "I'm surprised you tolerate me, sometimes."

"I want to learn. I hate that I don't know how to do what to you are very simple things."

"I'm happy to show you."

"I don't want to shower you with money," began Oliver. "Well, I do. But you'd be uncomfortable and I don't want to make you uncomfortable."

"I wouldn't let you. It's nice to be able to relax a bit, occasionally buy a luxury brand instead of the supermarket's own without worrying about the impact on your budget. But if you flooded me with it, I wouldn't know what to do with it."

"I love that in you."

I smiled and leant against him.

He kissed me. "You're still keeping up your job?"

I nodded. "I actually enjoy it. You're always going to get the odd awkward customer, but I get to hear about all the latest releases, latest on tour dates and gossip before things go on sale. I'd miss all that. And it's great when you're able to advise customers about other bands they'll like based on the music they're buying or finding a hard to find record. That's really rewarding."

Oliver was looking at me as if this were really fascinating news. "I'll see you later." He kissed me. "I miss you. When you're here, I don't notice how empty this place feels. That's what struck me about your old place, it seemed so full and not because it was so small either. It felt as if it were part of you. This place is never going to feel part of me."

My 'well, move then' went unsaid. I'd learnt things were never that simple with Oliver. The apartment was in his father's name so Oliver couldn't sell it. Although that didn't necessarily stop him renting somewhere else, it seemed a waste of money to do so. At least, it did from my point of view. I never asked Oliver about money, merely trusted it was more than I could dream of. I kissed him instead of replying.

"I love you."

I froze.

"I do. You're so sweet and uncomplicated and beautiful and you never make a big deal of anything." He kissed me. "Oh, I know, you're not ready to say it. But I really do." His eyes shone, child-like in his enthusiasm. "I'll get a take-away tonight."

"Thought you were supposed to be learning..."

"Then there'll be no washing up and I can have you to myself for longer." He finally began to roll his sleeves back down.

"You're too much of a temptation. I've a deadline looming." I reached out and touched his scar. "How did it happen?"

"You won't believe me." He looked away from me.

"Try me. You know I won't tell anyone else."

"I know. It's not that. It's difficult to explain. I did it myself."

"How?"

"I... I... was about fifteen and had gone to the kitchen. Can't remember why. But the cook had left a knife lying on one of the work surfaces. I picked it up, put my arm in water. The water was cold, my arm started to go numb. I cut. You won't understand, but it felt good. So I cut again. I don't know how long it took. But cook came back in, saw the reddened water, saw the knife, pulled my arm and knife out of the water. I felt faint, I remember that much. Someone must have called a doctor... It was dark when I came round. I was in bed, but still had my clothes on. Cook begged me not to tell my parents what had actually happened." Oliver shrugged. "I never did. They never knew. When they saw the scar eventually I told them I'd been walking, felt myself fall and caught my arm on something to break my fall. They swallowed it. Stupid, wasn't it?"

I intertwined my fingers with his. "It was a good job the cook found you."

Oliver didn't answer.

"Have you ever been tempted to do something like that again?"

He tried to pull his hand away.

"Oliver," I began, softly. "You've just told me you love me. Was this a one-off?"

"You know me. You've not found any other scars." His tone was dismissive.

I pulled his hand to my lips and kissed it.

When he looked at me again, his eyes were bright with tears. "I wish... No, you're so sweet. I couldn't put you through something like that. You're not going to find me cutting myself, I promise."

I didn't have anything to say, but kept hold of his hand.

Eventually, Oliver broke the silence, "Tonight, we'll take a break then tomorrow morning, we'll work. You have the desk, I'll have the sofa and we'll see who finishes first."

"First one to finish cooks dinner," I said.

"So, if I win, we'll go out."

"How does that give me an incentive to finish my assignment, then?"

Oliver thought. "If you finish first, I'll include dessert. If I finish first, no dessert."

"OK. You're getting to know me too well."

"I want to. You never talk about your parents."

"You just complain about yours."

Oliver shrugged. "They were distant. Everything could be solved with money. If that didn't work, more money would. You were closer to yours."

"Mum got a bit distant after Dad died. I was always closer to Dad. We both loved music. Oliver, I really must go. I don't want to be late."

"OK. One more kiss."

I looked up at him.

"It's got to last all day. I'm not going to see you until tonight."

"You're amazing," he groaned softly. A cancelled lecture had turned into a lazy morning in bed making love.

"You're wonderful," I responded. The chorus of *Some Kind of Stranger*, which I'd adopted as our song, was running through my head. Gary Marx had intended it as his version of *The Wedding March*. Andrew Eldritch corrupted it into a celebration of casual sex. The resulting tension polished it into a brilliant song, although the ambiguity remained. I preferred Gary Marx's intention.

Oliver kissed me.

I rested my head on his shoulder, turning onto my side so I could curl against him. Despite the warmth of our loving, Oliver felt chilly. I pulled the quilt over us.

"Dad loved that sculpture you made."

Sculpture? "Oh, it wasn't much." I remembered now. I'd found some bits of scrap metal, used them for welding practise then brought it back to Oliver's flat, not sure what to do with it but determined the other students weren't going to see it. I'd heard the panic in Oliver's voice as he'd realised he had less than a week until his Dad's birthday. Oliver saw the welded pieces and said it would be perfect if it weren't so dirty. I'd cleaned and polished it. Oliver had called it a 'sculpture', way too grand a word for what it actually was.

"You don't understand."

True, I didn't understand. "He liked it. I'll do a different one next year if we can't find something else," I tried to sound reassuring.

"Another one won't do. It has to be something different. But it's so difficult. What do you get a man who has everything?" he groaned.

I nuzzled his neck.

"You don't..."

"Stop torturing yourself," I interrupted, keeping my voice as gentle as possible.

Oliver looked at me then. I saw the tears in his eyes. I pushed his hair away from his forehead and kissed it. "I feel trapped. I hate it. I don't have to work but I want to. I try and be careful with money, but Dad bails me out anyway. I ask Mum to tell him to stop putting money in my account but she won't. How am I going to stand on my own two feet?"

"You are," I murmured.

"Not like you do."

"I don't have a choice. There's no one to bail me out. But you don't ask him to do this. He doesn't give you money because you need it. You are standing on your own two feet." I propped myself up so I could look down at him.

"You're so sweet," he said. "I want to cut adrift. Just you and me." He tilted his face up and I thought he'd kiss me. He closed his eyes. "But it's just a dream."

"It's not. We could do it."

"My little catalyst." He pulled his lips close together, making his mouth appear as a straight line. "What would I do?"

'What do you want to do?' seemed the obvious question, but I knew Oliver didn't know. "You design, I sculpt."

I was rewarded with a small smile. "But I couldn't..."

"You could run the finances for our own company. Find a small shop with room at the back for a studio. We could do mirror frames, candelabrum, ornaments..." I could picture it: mirror frames at the back of the window display with ornamental iron sculptures near the front, me welding something or other in the back studio and Oliver learning when to remain behind the counter to allow browsers to feel welcome and when to encourage a sale.

"But I wouldn't be much use. I'd just be hanging around, getting in your way."

"You wouldn't. You have to give it a go. You strangle everything before it's even been conceived." I kissed him, aroused him again. It was the only thing I could think of doing.

"Remember what you promised," I reminded Oliver as he paid the admission to the record fair.

"OK," he nodded. He took my hand as we turned into the actual fair. "Don't buy you anything without your agreement. I think there are just some things that I'm going to accept I can't understand."

"But if you buy me everything I want, you take away the thrill of tracking down something and the agonising over whether I can afford it. That's the whole point of collecting: those kind of decisions. If I could just buy it, it wouldn't seem so rare."

He shrugged. "Where do we start?"

The sports hall was two basketball fields wide and littered with trestle tables covered in record boxes. Some vendors had put up displays behind them to entice potential buyers. Most were collectors, selling off parts of their collections they no longer wanted or selling records they'd deliberately bought to make a profit on to use to buy the records they really wanted. A couple of stalls were staffed by second hand record shops, displaying their rarer wares in the hope of getting a slightly higher price.

I pointed at the first trestle table, "What do you see?"

"No display. No band names. Just alphabet labels. Nothing worth looking at. Let's try that one," he pointed further along. "It's sectioned by music type and he's got a decent 'alternative' selection," he whispered in my ear.

I raised an eyebrow: he must have been listening last night when I tried to explain how to look for rarities and how to tell a decent live recording from a duff one, without listening to the record. "Have a look then," I suggested. "I'm going to start in the other direction and we'll meet half-way. Don't buy anything yet. We'll compare notes when we meet again."

"OK."

I left Oliver gently flicking through the records. I already knew which stalls were the only ones worth bothering with, but lingered and browsed at a few others so that Oliver had time to look. I'd found an American import of a single complete with accompanying DJ notes.

Oliver looked as excited as a child in a sweet shop. "Found a couple of things," he said. "Get you a coffee first."

The sports centre's café was actually shut, but enterprising record fair organisers had set up an urn and were offering polystyrene cups of coffee with a complimentary plain digestive biscuit. Oliver was enchanted even though the coffee was no more than hot sludge and the digestives as bland as sawdust.

"What have you seen then?" I asked.

"It looks like an import compilation of the early singles. Black cover, red logo and lettering."

I nodded. "I've seen one too. It's genuine: a Greek import." I'd also heard that some of these imports were unplayable.

"This one wasn't warped. I did it: took it out of its sleeve, holding the edge against my thumb and resting the hole on my forefinger and held it up. Saw a black line."

I nodded again. The one he'd found sounded in better condition than mine.

"Saw a *Damage Done* single too."

Probably a copy, I thought.

"I wasn't sure, so I left it."

"Only three hundred and fifty were made originally and if one comes into circulation, vendors will keep them for special customers. The import's worth another, serious look." I kept my tone flat, but knew Oliver could see the excitement in my eyes.

"I think I'm getting the buzz you seem to get. Thank you for sharing this." He slid his arm around me and kissed me. He tasted of sludge and sawdust, but I didn't want this kiss to end.

We bought the Greek import Oliver found: his was in better condition than the one I'd seen and it turned out to be playable, plus the American import I'd seen. That night I cooked a hotpot and was laying the dishes out on the table when I noticed a single propped against a vase of lilies.

Not just any single, but *Damage Done*. My heart sank, how was I going to explain it was just a copy and I already had a mere copy?

"Check it out," said Oliver, grinning.

I picked it up and slid the single out, keeping it horizontal. "No warping," I commented, trying to delay the moment. It was a good copy, I thought as I turned it vertical. Then my jaw dropped. "The real thing! Thank you!" I managed to return the single to the safety of its sleeve before hugging and kissing Oliver.

"I thought you might be angry. But I knew how much it would mean to you. I wasn't sure at first. But then remembered what you said about the run-off. It's the right one, isn't it?"

"Yes," I grinned.

"Now I really do get the buzz you get out of these things."

I was clearing dinner plates, putting them in hot, soapy water. I heard Oliver come out to the kitchen and stand behind me, that close I could feel his breath glide over my hair. If I tilted my head back it would rest on his shoulder.

"Could you contemplate spending the rest of your life with me?" his voice was just above a whisper.

"Yes."

He turned me around to face him. "You really mean it." He kissed me, running his tongue over my bottom lip until I parted my lips for him. "When you graduate, we'll do it. Leave, just the two of us. Cast ourselves adrift. You can teach me all those practical things you do so naturally and I've been taught I only have to pay someone to do. And it'll be just the two of us. I've got something for you."

His expression reminded me of Dad's on my tenth birthday: someone receiving so much joy from giving something they know to be so right. I followed Oliver back into the lounge. He knelt on one knee and held up a small box.

It took several moments before I got the significance. "Engaged?"

He grinned. I wanted to pull him up and kiss him. But he opened the box and pushed it closer to my face. A plain white-gold band with a ruby that was twenty-five millimetres in diameter.

"It's beautiful," I breathed. I couldn't put it on.

Oliver took it out of the box, dropped the box to the floor and slid it on my finger. "I want to show this is real, not just some affair that I'll cast off when I graduate."

His eyes were brighter than the ruby. I placed my ringed hand over his heart. His hand covered mine. I remembered thinking how alive he seemed.

I hurried to the flat, mind already celebrating the end of lectures – at least until Monday – and spinning with the possibilities the weekend offered. Clumsily I opened the door and stopped.

I tugged the door closed and retched. Thankfully my stomach was too empty to bring anything up. My heart raced. I didn't think I'd ever catch up with it, let alone steady it again. But I had to do something.

I inched the door open, turned my back and, crab-like, sidled to the phone. It took several goes before my shaking fingers could manage to stab three nines slowly enough for the dialling system to actually dial.

What service did I want? My mind blanked. I saw a picture: white van-size vehicle with blue flashing lights. "A-am-ambulance," I stuttered the address, our address.

The voice on the other end was calm, reassuring even. I put the phone down and awkwardly crabbed back out, putting the door on the latch as I went.

Then my knees gave way. I huddled in the corridor, head buried in my knees, arms across my forehead. But the more you want to forget something, the more your mind's eye repeats it.

His feet didn't touch the floor. I hadn't wanted to look up, but I did anyway. He'd tied a rope from one of the beams and kicked the chair away.

Tears finally came.

The police were sympathetic. His family gave me a month to move out and asked for Oliver's ring back. I don't think I'd have kept it anyway. Most of that month I spent in the apartment, drifting from bed to sofa to bed again, dazed. A splinter of me knew I had to leave but the rest of me didn't want to. I didn't know a person could cry that much.

I told my Mum that Oliver and I had split. I didn't want the worry of her worrying about me, although it felt mean lying.

I needed another gig on my map. *Under the Gun* wormed its way into my head.

It took me three months to take the hint, having found a bedsit not unlike the one I'd left to move in with Oliver, and buried myself in studies.

The Gun Club had recently opened as a night club venue hosting mainly unsigned bands but one of the music papers had started sending along reviewers and in their wake would be A & R scouts.

It started as a friendship. Violet Kiss were support slot regulars: if a signed band didn't have a support act or a support act dropped out, Violet Kiss took their place. Their vocalist Ciaran bought me a drink after their slot. It became a habit. He knew I wasn't interested. I'd blamed a bad split. Logically I knew Oliver's death wasn't my fault, but that didn't stop me feeling guilty.

It was ages before Ciaran wore me down enough to agree to a date. Our first date was another gig and club afterwards. Surprisingly I remembered how to dance. Ciaran walked me home but I failed to invite him in for coffee, avoiding that whole 'should I let him stay or make him go, what if he drinks tea rather than coffee' scenario. It didn't put him off.

Physically Ciaran was like Oliver: tall and thin but Ciaran had dark eyes and let his hair creep past his shoulders, tied back during the day but allowed loose on stage. Oliver had kept his short and spiky.
Ciaran was talented: on stage he had a self-confident swagger that made glib, insincere lyrics drip with gut-wrenching emotion. Offstage he was full of ideas and lists of contacts. Basically Ciaran was Violet Kiss: he wrote all the lyrics, told the others what to play and decided which venues would be played, which record companies or journalists got sent demos and whether any resulting enquiries were worth following up. Ciaran shot for the stars but aimed for cult status: making enough to make the next album was realistic. I was intrigued by the idea of having a limited edition release of every single, every album.

Eventually I moved in with him: that old why are we playing two lots of rent logic. My final year at university and Ciaran was officially unemployed, since being even in a regularly gigging band didn't count as a job, and frequently managed to excuse himself from various job creation schemes. He had a flat above a corner shop which Jay, who did shift work in a care home, shared. However, friends and people who vaguely knew Jay or Ciaran kind of drifted in and out.

I thought I knew what I was doing. Well, you do when your friends think it a great idea and your Mum's the only one who disapproves. I cleared out the cupboard under the stairs, fitted it with a lock and kept my records in there, only taking them out to play and putting them straight back.

I crammed my clothes and books into the single wardrobe and learnt to love watching the stars through the glass ceiling of the skylight, stuck in the attic on the second floor. Jay slept on the sofa in the lounge on the first floor. The first floor also housed a bathroom and a kitchen that looked like a bomb site. I quickly learnt to avoid the sticky patches on the floor, to prepare food on a plate and periodically squirt disinfectant over the crumb and grease-layered work surfaces. The fridge, however, was always kept clean. The temperamental gas cooker had a permanent saucepan of Jay's bean and curry powder concoction usually eaten with over-boiled rice. Plus an eye-level grill that once caught my hair. It was at that point that I started having cereal instead of toast for breakfast.

Not only did every new song get dedicated to me, they were also about me. It was a great ego-boost at first: watching a song grow from scribbled notes on a scrap of paper to a full-blown live piece that an audience cheered for. Slowly, though, perhaps too slowly, I came to realise that my life wasn't my own anymore. Dead celebrities at least get to leave diaries or letters to show their side of things and generally biographers put their lives in context with their times. But I only ever lived through Ciaran's songs.

We began to have an agreement. I studied and worked part-time so that Ciaran would have time to compose songs. Ciaran had started to send out demos to A & R departments in an earnest but haphazard manner. The music press were beginning to review Violet Kiss gigs. It seemed a matter of time before Ciaran would be offered a contract. It seemed worth the hassle of trying to be polite to snotty-nosed shoppers when not studying and somehow still finding the energy to cook and attempt to clean instead of crashing straight into bed when I got home.

At least until one Wednesday morning at four o'clock when I was woken by a dog barking. It turned out Jay had brought a couple of friends back and the dog was unsettled by my presence. Never mind how unsettled I felt at being told I didn't belong in my home by a dog, even if it was an allegedly friendly rottweiler. I insisted the dog be tied up outside.

Little did I know that at the next gig, Ciaran was to proudly announce a 'new song'. I didn't pay much attention at first but caught the chorus:

Friends brought a dog home yesterday
An old softie, a former stray
He'd only wanted to play
But you insisted outside he stay
He whimpered, howled, wanted a way
Back inside where it was warm and dry
But you held firm, wouldn't sway.

The next verse described the dog's pitiful repertoire of howls. Not one mention of my getting up in the small hours and encountering a strange rottweiler on the stairs.

After graduating I got a job in an engineering company, sizing heating systems and providing technical quotations.

I always knew when Ciaran was composing. There'd be twice as many bottles of beer in the fridge. Then he'd start pacing the lounge frowning and tapping his finger against his lips. This is when I started wearing ear plugs.

Two days of pacing and he'd introduce a random 'I feel confined, I can't concentrate' shout.

On the fourth day, Ciaran would get the sporadic need to play a song, usually at full volume, for inspiration. Of course, inspiration doesn't work nine till five, but, in Ciaran's case anyway, between midnight and two in the morning. I found myself doing the odd line of amphetamines when the hours of inspiration extended until six in the morning.

After a couple of weeks, paper mountains would begin to appear. These I crept round. But, no matter how carefully I crept, he would invariably accuse me of disturbing one. Usually the one buried under two inches of dust, although I apologised anyway. In a rare interview, Ciaran complained that his useless girlfriend was such a hindrance when he tried to write. He didn't answer when the music journalist asked why he didn't just leave her.

For some reason I'd begun moving my records back to my Mum's. Something was telling me they weren't safe under the stairs anymore. Mum complained she'd only just got rid of Dad's records and now mine were hogging the record room. I promised it was temporary.

Rehearsals didn't offer any let up. I usually came home to an empty flat, cleared of food, except Jay's bean and curry powder concoction and nothing to say when Ciaran planned to be back. This was when I discovered Jay's concoction didn't actually taste too bad. Rehearsal room rent and band expenses ate my wages and his benefit payments. Since he'd already suggested I increase my hours or get another job, I still worked at the record shop on Saturdays, I knew raising the idea of Ciaran getting a part-time job was wasted.

Jay was on a sleep-in shift at the care home. The house was empty. Our anniversary, I had to count on my fingers, our ninth anniversary. Of course Ciaran was rehearsing. I packed my clothes into my bag.

I found a demo-tape, put it in the stereo and pressed play. Against a background of familiar guitar riffs came Ciaran's vocals.

She had heroin-chic
My girl
Skin so pale
It would bruise to touch
Like a delicate fruit
I could play xylophone
On her rib bones
Such a pity
She used to be so pretty
She had heroin-chic
My girl
She was good when she was earning
We could afford to do things
Would afford rehearsals
Gear for the band
Recording sessions
She was good when she was earning
Such a pity
She used to be so pretty
She had heroin-chic

My girl
With eyes like bruises
Purple and black
Dark circles swirling under
But things fell apart
She wouldn't earn no more
She held me back
Couldn't write no more
Couldn't play no more
Band nearly split
She had heroin-chic
My girl.

I wondered who she was. Probably an ex-girlfriend, I thought. If you dropped the lack of money complaint, it would have been a haunting love song. I took the tape out and put it back where I'd found it.

Once up in the attic room, I blew white dust off a mirror, stood it upright and looked at me. A ghost looked back. A skinny ghost with crow's-feet under her eyes.

I curled up under a chest of drawers, a large, ancient chest that stood on legs. Heard Ciaran come back, grunt and fall into bed fully clothed. As his snores filled the room, I crept out to write a letter, taking my bag with me. Perhaps one day I'll write my record of life with the misunderstood rock genius.

I put a piece of paper on top of the fridge, the only surface clean enough to write on, and found a pen. But couldn't think of what to write. Nine years and somehow the blank paper seemed best.

All the windows were closed. I turned on all the rings on the gas cooker and the grill for good measure. But I didn't light any of them. Ciaran will do that when he wakes up and reaches for his cigarette. I planned to be as far away as his record deal by then.

I plunged into work, continuing with my Saturday job in a record store and taking up a Sunday job with an estate agents, showing people round houses, as well as working any over time I could get from my engineering job. I felt good: I was too tired to think straight most of the time. I began to wish I'd insisted on keeping the ring Oliver had given me. I never heard a news story about a gas explosion or the death of a young rock genius from asphyxiation, so I guess either Jay came back in time to deal with it or Ciaran had woken during the night and somehow been alert enough to open the windows and turn off the gas.

Two years passed. I needed a break, another point on my map. I bought a ticket to Paris and a 'teach yourself French' programme. Afterwards I discovered Evanescence were touring and managed to get a ticket for their Paris gig: the advantages of working in a record shop.

The Zenith looked like a thousand and one other venues: big stage with speaker stacks, crowd barrier set a little way back, a couple of security personnel with ear plugs facing out towards the audience. I moved down to the front. The way the speaker stacks were angled, it was possible to stand alongside them and not get deafened. Then the wait...

Although the venue was filling up, people were gathering in small groups so there was no crush at the front and it was possible to maintain a small amount of personal space. The support band, I didn't pay much attention to: not their fault, my mind kept drifting. My savings were running out so I'd have to get a job soon. Paris had done me good: it seemed a shame to leave. I didn't get homesick but record-sick: it was unsettling not having them near me.

The opening bars of Evanescence's *Haunted* caught me by surprise. I hadn't noticed people crowding forward or that there were different personnel on stage. I leant against the crowd barrier. Voices joined in with Amy Lee's vocals.

My mind's eye saw Oliver as I had last seen him: neck at an impossible angle, body slumped but stiff, chair kicked to one side, feet not touching the floor. It was an image I'd never lose. My heart skipped a beat. I grabbed the barrier, rode the rush of anxiety. But the panic attack didn't come.

The crowd had got louder, joining in the chorus of *Going Under*. I didn't join in but it gave me a focus. The crowd's singing and arm-waving seemed to give the song a faster tempo and an urgency not in the studio versions. Finally, ready to join in, I was too late.

The collective mood mellowed with the quieter *Taking Over Me*. This was the song I'd add to my map: love lost, mourned, regained. I felt a chill on the back of my neck. I turned to look back. Three rows behind and about twenty people to my right, a tall, dark-haired man was looking in my direction, then got lost in the movement of the crowd. I shrugged: it probably wasn't me he was looking at.

I focused on the stage. I sensed, rather than heard, the band launch into *Everybody's Fool*. I remembered my ring and how alive Oliver had seemed when he gave it to me, the eagerness he had when he slid it on my finger. Why had he thrown that away? Wasn't it strong enough to prevent him from being overwhelmed enough to take his own life? I felt tears well and pinched my ring finger. I didn't care if I tore flesh, I was determined not to give in.

The cover of Korn's *Thoughtless* always turned my thoughts to Ciaran and the usual how the hell did I ever get involved? I knew it was pointless, the past can't be changed, but that doesn't stop the mind running through a thousand *what if* permutations.

As strings swirled and surged through *My Last Breath*, my palms became clammy. My heart fluttered into a faster beat. I went light-headed, even though I hadn't had a drink. I grabbed the crowd barrier as my knees weakened. My eyes caught the snaking movement of a wire as I bowed my head. I focused solely on that. All I could do was wait for it to pass. Experience told me I wasn't going to faint, wasn't going to buckle under or black out.

I could taste blood in my mouth. How long had I been biting my lip? The pain helped focus me. I heard the opening of *My Immortal* and glanced at my watch. I'd missed at least two songs and only half-heard this one. The audience were making up for my inattention by yelling the words. My breathing slowed, my heart rate was back to normal. A chill shivered my spine. Steadily I ungripped the crowd barrier and stood back on my feet again. Appropriately Evanescence launched into *Bring Me to Life*. Another song for my map.

The crowd were even noisier now, singing along, stamping with the rhythm. I caught the mood: there'd be two encores at least. I lost thoughts of Oliver during *Torniquet* and *Imaginary*. The gentleness of *Whisper*, even at almost deafening volume, helped keep me calm. While the cheering crowd knew this was the last song and wanted to make sure the band would remember Paris, I remembered the bonus track Missing, a new song. Against melancholy, low-key guitars and strings, Amy Lee's vocals were questioning, but emphatic, as if she were a teacher prising the answer out of a child who knows the correct response but lacks the confidence to actually say it aloud.

I let the song resonate.

The morning after found me sitting on the steps of the Sacre-Coeur, aware of yet ignoring people walking past, wondering what the hell to do now. Evanescence's *Missing* replayed in my head. I liked the sentiment: it felt like I was missing from my own life.

I heard a male voice and a shadow fell over me. I looked up, I'd been enjoying the sun's warmth, weak though it was.

"Hello," he said.

I know my mouth dropped open. He could have been Oliver's twin.

"Sorry, I startled you," he said in French and sat next to me, repeating it in English.

"I understood your French," I told him in French.

"You're English," he continued in French, pointing at my band-logo covered bag.

I nodded.

"Perhaps a coffee?" he suggested.

I shook my head.

"Stay there," he said.

I watched him walk away. A few moments later I watched him walk back, carrying two coffees and a bag.

"I got some crepes too. You look very pale. You looked very pale last night too. I saw you in the crowd but you'd gone before I got chance to speak."

"Thank you." I ate the crepes, discovering a hot apple filling. "M-m."

He smiled. Now I noticed he wasn't quite Oliver's twin after all. He had dark eyes and his hair was a very dark brown without the blue-black that Oliver had. He was also at least a couple of years younger than me.

"You look like someone I used to know," I offered, realising my staring must be off-putting.

"What were you thinking?"

"About opening a record shop."

He grinned.

I shrugged and took a sip of coffee. Now I'd said it, it didn't seem such a daft idea. What else did I know? "It's what I do, buy and sell records."

"You have a shop in England?"

I shook my head. "Worked in one."

"So you collect records?"

I nodded. "I've a map inside my head, Hamburg *Sister Ray*, Newcastle *Nine While Nine*, Blackburn *Stairway to Heaven*, Wembley *Temple of Love*, Brixton Academy *Ribbons*..."

"And it ends Paris *Haunted*?"

"And it includes Paris *Haunted*. Why should it end?" I wondered if there was more to his choice of song than it being a favourite.

"But the Paris map should be bigger."

"I need a job, if I'm to stay here more than a few days."

"I might be able to help."

"Do you work in a record shop, then?"

"No. I do marketing and promotion. But I know most of Paris's record shops. I could recommend which ones you should try, put in a good word. But you should aim higher."

"I don't think my French is good enough. And I'm happiest surrounded by shelves of vinyl or CDs."

He laughed. "I don't think there's any problem with your French. You speak it more naturally than I speak English. But, if you're determined, I'll help."

"Why? We've nothing in common."

"A taste in music, which is very important to you. I'll take you for dinner tonight, we can talk about it."

I opened my mouth to say 'No'.

He smiled. "Don't worry. It's not a date, just two friends. Something tells me you're sad about someone."

"How?"

"You keep rubbing your finger." He lightly touched my ring finger.

"Sorry, I must do it without thinking."

"He meant a lot to you."

I nodded. "I don't even know your name."

"Thierry."

"Thierry," I repeated. "It's been nice meeting you." I finished my coffee and stood up.

"But where are you going?"

He'd got me. Where was I going. "Back to my room."

"But we've not arranged dinner."

I hadn't even said yes to dinner, I thought. But I sat down again.

"Do you know...?" He rattled off the name of a restaurant then proceeded to give directions from where we were, obviously interpreting my silence correctly. "Eight," he finished.

I nodded, rapidly running my mind's eye through my wardrobe and trying to work out if I had anything suitable. I hoped my black, crushed velvet dress would suffice.

"Where is he now?" Thierry touched my ring finger again.

"Dead."

Thierry looked shocked then almost immediately rearranged his features into sympathy. "Accident?"

I nodded, not trusting my voice.

"I'm sorry," he said.

"You didn't know him."

"Let me walk you back."

"It was a long time ago..."

"But feels like yesterday," he completed.

"But you've not said anything about yourself."

"What do you want to know?"

Why you'd ask a strange Englishwoman out to dinner? I thought.

"You know I'm a promoter, I live in Paris, that we like the same music and your French is better than my English. I'd like to know more about you. Is that such a silly idea?"

"Perhaps not," I conceded.

"Which songs would you put on your map for Paris?"

"*Taking Over Me*, *Bring Me to Life*," I answered without hesitation, then wondered if they'd been wise choices.

He nodded. "He took over you and you need bringing back to life."

It sounded like a suggestion. Saying nothing seemed like a good idea. The rate Thierry was putting my life together, it would be another ten minutes before I found myself trying to explain the unexplainable: the wasteland of my time with Ciaran.

"Nothing will replace him. But it shouldn't stop you finding love again."

"I know you don't mean it that way, but it does sound like a greetings card sentiment."

"All clichés have a germ of truth at their core. Tonight, eight o'clock." He turned to go.

I watched him: envying his confidence, his ability to assume I wouldn't turn him down. I looked back at the Sacre Coeur.

Could I live here? For the first time where I lived was going to be my decision and I told myself I had to make it. I balanced on one leg, pointed the other out in front of me and made myself spin round. Let the tourists think I was mad: I needed a dancing movement. I stopped, facing where I'd started.

Yes, here. A good place to *Nine While Nine*. A life I was going to take charge of. I thought of Thierry. Why not? Love could feature. Let it start tentatively, like the opening bars, build to a surge of drummed beats. Stay there for a verse or two then extend to a swirl of strings. Steadily fall into a rhythm of verses and repeated choruses. But leave out the ad-lib to fade.

Singing The Classics

Tall Poppies

Literature can transport one to an inaccessible place or time allowing an artist to look on the world with eyes they would not otherwise have had the chance to see through. As songwriters we thrive on emotion as a fuel for melody and a starting point for the lyrical content of our songs. When there is no turbulence on the journey of our own lives we look to other art forms, particularly literature, to provide a gust of inspiration thematically and lyrically.

Being impressionable readers, the characters, concepts and style of a writer infiltrate one's thoughts during the period of time that it is being read, the work affects not only everyday thoughts but also the songs that are sung and the conversations had; I spoke in a Scottish accent for a week after reading *Trainspotting* by Irvine Welsh which in turn influenced my singing on one of our songs *Better off Dead*.

Just as Dorian Gray was poisoned by a book, the delicious wit of Oscar Wilde had a poisonous affect on our songwriting. Writing a song from the perspective of Basil in Wilde's novel, *The Picture of Dorian Gray* was a treat as we both had read and been inspired by the story around the same time. The elements of murder, vanity, overindulgence and eternal youth were all laid out for us and set against the exquisitely decadent interior of Dorian's abode. With all this in mind, Basil's perplexed voice in his final scene seemed to fit the wordless tune we had already written. Now when we sing it the memory of Dorian's golden hair, rosy cheeks and blood stained hands are happily recalled and the moral of the story given some consideration. Well, for three minutes at the most.

A Night In Tunisia

Tony Richards

Who are … 'they'?
  Good question.

*

What you have to understand is – if you don't already know it – jazz music, rather like life, isn't just the formless, spur-of-the-moment mess it at first seems to be. There are, in fact, certain famous numbers everybody knows, everyone can hum out loud, and any artist worth their salt has a go at their own version of at some juncture in their career. The most famous and most recorded has to be *'Round Midnight*, originally composed by Thelonious Monk and covered by every artiste from Charles Parker to Elkie Brooks – it even wound up being used as the title and the theme tune for a major motion picture.

Then there's Nat Adderley's *Work Song* – oh, a real toe-tapper that.

And then, of course, there's *A Night in Tunisia*. 'Cannonball' Adderley? Davis? They have all laid down their own versions of that one.

A night in Tunisia.

Which is precisely when and where we first met. On a hot and humid night out there, the sky all drenched with stars.

*

He never liked to be called 'Bob'. In the first place, probably, because 'Bob Biko' would have sounded like the tag of some stand-up comedian.

But most of all because 'Robert' wasn't actually his name.

He was born Royston Prince Hoyle down in Charleston, South Carolina, although his family moved up to Harlem when he was just five. Never liked the 'Royston' bit from the outset, and changed it to 'Robert Hoyle' when he began his musical career at seventeen. Then he changed his stage *surname* in 1979, out of sympathy when news of the killing of Steve Biko leaked out of South Africa, apartheid as it was back then.

That was back in his 'solidarity' phase, his 'roots' phase, call it what you will.

He went through a lot of different phases. Most good artists do.

*

When I heard he'd died, I put on the record almost straight away. An inappropriate record to accompany most deaths. And yet … the right one for his, from my perspective.

And in case you're wondering, this isn't going to be a ghost story as such. I've written a good few of those down the years, but this one's ninety percent real. Most of it did happen, in precisely the same way that I'm about to set it down.

So, which of this is the remaining ten percent that isn't based in fact? Well …

*

Somehow – and don't ask me how – Lauren had done it once again. She didn't even have the Internet to help her in those days, but she spent the best part of an afternoon scouring through the travel ads in the backs of the dailies, looking up stuff on Teletext, then getting on the phone. And by the end of it, she had booked us a holiday at half the normal price. Two weeks at the Hotel Splendid off in Gamarth – you pronounce it 'Gam-art' – which was on the Mediterranean coastline half an hour's cab ride outside Tunis. It was early in our marriage, and the first time that we'd ever visited North Africa.

The hotel lived up to its name and then some. It would, under normal circumstances, have been way out of our league in fact. Rich Arab businessmen would be chauffeured there for a drink, a meal, come evenings and weekends, and even the country's President showed up for an hour.

All the other foreign guests? Were conspicuously well-heeled, middle-aged and deeply sun-bronzed French and Germans, chunky gold watches, designer shades, and polo-shirts with alligators on them everywhere you looked. There was no beach, just big rocks that the green-grey sea beat up against. But the pool was massive, there were tennis courts – we were the only people out on them who were not wearing whites. Otherwise we'd hang out in the local *souk*, or head off by bus to Sidi-bou-Said, further down the coast, or the ruins of Carthage.

The waiters in the hotel's restaurant were utterly mild and charming. And, considering that this was Ramadan – a summer one at that, the daylight only starting to fail some time after nine o'clock – their good humour was remarkable. Since … what must it have been like for them? I still can't imagine. Serving food, smelling it right under your nose, and not being allowed all day to touch the smallest morsel?

There was a nightclub in the hotel's basement. But the whole first week that we were there it remained firmly closed. Due to the religious festival, we both supposed a little disappointedly. But right at the beginning of our second week …?

"They're open again! They've got jazz!" Lauren announced as we were passing by the entrance, off on our way to the restaurant again.

I gazed at the brand new poster stuck there on the wall.

JULY 11th TO JULY 14th. ROBERT BIKO, JAZZ SAXOPHONIST, AND HIS QUARTET. 10:30 P.M.

Robert Biko? The name rung a bell somewhere. Hadn't I seen it on a free-jazz album I'd got hold of in a bargain bin at *Our Price*? Playing alongside Archie Shepp or Sonny Stitt, somebody like that?

We went in for dinner, which was tuna *brik* and *cous-cous*. Then migrated through into the outdoor bar. The air had grown dim by this time and cicadas called. It was still pretty warm, and far closer than it had been during the daylight hours. We drank some wine and peered at the massed stars overhead, which were growing brighter as the last light disappeared. It was an amazing sky that night, as I remember.

The hour rolled around to ten twenty p.m., and we went down into the nightclub.

*

I woke up suddenly on my own, more than fifteen years later. Thinking, before my head had even lifted from the pillow, *He's still here!*

*

It was autumn, maybe a dozen years after Tunisia and late in the afternoon. The sky was overcast, and there was some damp in the air. Lauren by now had this job which took her to a lot of conferences overseas and, given the number of international organizations which have bases in Geneva, she was visiting the city maybe four, five times a year. It was only forty minutes from there to Lausanne. So I'd go with her when I could, and take the opportunity to drop in on Robert, if he wasn't away touring somewhere.

The train snaked gently through the low Genevan suburbs, and then gathered speed as it approached the countryside. There were vineyards all around me before too much longer, broad green fields speckled with pale dots that moved occasionally and were cattle. The dim shapes of mountains hung off in the distance. Buzzards circled, high above. Beside the track was Lake Geneva, *Lac Leman*, slate grey now with just a tinge of blue, the snow-capped French Alps rising on the other side.

I was alone in the carriage, and spread myself out. Had bought along a book to read, but something other than that caught my eye.

A newspaper had been abandoned on the seat opposite mine. And by the look of the headline – which was upside-down – someone well-known had just died.

I picked it up and turned it over. DEXTER GORDON EST MORT, it read.

Dexter Gordon was one of the principal saxophonists of his generation, the kind of jazzman who would play to a packed house at the Royal Festival Hall. And even if you know nothing about the music, then you still might have seen him. I mentioned that great Bertrand Tavernier film, *'Round Midnight*, at the start of this? Dexter Gordon played the leading role.

Only in French-speaking Europe, for all of that however, could the death of just a jazz musician make a national newspaper's headline. And it made me rather sad, since I had ten of the guy's albums. So I hung onto the paper when I finally got off the train, and had it in my grasp as I went quickly down the slope.

By this time, Robert had quit his studio flat on the Rue du Haldimand for a neat one-bed apartment in a far more modern block, half way down the gradient to Ouchy on the Avenue de Cour. It took me fifteen minutes to walk there. After which I buzzed. He let me up.

There's another thing you have to understand – if you don't already know it – not about jazz music this time, nor the guys who play it, but about the fans. When it comes to the all-time greats of our beloved musical form, the stellar superstars of it, we have a habit of referring to them all in the familiar, as though they somehow are, or were, extremely close friends of ours. So, Chet Baker is simply 'Chet'. Miles Davis is simply 'Miles'. John Coltrane is 'Trane', Dizzy Gillespie's flat plain 'Diz', and Charlie Parker's *always* 'Bird'.

So when Robert opened his front door to me I waved the newspaper at him and asked him, almost yelping, "Hey, did you hear? Dex is dead!"

He already knew of it. He looked from the headline to me, jutted out his lower lip.

Then shrugged softly and commented, "It happens to us all sometime. You can't stay here, man – they won't let you."

*

Who the *hell* are 'they'?

*

It was a broad, low-ceilinged area normally designed for dancing, except tables had been set up all across it now. We were the only tourists who'd come down here. All the rest? Were those businessmen I've mentioned in their dark, sleek suits, who'd come out from Tunis with their fiancées and wives. They seemed very still, I noticed, as though in a partial trance. The lowest of murmurs escaped them. I couldn't remember, ever, seeing such a quiet and moveless crowd. A closer look around at them gave me a hint of why.

Their faces were all glossy, all their cheeks puffed out a little and their eyes noticeably glazed. This was Ramadan, remember? They had gone the entire day without a single bite to eat, then, once the sun had set, had gorged themselves on flat-bread and *harira* soup. Which had had quite an effect on their blood sugar levels. They were drunk simply on sustenance, a phenomenon I'd never come across before.

They kept gazing at the stage in happy expectation, smiling gently, eyes like mirrors in the gloom. We found ourselves a table with a clear view. Lauren ordered drinks.

Three young local men in pale grey suits came shuffling out onto the stage, and took their places respectively behind the drum-kit, piano, and bass. They started tuning up, and took their time about it. We waited impatiently, the only people like that in the entire place.

A spotlight shone down suddenly on the microphone out front.

A voice announced over the tannoy, in clear English for some reason, "Ladies and gentlemen … Robert Biko!"

And out walks this tall, broad-shouldered black man, holding in his king-sized grasp a gleaming alto sax. Dressed with incredible stylish smart sharpness in a blue suit with a matching tie and a pale yellow shirt. His cuffs were evenly presented and a handkerchief was folded to perfection in his breast pocket. His shoes were cleanly buffed. His nails the same. There was not a hair nor a thread out of place.

Like so many black jazzmen – and I came to understand this only later – it was a pride thing for him. A desire to be taken seriously and a rebellion against stereotype. He hated any kind of sloppiness. Despised street-fashion when it came along, with all its baggy trousers and its back-turned baseball caps.

They had to get in a replacement pianist at short notice one time when he was playing here in London. When the guy turned up, it looked like he'd been wearing the exact same clothes the past couple years. Filthy sneakers. Badly crumpled, grubby jeans. A maroon woollen cardigan that had half-way unravelled. Robert was polite enough to him while he was present … but I can still remember clearly the look of disgust on his face once the man had gone away.

Smartness was synonymous with self-respect in Robert's mind. And – whatever life threw at him – he always possessed that.

*

"Hey, did you hear …?"

*

I have no musical talent whatsoever, but I have one claim to fame in that regard.

About six months before the 'Dexter Gordon is Dead' evening, Robert had just finished cutting a new album. And, for some reason, was at a total loss as what to call it. He was sitting in his new apartment, literally racking his brains, when his gaze fell on a book that I had sent him.

He always liked to read my stuff. And I had posted him a new tale in the *Twelfth* – and as it turned out final – *Orbit Book of Ghost Stories*.

And so? He called the album *Ghost Stories*. I beamed hugely when he phoned me up to tell me that.

*

You must have heard the term 'infectious grin'? He had one to a tee. He stopped in front of the mike, cast his gaze across the audience. And, satisfied with what he saw, broke into the widest, laziest, and most unaffected smile you could imagine. Everybody – including ourselves – could only smile right back.

I can't remember what he said, exactly. Nor the first couple of numbers that he played. What I *can* recall is the way the three local musicians struggled to keep up with him.

He played like a bird in flight, soaring and then swooping, only to next spread his wings and ascend to new heights. He spiralled on thermals of inner feeling, let an unexpected draught of creativity take him to a new place entirely. His eyelids were gently closed, his shoulders bowed with the strain of his efforts. Riffs and licks exploded from him, dazzlingly bright.

His backing band? Just looked more nervous as each minute passed. They were actually sweating, glancing helplessly around at each other with their eyebrows raised.

Don't get me wrong here. Robert wasn't an ungenerous performer. Every so often, he'd glance back and realise the trouble they were in, then slow his pace a little and allow them to catch up.

But then some brand-new flight of fantasy would take him over. He'd be off again, forgetting them. Lost only in the music.

By the time that he was half way through his set, the audience had been completely roused out of their torpor. Were shouting encouragement, applauding wildly at the end of every number. Robert nodded modestly and gave them a dose more of that infectious grin.

"We're gonna finish up now," he announced at last. "And, seeing as where we're at, what better tune to finish with than this one?"

The band knew where they were at last. The drummer took his place behind a set of congas and set up a backing beat. The pianist came in next, low and insistent. And finally, Robert lifted his mouthpiece to his lips again, and *A Night in Tunisia* came skirling out.

The entire audience was on its feet by this time, Lauren and myself included.

It was over. Robert and the others bowed, then emptied from the stage. We settled back down, chattering busily now, the adrenalin of the performance coursing through our veins.

Except … some fifteen minutes later, Lauren happened to glance across to a table in the corner. "There he is!"

Still dressed as he'd been on stage, he was sitting drinking quietly with a small brunette who turned out to be, back then, his fiancée.

We wandered across cautiously, not wanting to intrude. Said things to him like 'Great set, man! Terrific set!' and reached across and shook his hand.

"You guys English?" he asked us, and he looked slightly relieved when we confirmed we were from London. We realised in that moment that, apart from Birgit, he had no else to talk to.

"Why don't you join us for a while. What'll you have to drink?"

We were faintly surprised but accepted, settling down across from him. And started to converse. About? The hotel we were in and its surroundings, where exactly we lived and where else we had been. And then the subject turned to music. Jazz, of course.

And, during the next couple of hours – by that unguessable magic that a hot, close night in a foreign country can sometimes impart to life – we became firm friends.

*

This next bit happened a few years later, but is far too relevant to put off any longer. It's a perfectly true story about man's inhumanity to man. I still can't believe that things of this sort happen, but they do.

In between us visiting him and vice versa, we'd all three of us go up to see his then-fiancée Birgit, who lived in the Swiss capital, Bern. There was no need at all for us to book a hotel, she told us the first time that we went there, since she knew some people we could stay with.

It turned out to be a gorgeous city, its centre a medieval fairytale full of arcades, old statues, and spires. Birgit's friends – Astrid and Ivan – lived in the best part of it, the embassy district. Astrid had been married to a leading surgeon once upon a time, and come off splendidly in the divorce. So she now inhabited, with her bohemian boyfriend, a truly massive townhouse, an ornate wrought-iron staircase spiralling up the core of it to scores of wooden-panelled rooms. Most of these she let to students, so that at least a dozen people sat down at the dining table every single evening.

She and Ivan were both in their fifties, and extremely unconventional inhabitants of such a neat, smart, rather stuffy district. She had been a beatnik in her youth, and still dressed mostly in plain black. As for Ivan? As the name implies, he was a Russian. Was an aging hippy too, his thin hair trailing half-way down his back. He dressed in an odd rag-bag of ethnic clothing and smoked skinny little Indian cigarettes tied up with cotton at the filter end. But he turned out to be highly intelligent, cultured and thoughtful, as well. He could speak and read High German, and discourse on any of the arts.

Which he did, for the first couple of hours at least of our very first meal together. During which, several bottles of red wine mysteriously disappeared.

By ten o'clock, his speech had become pretty slurred. And by eleven, he was fast asleep, his head lain on the table.

When precisely the same happened the next evening, it became pretty obvious that Ivan had a problem.

Astrid might have been a freer spirit than her neighbours, but she was still Swiss. And so, the next day over washing-up, she apparently felt obliged to try an explanation.

So she told me Ivan's story.

He was by birth Jewish, and while still in his twenties he had emigrated to Israel. There, he'd settled happily until he was conscripted. He didn't like the army much, but things were to get even worse. The Yom Kippur War came along, and he found himself in the thick of the fighting.

A gentle and cerebral man, the sights and smells of battle sickened him. So, once it was all over, he decided he was moving to America instead.

Remember the date? 1967? Like a lot of people who live a life of the mind, Ivan wasn't paying attention to his surroundings properly when he visited the US consul.

"You've got military experience, I see?" an attaché asked him, glancing down his application form.

Ivan got his citizenship in something near to record time. Flew out to New York. Put his hand over his heart, recited the Oath of Allegiance.

And, as soon as the last word of it had dropped from his lips, he found himself conscripted again. He was off to Vietnam.

"You know who were the worst amongst his comrades, yes? Those white, clean-cut, college football types? They'd shoot people for no reason and think that it was funny. Or they'd cut a prisoner's head off and play catch with it. Only the black soldiers were decent. That's one of the reasons Ivan enjoys seeing Robert."

A year of this awfulness came to a head with Ivan being captured by the Viet Cong. And how did they treat this mild, pensive, cultured man who didn't even want to be there in the first place?

Astrid's face turned away slightly and her voice went very stiff.

"They buried him alive for three days. Not even in a box, you understand? In the raw earth, with just a bamboo pipe to breathe through. By the time they dug him out again …?"

She could only sigh and shake her lowered head. "He's a good man. But finished."

I could scarcely take in what I had just heard. Tried to imagine how it must have been for him during those seventy two hours. Dead yet not dead. Clutched in the grip of the very earth itself, entirely unable to move. The soil pressing in at your mouth, your nose, your eyeballs, and your head all filled up with a soundless scream.

I tried to imagine it for a long while. Then I tried to stop.

How's this relevant? You'll see.

*

Robert was modest, didn't disclose a lot. And so I found out most about his career by just buying up his records and then reading the sleeve notes.

He *had* played with Archie Shepp *and* with Sonny Stitt. He was acknowledged, in fact, as one of the founders of 'free-jazz', though later on he was disparaging about that whole adventure. He'd started as a flautist before switching to the saxophone. And he'd had a string of three hit albums with Atlantic in the Seventies.

Like so many African-American jazzmen before him, he had finally tired of the urban USA and made the exodus to Europe, leaving behind an ex-wife and three children. He'd lived in Paris first, for a few years, before moving to Lausanne.

He and Birgit had a kid too, but they finally split up.

Before he started on his jazz career, he'd had a brief spell as a boxer. He only mentioned it in passing, and the subject never came up again. Except once.

One day he was in London, maybe six years after that night in Tunisia, and I casually mentioned the recent, infamous Chris Eubank-Michael Watson fight. The one which finished up with Watson seriously brain-damaged.

Robert's normal calm expression disappeared beneath a furious scowl.

"Both of those guys black?" he asked me, with rather more sharpness than he usually would ask me something.

Mildly puzzled, I just stared back at him.

"Two black guys whalin' on each other till they're almost *dead*!" he burst out fiercely. "Oh yeah, white folk just *love* to watch that!"

So I suppose it doesn't take much of a genius to figure out why he gave up on boxing.

*

There's something else you have to understand, if you don't already know it. Robert was the first jazz musician who I became friends with, but not the only one. Usually, I'd get to know them the same way, go over and congratulate them after a good set, or else I'd know someone who knew someone who knew someone well-known.

But the point about them is that when it comes to times, dates, places, life in general, they are flotsam, they just mostly drift. Bump into you or not. Linger for a while, or wander off elsewhere. There's no rhyme or reason to the way they live their lives – they're as impetuous and improvisational as their music can be.

Lauren picked up *Time Out* one day, about ten years after Tunisia, goggled at the 'music listings' page, then told me, "Robert's coming over! He's playing the Jazz Café on …"

She read the date, and looked severely disappointed. By this time, she had already got that same job that involved a lot of foreign travelling, and she was out of London the whole week.

But the point is this. He was playing one of the best venues in town and, though he'd call us on the phone on the most casual of whims, it hadn't even occurred to him to actually let us know.

I turned up at the Jazz Café some half an hour before the set was due to start. Scoured the whole ground floor of the place. Couldn't see him anywhere. And so I went on upstairs to the balconied section.

There he was, sitting at a table with his new quartet, all black American exiles like himself. As I approached, he caught sight of me in a wall mirror and smoothly looked around.

I'd expected him to be surprised, but he just wasn't. Not at all. There was not a trace of startlement or puzzlement in his happy, mild expression.

As though … we lived just around the corner from each other, and he'd been expecting me to show up the entire time.

"Hey, man!" he grinned. And pointed to an empty seat. "Set yourself down. What're you having to drink?"

What I'm really getting at is that, if jazz musicians never let you know what their plans are, it's generally because they have none. I wouldn't realise how important that was until just before the end.

*

He visited us in London several times. Firstly at the fourth-floor walk-up that we had in Bayswater, but after that in West Hampstead, on the first floor of a vast Victorian Gothic house just off West End Lane. It had a double bedroom that was ours, and a much smaller second bedroom half-filled with the big, grey-painted metal office desk that I still write at. There was a futon sofa-bed in there, and he was quite happy with that. The few nights we remained at home, he'd turn in early, maybe ten o'clock. And sit there for the next couple of hours, writing down new music scores that he'd later perform. He didn't need a harmonica, or even a tuning fork. The music would just pour from his head straight down onto the lined paper.

Mostly, though, we'd visit him in Lausanne, a miniature Paris set on a low mountaintop. He lived at number 6 Rue du Haldimand, just around the corner from the University.

The first time that we went there, he met us at the station and then led us through the town's bustling centre. We went up the stairs and in through the front door. And I stopped, looking round surprisedly.

It was a studio apartment. A large one, with an elevated section for the bed. But a studio apartment nonetheless. Where were we going to be staying, exactly?

Robert took in my numb expression. Grinned, then told me, "You guys take the bed. I'll sleep on the couch."

But we were here the entire *week*.

I opened my mouth to protest, but the look in his eyes forbade it. And that's the way it was for the entire seven days, without the slightest grumble or complaint, not a hint of it, on his part.

In the mornings, Robert would teach class at the local music school, which gave us a chance to do some sight-seeing. He'd be back by one in the afternoon, and then we'd spend the rest of it hanging round some bar or other, bumping into his numerous friends, or else we'd take the funicular Metro down the entire way to the lakeside at Ouchy, an Edwardian spa-town in its day.

In the evenings? Usually, we'd dine at the little green-frontaged bistro just around the corner, and then go up through the Old City, across the Pont Charles Bessières, and stride along the Avenue Mon Repos to the Black Note Club, where Robert played.

We'd head home come three in the morning, the town completely quiet around us now. The streetlights made the paving stones look amber-coloured. And it would strike me, occasionally, that perhaps we were abroad on some nocturnal Yellow Brick Road. A night-life road. A jazz one.

Leading to some bright, jewelled city? No. In jazz there is no destination, just the road itself.

*

"Hey, did you hear? Dex is dead!"

"It happens to us all sometime. You can't stay here, man – they won't let you."

He looked faintly sad a moment. But then that grin of his came flooding back. Neither of us had actually known Dexter Gordon. He might be gone, but we were still here, and that was all that really counted so far as he was concerned.

There was a little more grey around his temples than the last time that I'd seen him, but otherwise he was exactly the same. The precise same person that I'd met all those years back in Tunisia. He led me through into his kitchen, where he was preparing an early supper, mussels cooked Provencal-style, on pasta. We chatted generally as we ate it, then went to a local bar. But it was almost empty, very quiet and dull, and so we only stayed some forty minutes before heading back.

He'd given up smoking by this time so, every half an hour or thereabouts, I would go out onto his small balcony, smoke a Gauloise and gaze at the vast surface of the lake below me in the darkness. And then pitch the finished butt over the railings, watch it explode like orange fireflies on the paving stones below. And then go back in, and resume our discussion.

We talked about what we were doing these days – he had quit his job at the *école* and founded his own music school, devoted just to jazz. He told me all about his kids – both the grown up ones back in the States, who he spoke of with genuine pride, and the newer one in Bern. And then we set about putting the entire world to rights.

When we finished up at last, it was about four in the morning. He pulled out the sofa-bed for me, and both of us turned in.

The next morning was bright and pleasant. He rode with me on the tram to the station. He had work to do, and his stop was the next along.

I got off with my overnight bag. Turned around as the doors hissed closed. Raised a hand and waved to him as the tram pulled away.

He did likewise, flashing me that same infectious grin I'd seen when I'd first met him.

And then the tram-rails moved off at an angle. The morning's soft, clear light made the glass turn reflective. He was lost from view.

I turned around and crossed the road towards the station, never realising once that this was the last time I'd ever see him.

*

The next time I was back in Lausanne it was very early in the Spring. Unseasonably warm and bright though, with a lot of trees already bearing blossom. I was grinning as I walked down the hill from the station – for once, I'd not phoned ahead, and I was planning to surprise him.

I turned right at the Avenue de Cour, and a few minutes after that was outside his apartment block. I reached out for the buzzer, and then noticed the front door had been left open. So I went inside.

There was something not quite right. Don't ask me how, but I could somehow sense it. It just didn't feel as though Robert was still around.

I looked at his letter box, and that confirmed it. His name tag had been replaced by a new one, a Swiss-German name.

I buzzed up all the same. Several times. No answer. All the while, the truth of it was sinking slowly in. He'd been talking about moving the last time we'd met. And now? He'd gone and done it and, in typical fashion, hadn't thought to let us know.

He'd mentioned, several times, the possibility of setting up in Fribourg, Germany, for a few years. He'd even toyed with the idea of Geneva itself. I tried both cities through directory enquiries, and got no result either for a Robert Biko or a Royston Hoyle. We'd long ago lost touch with his one-time fiancée, Birgit. Astrid and Ivan had emigrated to a small Greek island several years back. And the Black Note club had, by this time, closed down.

All of which was bad enough. But a couple of months later, Lauren and I moved as well. We left a forwarding address with the couple who bought our flat, but it was all that we could do.

We'd scour *Time Out* occasionally to see if Robert's name turned up. And, any time we were in mainland Europe, I'd look through the entertainment sections of the papers in case he was featured on their list of dates.

There was nothing. Where'd he gone? We had no way of knowing.

Life – and especially life in a city like London – just moves on, however, like a steamroller at break-neck speed. We had our work and other friends, places to go and people to see. And in time, memories of Robert were slowly jiggled to the hindmost of our thoughts. I'd still play his albums every so often, and wonder where he'd got to. But then realise I had a dozen other things to do. The phone would ring. I was due out somewhere. I had the last draft of a new story to complete.

It was only about four years later – I was putting together my own website – when it suddenly occurred to me that perhaps, by this stage of the game, Robert had a website of his own, or at least was mentioned somewhere.

I was surprisingly nervous as I worked the keyboard. All those memories had suddenly come flooding back. And could it be ...?

On Google, I typed in 'robert+biko'. A list of addresses almost instantly popped up.

I clicked on the first one. And two seconds later, his photo was right there on my screen.

That infectious grin was still there, but his hair had turned completely white. My eyes slipped across the bio underneath his photo, taking in the fact that he was twelve years older than I was. Somehow, I'd never really noticed that, it had not even occurred to me, before.

He had not moved to Germany *or* to Geneva. He had gone back to New York instead. He was teaching one day a week in Boston, and playing gigs the rest. And was now living in the Village, down on Bleecker Street. One more call to directory enquiries and I finally had his number.

It was now six o'clock in the evening. Which made it, in New York ... midday? I punched the digits in.

A feeling overtook me as I listened to that slow bell ringing on the far side of the ocean. There was something definitely not quite right again. The ringing sounded ... far too shallow, flat in tone. As though there were something missing.

This was all happening so quickly, and I tried to tell myself that I was being stupid. But the last time I had felt that instinct, it had been just inside Robert's block on the Avenue de Cour, when I had known deep in my gut that he was no longer around.

Someone picked up.

"Yes? Hello?"

It was a black woman's voice, a reasonably young one in so far as I could tell. He had a new female friend, I tried to tell myself. But …

"Who is this?" I asked her.

"This is Kisha Biko," she replied.

I recognised the name immediately. We had never before spoken, but this was Robert's eldest daughter. He had mentioned her a whole lot that last evening in Lausanne, telling me proudly how well she was doing for herself. I think she worked in the Mayor's office, or something like that.

"To whom am I speaking, may I ask?"

I explained to her who I was and how I knew her father. But I couldn't help noticing that the information didn't seem to be sinking in properly. Her responses were rather vague. She sounded very distant, and it wasn't just the line.

"I'm just here picking up a few of Daddy's things. The funeral was yesterday and – "

Funeral?

The sole reason I could believe what I was now hearing was that my instincts had already warned me of something like this.

I felt the carpet dropping out from underneath me all the same, and I could scarcely keep my balance.

"You didn't know?" Kisha was saying.

I reminded her – my voice stumbling and hoarse – that Robert and I had been out of touch for a few years.

"Ah," she murmured. "I'm sorry to have to break this to you, then." Taking a few moments more to gather herself properly, she told me what had happened.

He'd been perfectly fine. His usual self, the way I'd always known him. He had gone up to Cape Cod to play a small festival there. Checked into the hotel they'd booked him, still perfectly fine. Gone into the restaurant for his evening meal, and then decided to turn in early.

He had never woken up again. His heart had simply stopped.

Then Kisha told me where the funeral had taken place. How many people had attended. And how emails, telegrams, and flowers had turned up from half around the world. All the friends that he'd made. All the people who had known him and admired him.

She had started crying softly by this point.

"I'm so sorry," I could only mumble. "If I'd only ..."

What? Thought to use the Internet a little sooner? That wouldn't have prevented anything. Except this sudden awful emptiness, perhaps?

There came back a faint snorting noise, as though she'd wiped a palm across her face and tried to pull herself together.

"Thank you," she said. And then, "Oh! That's odd!"

I waited, my head still spinning, for her to continue.

"There's a book here, by the telephone. I think a British paperback. *The Twelfth Orbit Book of Ghost Stories*. He had an album called that once, *Ghost Stories*, but I didn't think he read this stuff."

I heard her flip the cover open. "Hey, it's signed. This you?"

I can't remember, either, how our conversation finished up. I wanted to sit down now, since my legs had become very weak.

*

Lauren was away all that week, off at a big international conference in Montreal or some such place. When she called me that evening, I did not tell her the news. Wait till she gets home, I'd already decided. Not over the phone

I poured myself a scotch though, and I did put on an old tape of *A Night in Tunisia*, a tune thumping and insistent as a steam train. It was a live recording from some ballroom in Southern California in the Fifties. Walter Bishop. Walter Yost. Roy Haines. Cran Candido. Dizzy Gillespie on trumpet. Charlie Parker – 'Bird' – on alto sax.

You could hear the crowd in the background, simply murmuring at first. But, after the first few minutes, they were applauding and yelling with approval.

I poured myself a second and then a third scotch, remembering all those evenings with Robert, all of those terrific gigs he'd played. How could anyone just go to sleep like that and not get up again? I was starting to get slightly angry. How could he just *go* like that, when I had only just caught up with him again? I'd wanted *him* to pick up the phone. I'd wanted to say "Hey, man! What's happening?" and hear his big, infectious grin break on the transatlantic line.

I kept on pacing back and forth and getting more worked up and drinking more, until I'd finished up the bottle.

I don't remember how I actually got to bed. But, once there, I had the strangest dream.

I had become Ivan, that aging Russian hippy back in Bern. The Viet Cong had captured me, and buried me alive. Worms and grubs brushed up against me, and the soil was damp and warm. I tried to move, but couldn't shift a muscle. The earth pressed against my eyeballs, tried to push its way right up my nose. But the worst thing of all was that I didn't dare open my mouth, which was unbearable, because I needed so badly to scream.

But the next moment, I wasn't Ivan any more. Instead, I was Robert, buried and yet still completely conscious. Simply lying there.

I woke up very sharply, thinking to myself, before my head had even lifted from the pillow, *He's still here*!

*

Call me crazy if you will, but the feeling hung around me all of the next day. The same kind of instinct I had had at the apartment block and when I'd yesterday been listening to that ringing phone. Perhaps it was because we'd been so much on the same wavelength, but I seemed to have developed this sixth sense. Just *knew* if Robert was around or not.

And that sixth sense was telling me, right now? That he was present still, somehow. That he had somehow not departed, as he should have done.

It was foolish, nonsense, the worst possible case of wishful thinking. But it just wouldn't let go of me, clung to me like an angry crab, bothering me so terribly I couldn't do a thing all day.

And when I dreamt again that night, it was a similar bad dream. I was Robert again, but I wasn't lying placidly this time. I wanted to get out and move around. I was struggling to scream beneath the earth.

Only half-awake, I rolled out of my bed, lurched to my feet. And then I just stood there, shivering and sweating, with my eyes clamped fiercely shut.

Somehow – I just *knew* it – he'd remained behind. And was, right now, trapped underneath the ground out in New York somewhere.

The knowledge was like a ball of concrete in me by this time, paining me terribly, wholly impossible to ignore.

And so … what was I going to do?

*

This was the most bizarre thing that I'd ever done in my entire life – I fully knew it. But I also understood that I had little choice. I simply had to get out there.

Heading down the motorway – the night air close and smoggy – I phoned ahead on my mobile. Yes, there were some free seats on the next United flight to JFK, and I could make it in good time. I pulled onto the hard shoulder and read out the details of my credit card.

Impatient hours later, I was stepping out onto the tarmacked soil of Queens. The time? Around one thirty in the morning here. There were a few cabs waiting. I approached the first one in the line.

In any other city, the driver might have looked surprised when I told him where I wanted to go at this late hour of the night. But this was New York – a fare was a fare. He simply pursed his lips and shrugged, then took me.

It was one of those enormous cemeteries which sprawl across the borough like some macabre golf course. Was set mostly on a slope, so that the headstones ascended in pale tiers above me. It was hotter and even muggier here than it had been in London, such a thick haze on the night air that the distant outline of Manhattan could barely be made out.

There were no railings, just a brick-built wall some five feet high which I climbed over easily. I'd brought a flight bag with me, with a few odd items in it.

A small torch, for instance. When I switched it on, I felt slightly dismayed. Not only were there literally thousands of headstones, but a fine mist was now gathering about them. Tendrils of it swarmed about my ankles when I looked down. And I hadn't even thought to ask Kisha which section he was buried in, so finding him was going to be a good long job.

I set off all the same, casting my gaze everywhere for fresh flowers and newly-turned earth.

It must have been more than an hour before I finally stumbled across his stone. His family hadn't used the name he had been born with, I was pleased to see. They'd had engraved the name that he had chosen for himself, and paraded on spot-lit stages half across the world.

In loving memory of
ROBERT BIKO
composer, musician, and father
1942-2004

"Hey, man," I said, finally relieved, and sat down.

I could almost hear him breathing underneath the earth. What exactly was he doing down there? Lingering, because the mood had taken him to do so and he had no other plans?

What should I do? He couldn't stay here. He was probably all right at the moment, but what about later, when the box rotted and the soil came tumbling in? Then, he'd be like Ivan, and I couldn't bear the thought of that. I was his friend. He was relying on me, even if he didn't know it. I just had to find a way to persuade him to go.

Maybe some music would stir him into action. It always had done in the past. I'd bought that same tape with me, the Parker/Gillespie session, along with an old, beat-up portable cassette player. And so I laid it in front of the headstone, switched it on.

A Night in Tunisia came flooding out again, for the last time.

I closed my eyes at that point, and then began talking gently to him. Ploughing through the past and reliving old memories. That first night in Gamarth, all the evenings since. That time that I'd turned up (un)expected at the Jazz Café, and the way that Ouchy looked in the late afternoon sunlight.

Perhaps, if I ran through all of it one final time, then he would realise that the hour had come, at last, to let it go.

It took me several minutes to realise that something had changed. The music … was no longer as it had been. It was still *A Night in Tunisia* playing, but when I listened properly, I realised there was just a saxophone now. No Dizzy and no backing band, no congas by Cran.

My eyes snapped back open. And I almost scrambled backwards at that point. Because the little spoked wheels in the cassette player were no longer turning. The tape had fouled, I could now see, big tangled loops of it protruding from the lid.

The music was by now coming from underneath the ground. They might have buried his sax with him, but I don't think it was that. Rather, it was coming directly out of him, directly from his soul.

I took in what was happening with a drained, bloodless amazement, and then got up to my feet, angry again.

"You can't *do* this Robert!"

His playing just got louder.

"You just can't – ". I turned around on the spot, trying to think how to say this.

"You remember what you said to me the day that Dexter Gordon died? I can still recall your exact words. 'You can't stay here, man. They won't let you'. So, you think the rules have changed? What the hell are you trying to *do*?"

The music stopped for a few moments, as though he were thinking. Then resumed more fiercely than ever, filled up with a savage intensity by this time. Fired, ablaze with impertinent life.

I understood now. He wasn't just hanging around, not loitering like flotsam the way he usually did. He was remaining here because this whole business was so unfair. To go to sleep like that and, without warning, simply not wake up again? Where was the justice in that? He had so much music to compose and play still, and so many places left to go. And all of that potential had been casually snatched away from him.

Whose justice was that? Who were the 'they' who just won't let you stay here?

I was shaking now, my own thoughts feverish and verging on the crazy … when something new caught my attention. There was something moving at the corner of my vision, and I'd thought I was alone out here.

The mist, which had grown slightly thicker, was starting to coalesce in places. Starting to form expanding, pallid blotches.

Within seconds, I realised there were dozens of them. Growing ever larger now, and gradually taking shape.

I *did* stagger back a little, my heart hammering, my breath turned solid in my throat.

There were several ranks of them, their features becoming apparent. Was there the faintest glow about them? I couldn't really tell you. I was too astonished to take that kind of detail in.

Human faces were now being formed out of the massed condensation. Limbs, and even fingers and toes, all melded into view.

And, once they were whole, these beings began to move towards me.

There was nothing threatening in the way they moved. Rather, they approached respectfully, making not a sound.

The first rank seemed to be babies, with massive heads and tiny digits. But they walked entirely steadily on their hind legs. There was a quality about them that was unlike any normal infant. Their large eyes shone with intelligence. Their brows were creased with thought. Their lips kept pursing and their fingers flexing, as though they all wanted to…

Wanted to do what, exactly? Play an instrument, the way that Robert had once done?

The second rank were six or seven years of age. Boys and girls, of all races and colours. Clutching in their hands recorders, triangles, and penny whistles. All of them just starting out, I numbly realised, on the same road Robert had travelled along.

And the third and last rank? They were all in their pre-teens. And they were holding proper instruments this time, clarinets and oboes, violins and trumpets …

And yes, saxophones.

I had thought at first they might be ghosts. But now, I recognised the truth of this.

They were not the lost souls of the dead, quite the opposite, in fact. They were the spirits of those still to come. Of all the talents waiting in the future.

They were not even looking at me, I realised.

I went back a few more paces, staying very quiet myself. And watched, as they gathered by the side of Robert's grave.

'You can't stay here, man – they won't let you.'

These were 'they', I now took in.

And why did they require him to go? Because they needed their own spot. Their time. Their debut. Their career. Their turn. No one could just remain here and deny a place to one of them.

Robert's saxophone, still playing beneath the soil, had become uncertain, muted.

The mist-children just stared down silently and waited.

After another short while, the tune faltered to a stop.

I don't think I was breathing at all by this time. I was still shaking, though. What exactly would he do? Which direction would he choose to take?

I got my answer finally when a last extended lick came blasting out from underneath that gravestone. The most beautiful short flurry of chords I'd heard in an entire life of listening to jazz. All the spirit, the soul and humanity Robert had ever mustered were contained in there, and a dozen other things as well.

It was fireworks at New Year's Eve. It was dawn's rise on the ocean. It was a sudden flight of birds against a sky of azure, and the crackle of a log fire on a freezing night. It was making love for an entire weekend in Paris, stepping out into Manhattan your very first time. It was being drunk and very happy, and being at some fiesta in Spain so wild that you were simply drunk on that.

It coruscated, seemed to burn my eardrums, and it scorched the very air.

And ... as it finally echoed away into silence ... then that instinct I'd developed kicked in once again.

He was gone. I knew it just as well as I'd known that he'd remained here.

The mist-children? Remained in place another moment. And then...?

They smiled simultaneously, a thankful if faintly apologetic smile.

Then they swiftly faded, until there was only mist again.

*

And I know what you're all thinking now. The death of a close friend is hard to take under any circumstance. But when that friend dies out of the blue, entirely without warning, there are always things you wish you'd done earlier, thought of earlier, said to him while you still had the chance. A yawning, guilt-edged void is left. And, the mind being what it is, half-formed dreams and imagination soon rush in to fill the void.

There is – in fact – another way of looking at it though. There are certain religions in the world, certain philosophies which hold that our genuine existence lies elsewhere entirely. That this place we call the world is no such thing in truth, and this thing we call life upon it is merely a passing dream, of little consequence.

And if that's true then, in spite of my claim at the beginning, none of this is real at all.

Including my setting it down on paper.

And you reading it.

*

By the time I'd climbed back over the wall my face was wet with tears. They were stinging my cheeks, and my eyes were burning.

It had to be four in the morning by now, still dark if it wasn't for the streetlights. A car hummed by in the distance and was gone.

You couldn't see even the faintest outline of Manhattan any longer, the mist had spread everywhere. But it only rose to chest height.

I set down my bag, tipped back my head. Above me, the sky was a clear, deep, purplish black, entirely filled with stars.

I could have been anywhere right then. New York? Tunisia? Lausanne? What did it matter? There are a hundred thousand places in the world with humid, star-drenched nights like this one.

The kind of night during which anything might happen, and occasionally does.

In loving memory of
ROBIN KENYATTA
composer, musician, and friend

how the boy least likely to became

jof owen

i remember being read *how the whale became and other stories* by ted hughes when i was about five years old, and then i remember reading it to myself all the time as i got older. i used to get the stories of creation in it confused with the stories in the bible, and it wasn't until i was older that i realised most of the ideas about creation that i'd thought were biblical were in fact just things i'd picked up from *how the whale became and other stories.* when i was young i was always drawn to things that were written from the perspective of things that weren't human, books like *animal farm* by george orwell and oscar wilde's short stories. i still am drawn to that sort of writing. when i was writing the first album i was reading *you're an animal, viskovitz* by alessandro boffa and *i am a cat* by soseki natsume. all these books somehow seem to say more about the human condition than any books written from the perspective of humans. i don't know why that is, but often when i'm writing i try to write from the perspective of an animal or a something else, like a balloon or an egg, instead of trying to write as myself, and it always seems to end up being more true to me than it would have been if i'd tried to write it as myself. when i write like a tortoise it always ends up being a much more honest reflection of the way i am as a human being. i'm not sure why. maybe it's because i often feel at such a distance from the rest of humanity, or maybe i'm just more like a tortoise than i am like a man.

In The Pines

Rosanne Rabinowitz

1. The longest train (Georgia, 1875)

Where is he? Where is he? I still look for the rest of my husband in the wreckage that remains. I only find shiny lumps of coal, a twisted length of iron, a chunk of wood, pieces of machinery.

They wouldn't even let me see Sam's head. It would have been my last sight of him. They told me the head was 'without a scratch'. So why can't I see it?

"You wouldn't want to see the look on his face. He must have seen that crash coming up, and he couldn't stop it."

'It isn't a pretty sight', they said. But he never was pretty. I didn't love him for being pretty.

He was the only one on the train, driving through to Tennessee. He'd had no rest since his last shift, but the company ordered him to do the run anyway. Coal and wood needed hauling. Factory owners up North were waiting for their fuel.

I grew up in a country of trees. I know silver birch. I know the squat branches of old apple trees and the smell of fallen fruit in the sun.

When I walk through the birches and oaks long enough, I feel the change in the air. It turns colder, and it carries a scent that is clean and raw. No more crackle of twigs or crunch of leaves under my feet. The dark pines rise up above me, the ground is covered with their needles. When I was a girl I thought that those needles should be sharp, like sewing needles that go through cloth and draw spots of blood from your fingertips.

But the needles beneath the pines are soft, covering ground where nothing else seems to live.

In the hidden swamplands south of here, the pines were giant cedars that stained the streams red-brown like tea. I've never been there, but my grandma and grandpa told me stories about the place and I can see it in my mind.

Pines stand in the deepest part of the forest, they guard faraway hollows and moist lands. They stay alive even in the winter, the only green when snow coats the ground and everything else is brown and black.

How can they live when everything else dies? I used to think that the pines must take all the green, all the sap from the other trees. Maybe they take their life from the living things that move and struggle beneath their branches.

There are also pines at the top of the hill where Sam is buried. But these are thin trees with half their branches bare. They are bent by the wind, bent by their vigil. I sit under them by his grave, and wait for him to tell me where to find his body. I have done this for days, though I know I have work to do. 'This can't go on much longer,' his brother told me. It won't.

I can't bear thinking of his head buried there, his body lost without the head. When I look at the headstone and the length of ground in front of it, I laugh with bitterness. There's only a head there, do you need that ground just for a head?

Sam was a big man. When we married we had to make a new bed that would be long enough for him.

"Only the best pine for us," he said.

We went into the deepest woods, where trees grew so close together their branches tangled into a roof above our heads. Two of his brothers came to help us. We chopped and sawed and got a good tree down. The sun came through the hole we'd made in the roof of the forest, falling into moving spots of light that looked alive.

Sam pointed out 'rings' on the stump that was left. He said they tell stories about the tree, and maybe they can tell you things about people too. Perhaps there is a forest somewhere with a tree for each of us that tells everything about our lives.

When I looked at the rings inside our tree I couldn't see where one began and the other ended. They were all of one piece like a rope coiled up in a barn. I kept staring at the ring and I was sure it had a story to tell like Sam said. His brother Tom said he'd been a carpenter for years and he never had a tree say shit to him about anything. Maybe the smell of the sap was going to both of our heads and making us see things.

Later, we turned the stump left by the tree into a seat where we could rest whenever we went walking through those woods. We polished the surface and made it smooth; kept cutting back the weeds and small branches trying to start up again. There was barely enough room for the two of us, but we didn't mind sitting very close.

Later, Tom made Sam's coffin. As I walked behind it, I listened for the sound of something round rolling in the big empty box.

How many times have I seen that train go by?

I was a little girl the first time I watched it rumble through the pass. This machine bellowing smoke and steam awed me much more than tales of God in Sunday School. Its rhythm was a pounding I could dance to if I dared. Car after car went by. One bearing stacks of logs, the next full of coal. Mysterious cargo covered by burlap, another load hidden in a closed car.

The train snaked its way through the valley. One morning I watched it from beginning to end. Was it just when the birds began singing and the rooster crowed that the first car passed? Maybe the caboose passed when it was well past breakfast time and I was shouted at for shirking chores. It was worth the shouts and scoldings. I just had to see it.

Later I was filled with pride when Sam started to drive that train, amazed that he could hold that thundering hulk of steel under his control. How lucky he was to ride such power across the valleys instead of going below the ground to dig coal in darkness.

Now, I'm only thankful that we didn't have children.

I start singing to Sam in a tune I must have heard before. I want to tell him how I felt when I was a child watching that train go by. Time takes so long when you are small. How can I say that? There was a post in our hollow to mark six miles from the last town, and I used to stand close enough to feel the train pull at my clothes and hair as it went by. *The longest train I ever saw went down that Georgia line. The engine was at a six-mile post, the cabin never left the town.*

The tune tugs at me in the same way. My uncle played the fiddle, and the banjo too. As if he is standing in front of me, I see how the bow slides across the strings and gets them to make that sound.

When I was little I thought there were strings inside each person that can be pulled and twanged and moved in the same way.

Of course, I knew what insides look like from seeing animals slaughtered. I knew what they felt like to touch as soon as I started to help my ma gut chickens. I saw plenty of folks hurt or killed, like the soldiers I found in a ditch during the war. They were mangled so bad I couldn't tell if their uniforms were blue or grey.

Our insides are soft and squishy, all the shades of red and liquid. I once believed that the strings were hidden in there.

But these days I think there is only an empty place inside me, so empty that there is no end to it. Imagine the whole of the night-time sky held in a body, but there's no stars, no moon. There's nothing at all, just a nothing that goes on forever.

That's what the music makes me see. Yet it also makes me feel the wind, the needles beneath my feet and the grit under my nails from touching Sam's gravestone. There's the train winding through the valley, a train that goes on as long as the empty sky.

The colour of the air changes from dusky grey-blue to deep green night. I smell a whiff of salt and fish that don't belong here. But it's gone in a flash, and only the music I'm seeking remains.

The tune brings words to me. Where did I first hear it? From my grandma, or my pa when he worked in the yard? Perhaps I stopped hearing it when he was killed, or when my ma passed away. But it's coming to life again with my husband's death. *Your head was in the driving wheel, your body was never found.*

Would he want to hear this? Yes, because he wouldn't want people to forget.

Finally, I tell him that I'm saying good-bye.

As I leave Sam and head towards the woods, I remember the tales from our old home in the swamp. Is there another place like it? Some people there had been slaves finding the way to freedom by the stars, but they didn't go all the way north and found a home among the great cedars. Other folk were Cherokee, still others brought as servants from across the sea, Irish and Portuguese. The blood of all these people flows in my veins and their songs fill my ears.

That swamp was drained, or turned into plantations by the lumber companies. My people fled again, this time to live here in the mountains.

Now it's time for me to leave. I can set out north, all the way this time. Or I can walk into the pines, deeper and deeper until I come into the open again. Another old melody goes through my mind as I walk, a song of escape. *"When the sun comes back and the first quail calls, follow the drinking gourd..."*

But here the trees hide the stars, so there's no sign of the drinking gourd or the twins. My grandparents fled like this from government men who drained their cedar swamp. They had to hide in the woods and mountains and make another life, but they also had each other. I only have a new song that hasn't been finished, a song of sorrow and a place in the black heart of the pines where no one can find me.

2. Jersey Devil (New Jersey, 1973)

"My girl, my girl don't you lie to me
Where did you sleep last night?
In the pines, in the pines where the sun never shines"

Linda tried to find a more comfortable position on the grass and closed her eyes as she listened to the band. Despite her deep gravely voice, the singer was just another white Jersey girl not much older than Linda herself. Not an old blueswoman who'd lived a long life of struggle and grief, or a hillbilly girl drowning her sorrows in a still of moonshine.

But that singer came out with notes that reached inside Linda, grabbed her guts and *squeezed*. Could she be the only one affected that way? Look at those happy families sitting on blankets with the remains of their picnics. Over there, kids just a little bit older than her, lucky to be out of high school and having a life. Laughing.

"Hey, there's room on our blanket!"

This guy was talking to her. He was leaning back, his long body stretched out. He held a joint in his hand. His dark hair was tied back in a ponytail, but ends of it came loose around his face. He wore a silver earring, which gave him a kind of pirate look. Maybe he looked a little like that Pentagon Papers guy, Daniel Ellsberg, except younger and cooler. She'd put pictures of Ellsberg on her wall when he got busted a couple years ago for giving the papers to the *New York Times*.

Next to the guy with the joint, an older woman with grey-streaked, curly Afro-style hair nodded with encouragement. She was quite round, but in a pretty way.

"There's plenty of room," the good-looking guy said again. He handed Linda the joint. She took a deep drag on it, passed it back. She'd only smoked pot twice before with Martine, but it didn't really do anything. Some kids at school smoked it all the time. They cut classes and hung out in the patch of woods near school. Linda cut school too, but hid in the local library instead.

The library people must have thought she was doing a project there. But school projects never involved reading Kurt Vonnegut or Hermann Hesse or poems by Ferlinghetti. No one in her school read books like that.

No one she knew ever read her kind of books, except for Martine.

"Thanks," she stammered as she inched her butt onto their blanket. She kept her eyes on the band. She didn't want to be caught staring at that guy next to her. The fiddle player had a bright red beard and sticking-out red hair. The singer was thin and blonde, with baggy jeans she kept pulling up. Like many women here, she didn't wear a bra. When she stood under the spotlight you could see her little nipples through her thin blouse. Some of the pot-smoking girls at school didn't wear bras either.

No way Linda could get away with that. Even after she'd lost weight she still had big tits. If she went to school without a bra the guys would be singing '*Ug-Ug-Ugly Linda*' all day.

"In the pines in the pines
Where the sun don't ever shine
And I shivered the whole night through…"

That song was making her shiver too. It made her quiver inside like Jello. It reminded her that she was alone. It made her think of Martine's

Mom on the phone last week, telling her that Martine was dead. From an overdose. Then she slammed the phone down, as if Linda had given Martine the drugs and it was all her fault.

Martine had been Linda's only friend, separated by twenty miles of the New Jersey Turnpike. Recently Martine had been very busy with boys. Boys never noticed Linda, unless it was to point and sing *"Ug-Ug-Ug-ly Linda…"*

Fuck them. They're just immature jerks, Linda thought. It's not like she's even fat anymore. She hasn't been fat for over two years. So what's their problem? They're just jerks.

"You OK, kid?" It was the curly-haired woman. Linda didn't like being called 'kid'. But the woman had a kind face, with warming brown eyes behind little round glasses like John Lennon's.

"Yeah," Linda mumbled. The joint came around again. The pirate-guy's fingers brushed hers this time. *Wheww!* That tingle started in her fingertips and went straight up her arm and everywhere. It twisted like a blade, a good kind of blade. He smelled like fresh tobacco, though there was only grass in the joint.

"The longest train I ever saw
Went down that Georgia line
The engine passed six o'clock
And the cab passed by at nine"

There goes a harmonica, like the whistle of a departing train. And the fiddle player came in with a sound that was rough and scratchy, but sweet.

"I've seen you before," the guy said. "My name's Phil, and this is my friend Kerry. You've been at *Change Your Mind* bookshop in Madison. You were with a dark-haired girl…"

"Yeah, Martine is – was – her name." Phil didn't notice Linda's change of tense. Good. She didn't want to explain. Not now, though she only came here because of Martine. Linda didn't even like folk music. She preferred David Bowie and Alice Cooper. And the Jefferson Airplane.

Folk music was kids' stuff. Songs they made you sing in school like 'This land is your land' (no, it's *not*).

But Martine had loved folk music. She said she'd take Linda to this festival and show her what it's really like. Martine had the same olive skin as Phil, but she wasn't thin like him. She had a graceful, pear-shaped body and green eyes. Martine understood her, and Linda thought she understood Martine. Maybe she didn't do it well enough. Why the fuck did Martine take that shit and leave Linda alone?

And now Linda's here and she's met Phil. She almost felt guilty about meeting this cool guy, with Martine dead. But Martine would *want* it to happen. Martine had worried about her not having friends to hang out with at her crap school full of bigots and junior Republicans. Martine would be so pleased. But Linda better not think about that too much. Martine *wouldn't* want her bursting into tears and ruining her chances.

Phil was handsome, a really mature guy who must be in his 20s. Maybe he'd like her. People said that Linda looked older because she was tall. Maybe she wasn't pretty, but at least she didn't look like a dim cheerleader type from Fuckwit Township, New Jersey.

Her father had to give her a lift to the bus stop so she could come here. You couldn't do anything without a car. You didn't have *towns* in her part of New Jersey, just town*ships* that were stretches of highway, shopping malls and streets of spread-out houses.

Martine lived closer to New York, where the transport was better. She used to get on a bus when she wanted, then come home. Her parents were strict Catholics but at least Martine was able to go to a bookshop or listen to folk music in a park without it turning into a federal case. Linda had to promise that she'd get a bus back before midnight and phone from the bus stop. When her brother was her age he never got this hassle. Boys didn't. It wasn't fair.

They say that life isn't fair, but that doesn't mean you can't try to change it.

She can't wait to get away.

New Jersey *sucks*.

"My man he was a railroad man
Killed a mile and a half from town
His head was found on the driving wheel
His body was never found"

This wasn't kid stuff at all. Where did her man's body go? It was gross about that head, but she wanted to find out more. It was like the woman in the song was tugging at her sleeve needing to tell her story, and Linda needed just as much to hear it.

"Who's that playing? What's the song? They must have been in a bad mood when they wrote it."

"It's an old, old song," said Phil. "That band didn't write it. They're the Raritan Ramblers from New Brunswick. They wouldn't know a pine forest if it smacked 'em in the face."

"No pine forests in Jersey," agreed Linda, "unless you go to the Delaware Water Gap."

"Hey, I can tell you're a North Jersey girl," said Kerry. "Haven't you been to the Pine Barrens?"

"No, it's south of here, isn't it?" Linda sucked at the joint when it came her way again. South Jersey didn't interest her. North was what mattered, north to New York City where her family originally came from, and where she'll return. Now she's sixteen she'll try to get a job at the library, save up money and then *go*.

"I come from South Jersey myself," said Kerry. "Closer to the shore, not really in the Pine Barrens. But I know the area, always found it fascinating compared to all the crap amusement parks and arcades down my way. When I was a kid we used to dare each other to spend a night out there. I was too chickenshit. Then." Kerry grinned. She was missing a couple of teeth.

People cheered when the song finished. When the group returned for an encore, the singer explained that they'd run out songs – but they'll do *In the Pines* again.

"I never get tired of hearing that song," said Phil. "It's a classic, whether it's played with a high lonesome sound or low-down and bluesy. It made me cry the first time I heard it."

Oh! Linda felt herself melting. This guy is really *sensitive*. "I don't know much about folk music, so this was the first time for me. What's it about?"

"It can mean all kinds of things," said Phil. "There are versions from different times and places, so there's no *right* answer. The head could be on, or in or 'neath the driving wheel or driving gear. It has also been found by the firebox door! Sometimes the train isn't in the song, but the guy loses his head all the same. Sometimes it's the girls' father who gets killed – or the girl herself."

"Other versions say 'Black Girl'. Some say it's about a lynching," said Kerry. "But a 'black girl' or 'dark girl' in traditional music can also mean a mysterious brunette who doesn't play the game!"

"Lynching or train wreck, life was hard," said Phil. "And it's still hard in many ways, that's why we listen to those songs."

Linda watched the tops of the trees around the stage sway in the breeze. The chords and notes were turning into ropes twining around her legs, twisting around her body. The trees seemed to sing along. A hoarse refrain came from the earth as if its stones were grinding together and making the music. Her heart beat along with it, much too loud in her ears.

It must be the pot. It had only made her cough before, she never knew it could do *this*. She heard each instrument clear and full, she revelled in the blend as they came together. She felt fragile and small in the music's power. Just like the longest train, it could crash and crush her. It could also take her far away from New Jersey wherever she wanted to go, or drag her to the place she feared the most.

She wondered if Phil and Kerry guessed this was all new to her. What if they asked how old she was? She wouldn't know what to say. But who was asking? They just accepted her.

Who is she anyway? Linda, Linda.

When does Linda start, and where does she end?

Linda stared at her hands in front of her, and flexed her fingers. Did she finish at the tips of her fingers? But she felt the vibration of the singer's throat as if she was stroking it; she could touch the wind in the trees and it was part of her too.

Why would that woman run to such a dark and cold place? Was she hiding, was she scared that her head would end up on a steering wheel too? Was a driving wheel the same as a steering wheel anyway? Who wanted to know where she'd slept last night?

Kerry and Phil passed around great slabs of carrot cake. Linda had tuna sandwiches in her bag, but the cake was more tempting. She ate it crumb by crumb. It was moist and dense, the creamy icing tangy and smooth.

Other acts came on. Phil's mouth was near her ear when he told her who they were, that they were much more famous than the Raritan Ramblers. His breath against her ear made those sparks fly again. Each one fizzed, then melted like a snowflake and formed again when he spoke, when he was close. It could go on and on if they ever did it.

Doesn't pot make you horny? But it's not only that, it's *him*. It's the night, it's the mournful music making her want to draw him close.

She shivered again as that plaintive chorus of *'In the pines'* kept coming back to her while the famous people were singing other songs.

Linda had no idea what the time was, but she had a horrible feeling it was time to leave. She stood up and brushed off grass and crumbs. "I better go catch my bus home. It was great talking to you guys. Maybe I'll see you again."

"Are you sure you can get your bus? It's almost midnight," said Kerry.

"Shit! It didn't seem that late. Shit!"

"Hey, don't worry. I know it's hard if you don't have a car around here." Phil patted her arm. "You can stay at our place in Madison if you want."

"Oh, are you roommates?"

Kerry and Phil exchanged glances like they were sharing a joke. Then Phil winked at her, letting her know the joke wasn't about her.

"Well, it's more like a commune," said Kerry. "A group of us live there."

"I didn't know there were communes in New Jersey. I thought you have to go to New York for that."

"There are communes everywhere," said Phil. "Even here. There's more to Jersey than meets the eye."

Linda was pleased with the day's second invitation. Then she remembered that her parents were waiting for her to phone from the bus stop. "Yeah, Phil, that sounds great about staying at your place. But I've got to call…"

No way can she talk about *parents*. "I've got to phone my friend who's expecting me back tonight. You know, my roommate. Can I phone from your place?"

"We're not going there straight away," said Kerry. "First stop's a little party out in the Pine Barrens. But we can find a phone booth on the way to this party. It'll be friends of friends I knew from college. I just went to Glassboro State, while some of these guys come from Princeton. But they're different. Science guys who like weird experiments, loud music and parties."

"I'm – I was – crap at science," said Linda.

"I don't think you need to know much science to party with them."

She told her parents that she'd met a friend at the festival – from the bookshop over in Madison remember? First it was: who is this friend? What's her name, where does she live, what's her telephone number? But still, she had another *friend* for once. And this *friend* had other friends who were students from *Princeton*.

Princeton boys? Her Mom was over the moon. Of course you can go.

Linda folded herself into the backseat of an ancient two-door sports car bearing a bumper sticker: *Don't blame me, I'm from Massachusetts.*

She'd been the only kid at school who was against Nixon last year, so she might as well be from Massachusetts too.

Maybe she'll head *there* after high school.

Linda peered out the window as they drove. The road signs flashed names she'd never seen in family trips to the shore. *Mount Misery Road. Ong's Hat.*

"That's a funny name. Ong's Hat!"

"Oh, there's a story to that," said Kerry "This guy called Jacob Ong flung his hat in the air, and it didn't come down. Some say it got stuck in a tree, but others say it went into another dimension. That kind of thing often happens in the Pines – allegedly."

"Yeah, sure!" Linda snickered. They were passing a bar, marked by a sign showing a grinning red devil with an overflowing mug of beer in his hand and the legend 'I partied with the Jersey Devil'.

"That's the second bar we've passed called the Jersey Devil," Linda observed.

"There's a dozen bars round here with that name. He's South Jersey's most famous resident," said Phil.

"Never heard of him!"

"What? I thought even North Jersey people know about JD!" Kerry seems truly shocked. "We're heading towards his native habitat, maybe you'll get to meet him!"

"Kerry's just pulling your leg. Ain't no such thing!"

"I believe in JD! It's a good old story anyway."

"Tell me about it." Linda was getting to like Kerry's tales.

"Some poor woman in the eighteenth century had twelve kids, see. When she was pregnant with her thirteenth she cursed the child and said, 'let this child be the devil'. And first he looked like a normal boy baby, but he grew horns, tail, got wings, the works. And he hangs out in the Pines. But some people say he's an evolutionary throwback from an isolated bog."

"Like the Loch Ness monster?"

"Maybe, but Nessie stays in her lake and doesn't go flying about and getting into mischief," said Kerry. "JD's a winged reptilian creature. He makes a lot of noise. Some say he attacks travellers, others have him going through peoples' garbage and stealing chickens. In 1906 he got bored in the Pines and rampaged around Trenton and Philadelphia, where he attacked a streetcar. It was in the papers."

"That means it must be true, eh?" Linda giggled.

The car made another turn, the road thumping and bumping beneath the wheels. They were driving through a forest of stunted, twisted pines. White sand between the mini-pines gleamed in the headlights. Another turn, back on a road between oaks with wide-spreading branches that scratched at the sides of the car.

Phil turned the radio on to a station coming from Philadelphia, and sang along with another quivery, bluesy song: *"Let him go, God bless him, Wherever he may be, He can travel this whole world over, and never find another girl like me."*

She always liked the mournful melodies the most, and it seemed Phil did too. Maybe he was sad, like her. Perhaps he had a friend who died, or maybe he had that sad bit inside him that didn't seem to come from anywhere.

They pulled into a clearing with a scattering of trailers, cabins and shacks and those big tee-pee things. There were chicken coops, but they didn't appear to house chickens. A few children crawled out of one and waved fizzing sparklers.

"Here we are," announced Kerry. "Here's the party!"

People gathered around a big campfire. Strings of Christmas tree lights glowed between the trailers, speakers were placed around the clearing as well. As they got closer to the group Linda heard *Ohio*, that song about student demonstrators shot by the National Guard. Though it was an angry song, its defiance and rhythm also made her want to dance. But everyone was just sitting around and talking.

"C'mon, Linda. Let's go near the fire," suggested Kerry. "Oh, here's Sunny and Joel!" A short woman in a long Indian dress came over, along with someone who looked like a bigger version of Cousin Itt from *The Addams Family*.

Kerry gave Sunny a hug and explained: "We went to Glassboro together, but Sunny went on to bigger and better things as Princeton's token Piney."

"*Ex*-token Piney," Sunny corrected. "They've called our thesis 'seditious nonsense' and we're out on our asses! But they haven't come up with a replacement. After all, you can't get any Piney-er than me. I'm even a descendant of the woman who gave birth to the Jersey Devil."

Kerry nudged Linda. "I'm part Scottish, so maybe I'm related to Nessie."

Joel looked up from under his heap of hair. "Yeah, the resemblance is obvious. Check the profile!"

He did speak a little slower than Cousin Itt, in a strong Brooklyn accent. He chuckled briefly, then lapsed into silence and stared at the ground.

"Don't mind Joel," said Sunny. "He overdid the weed. You know the kind of things he worries about when he gets paranoid."

"Hey, Joel, you always make me think of that joke," said Phil. "How do you know when a mathematician is being outgoing? He looks at the other guy's feet!"

"I object to that," said Joel. "I'm a *physicist*, and I've got a joke for you. An engineer, physicist, and mathematician go to a motel..."

Science kids at school were really straight, Linda thought. Always peering into a microscope or a test tube, not caring about what happened around them. Sucking up to teachers so they can go to a college with fancier telescopes. Can you really be a scientist *and* a hippy? Linda pushed her hair behind her ears, as if it would let her hear and understand all the chatter buzzing around her.

"…connecting between two or more resonant spaces – "

" – multiple realities in the same spatial location, but slightly out of phase."

"…dissonant symmetry."

She felt more than slightly out of phase herself. The words echoed in her head until they meant even less than she thought.

"…our skin is a boundary but so much can cross it."

Who said that? She stroked her arm, imagining what she wanted to cross the barrier of her skin.

Meanwhile Sunny was saying something to Kerry about *quantum voodoo*.

"You always were an intense chick, Sun." Kerry was laughing.

Are these people too busy talking shop at parties to do any dancing? And Joel was finishing his story "…and the mathematician said 'a solution exists' and went back to sleep!"

Linda was getting tired of standing so she went to sit on a log near the fire. When Joel slumped down next to her, she was surprised but pleased.

"Hi there," he said. "I've not seen you before. So you're a friend of Phil's?"

"Well, I just met him tonight. At the folk festival."

"Good old Phil. He's always meeting people and bringing them round. He's a great guy. I've known him for years. Kind of a charmer, but he means well."

Charmer. Is he warning her? Does that mean he *knows*? The idea that anyone could *know* mortified Linda. Better change the subject so she doesn't look so keen.

"Sunny said you get paranoid," she said quickly. "So do I! What do you worry about then?"

Joel looked at her and blinked. "It's not paranoia. It's facing the truth. The universe will freeze, though the sun might swallow us up first. We have no escape. At the most we can delay our miserable end by a few million years. Unless…There may be one way out, but *they* –"

"Is Joel bending your ear? He's always such a big laugh at parties."

Phil ruffled Joel's great volume of hair and sat down next to Linda.

Kerry and Sunny joined them on the log too, now talking about pals from college. As Kerry chatted with her friend, she took hold of Phil's hand. It startled Linda. But she held Phil's hand in a loose kind of way, as if they were just good friends. Phil did introduce Kerry as his *friend*. Martine used to hold Linda's hand sometimes. It first felt weird. Then she realised it must have something to do with being French. Kerry looked like she might be partly Italian, and maybe that's how Italians do things too. She wished she could be French or Jewish or Italian. *Something*, not just a boring American Twinkie-eating WASP.

She started shifting back and forth on the log. She looked around. Two women were dancing together – to a slow song. Were they...

Whatever you do, don't stare. But where will she look instead? It would be worse if she got caught staring at Phil.

Martine always knew her way around places like this. The first time Linda went to *Change Your Mind* people were sitting around the desk, talking about going to an anti-war demonstration in New York. Linda wanted to join in, but there wasn't any room left to sit there. Martine was in that group too.

So Linda went to look at magazines. She picked up one with a cartoon on the cover showing a man in a suit running around with a butterfly net outside a school. He was trying to catch the kids who were running free all over the place. That must be why the magazine was called *Outside the Net*.

Inside was a poem by a high school junior who later committed suicide. This kid drew to express the things that pushed inside, he wanted to carve it in stone or write it in the sky. At school he had to sit in a square brown desk, but he thought it should be red. He hated to hold the pencil with his arms stiff and his feet flat on the floor, the teacher watching. He drew a yellow picture, and it was the way he felt about morning.

But the teacher said he should draw pictures like the other boys. So he wore a tie and drew rocket ships and airplanes. But he was messed up by it.

Linda later read that poem over and over and knew those last lines by heart:

"He was square inside and brown
And his hands were stiff
And he was like everyone else
And the things inside him that needed saying
Didn't need it anymore
It had stopped pushing
It was crushed
Stiff
Like everything else."

"Hey Linda, can I get you a drink?" Phil pointed to the biggest trailer. "There's lots of cold beer in there."

While Phil was getting the beer Kerry gave her some brownies – hash brownies, she said. Linda ate half of one, and put the rest in her bag. When Phil came back with their beer he sat down next to her and asked if she was OK.

"You seemed quiet. Hope you don't feel left out. I know what it's like being a stranger." He smiled that crooked smile.

She wanted to tell him everything now. She *had* to.

"You know that girl I was with at the bookshop?"

"Yeah, Martine."

"She was my best friend and now she's dead."

Those words sounded so short, so final. *Now she's dead.*

"Hey, I'm sorry to hear that. Really sorry."

"She OD'd. Her parents blame it on her friends. They hung up after they told me on the phone. Well, they did give Martine shit about going to church, being Catholic and going out with boys. Sometimes they drove her crazy with that stuff and it got her down. But they'd been OK in their way. They invited me to supper and made French food. They're French, though Martine was born here. And all the time I'm wondering what happened, why it happened. It must've been an accident but what led up to it? And I keep wondering if I could have done something to stop it."

Phil put his arm around her. "That must be terrible."

Linda was trying not to cry. Sometimes, it was harder when people were nice to you.

It had been like that the first time she met Martine in the bookshop.

Crushed. Stiff. Like everything else.

First, a single tear rolled down her cheek.

She sniffed and wiped it away. But tears just kept coming. She always knew there was something wrong with her. This was it.

Square inside. Everything in you just scooped out.

Martine came and asked her if she was OK. Linda felt like a fool. But Martine took her into a little room with lots of comfy cushions. They ended up talking all afternoon.

Linda didn't want to cry this time. Her voice was shaking but at least she was able to keep talking. Phil held her and stroked her hand and even though she was so sad, she felt wonderful. He leaned forward and his lips just brushed her cheek, though her hair was in the way.

Talking to Phil made everything feel lighter. Soon she was telling how Martine had helped her with her French homework and then taught her the best French swear words.

Phil seemed to enjoy her collection of French curses. He stopped giggling and taught her some things in German.

She knew she could be a laugh sometimes, and maybe that was why he liked her too. It made her feel warm and oozy to think of that. He really did like her. He didn't treat her like she was just a kid.

"Hey, I'm getting hungry now, are you? There's food in the trailer too. I'll be back!"

Linda waited for Phil to return, but he was taking a while. She needed to find a toilet. Could there be one in the silver trailer with the beer?

The trailer was crowded with people who probably needed the bathroom too, so she kept walking up the path. There was a light twinkling in the woods. Perhaps that was a cabin or an outhouse. The music from the party filtered through the trees and she heard the Jefferson Airplane singing about how people will rise up against the government in 1975. Only two years to go!

Maybe she'll go back and dance, especially if they play *Volunteers*. Maybe Phil will dance with her.

The thought made her stride ahead into the moonlit woods.

She heard rustling and murmuring from the trees on her right. She was about to avert her eyes to the path in front of her and walk on, then she recognised one of the voices. Phil? He'd gone for food, but that trailer must've been crowded for him too. But who was with him?

He had his arms around someone; they swayed together.

A quick sickness stabbed Linda in the stomach. He'd liked her. Remember those fingertips brushing, that quick squeeze. How he hugged her as she told him about Martine.

She should have walked on. But she was rooted just like those crazy stunted trees they passed in the car.

She heard a low chuckle. *Kerry?* Phil and Kerry were together? She thought they were just friends. She thought Phil liked *her*.

Linda stepped forward to flee, but made a loud *crack* when she put her foot down. The couple separated.

"Hey Linda! You OK?" Kerry emerged from behind Phil. Her hair was sticking out, looking even greyer in the moonlight.

She wished she could dissolve in a puddle like the wicked witch of the fucking West. Melt away, after being caught out. But Kerry was smiling at her.

Phil grinned and gave her a thumb's up.

"You lost?"

"Yeah, I was looking for a bathroom, but the trailer was packed and I couldn't wait. I saw a light and thought there might be an outhouse or something."

"That's an old clubhouse they use. There might be a toilet. But they keep a lot of stuff there so it's probably locked. You just might have to use the natural facilities."

"Yeah, I remember how to do that. Cover your shit with leaves. Fucking Girl Scouts!" Linda couldn't stop herself from talking nonsense.

"I went to Scouts too," said Kerry, "but it was a long long time ago."

"I hated Girl Scouts," said Linda. "My parents made me go 'cause they thought it would be good for me and I'd stop being 'negative'."

The two of them were being *too* cool about it. Phil must think she was just some kid he could pat on the back when she cried. It didn't even occur to him that she'd be upset to find him with Kerry like this.

"I gotta go," said Linda.

"See you later," said Phil. "Let us know when you want to leave."

She started to walk, but she couldn't stop herself from looking back.

They were hidden by trees now, but seeing nothing was worse.
Then she ran.

On each side of the path the columns of pines didn't move a needle, though the breeze moved strands of hair into her face. She walked towards the light and found it. A single bare bulb surrounded by moths and gnats above the door of a single-level building. It didn't look like it would have electricity, but those hippies managed to wire something up. A faded sign said it was a *Rod and Gun Club.*

Phil's a charmer, but he means well. Joel must've seen *it* in her, all her thoughts and desires. She'd been making a fool out of herself.

She knocked, then banged at the door. It's locked, fucking *locked.* With a final bang she ran again, further into the woods.

As the path narrowed, the trees on each side reached over to each other to make a tunnel. Where did it lead? Not back to the party, to failure and humiliation. They all must be laughing at her now, that silly lump of a girl who took a shine to Phil. They were nice to her, but it was only because they felt sorry for her.

So people get scared to stay out in the Pines at night?

She wasn't scared. She'd put on insect repellent at the festival. She's got sandwiches left. And hash brownies.

Why did that woman in the song run into pines?

She was beginning to understand why.

Linda thought she'd been following a path. But now she made her way through random spaces between the trees.

Soon she heard a stream, and she moved towards the sound. The trees were so close together, like bars on a prison. Some were half-bare, limbs twisted like pretzels.

No leaves rustled, no animals scampered. Silence filled the forest.

She was getting hungry. She took out a sandwich and took bites out of it as she walked. The mayonnaise in the tuna salad had turned the bread soggy.

The ground was also getting mushy. Little puddles formed between her footfalls. Then a space showed between the trees. She walked through it to a clearing where she found the stream, widening into a broad patch of water like a pond.

She rested at the edge, and took another bite. Here there were white birches, pale like skeletons with pines among them. Some of the pines had no branches at all, only clumps of needles sticking out from the trunk. They made her think of pictures of thalidomide children she'd seen in *Newsweek*. There was a patch of ground in the middle of the pond covered with the white birch-bones and one single twisted pine tree. On the grassy bank opposite, tall dark ranks of pines extended to the places she couldn't see.

She never thought she'd be eating a tuna sandwich alone in the woods at night. She always ate her lunch alone at school. It was what she knew. But she never knew what it's like to look at the sky and see no one else under it, no one at all. She finally found a place behind a tree and squatted. It would be easier doing this in a long hippy skirt.

Linda felt like she was being watched. Not by a person, not even by an animal. It was the place itself, poised and waiting. She listened for a breeze, for anything. She began humming. *"In the pines, in the pines where the sun never shines…"* She thought of her only friend Martine, slumped dead over the desk in her room, stretched out on the bed or lost somewhere…

She walked along the side of the pond, slow through boggy land. Good thing she had on hiking boots. She wore them everywhere because she liked the way they looked.

The thalidomide trees gave way to cedars as wide as barrels. Their branches arched and looped over dark water. A flowerpot was hanging from a branch of the biggest one, but there was nothing left growing in it.

A clean spicy wood smell filled the air. She knew they were cedars from that smell, because Martine used to burn cedar-scented incense. The fragrance went to her head and her humming turned into the song itself.

People used to say she had a good voice. Her parents urged her to try out for the school choir. Made her. She got in. But her singing never blended in with the school anthem, the national anthem or any other stinking anthem. She quit before the Christmas assembly because she hated the carols, especially those warbling high notes in the 'Gloria' choruses.

In The Pines was a song that went low. She pushed those low notes out with deep breaths, and the high ones came piercing and forlorn. *"My girl, my girl, where will you go? I'm going where the cold winds blow..."*

The emptiness of the forest gathered her notes, and waited.

Out of the sky came another voice if it could be called a voice, another note weaving between and below her song. It was soft at first, a thread of dissonance. But it rose, and kept rising into a shriek. It was distress, it was a threat. It wasn't human, and it wasn't like any animal she'd ever heard. She's seen films. She's been to the zoo. So she knew what a lot of animals sounded like, and this wasn't one of them.

It could have started from many throats, but came out of only one mouth.

It came from far away, but it was getting closer.

It was here, with a beat of wings cracking the branches above her.

It landed in front of her, under a cedar tree.

It had a face like a horse, but without the attentive expression of a horse. It was a blank face, made of two flat planes of bone on a long thick neck. It had curved ram-like horns, a long body covered with scales. They gleamed in a liquid but murky way, like the puddles between the trees. It had hooves on its back legs and claws on its forelegs, long leathery wings like a big bat's. It reared up on its back legs and held up two short front legs, with claws extended.

It let loose its cry again, starting with piercing mournful notes and subsiding into a low and hoarse rumble.

Fuck! This must be the Jersey Devil. It's *real*. And it's not holding a beer and inviting her to party either.

What can she do? Where can she hide? Her heart was banging, she could hardly draw her breath in and out. It hurt her ribs. But –

She didn't believe in devils, so it must be an animal. And wild animals don't usually attack people unless they're cornered or scared.

Can't you talk to animals to calm them down?

"Hi, are you the guy called the Jersey Devil?" She made her voice low and soothing, the way she used to talk to the dog at Martine's. Their huge Airedale was always in a huff, but he was soon wagging his tail whenever Linda came round. Martine's Mom thought Linda had a way with animals. She sure hoped so.

"Where do you come from? Oh, what am I saying? Of course, you live here. Sorry if I disturbed you."

Just keep talking. Anything. Animals don't understand what you say, but they'll listen to the sound. It'll hear that you don't mean any harm. Or is it a 'he'? According to Kerry's story, JD was born as a human boy. She wasn't sure about *that*. Male or female didn't seem to apply here.

"I guess I wouldn't be happy if someone came crashing into my home, making lots of noise. Was my singing that bad?*"* Her heart was slowing down. At least this blabbering was calming *her* down. She must *not* panic, or the clawed creature will smell it. "Or maybe you didn't care for the song… You know, the one I was singing…*In the pines in the pines where the sun never shines.*"

The creature cocked its head to the side and let out another yelp that climbed into a crescendo. Just listening made a pressure form in her chest. It made her feel sick. Everything about this creature seemed so *wrong*, as if it was put together to fit another place.

It lunged.

Linda stepped back and her foot got stuck in the soft ground. She put out an arm to break her fall and her sandwich flew from her hand. She cowered on the ground in the shadow of its wings as it stepped forward.

A clawed foreleg reached out for a piece of sandwich. The creature sat back on its haunches as it quickly disposed of it. Then it grabbed the other half. Thank fucking goodness it found that sandwich more appetising than me, Linda thought.

"Liked that didn't you? Here's another one," She reached into her bag and threw her remaining sandwich towards the beast. "And look, here are some cakes."

There go the hash brownies. Maybe it'll get good and stoned.

When all the food was gone, it began to make a barking sound.

"No, sorry that's all I've got. I'll bring more next time. Maybe I should just be getting on my way. Thanks for your time, mm, uh, do you mind when people call you Jersey Devil? I mean, I don't like it when people call me Ug-ug-ugly Linda. You know, like that sappy Paul McCartney song? It's crap, that song. Everyone knows John's the only old Beatle who writes good songs now. My favourite is *Working Class Hero*, but you never get to hear it unless you have the album. All the radio stations banned it 'cause he says *fuck*."

She was starting to feel like someone else, someone who knew what to do. It was like swimming to the top of a huge wave and riding the crest of it.

But where does the wave go?

Just keep talking. Pretend this scaly thing's just a grumpy Airedale.

"Even WNEW banned the song, and they pretend they're *so* cool. But John's right. We get stuck in schools where you don't learn anything except how to conform. They only prepare you to take orders in some crap job or fight wars for corrupt politicians. They brainwash you with religion, TV and bullshit…"

Then the creature howled. It seemed as if each howl floated somewhere so desolate it could never be seen.

"OK, OK, sorry, so you're not a John Lennon fan! I thought you came to tell me to shut up when you flew over here, but maybe you really like *In The Pines*.

She began to sing that song again.

"My girl, my girl don't you lie to me, where did you sleep last night?"

She didn't remember all the words. But didn't Phil say that people made up their own words as they went along? *"Her body was on the driving wheel, her mind was never found. Martine, Martine why'd you die on me?"*

Every sound the Jersey Devil made clashed with her singing. It would have given the choir teacher a heart attack. It didn't make her feel that well either.

Yet the sounds belonged together.

It was singing of its own loss too. It was singing about being lost, of fleeing to darkness – the only place it could ever make its home. Light was for other people. Not for Linda. Not for the Jersey Devil.

The creature keened. She felt as though something was about to split in her chest. Notes floated from the trees like needles, like leaves. The minor chords tugged and unravelled her. The pines were full of voices. The noise released them, as if they had been trapped in ice and amber now melting.

Sound waves never die. She remembered that much from science, taught by greasy Mr Gerber. So where do they go, when the person making the sound is dead?

When the creature came closer, this time she wasn't afraid. It stretched out, now resting on its front legs. It lowered a wing, and looked at her with eyes too big for its face. They were flat, yet facets below the surface shifted. She was sure those eyes were meant to see another kind of light, and the Jersey Devil was trying to find it. And it seemed to want her to sit on its back.

"No, no I'm too heavy," Linda protested. "I don't think it'll work!" But it waited, and barked with impatience. It wasn't going to give up.

When she sat astride its back, she was overwhelmed with the smell of swamp. Yet there was a clear sky scent too that must have clung to it when it flew. Its scales were surprisingly warm and dry. She tried to find something to grasp on its narrow back. She wasn't aware of lifting into the air. The lurching movement didn't come as a result of flapping wings, or putting one foot ahead of another. She wasn't aware of going *up* or *down* or *sideways.* Yet they moved.

The air was full of angles and curves, suffused with a green light as if she looked up through a pool of water covered with lilies. Branches surrounded her and pine needles pressed against her, each one bringing a stab, a spark. Each needle falling off made a *ping*, a ring like a glass singing before it broke. Everything smelled of sap and wood. The pines spread below her feet, an ocean of trees cut with the shine of waters, fringed on the horizon by a darkness that might be the Atlantic.

Then they angled in a direction that could have been 'down', for the trees were coming close again. "Where are we going?" Linda whispered to the Jersey Devil.

It didn't reply. Even if it spoke to its own kind, it didn't know her language.

But she could guess the answer.

In the pines, in the pines where the sun never shines.

3. High lonesome frequency (Cornwall, 2015)

Look, there's two blokes in brand new hiking gear. Poking about, but trying not to appear that way. Too studiously casual to be officials or property developers. They're not tourists – too sombre, too intent.

This isn't actually our land so I can't tell them to fuck off.

I don't want them to see me. I walk faster down the hill. I have work to do, so I'll just ignore them.

I only need to duck down a little at the entrance of the cave, stepping through the fringe of bluebells, ferns and foxgloves that grow around it. The afternoon sun throws light into the passage, showing fractal patterns of moss and lichen over the dry-stone walls and the stone slabs that make up its roof.

"Alright, mate?" I nod at the figure carved into a boulder near the opening, a man with long hair and raised arms, the left side of his face flecked away. Some heritage people from Penzance come to look after him, but he's showing his age – a good 2000 years or so.

I follow the passage as it curves deeper into the earth and I turn on my torch. As I descend the sounds of buzzing bees and squawking birds fade away with the light.

In the main chamber I sit down with my back against the wall. I take my laptop out of my rucksack and let it boot up.

There's plenty of time before our interview tonight. So I open a page of equations that have been pissing me off for days. The light my computer sheds on the walls of the cave is not at all harsh or out-of-place. I've found yet one more use for something that was obviously built to last. This iron-age hideaway might have been used for rituals or to store grain. Smugglers and wreckers took advantage of its protection. There are stories of Saxon massacres and witches' sabbats here, though if a coven consists of thirteen those parties must have been standing-room only.

"Resonance, resonance…" I mutter, as if simply repeating the word will achieve something. Maybe the Celts chanted a lot down here, but it obviously didn't do them much good. I had a semi-mystical phase myself. But it only went so far, like everything else.

A few days ago I gave another set of equations to the musicians. The only result was a headache when I ventured into their studio. Let's see, if two people have headaches with the exact pattern of pounding pain, can they share their thoughts? Try that for an experiment!

I scan the figures and symbols again, but I see no completion. Something's missing. I sigh and close my eyes. I try to imagine vibrating strings tied up in knots and how I can put that in numbers; and the ways I can translate and express those numbers in music and in colour. But my surroundings fill my mind instead.

So far I've not seen any ghosts of witches, smugglers or Celtic warriors down here. Ghosts don't interest me anyway. But often I sense a shifting in the stillness of this place. It's like I'm sat in a traffic island that's deadly quiet at the centre, but there are vehicles whizzing around it. I'm trying to hitch a lift but no one's stopped. I can't even see the cars but feel the breeze and smell their 'exhaust' as they go by.

What I really smell is earth and stone, damp dirt and dry dust together. It's a scent of time passing. There is rot and decay, fresh growth that extends roots from the ground above; the lichen and moss as it clings and penetrates the walls. Particles of stone falling off and crumbling. There is something else, a clean, almost-medicinal smell like pine. I breath deeper, let it fill me, let it expand. The space around me also expands as I breathe, my confined room opening up until I'm in the centre of a hub that spirals out in countless roads and paths.

I still can't catch what passes by, or where the roads go.

Then there is someone, just walking in a place where everything else moves so fast. A tall, strapping woman with curly dark hair, a smile with a promise of mischief. Her sights are set ahead. I'm afraid she'll get knocked down by the traffic. Though I can't see it, the traffic must be dangerous because I feel its sucking undertow as it goes by. But she walks forward, calm and set on her goal.

Except for the silver in her hair, she looks just like me. I dye mine these days.

I know her name. *Esther.*

I'm hit by sadness, feeling a loss that came before all others. It wells up uncontrollably, a hidden spring of salt water.

Then I'm staring at my screensaver, a photo of our big black cat Schrody.

When I emerge outside, the sun is already setting.

"Briony, you were down that fuckin' *fogou* again." Deb doesn't usually swear, but in this case she can't resist a bit of alliteration.

She's already working her way through a pile of washing up. "I know when you've been down that hole. You're always late."

"Sorry, I just lost track of time. It happens there. But I get ideas too."

"What idea did you get this time?"

"Oh, I'll tell you later." This isn't the time to tell her I saw my twin sister – who had died shortly after birth. I don't know if it's a vision –

my unconscious grasping something that could be there, but hidden – or simply a wistful dream. I've never told Deb about Esther. Why should I? I was just born, what would I remember? I only heard stories from my parents and I used to wonder about her. Then I stopped thinking about it when I became interested in mathematics and boys.

Perhaps stress brought it on. This interview, maybe.

I used to be good at interviews. I'd made presentations, sweet-talked grants committees, appeared on talk shows and gone on book tours. I admit I enjoyed the attention. I was full of *chutzpah* and I knew the *craiq* too. I got that much from my Jewish *and* Irish Catholic background, along with a great multicultural helping of guilt and repression.

The woman who's interviewing us – Linda Brooks – used to be famous too. Years ago she was a top war correspondent. She went missing in action; then she was found. Now she only writes occasional articles about health and mental health and women who do unusual things. Deb said that Linda's last article was an excellent piece on services for torture survivors. So Linda should be very worthy. No headlines like 'Curvy quantum cutie' from her. I shouldn't worry.

Deb is playing some of my old music, *Nirvana Unplugged*. It always amazes me when young people listen to music I loved when I was even younger and full of angst. I'd just moved to London and started university. I was living in a grotty bedsit with one ring for cooking my baked beans, etcetera etcetera – the whole scene.

Despite her taste in depressive 1990s rock, Deb's always been upbeat. Somehow, she skipped the miserable phase. People like that seem to come from another planet – bless 'em.

"Oh hi, I guess I'm early! I was afraid of getting lost and I *hate* being late." A bright gee-whiz American voice chimes at the door.

This must be Linda: a tall blonde woman in a brand new Climatex outdoor jacket – trendier than the stuff worn by the maybe-spooks I spotted this afternoon. I can smell the newness of the jacket from here. My eyes are drawn to her lime green knee-high wellies.

Who let her in without warning us? I'm not ready.

Deb holds up her plastic-gloved hands. "Oh hi you caught us by surprise! Sorry about the mess, but we weren't expecting you until later. Just let me turn the music off."

Linda is clearly shocked at the state of our kitchen. The clutter, cupboards open, plates and cups still in need of washing. What did she expect? A laboratory?

Linda isn't what I expected either, kitted out in full retro-cool London-luvvie-roughing-it mode. But what did I expect – a flak jacket?

"Never mind," I say. "Have a seat." I point to the armchair by the bay window. But it's still occupied by Schrody, who often gets mistaken for a cushion. I scoop her up and onto the floor. She lets out an indignant *miaou* and stalks off.

Linda looks likely to do the same as she scrutinises the chair.

"Sorry Linda, are you allergic to cats?" I ask

"No, I'm not allergic, just…" Linda brushes at the cushion and finally lowers herself into it. "It's OK."

This woman fussing about a few cat hairs was once dodging bullets? But then, that was years ago and I've changed too. She must be older than me, somewhere in her fifties but seems younger. With her jacket off, she has that raw, incomplete look that large-boned people get when they're too thin.

"Perhaps we can get started." She's all business, leaving out the introductory remarks about the weather, her guesthouse accommodation and the long journey from London. We don't even have time to offer a cup of tea before she takes out her I-Voice and switches it on.

"So Ms… Dr…"

"Call me Briony. And this is Debjani," I add. "A physicist working on our project. She also co-authored the second book."

Linda gives Deb a big smile with teeth gleaming like piano keys, but her eyes are only on me as she gets her machine going. "As you know, *The Review* wants a human interest rather than a technical angle. I'm not a specialist myself, but I did find your books fascinating and liked the fact they were written for a lay audience. Your work on time travel, alternate universes and dimensions sparked a lot of debate. Then you disappeared… What have been up to in the last eight years or so?"

"Well…" I find myself staring at the contents of a teacup that had escaped the washing up. Get a grip! You're not telling the woman's fortune. "Well, I needed a change. Being a celebrity scientist was getting in the way of the real science. And I was thinking beyond pure mathematics, and wanted to explore other symbolic systems and other disciplines that embrace all the senses. Abstract formulas showed the way, they gave me the bones, but where was the flesh?"

Is that a snort of suppressed laughter coming from Deb at 'flesh'? No doubt she's thinking about some earlier 'experiments' I told her about. I'm reminded of our age difference in moments like this. I give her a discreet nudge with my foot and carry on: "It's been said that the separation between science, art and music is relatively recent. But we wanted to take these connections further and see how 'art' can actively aid scientific exploration, particularly in areas that are new and a bit strange. So we got together with artists and musicians and settled here. I was drawn to this place on my first visit, and blew the advance from the second book on a rundown old wreck. But we did a lot work. Not bad, is it?"

I point to the bay window and its view of the valley, a lush swathe cut into arid cliffs and windswept fields.

"It's lovely," says Linda, "but wouldn't you find it isolated after being at the centre of things? You were at the top of your profession at a relatively young age. Why did you suddenly withdraw and give up your academic position in London?"

"I could ask *you* a similar question!" I snap back without thinking.

"Briony just needed more space to do her work. We all did." Diplomatic Deb jumps in. "We just wanted to get on with things, working as a group. There are about twenty of us coming and going. Some of us still teach or do research or other part-time jobs, but what we do here is our main interest."

I will give Deb credit for *not* mentioning that some of our lot still sign on, or our ways of dealing with those electronic job-seekers' implants! And I'm also thinking that it's time to stop. I can see my *spiel* getting disjointed and my ill-temper taking over. I've fallen out of practice, I really have. It won't be fair on Deb to get stuck with playing good cop to my bad one.

I want to talk about the work we do together, now that I've done my job as a formerly famous person by drawing attention to it. But with the way that silly cow's been ignoring Deb, I don't know how much good it will do. I really don't trust this woman.

Maybe I'm just getting to be an old cynic. I shouldn't ruin it for the others. *Try* to be nice.

"Linda, maybe we can show you around." I suggest. "And our musicians are playing in the local tonight. You might find that more illuminating than listening to me! You're here for the weekend, so we can go into more detail later. Let's have a break and a cuppa," I put on the kettle and get some mugs onto the table.

Linda picks up a mug and furtively examines the rim. "What music were you playing when I came in?"

"Just Nirvana," I say.

Linda shrugs. "I have big gaps in my musical knowledge, since I was out of the country a lot in the 90s. Some old stuff is really new to me. It sounded OK."

"You like it? I'll play my favourite song from that album." Deb puts the music on, then goes foraging for biscuits while Kurt Cobain begins to rasp and wail that old song about headless bodies and hiding in the pines where the sun never shines.

Linda stops her inspection of the mug, putting it down with a thump. She looks like she's just been punched in the face. She's shaking. She puts her head down, her eyes behind her hand.

Deb runs to her rescue. "Linda, you alright?"

Linda doesn't respond, except to hide her face more.

"Maybe you need something stronger than tea," I suggest. "Would some whisky suit you better?" I take a bottle of Jameson's from the cupboard and pour a healthy amount into a glass.

Linda reaches for the whisky, with a muffled 'thanks'. Suddenly she takes her hand away from her face. She tips her head back to swallow it, fast. Her face is white, her eyes reddened but otherwise she is still in control.

"I never heard that before," she says in a flat voice.

"Eh?"

"That version of *In the Pines*. I collected them in high school. I worked part-time in a library and spent my wages on old records instead of saving for college. There's about a hundred recordings of that song – Hank Williams, Joan Baez, Leadbelly, Dolly Parton, Bob Dylan, Bill Monroe. I was so obsessed, I got ill. Ended up in the hospital.

"But I got better," she adds quickly. "Completed my high school equivalency. Went to college, grad school, became a journalist. I pulled through."

"It's an intense song," I comment. "Marianne Faithfull has sung it too, so did Hole. But Cobain's version is just... You hear it and think: he sounds like he's really going to do it."

Maybe that wasn't the right thing to say, because Linda looks even more disturbed. "I'm really sorry about this," she says. "It's not really professional, is it?"

"Don't worry," says Deb. "Maybe we're not so professional either."

"I first heard that song at a folk festival when I was sixteen and met people who took me to a party in the Pine Barrens. It's like another world there, though you're only a couple of hours from New York and Philadelphia. We visited a bunch of hippies living in yurts and trailers. They were into science and weird physics, some Princeton dropouts who took too much acid. I was... a friend had just died and I got upset with the people I came with and ran off. It was almost like the song, someone I loved had died and I spent the night in the pines."

"I had a friend who died when I was a teenager," I say, pouring a whisky for me and Deb and another for Linda. "She got killed in an accident at work. Another crashed when he was joyriding. Bad things seem to affect you even more at that age."

Linda's now keen to tell more about her teenage nervous breakdown. "The shrinks said I was a classic obsessive-compulsive. Keeping order was a way to stop things from *slipping*. But I snap out of it in the face of danger, real danger. Everything's clear then. That's why I was good on the frontline. But then it stopped working..."

Like many Americans, Linda seems to enjoy revealing highlights from assorted therapy sessions. But she still doesn't say what happened in the Pine Barrens.

After another round of whisky we head to the pub. On our way I point out the art building, dwellings and music studio. "We have the studio heavily soundproofed. The music boys – and they always seem to be boys – have a band called the M-Theories. Like the M-People, geddit? The landlord invited them to play when he heard them talking about music, but I'm not sure how they'll go down at the local."

"Briony's tastes are a little old-fashioned. *I* think they're good," said Deb.

I shine a torch on the path ahead as we go deeper into the valley, surrounded by flowering rhododendrons gone feral, clusters of ferns that stand higher than our heads. A few designer houses with angled window-covered wings perch on the ridge above us, looking like giant dragonflies. In their way they are beautiful, but not a good sign of things to come.

"When we bought this land, this was a deserted valley among the rocks far from a town or railway line," I tell Linda. "Only a few fishermen and some old hippies lived here, and the fishermen were getting fed up. Later came some low-key guesthouses and holiday cottages. But now developers want something big. We've got police looking for drugs every other night, and the developers have people in the council making up planning violations as we speak. There's also been tapping on the phone, suspicious people lurking about. We suspect that it's not only our prime real estate drawing unwanted attention, but also what we're doing."

"A couple of centuries ago, this valley was a hide-out for brigands and smugglers," Deb adds as we come down to the stream. "I like to think that in our geekish fashion we've been carrying on the tradition!"

If only, I think. If only the authorities really had something to worry about! They might believe we're onto some great subversive free-for-all dimension-bending science they have to stop, control or use for their own purposes. But we're not getting closer. Still, it's better we tell people what we're *trying* to do, rather than the wrong people find out and keep it to themselves.

We stop for a while at the bridge across the stream, look down at water rushing around moss-coated stones. If you follow the stream a mile to the sea, it swells and tumbles down the cliffs in a noisy, multi-tiered waterfall. Even here, mist and spray wafting from the bubbling, bashing water casts a layer of pearl over the green. I shine my torch on it, searching for a rainbow of colours from a spectrum I've never seen.

I caution Linda to avoid hitting her head at the entrance of the building. "It's a very old pub, 18th century I think. But like a lot of people around here, the landlord's family dates from the 1960s."

Linda is very impressed with the house brew, beer of an amber-honey colour with a head that's pure voluptuous cream. I let it slip down my throat as we watch the band setting up.

It's not the main session night, so our M-Theories won't face the usual rowdy lot here for Irish music, fiddle tunes and jigs. Still, people arrive from isolated cottages where fishermen and tin miners once lived. A few punters get off the bus that stops here twice each day.

There's old Jake with his dog, an alarming Rottweiller-Doberman cross that's really the soppiest animal outside of a Disney cartoon. A few of the session regulars, old-timers and the more settled incomers like me and Deb.

There isn't really a stage, simply a space at the front. It's all very cheek-by-jowl at sessions where fifteen musicians might materialise out of the woods. Tonight, there's a keyboard player, electric violins and two standing basses. There's a drummer whose kit gleams with extra gadgets, surfaces and snares. Someone else twiddles two dials and flips switches back and forth on a big black box while alternately twanging a tuning fork. I hope there'll be some improvement with the new equations, despite their flaws.

Ben, who plays standing bass, introduces a song. "While we're getting the dimensional resonator tuned I'll tell you a little about us."

"A what?" Linda frowns, then pulls a notebook out of her bag.

"I guess we're different from what you usually see here!" Ben continues. "We aim to pluck more than guitar strings, though guitar strings help. The strings we're plucking and the membranes we're hitting exist in ten and eleven-dimensional space. We want to twist them, braid them and roll'em into a ball! This song gets into the heavy stuff – we call it *Dark Matter*!

Then it starts. Ear-splitting waves, poundings, electronic burps, gurgles and screeches piling onto each other. It has an effect like a massive hunk of chalk dragged across a slate that might be called 'Earth'. Deb is nodding and grooving to the din, but Linda is looking truly stricken. Then she seems bored. She plays with a packet of crisps, as if the rattle of crumpled paper was more pleasing to her ear.

The dog starts howling. Ben must be taking that as a compliment, because he grins and whacks the strings of his standing bass with even more enthusiasm.

Then Linda laughs. It's the first time I've heard a proper laugh from her. "What a bunch of hippy shit!" She's laughing so hard she almost falls into the sawdust on the floor.

Despite my own reservations, I feel compelled to defend our lads. "Look, they're weaving physics into music, trying to cross dimensions with chordal structures, frequencies and harmonics." I raise my voice so she can hear.

"You're bullshitting me. I don't care what dimension they're from, it sounds like shit."

I give up. "OK, they do. But it's an experiment. And maybe they should keep their experiments in the laboratory or the studio, and not torture that poor dog with them. But sometimes you have to get things wrong before you get them right."

"But it's elitist rubbish to assume that the more obscure, tuneless and annoying you get, the more revolutionary and provocative you are!"

"They're not trying to annoy anyone. Most people writing *seriously* about parallel universes talk about using great machines and messing about with massive charges, energies and black holes. But what about other methods of finding a way through, of achieving resonance? Maybe there are things we can do in our own garden shed – with materials we have at hand, with our imaginations and creativity, with voices, visions and instruments that can prepare the way. Our approach is very DIY but the results might not be something you can sing along to."

"Why the fuck not?"

I don't have an answer to the question. *So why the fuck not?*

I'm mulling this over when Linda gets up and returns with more drinks. She takes a long draught of her beer, emerging with a foamy moustache. She wipes it off with the back of her sleeve. She's definitely not the same woman who walked into our house today.

The M-Theories are lurching through another discordant composition. Someone's trying to calm the dog.

"Why don't you play a goddamn tune!" Linda bellows, brandishing her pint.

"Linda, no!" Deb lays a light restraining hand on Linda's arm. "Shh-shh."

"Shhsh yourself Deb," I tell her. "I know you enjoy this stuff, but is it going anywhere? Just another bunch of geeks pissing about! Maybe our musicians need to be challenged."

Ben and the others are still twiddling their strings. They relish a bit of opposition, a bit of negative energy they can transform. Perhaps they're hoping the dog will howl again. The drummer stops. The guy on the dimensional resonator carries on. I can't hear what comes out of it, but the dog certainly does.

"Yeah, play some tunes!" I call.

"Alright," Ben agrees. "Maybe the music of the spheres isn't right for a night down the pub after all. Anyone know some tunes? Grab an instrument and join us."

One of the regulars rises to the occasion and picks up a violin. "Requests?"

I get an idea. "*In the Pines*?"

I make my suggestion a question, not sure what Linda will think. Does she get upset *every* time she hears it?

Linda glances at me, then down into her pint before another big swallow. "Yeah, why not? It's a beautiful song, it only took me by surprise before." She raises her voice again, shouting to the musicians.

"Yeah, play *In the Pines*!"

"Right." He begins scraping out the song. He plays it rough, torn from the belly of the instrument. There is discord in this too, but at its heart lies the melody.

My girl, my girl don't you lie to me,
Where did you sleep last night?

When he gets to the chorus, Linda is already singing along. Her voice is surprisingly strong and tuneful, however slurred her words. A hush falls. The barman leans on his elbows, just listening. The dog's ears prick up, but he stays quiet.

Before I know it I'm singing too. My voice is off-key and hesitant, but it fits in. The music blends with the rush of the stream beneath the bridge, the world outside becomes another instrument.

I've heard that song many times, usually the Nirvana version. But this is the first time I feel it. The electrified violin and standing bass, our own physicist-designed drum kits bring a new rhythm to it that beats beneath the soles of my feet and makes the bottles at the bar rattle. The dimensional resonator must be doing something in the background, though I don't know exactly what.

As the chords change there is a shift in me too, a bittersweet taste in my mouth. The bitterness stings. The sweetness makes me ache, ache to hear more of it. I am sucked into the darkest blue oscillation. I reverberate inside it, every cell pitched to that high and lonesome frequency that I am sharing with so many unknown others. My heart vibrates at a perfect pitch. The pitch is answered; it's found its match. I close my eyes and I see…

Scrawny pines at the top of a hill, bent by the wind. A woman sitting beneath them, facing a grave. *Where is he?* Twisted trees you can hide yourself in, staining the waters of a swamp.

The song cracks an egg open, letting everything out. *Where is he?* Where are my friends who died before they reached eighteen? I think of a would-be boyfriend blown up on a bus on his way to our second date. Lives never lived, potential not realised. Parts of me are missing, like the husband's body that was never found. *Where is he?*

Where is she? Where is Esther, the twin who shared everything with me long ago? I only know now how much I can still miss her.

Does sorrow have a frequency, does longing and pain? It is a strong one.

The sound of the stream is louder, almost a roar. Am I still in the pub? Deb sits across from me but doesn't seem to notice me. No, I'm not in the pub. Yes, I am. But the pub has expanded, and it contains a forest. It contains a world. Dark, rolling hills, the pines. Someone once wrote that each human creates from birth to death a double furrow of light and sounds; so do events, music and movement. I am falling into a furrow now.

I'm sitting on a seat formed from the stump of a tree. When I get up, I run my hands on a smooth, polished surface. The polishing brings out the pattern in the wood, a spiral instead of concentric rings. I run my finger around the spiral; the end of it loops back to the centre and begins again. I can't tell the age of this tree.

I realise I have company. Linda, lime wellies and all. Christ, Linda. She must be freaking out.

But she's only pulling her hood up as if going for a stroll. She seems very much at home though her cheeks glisten with tears. She gives a sigh of something that sounds like resignation.

Maybe she's stunned. I should explain what's happening, even if I'm a bit dazed myself. I want to skip and cheer. What a brilliant discovery. But I'm also tuned to the frequencies of loss, ready to cry. I have to keep it together.

I try to be reassuring as we walk along a path. "It's alright. We just need to stay calm. We never left the pub, but that pub shares space with another place, or many places coincide in the same place as the pub. Think of radio waves. We are surrounded by them, but you can only tune to one frequency. But what if we have more than one radio on? After so much faffing it took a simple folk song to achieve this… this resonant coupling, this connection! Brilliant, brilliant – Jesus Christ! What the fuck is *that*?"

There's a flash of grey and green wings through the upper branches of the trees, an eerie cry rising and descending scales not meant to be heard by human ears. Something lands in front of us, a very badly-designed dragon with a head like a horse with bone disease. It spreads its wings and shrieks and glares with red eyes.

"What the…" I stutter. Take a deep breath, try to listen to something other than my heart in my ears. Curiosity should win over fear.

Those eyes transfix me. They have another colour besides the red. I don't recognise it. More than one colour there, but they don't blend. They are just *in the same place*. Maybe the creature isn't glaring after all. But what is it looking for?

Linda pats my arm. "Don't panic, it's only the Jersey Devil. I've met it once before. It'll be fine if you give it something, you know, make friends. The poor thing's just lost. I don't know why it stays stuck."

The poor thing is making a racket far, far worse than Ben's first few numbers.

"Good thing I still have some crisps." Linda opens a packet and tosses them towards the noisy monster squatting yards away from us. The Jersey Devil snaps up the crisps, devouring the packet along with them. It flies away, disturbing branches above us and shaking a shower of pine needles loose.

I'm beginning to understand more, the part Linda didn't talk about. "Is this where you went that night in the Pine Barrens? And it was just by accident? You seem so relaxed about it now." I look at her with new respect.

"I'm not so worried *now* because it'll wear off and we'll be back. I know I really lost it back in the kitchen. But now that we're here…" Linda shrugs. "The hard part is after you come home and try to live a normal life. That was my undoing both times. You think you're on a sidewalk, but something shifts and you feel it rocking like an ocean swells beneath it and huge waves are about to crack through. You suspect everything, see a different form flexing beneath every surface. Sometimes it even felt like there's another person in the same space as me. The second time I got caught was in Bosnia. But in the short term, we'll be OK."

"Deb must be worried about us!"

"She might not even notice we've been gone. On the other hand, it might be weeks to her. We can't think about that now."

Linda puts her fingers to her lips and whispers. "If you listen to the trees, you'll hear the song in so many ways. Not all in English, but you'll understand them."

There's a high, silver hum from the needles. Each one a spark of light, a membrane of someone's universe ending. The needles fall over us as we walk, they hum beneath our feet. Slivers of strings form minute melodies. Each one is a high lonesome frequency, cutting into you like a diamond.

Even now, I'm thinking: *You must observe. You must collect samples, you must collect data.*

But the rest of me is full of the song, and the sorrow that formed it.

A rhythm underlying our steps and our breath becomes louder, until it swells outside of us and fills the air. We walk faster, as the sound comes faster too. The trees are so close together we have to struggle our way through them, as if the fragrant pines had turned into a cage. But there is light ahead, moonlight, starlight showing through the trees. *What would the stars look like here?* I must get into a clearing to have a good look.

"Don't run," cautions Linda.

But already I see where ground drops in front of us, and we come to the edge of a steep valley. I expect to see the stream, or the sea pounding down below, but there is only a railway track. And then we hear the vast noise of the engine.

Below, an ancient steam train makes its way, clouds of smoke reflecting back the silver light. The metal moves with a groan, as if the machine protests. Some cargo cars are covered, others carry gleaming heaps of black anthracite. Carriage after carriage passes. There is still more of the train beyond the horizon.

Linda recites softly: *"The longest train I ever saw, Went down that Georgia line, The engine passed six o'clock, And the cab passed by at nine"*

All the windows are covered, no lights on. Faster and faster, the clack-clack swells. There is always more of this train. Perhaps it will loop back on itself with no end, ever.

Linda is watching, her face unreadable. Has she seen this before?

"Briony, I believe you," she finally says. "When you told me that the song put us in synch with signals and waves elsewhere, I believed that. Why do you think I wanted to interview you? I wanted to find an explanation, and hoped you had one. But tell me – can't we do the same thing with a happy song? Imagine how wonderful that could be."

Wonderful, yes. But I remember the kind of music that clutches at you deep inside and hangs on. I think of how it takes a high lonesome sound to reverberate through a void and bring you to the other side of it. I think of a bass that thunders in sorrow. That is where the power lies.

"Sorry Linda, but I think that minor keys are the only ones that *work*."

Time Travel

Chris T-T

Give me time. Stories take place in time just as strongly as in place, from a single day (*Ulysses*), to the lifespan of humanity (*2001: A Space Odyssey*), encompassing as many time-spans in between as there are different stories. And I think that's what draws me to fiction, as an influence. I switch off – or quickly get pissed off – when a pop song's lyrical content only exists within a single frame of thought-process, when a basic expression of feeling (that he fancies her, or whatever) is re-occupied over and over in a solo strand of narrowband reverie. Too often, time goes missing from the equation – the songwriter literally loses the plot.

My musical composition is basic, using a box of melodic, rhythmic and sonic tricks, plus a fairly limited ability with structure, to build tracks. Yet where words are concerned, something else is also at play: I find myself focusing a kind of sub-editorial craftiness onto initial ideas that (honestly) floated in from somewhere else. And it's immediately obvious (to me, anyway) that these ideas could as easily form starting points for stories as songs. So I'm inspired to write by literature because, when the ideas come, they have plot, characters, emotional unfolding and surprise twists. They have time.

Haruki Murakami's *After The Quake* collection is where I'd like to reach as a lyricist. The short stories are all connected to the real Kobe earthquake, yet, although each one skirts the edge of the true-life drama, the whole book drenches the reader in the human repercussions of the disaster, or any disaster, or human nature as a whole. I want my songs set in London to capture the city in time, so although each is self-contained, a grand Cinemascope picture can sneak up on people later. I'd like to think of a listener tricked into a more complex experience than they bargained for, when they hit 'play'.

And again, that's a story-making process: asking yourself where and when and what might happen next. I find it ludicrous that so often, we (songwriters) stretch towards that weirdly dull universality of expressing a 'feeling we all share', in as conceptually undemanding (i.e. direct) a way as possible. As a punter, I really don't want a song to re-explain guff I already dissected a thousand times, what I want is a balance of escape and rediscovery; the magical re-sampling of the world in different hues, from different angles, which is only possible when you throw the passing of time into the mix.

The Barrowlands' Last Night

Philip Raines and Harvey Welles

It's the last night of the Barrowlands, and just about everyone is here.

From the middle of the hall's capacity two thousand, Cam observes two crowds. From one city, hipsters – the indie record shop assistants, freelancers for *The List* – and the usual West End culture vultures. From the other, clumps of young-team neds and the goths Cam used to hang out with. Only an event like this could pull together people who would never see each other in their everyday lives. It's the first time Touchpaper have played here since the trouble two years ago – a brave gesture, but how could they resist. It's the last night before the velvet curtains and carpets are stripped from the old ballroom, the lightbulbs cored out of its famous neon sign, and the demolition experts move in to check stress points in the structure.

Cam heard about the Barrowlands finally giving way to the developers months back. Like everyone else, he wasn't that surprised. The violence had pretty much killed it. For over a year now, most people could talk about how legendary the Barrowlands was but couldn't pick it out on a map. That was why the place was full. Somewhere in their lives, everyone knew that the Barrowlands was one of the last places they all shared. After tonight, these two crowds would never see each other again.

The audience is on the point of boiling. Fans pressed around Cam chant *Touchpaper*, hooting whenever they see a silhouette on the walkway leading up to the stage, but it's not just anticipation. Nerves are thick. At the metal detector downstairs, the Rock Steady security patted down Cam's combats and loose Rockitt shirt like they were American cops on a drug bust. Hands punched shoulders and tore hooded jackets in the mash at the concessions stall. There was a fight in the toilets, and now up on the ballroom floor, two girls in *Nightmare Before Christmas* T-shirts are screaming at each other over a cigarette lighter.

The girls are drowned by a roar all around them. Bodies surge and Cam is carried forward. Tall for a fifteen-year old, skinny enough to fit into the breaks in the crowd, he still has to bounce up and down to see what's going on. He glimpses the band coming through the dry ice on stage: Wafa Idris, Touchpaper's singer, baptizing herself after the first Palestinian female suicide bomber; John Brown on guitar, Gerard Winstanley on bass, Fidel on drums, expressing the band's revolutionary agenda in their own nicknames.

But Cam doesn't waste time watching the stage. He scans the crowd, sweeping the floor in sections as he pogoes for better views. He's been told he'd be at the edges at the start of the show, and yes, there he is – right on the far side, just below the step leading to the bar. All Cam can see is the back of the man's head. There aren't any distinctive tattoos or strange hair tags to set him apart. *He won't look like much, but you'll just know* – Marty's words, and he's right. His intent hangs out of him like – like Cam's does at a perfume counter in Frasers.

Someone saw him at the System Of A Down gig in June, but then that fight started and he was lost in the rush. Cam knows that there have been other sightings over the years and there may be more in whatever places he's drawn to in future. But Cam knows that tonight is his own last chance to find the Mosh Demon.

Wafa shakes her dreads. After their last time here she should be nervous, but she snarls into the mic – Welcome to your last night, Glasgow. 'Glasgow' shouldn't mean much to most people here anymore, but as soon as John Brown chops out the opening riff on *Calamity*, everyone jumps into the air and at each other and out of their lives and for a few hours, it's Glasgow again.

It's the last night of the Barrowlands, and even the Mosh Demon is here.

So where is Cam's brother then?

*

Waiting in the long line outside the Barrowlands to see Touchpaper's debut in Glasgow, Cam and his brother, Paul, listened to Paul's mates arguing.

"No debate. Paddy's Market is gone."

Mustafa scoffed. "What are you talking about, Kenny? I was there last weekend. Got a nice pair of Pioneer headphones for a fiver."

"And where exactly were you?"

"Behind Kings Arcade. Don't you remember us all bombing down there last year? Where else would Paddy's Market be?"

"That whole area became new flats in December. You're sleep-walking on the weed again, Mustafa. Big red spike on top, waterfall in the lobby – even you must have seen the new building. It was about time they cleared out that rat-run."

"And when did you start defending those yuppie farms?" Mustafa challenged Kenny. "Maybe since you started working at the call centre? Yes sir, no sir, can I drop my trousers now sir?"

"A job's better than getting stoned on the dole. Nowhere deserves a bit of lip and blush more than Glasgow."

"Maybe," Paul intervened, speaking for the first time. "It's just a shame they couldn't keep both."

The pulsing neon of the Barrowlands sign raised the sadness in Paul's face like secret lettering. Staring at him, Cam couldn't deny that something had changed in his brother. With his hair cut short and his new taste in M&S white shirts, a lot of Paul's old friends thought he was clipping the interesting edges off his life so he could fit into some new pigeon-hole none of them could understand. They wondered whether Paul had decided to get dry-cleaned and go straight. But Cam was sure he knew better – Paul's ideals might have morphed to fit the new shape of the times, but they hadn't changed substance. Cam knew nothing could sap Paul's passion for Glasgow.

Ash came back along the line, ignoring the comments about her full-on black goth evening wear. "No-one's scalping any spares, Cam."

"Shit, Ash – Touchpaper finally come to Glasgow and we can't see them. I told you – e-bay."

Ash stuck her tongue out at Cam.

"Just as well," Paul said. "There's been fighting right through Touchpaper's tour. Don't want my little brother caught up in any trouble."

"So why are you going then?"

That silenced Paul, which was fine by Cam because he hated Paul doing Big Brother in public. Ash would rag him about it afterwards and it would probably get back to Viper and the others. He should just tell Paul to fuck off, but he was so deeply awed by his brother he couldn't even do that.

"Didn't you know?" Mustafa said, winking at Cam. "Paul's after the Mosh Demon. Tell your brother what you told everyone in the newsgroup. About the twisted firestarter. The patron saint of bangers." There was a nervous silence between them when Paul said nothing.

"Anyway, if you're worried about getting into fights, Paul, you should have kept your Glasgow Gather nights going," Mustafa continued. "Never any trouble at the Gathers."

"Yeah, whatever happened to them? They were fantastic events. They really brought people together from all over."

"Got too tribal in the end, didn't they," Mustafa told Kenny. "You invited one group, another wouldn't turn up."

Paul just shrugged. "Anyway, nothing brings people together like the Barrowlands."

The Barrowlands doors opened suddenly and there was a scattering of sarcastic applause as everyone baby-stepped forward. Ash tugged Cam's jacket. "Come on, I know a place where we can get a carry-out. Let's go back to Viper's and get drunk and listen to Touchpaper for free."

Cam looked back at his brother, but Paul was already beyond the venue's doors. He was glad he did look, otherwise he wouldn't have caught sight of that expression on Paul's face. So when Paul's friends later described to Cam's mum what had happened after the riot started and the police explained that no-one of Paul's description had been taken to the hospital or the station, Cam didn't worry too much about other people's theories. He just knew what he saw: that determined look on his brother's face. Exactly the same look he had when they were both very young and they had lost their mother in Braehead and had to make their way home alone.

Paul knew where he was going.

*

The Mosh Demon always wears the same clothes: an old-fashioned, faded white shirt, the kind with attachable collars, seersucker trousers, black brogues polished to a dazzler. He's older than most people here and Cam would have tagged him with the hipsters but the man never pays attention to the music. That's not why he's here.

Touchpaper aren't bothering with their new album – they sense the atmosphere won't accept anything else, so they ditch the setlist for crowd-pleasers. As the Mosh Demon moves towards the centre of the Bounce, Cam shadows, waiting for him to make his move. He's picked the right spot – a pair of bullet-heads with bulging neck muscles. A lightning dart and the Mosh Demon shoves one bullet-head into the other, then propels himself into the shelter of the Crush. The bullet-heads don't take offence – it's the excuse they've been looking for and they start slam-dancing, grabbing each other and anyone else within reach into a whirl of spinning bodies and fists. Other hard-ons move in while bystanders stumble away. There's a cascade of shoves and insults, small eddies of anger ricochet through the crowd.

There will be two or three incidents like this. This is just the Mosh Demon stoking things up. The real riot action is yet to come, something Cam knows from reports Paul logged ages ago in his urban renaissance newsgroup. At first, Cam went to the newsgroup in case Paul was still placing messages, but stayed to read his brother's secret history, tracking the legend of the Mosh Demon.

The legend is that the Mosh Demon is only ever seen in Barrowland gigs and only ever at gigs that lead to serious trouble. Maybe he has a life outside the gigs, but he's never seen arriving or leaving the venue. He only seems to exist on the ballroom floor.

He's edging towards the right of the crowd, so Cam finds the gap between the Bounce and the Sway and keeps step with the Mosh Demon. Knowing his way around mosh ecology helps, something else he has to thank Paul for. Right up against the barrier, where security are freeing those fainting from heat exhaustion, is the thin layer of the Crush, the hardcore devotion where nothing moves. Further back is the Bounce, a zone of ever-changing thickness through which fans rotate, dancing and screaming for a few songs before stepping back. Between the Bounce and the Sway, there's a firewall of empty floor to allow for the Bounce to shift suddenly back and forth, and then diminishing zones of intensity – through the nodding heads of the Sway to the dark mass of the Still – all the way to the mixing desk at the back of the ballroom. Paul told him this for his own safety, but with every gig he's gone to, Cam appreciates more the careful balance of forces in mosh dynamics. Each of the zones is unstable, each threatens to swamp the rest and overwhelm the gig. The Bounce could sweep forward and cause serious harm to anyone in the Crush. The inertia of the Still could infect all the zones with a poisonous chill. True equilibrium is rare.

Cam finds a space in the Bounce and joins the heaving as Fidel thrashes out the beat for *Pain Barrier*. A girl beside him steadies herself on his shoulder and they leap together in one of those moments of perfect synch with the song when Cam feels the music passing right through his body, the crowd, the building, the city, rearranging the atoms so that everything can fit together for a single instant. He forgets the Mosh Demon for a few seconds, looks up to the stars embossed on the ballroom's ceiling, then over at the girl.

He recognizes her right away. It takes Ash a few heartbeats to register him too. The Bounce holds them together, but Ash takes her hand off his shoulder.

Her black hair's got a Bride of Frankenstein white streak now, but under the kohl and piercings, she hasn't changed much since their last fight. He wonders how he looks to her now. Inside here is the only place that either of them would recognize each other. Out there, they'd look straight through – though chances were, they wouldn't run into each other in the first place.

Over the feedback of John Brown's guitar, Wafa tells them, "Barrowlands, you're the best in the world!"

Someone shouts, *Fuck off!*

Head-bangers wedge between him and Ash. Cam is suddenly part of a block of people that jerk backwards. He's off his feet, borne by the mob as he desperately tries to connect with the ground. The wave of people comes to a dead halt and Cam goes down into a sudden space. A mosh abhors a vacuum and there's a rush of fans forward again. Cam instantly puts his elbows up to protect his face and curls into a ball. Someone is trying to use his thigh for a leg up.

Strong arms yank him up, and Cam's feet spasm as he kicks away the people around him. The arms won't let go, pull him backwards through the Bounce, across the gap into the Sway, to safety. He takes deep breaths and tries to control the shaking, but the arms are still tugging.

Cam finally slaps away his rescuer's hand. "Fuck's sake, I'm OK now."

"No, you're not," Paul says.

*

In the year after the Touchpaper gig, Paul wasn't the only thing that disappeared. But things weren't really vanishing – just being rearranged.

Like his family – well, only his mother now. When Paul was there, three was enough for a family because Paul made sure that any group he was part of became a community. But even before he left, his mother was losing interest in everything. It got worse with Paul gone – but her hold on things didn't exactly go. It seemed misplaced, as if she knew it was around somewhere. She sipped Baileys from a mug and watched afternoon cookery shows while Cam took the train in from Barrhead and stole bottles of *Chanel* from Frasers. When he brought them back as gifts, his mother smelt hungrily from the bottles as if they could give her what she was looking for, but she always abandoned them on top of the television, disappointed.

When Cam was up in town, he used to keep watch at Paul's old hang-outs – just in case. The Community Centre in Maryhill. Queen Margaret Union in the University. A few places in the West End like Tchai Ovna where Paul used to organize poetry slam and acoustic evenings. Then he would meet up with Ash and hang out along Great Western Road, looking through the shop windows of places like Isis at all the cool gear they couldn't afford.

"Tchai Ovna?"

Ash looked at him strangely. "You didn't tell me we were going over there."

"What do you mean? It's just around the corner."

"No – *there*. Kentigern. The other Glasgow."

That rang a bell. Something about it on one of those current affairs programmes his mother watched. He wasn't arguing, but Ash had a point to prove. She marched him down the alley off Otago Street and showed him Tchai Ovna, but not the one that he'd been in that morning. This teashop was boarded-up, like the surrounding buildings.

"*This* is St. Mungo," Ash said, then challenged him. "This is my home. Is it yours, Cam?"

His home was wherever Paul's was, but he didn't know where Paul was so he didn't know anymore. Cam tried to tell Ash that Glasgow was his home, but the more he started taking an interest in the city, not just thinking of it as a potential hiding place for his brother, the more he saw that his home was fading. Kentigern and St. Mungo had always been there, lying side by side. One street would be swish new apartments, the next sinking tenements still black with ancient coalfires. Kentigern was always the city looking forward into the future's bright lights, the City of Culture, of Art & Architecture, of conference centres and harbour redevelopments. St. Mungo was a city of high-rises and joy-rider graveyards, the smell of the abattoir along Duke Street, the sound of arson in the wasting dockyards. Now the two cities were splitting, as if an earthquake had shaken them loose or the glue binding them had yellowed and flaked away.

Cam found that you could cross back and forth at certain common points – the Buchanan Galleries shopping mall, the Barrowlands, though there were fewer of them each week – but Ash and Viper and the rest of his friends liked to roam St. Mungo. They felt out of place in Kentigern's designed green spaces and cleaned-up industrial dereliction. They liked to climb to the top of the loop of half-built motorway at Anderston and throw empty *Miller* bottles at the signs arching over the M8 out of St. Mungo.

But when they were asleep in Mustafa's Haghill squat, Cam would slink away to Kentigern. He was convinced that was where Paul had gone, but that wasn't the real reason for slipping back and forth across the border. Wandering through the business district around Bothwell Street at lunchtime, he was amazed at how directed and upbeat everyone looked. Even at night, it was bright young people coming out for a drink in groups, not the lone prostitutes Cam was used to in St. Mungo. While Cam couldn't live all the time in Kentigern – he couldn't take the relentless optimism – he liked the change.

So he swapped his black for baggy and hung out with skatepunks, who preferred the long, smooth walkways of Kentigern corporate headquarters to the broken pavements in St. Mungo. Part of him thought that as Paul used to be into skateboarding, they might have seen him.

A smart idea, as it turned out. He was with Marty, skateboarding across the pedestrian bridge over the Clyde. Cam had difficulty getting into rhythm – it was still too strange to see the twinkling lights of the new river walkways and cafés. That was where Marty told him.

"Someone saw your brother."

Cam flipped off his board. "Where?"

"Barrowlands. System Of A Down gig. I showed Aziz that picture you gave me and he remembered because there was a fight and your brother was pulling kids out of the trouble."

That sounded like Paul. "Did Aziz see what happened to him?"

"No. Aziz just got out of there. He didn't want to mess with that other fucker."

"What fucker?"

"The Mosh Demon. He was there too."

A month later, just after the news percolated out that the Barrowlands was closing down, posters for Touchpaper's new tour started appearing. The concert promoter was shrewd enough to only put them up in St. Mungo, knowing that the tickets would sell out quicker in Kentigern by word of mouth. Sure enough, *The List* talked the band up after their 'infamous' last gig in Glasgow and Kentigern's tickets went in days.

Cam went to St. Mungo for tickets. "Are you going or not?" he asked Ash after she'd been sulking for days.

"Amazed you saw the poster."

"What the fuck are you talking about?"

"You've never really been in St. Mungo, have you, Cam?"

Her face was puffy with either being drunk or crying before he got there. "Just fuck off back to Never-Neverland!" Ash screamed at him. "You always were a happy goth."

By that point, few ventured out of Kentigern – or went in the other direction. People seemed to understand which city they belonged to. Cam didn't want to make up his mind and was able to make some money scalping tickets to Kenny in Kentigern, using the money his mother had put on top of the television after she'd finally left St. Mungo for wherever.

But he kept one ticket back for himself.

*

At the edge of the Still, Paul and Cam stand, ignoring the band, almost ignoring each other. Paul's on the dancefloor, Cam's on the step up, slumped against a pillar. It's too noisy to make sense, which is fine because Cam's not sure if he wants to hit or hug him.

Eventually, it comes out as both. "So where the fuck have you been?"

Paul shakes his head. "I've been here, looking after people."

"You should have looked after Mum."

By which he means *him*, but Paul won't say anything, so Cam spins around and is about to head for the throng around the bar. "Still Guinness, right?"

Paul stands at the edge of the ballroom floor, right up against the step, as far as he can go. The sadness on Paul's face catches him – and then Cam understands. White shirt. The hair. Everything just as it was.

"What's wrong?

"I told you." Paul kicks the edge of the step, his boundary. "I've been here."

They move as far away from the music and the crowd as they can, way at the back by the sound desk. People push past them, splashing drinks, sometimes crying or holding their heads, so Cam finds it hard to listen as Paul tries to explain. It's easier to imagine the words coming from Wafa, so Cam doesn't look at his brother, at the heavy bruising across his face and the cut above his eye that can never heal, but only at the stage.

Wafa tells him: People come together because they're looking to be something bigger than themselves, something strong. Cities and gigs, families and crowds, everyone's drawn to that power. It's a force that can set a time in stone or trigger a revolution, it can unite a city or drive apart two communities. It's people refusing to give way in Prague and Bucharest in 1989, it's spectators flying in panic in Amritsar when troops opened fire in 1919.

And at its most intense, when the need is greatest, it can summon. Paul touches his arm. Cam can almost feel that force, making his heart want to fly apart into pieces. "I'm sorry" – Paul's voice, clear in a sudden gap in the music.

Then Paul looks up – dog radar, picking up a secret signal – and he looks around. Cam sees it too. The mosh ecology is changing – the same zones, only now through some remorseless osmosis, the Barrowlands has divided right down the middle, two crowds pulling apart from each other. Their Stills are starting to edge towards the exits at the back as the two sets of Bounce range all over the floor, spinning with the frustration of something that doesn't want to be held back.

Only one person moves back and forth across the boundary, his head bobbing as he throws punches and nips back through the crowds. The band can see the Mosh Demon, and Wafa glances at the line of security along the front of the stage, but they can only stand and watch the audience with growing fear as plastic tumblers are hurtled from one side of the ballroom to the other.

Wafa makes a decision. "Barrowlands, this is our last song." She nods to John Brown, who starts their anthem.

"Who is he then?" Cam asks.

"He's angry, but he doesn't know what at," Paul tells him. "He drinks inside all day and all night screams in the streets. And he refuses to let go."

"You won't let go either. You can't keep holding it together, Paul."

Paul pushes himself away from the barrier. A boy nearly slips to the ground just in front of them, but Paul holds him up. "Get out of here, Cam."

"But where to?"

"Glasgow, I don't know. Just go."

But Glasgow is gone.

*

It was at the end of a run of gift days in February. Paul called up everyone he knew and set the tribal lines humming in dozens of spiderweb directions throughout the city. He let his twelve-year old brother, Cam, carry the box of records, and Cam was proud as he lugged it up the long slope of the Necropolis in the midnight darkness. Paul's reflected glory made the little brother stick out for a change. Viper and his mates were impressed – so was the new girl with the Emily Strange handbag.

No lights – just the two turntables, the records and Paul's renegade sound system. A friend of his DJ-ed as people began to stream in from all over. Goths, young-teams (neds and Pakistanis both), football fans straight from the pub, indie kids, a stray hen party – all dancing between the gravestones to the mishmash of records Paul set-listed, all plugged into the network that Paul had been stitching since he first started sneaking into clubs. They wouldn't have long before the police caught on, but Paul had look-outs, even taking turns himself at John Knox's monument at the crest of the Necropolis.

Cam danced with the new girl – Ashley – a couple of times. She had a bottle of cider with her so they went up to the monument to share it with Paul.

Glasgow spread away from them either side of the slur of the Clyde, which was already starting to shine with pre-dawn glow. Its skyline was spiked by a history of ambition and failure: the University of Glasgow's neo-gothic spire, which always looked half-finished to Cam; the Anderston shipbuilding crane, memorial to past industrial epics; the slender tower of the Glasgow Science Centre, a peg holding down the future.

"I hate that science tower," Ashley said.

"Why?" Paul asked, surprised.

"It's always breaking down. I mean, look at it – a giant hypodermic needle. What's the point?"

"At least, someone's trying. What would you do? Let the place fall apart?"

"And what makes you think it won't anyway? What would *you* do?"

Paul took a long swig of the cider, looking to Cam as visionary, as unrelenting, as the stone city fathers around them.

"Preserve the best of it. Burn out the rubbish. And put up something fucking amazing."

Ashley smiled sourly. "Well, we agree about the burning."

Cam drank too much cider, but kept dancing. A look-out shouted and Paul scrambled down the hill, telling the DJ to cut the music, grab the equipment, everyone to scatter. A few ran, but the rest linked arms, started running back and forth, crashing into gravestones.

"Come on!" Paul shouted at him, ever keen to avoid any trouble.

But trouble was the whole point. The skyline was teetering, as if the whole city was on the verge of falling down or straightening up or both at the same time. A spinning top delighted it was out of control, neither forward nor back, but deliriously round and round.

He wanted to explain to Paul, but he was too drunk to get the words out. Cam didn't want to stop.

*

Everything is Crush and Bounce now. Tempers are too frayed to re-knit. People are shoving out in all directions. Young teams move in packs across the floor, circling each other and jabbing at anyone in their way. Thrashers head-butt forward in violently straight lines. Small knots of fighting form and burst apart, the crowd suddenly constricts into super-dense balls, and through it all, the Mosh Demon, pushing here, kicking there, and Paul, separating punch-ups, pulling kids from under foot. The band doesn't seem to care and play their last song as if the crowd's seized their nerves and won't release them.

Cam tried to get out earlier, but one exit has been locked and the main doors are jammed with people fleeing and slipping on the stairs. Now he's just following the host of refugees ahead of him, moving towards the bar, hand on the back of the person in front, someone behind holding his belt. A man pulls Cam away from the others, whirls him around so they're facing.

The Mosh Demon always wears the same clothes. He's still clean shaven and his hair is slicked back in the rockabilly style of his youth. He has none of the bruises that Paul has, but his skin is pale, like a freshly-painted room locked up for a century, and his knuckles are scabbed and scored with dirt. His teeth could almost be humming from how tight they're grinding. For a moment, Cam thinks he must be blind from the way his eyeballs have rolled up inside their sockets, but that's just him wincing, as if the punch he's about to throw is going to hurt him more than Cam.

Cam should duck – or run – or whimper – but he hears Fidel still stomping up on stage and Brown and Winstanley locking into a rhythm. He moves on instinct. The fist comes forward, Cam comes around it, letting the Mosh Demon's arm loop through his and using the force to spin around, once twice, skip-to-my-lou, and he hops forward. The Mosh Demon growls but the people around them are laughing – so Cam keeps gyrating, locking arms with the nearest man, a full circle, onto a rocker, then a girl in a pink-and-white tracksuit, then a fierce boy wearing a Celtic top. Each time Cam takes a partner, he smiles goofily, his partners look surprised or start to struggle, but as soon as he spins them around, they relax, they see what he's trying to do, and they take their own partners.

What is he trying to do?

He has a chance to get out – when he gets close, Cam can see that the doors are clearing. He can leave – but he doesn't want to. The music's stopped now. Wafa is trying to persuade everyone to go home, but no-one else wants to either. They want to dance, and the impromptu ceilidh gets fiercer. Cam's arms are bruising, some of the thrashers are spinning into slam-dancing, and there are still fights at the edges, but no-one cares, they just keep dancing. Cam moves from stranger to stranger. He spins Ash at one point, and they both scream together and spin as fast as they have to for take-off, but they still let each other go and move onto new partners.

Cam sees Paul – running around the outside of the chains of dancers, picking up whoever slips, trying to persuade them to leave, still terrified that this would collapse into something horrible, unable to accept that everything was always going to fall apart and come together. Cam sees the Mosh Demon too, helpless at the heart of the ballroom, surrounded, battering whoever he can reach, able to do nothing more than start small chain reaction fights that quickly peter out into fits of laughter.

Cam sees everyone – teetering. It could be a fight. It could be a step-march to a new dawn. The equilibrium is on the edge, swaying like a drunk on the way home for a good night's rest or ever roaring on the way to the next pub. Cam jumps up and bellows because the tension is wonderful. He sees that it's the last night. It's always the last night, and it's never going to end.

Lower East Side

(revisited with reflections)

Chris Stein

Moving back to the lower east side of New York City thirty years later has in an odd way diminished aspects of nostalgic ache that I am usually afflicted with… somehow the sweeping changes have created a warp in the space-time fabric that relates to these feelings in my sentimental vision… I feel to be dropped into an alternate universe, a somehow flattened and cleansed version of its former self that although recognizable is still such a totally different place… I walk around the various streets; there isn't a single block that doesn't have some connection with the past, indirect or otherwise… I see an overlay of the twilight former place but what I fondly remember as a dark world of danger and intrigue is transformed into a realm of dappled sunlight and shady lanes and I can only wonder how this alteration is reflected in all of the layers of the modern world…

First we are dumped into the midst of some various symbolic local drama; directly across the street from where we are is St. Brigid's church; built in the 1850's by those escaping the potato famine in Ireland, it's a simple pretty old place with really big arched windows… it is perhaps the oldest of some six hundred churches designed in the US by one Patrick Keely... it is an inevitability that it will be torn down, probably replaced by a large condominium, that is, expensive living spaces for the newly arrived hip gentry... around the block from the church is P.S. 64, an even more beautiful old school house that for the last twenty years was home to a radical Puerto Rican community center: Charas/El Bohio... in 1998 another of mayor Giuliani's acts to better the city was to sell the building to a private real estate developer for three point fifteen million dollars, a tiny fraction of what the 135,000 foot property is actually worth... since then the place has been boarded up as the developer attempts to stave off the landmarks commission... the political details of this particular stand off are truly disgusting, take my word for it...

But even the landmarking of a place is so much bullshit, still its about money... a few years ago Poe's little house near Washington Square was pulled down by NYU to make way for a dorm or some such... there seems to be more protest over Brigid's than Edgar's place but it is just as hopeless a case...

My earliest memories of alphabet city, whatever, are of the end of the immigrant neighborhood system... in the sixties there was still a really diverse racial mix: eastern Europeans were still part of the equation and one would come upon odd little shops run by elderly couples. I bought a motorcycle jacket that was likely made in the forties or fifties for five bucks in a dusty store front that was piled with old clothes... the atmosphere was so dense for me, a mix of magic music and hidden art... the *East Village Other* was the local periodical of note and anarchic freedom personified... the artistic character of the neighborhood was in a direct line to the Beats and the jazz era of Slugs... my friend's older sister rented a one room apartment on twelfth street for twenty four dollars a month, that might have been in 1965, four years later my first avenue apartment cost about a hundred dollars a month for four rooms five flights up... There I had fanciful visions of the apocalypse brought on by witchcraft, the smoking ruins of Manhattan occupied by the remains of the downtown youth culture...

But not to be... some correlation of economy and art, as America pulled itself out of recession things swung in an opposing arc to my daydreams... heroin use became no longer the province of the few... in ten years the lower east side rapidly declined into violence and neglect… one day in about 1971 I came downstairs and ran into a friend whose name I have now lost… he was dressed in mostly dirty brown leather with a matching dirty brown leather cowboy hat, he was armed with a shiny silver decorative axe, the type one hangs on a wall in a den… he told me that he knew where there was a treasure of sorts, that 'somebody like you' would appreciate. I went back upstairs, got my camera and we started our little journey into the jungle… in spite of it being early afternoon the jungle was in full swing and I feared for the safety of my camera as I thought I saw it being occasionally eyed… the streets and stoops were crowded with hordes of kids, people looked at us, somehow recognizing our out of placeness… we arrived at what my friend announced was the destination, deep in the midst of the alphabet, between avenues C and D maybe on fourth or fifth street… the 'treasure' turned out to be the gaping broken window of a hastily vacated first floor apartment… someplace I have a picture of him squatting on the window sill axe in hand… we climbed in and observed the utter destruction of somebody or others at one time vaguely ordered existence… had the police raided the place? an earthquake? total destruction, piles of furniture, papers, dishes etc. etc. I didn't find anything at all of interest to me and we left… the point of this anecdote being I think that this seemed all quite regular at the time… these memories are shadows, they crowd around like people trying to get off a crowded train… our lives in those days were different… where did the transition begin? with Viet Nam winding down? is there a connection between the psychic life of the Lower East Side and American imperialism? with the rise of right wing corporate agendas?

I always saw it coming but its different and I feel like all the old guys who came before me whining about the good old days or in this case the bad old days but again there's a difference… to be hip was once a hidden commodity that needed some effort in its pursuit… we had a vast world of conservative life with a small out group, I think Marshall McLuhan is one of many people who stated the obvious; 'that one can't have an in group without an out group'… now everyone in New York, in the West, is hip… it's become the standard of style and design by which reality is measured… hipness is marketed and sold to the masses at crazily inflated prices, it used to not cost anything to be hip, in fact paying for it was contrary to the ideal… 'what are you rebelling against'

is still the question but the answer today seems to be 'nothing'...
everyone at the little demonstration to save Poe's house wanted to know
how an alleged institution of higher learning, namely New York
University could be responsible for the destruction... wouldn't any
school be absurdly grateful to have this bit of American history on its
campus? How can we have a future without a past?

We in the west are falling deeper and deeper into the bottomless pit
of the greed and spectacle culture... everybody knows who's waiting at
the bottom and if we get there he's not really gonna be very sympathetic.

Contributors

Marion Arnott is a Scots writer whose work has appeared in *Peninsular Magazine*, *QWF*, *West Coast*, *Northwords*, *Books Ireland*, *Hidden Corners*, *Chapman Magazine*, *Scottish Child*, *Solander*, *Crimewave* 4& 6, *Hayakawa Mystery Magazine* (Japan), and *Roadworks*, as well as the anthologies *Year's Best Fantasy and Horror 2002*, *Best British Mysteries* (ed. Maxim Jabukowski), *The Alsiso Project*, *The Elastic Book of Numbers*, *Nova Scotia – New Scottish Speculative Fiction*, and *Cafe Ole – Too Hot To Handle*. Her first short story collection, *Sleepwalkers*, was published by Elastic Press in 2003. She is the recipient of the 1998 Philip Good Memorial Prize for Fiction (QWF), and also the CWA Short Dagger Award 2001 for her story *Prussian Snowdrops* (and was also shortlisted in 2002 and 2003).

Jean-Jacques Burnel is one of the founder members of The Stranglers, a band which is now in its thirty-second year and whose sixteenth album, appropriately titled *Suite XVI,* was released in September 2006. He is also a 6th dan in Karate and teaches in the City of London.

Editor **Gary Couzens** first started watching *Top of the Pops* in early 1973 at the age of eight, when Slade and Sweet were at number one. He cannot sing but, as one of those post-forty things, is learning to play the bass guitar. In the meantime, he has had thirty-five stories published in *Fantasy & Science Fiction*, *Interzone*, *Crimewave*, *The Third Alternative* and elsewhere, eighteen of them being collected in *Second Contact and Other Stories*, published in 2003 by Elastic Press.

Rebekah Delgado is co-singer/songwriter/guitarist in Ciccone. Their acclaimed first album *Eversholt Street* was released in 2004. Their next album is on the boiling pot. Their online presence can be found at both www.ciccone.co.uk and www.myspace.com/ciccone. Rebekah and the band can be contacted by e-mail at ciccone@ciccone.co.uk.

Becky Done is 25 and lives in Norwich where she graduated from the School of Art and Design with a cultural studies degree. She is currently seeking a publisher for her first novel. *Tremolando* is her first published story.

Andrew Humphrey has been widely published in the Independent Press over the last five years, most notably in publications such as *The Third Alternative*, *Crimewave*, *Bare Bone* and *Midnight Street*. His debut collection, *Open the Box and Other Stories*, was published by *Elastic Press* in 2003. His first novel, *Alison*, a taut psychological mystery, should be published by *TTA Press* in the near future. He has two sons and lives and works in Norwich.

Emma Lee's poetry collection *Yellow Torchlight and the Blues* was published in Autumn 2004 by *Original Plus*. Her short stories have been widely published in the UK, USA and on-line as well prize-winners in competitions. She has given poetry readings at venues such as Leicester City Football Club, Leicester's Guildhall, Loughborough University and various bookshops. After a knee-injury cut short a potential figure-skating career as part of the chorus line in *Holiday on Ice*, Emma settled in Leicester where she lives with her husband and young daughter.

Lene Lovich is a singer and writer of songs. In 1979, she had chart success with the hit single, *Lucky Number*. Along with her musical activities she has been a campaigner for animal rights and is on the board of directors for Peta (People for the Ethical Treatment of Animals). She encourages anyone who is against animal cruelty to visit their website at www.Peta.com. Recently, she has released a new album: *Shadows and Dust* (stereosociety.com).

Gary Lightbody is the singer and chief songwriter with Snow Patrol, who struck the seam of commercial success in 2004 when their unforgettable anthem of love and longing *Run* was released, reaching number five in the UK charts and propelling their third album, *Final Straw*, to number three – going on to sell 1.2 million in the UK alone, and winning them an Ivor Novello for Best Album of 2005. After a decade together it was the culmination of years of faith and hard work. Their most recent album, *Eyes Open*, came out earlier this year and has hit the number one spot twice since its release. Their website can be found at www.snowpatrol.com.

Sean "Grasshopper" Mackowiak was born in Dunkirk, New York in 1966. He graduated from Dunkirk Public High School in 1984 with an award for Excellence in English Literature. He attended The State University of New York at Buffalo from 1984 until he graduated in 1988 with a Bachelor of Arts joint degree in Communication and Media Studies. At UB, he studied with Robert Creeley (New York State Poet Laureate from 1989-1991), Paul Sharits (Fluxus artist and Filmmaker), Tony Conrad (Minimalist Composer, Filmmaker, Video Artist) and Charles Keil (author of Urban Blues). He attended The New School For Social Research in New York City from 1990 until 1993 and graduated with a Master of Arts Degree in Media Studies. Grasshopper is a founding member of the musical group Mercury Rev (formed in 1988) and has released six albums with the band since 1991, including the acclaimed *Deserter's Songs* and *All Is Dream*. Touring with Mercury Rev has taken him around the world numerous times. Grasshopper has also recorded a solo album with his "Grasshopper and the Golden Crickets" for the Beggar's Banquet Record label, as well as a side project "The Harmony Rockets", which appeared on the Big Cat label several years ago. In the past, he has contributed music related articles to both RAYGUN and ESOPUS magazines. Currently, Mercury Rev are working on their seventh musical release. Grasshopper has called Kingston, NY his home since 1995. He serves on the Board of Trustees for the Kingston Public Library. He has one dog named Dutch and a cat named Nico.

Tim Nickels entered the conservatoire in 1960. His research into obscure Victorian scientific societies led to his first recording (*English Soil: Theme & Variations*) on the prestigious Elastic label. Tim spends his days in the practice room humming Alice Faye tunes, a glass of lemonade and the *Dictionary of Organ Stops* his only companions.

jof owen sings and writes the words for the boy least likely to. An indie pop group from the sleepy village of Wendover in Buckinghamshire. Their self released debut album is called *the best party ever* and was described by Rolling Stone as sounding like what would happen 'if all your childhood stuffed animals got together and started a band'.

Rosanne Rabinowitz's published fiction includes stories in *The Third Alternative, Roadworks, Midnight Street* and *The New Review* at www.laurahird.com – with another (also musically-inspired) story due in *PostScripts* next year. She has contributed to anthologies *The Slow Mirror: New Fiction by Jewish Writers, Deep Ten* and *Café Ole: Too Hot to Handle*. Her reviews and articles have appeared in *TTA, Interzone* and *The New Review*. She lives in South London and sometimes works as a freelance sub-editor. Other forms of toil include stints as a life model, oral history researcher, part-time mental health worker and full-time dole claimer. She is a graduate of the Sheffield Hallam University MA in Writing and belongs to the T Party Writers Group. And deep in the buried past she had been known to play bass in two obscure but very groundbreaking Brixton-based bands – the Sluts from Outer Space and Bag 'O Shite.

Philip Raines is a member of the Glasgow Science Fiction Writers Circle, and with Harvey Welles, has been published in *Lady Churchills Rosebud Wristlet, Albedo One, New Genre* and *The Year's Best Fantasy & Horror*. When he grows up, Philip wants to be a band that has a rider including the lost album by My Bloody Valentine, the sunken city of Atlantis and all the dream stuff that gets lost when you wake up in the morning. He'd play kazoo in that band and the band might or might not be called the Fischer-Price Explosion. He lives in Glasgow, where all good bands go to play in the Barrowlands.

Tony Richards is a Stoker Award nominee and the author of four books – the fifth, *Going Back*, is due out from Elastic Press next year – and over sixty short stories, his work appearing in *F&SF*, *Weird Tales*, *Cemetery Dance*, *The 3rd Alternative*, and *Dark Terrors* amongst others. Widely travelled, he often uses the places he has visited as settings for his fiction. He is currently a full time freelance writer, and lives in North London with his wife. You can find out more about him and his work by visiting his website at www.richardsreality.com

Iain Ross is a member of Bearsuit. Since playing their first gig in 2001, the band have notched up three Festive 50 top five hits and three Radio 1 sessions on the legendary John Peel show. A string of obscure vinyl single releases on several indie labels lead to the late great DJ championing the band in the last few years of his life, and meant they could gig their odd pop around the UK before they ever garnered a record deal. The band released their debut album *Cat Spectacular!* in the UK (fortuna pop! records) and America in March 2005 (microindie records), and in October 2005 they launched their 'long lost' debut album *Team Ping Pong* on the Fantastic Plastic label. So it came out AFTER their second album. Hey, what're you gonna do? Life is chewy sometimes. New material is being worked on for a THIRD album (which if previous form is anything to go by, may well come out after their fifth...). Their most recent single, *Steven F***ing Spielberg*, has had airplay on radios 1, 6 and MTV2. Bearsuit are currently embedded in the studio in the misty fens of Norfolk, recording new songs, including one about a dirty old crow. They can best be described as a stop-start boy-girl twee-rock cutie-killer six-piece with everything from cinematic waltzes to catchy electro disco and hard punk screaming riot grrl noise. Comparisons have been made to Huggy Bear, Belle and Sebastian, and Sonic Youth.

Nels Stanley lives in the West Country. This is his thirteenth short story publication, and first in an anthology. He regards this as a milestone, as it'll be the first piece of his published fiction which he'll be able to prop his bedroom door open with. He does lots of things, none of which pay very well. He could tell lots of hair-raising stories about interviewing Indie also-rans in back rooms of shitty pubs, but knows that no-one cares, really. Although he still has the tape of the time that he had to interview Crispin from Kula Shaker and the guy sat in the dark for an hour chanting a mantra and ignoring everything that was said to him about his latest album; he plays it from time to time to keep himself warm in his rapidly approaching senescence.

Chris Stein formed Blondie with Deborah Harry back in the early seventies, and the band enjoyed worldwide chart success with a string of hit singles that often broke new ground: *Heart of Glass*, *Atomic*, and *Rapture* to name but a few. After a sixteen year break, the band reformed in 1999 releasing *Maria* which topped the charts in 14 different countries. Their most recent album is *The Curse of Blondie*. Chris can be found at http://www.myspace.com/esxp and Blondie's official website is at www.blondie.net.

Chris T-T is a UK-based indie artist. He's released five studio albums and a pile of singles and EPs, the most recent being folk protest mini-album *9 Red Songs* (2005). Chris's next release will be the final part of his 'London Trilogy' of albums, which so far includes *The 253* (2001) and *London Is Sinking* (2003). Chris is married and lives in Brighton. His website can be found at www.christt.com.

Tall Poppies are a Perth / London based melodic guitar pop act fronted by twin singer songwriters Susan and Catherine Hay. They have written and produced the debut album *Thursday* and are performing in the UK. They can be found at either www.myspace.com/tallpoppies or www.thetallpoppies.com.

When he grows up **Harvey Welles** wants to be a roadie for bands that don't tour. He lives in Milwaukee.

Currently available from Elastic Press

Open The Box by Andrew Humphrey

With quiet understatement and beautiful characterisation Andrew Humphrey examines the complex link between relationships and abandonment, resulting in an important collection of thirteen stunning stories.

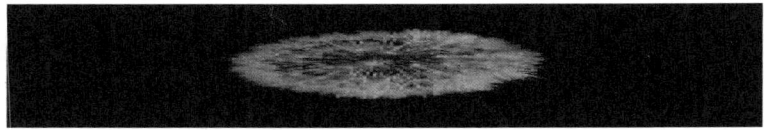

Second Contact by Gary Couzens

Exploring the twin themes of time and identity Gary Couzens manipulates our sensibilities in a major collection of nineteen powerful stories, drawing on the fascinations that dwell within the hearts of us all.

For more information visit:

www.elasticpress.com

Currently available from Elastic Press

The Sound of White Ants by Brian Howell

Taking the iconographic images of the schoolgirl and the salaryman, mingled with the bittersweet experiences of the sexually repressed, Howell explores beneath the plastic veneer of contemporary Japanese society; revealing a world caught precariously between its future and its past.

The English Soil Society by Tim Nickels

Here are stories that defy easy categorisation. They might be folktales from an alternate world, modern-day myths or eccentric fables written by creatures under the earth or from the stars. Their elusive, amorphic qualities and dextrous, lullaby prose, expresses both the personal and collective anxieties which affect us all.

For more information visit:

www.elasticpress.com

Currently available from Elastic Press

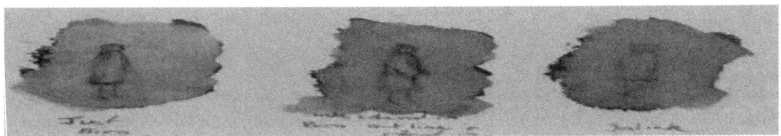

The Last Days of Johnny North by David Swann

Dave Swann is, without doubt, one of the most vivid short story writers in the UK today. He brings the landscape and voices of the North to life with an energy that catapults his characters into the universal. Pathos. Irresistible comedy. The raw and beautiful stuff of everyday life. It's all here.

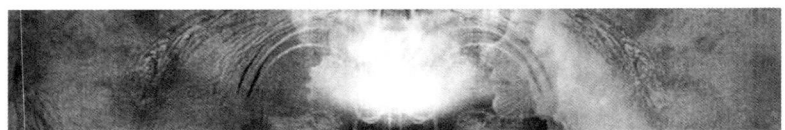

The Ephemera by Neil Williamson

Neil Williamson's collection of bittersweet tales features fourteen stories of impermanence: from the ends of love affairs and the brief sanity of wartime convalescence, to the fading away of old languages and the dying of humanity itself.

For more information visit:

www.elasticpress.com

Currently available from Elastic Press

Unbecoming by Mike O'Driscoll

Mike O'Driscoll plays with our imagination and expectations. What results is a strangely brewed cocktail of terror: dark, dangerous, and sometimes downright dirty, O'Driscoll's stories get under your skin and into your head, where the freedom to prowl the peripheries of your consciousness becomes addictive. Uncompromising and unflinching, this is modern horror at its very best.

Photocopies of Heaven by Maurice Suckling

In Maurice Suckling's debut collection slices of life react and interact against a consumerist background where expectations of what we are and where we should be going are frequently in conflict with reality. Combining traditional storytelling, vignettes, emails, text messages, and a cartoon, Suckling reinvents the short form for a society that has replaced its gods with technology, yet still prefers the permanency of love over a quick cyber fix.

For more information visit:
www.elasticpress.com

More quality fiction from Elastic Press

The Virtual Menagerie	Andrew Hook	SOLD OUT
Open The Box	Andrew Humphrey	£3.00
Second Contact	Gary Couzens	£5.00
Sleepwalkers	Marion Arnott	SOLD OUT
Milo & I	Antony Mann	SOLD OUT
The Alsiso Project	Edited by Andrew Hook	SOLD OUT
Jung's People	Kay Green	SOLD OUT
The Sound of White Ants	Brian Howell	£5.00
Somnambulists	Allen Ashley	SOLD OUT
Angel Road	Steven Savile	SOLD OUT
Visits to the Flea Circus	Nick Jackson	£5.00
The Elastic Book of Numbers	Edited by Allen Ashley	£6.00
The Life To Come	Tim Lees	SOLD OUT
Trailer Park Fairy Tales	Matt Dinniman	SOLD OUT
The English Soil Society	Tim Nickels	£5.99
The Last Days of Johnny North	David Swann	£6.99
The Ephemera	Neil Williamson	£5.99
Unbecoming	Mike O'Driscoll	£6.99
Photocopies of Heaven	Maurice Suckling	£5.99
Extended Play	Edited by Gary Couzens	£6.99

All these books are available at your local bookshop or can be ordered direct from the publisher. Indicate the number of copies required and fill in the form below.

Name_____
(Block letters please)

Address_____

Send to Elastic Press, 85 Gertrude Road, Norwich, Norfolk, NR3 4SG.
Please enclose remittance to the value of the cover price plus: £1.50 for the first book plus 50p per copy for each additional book ordered to cover postage and packing. Applicable in the UK only.

While every effort is made to keep prices low, it is sometimes necessary to increase prices at short notice. Elastic Press reserve the right to show on covers and charge new retail prices which may differ from those advertised in the text or elsewhere.

Want to be kept informed? Keep up to date with Elastic Press titles by writing to the above address, or by visiting www.elasticpress.com and adding your email details to our online mailing list.

Elastic Press: Winner of the British Fantasy Society Best Small Press award 2005